BREAKING THE RULES

A summer road trip changes everything in this unforgettable sequel to *Pushing the Limits* from phenomenal bestselling author Katie McGarry

For Echo Emerson, a summer road trip out west with her boyfriend means getting away and forgetting what makes her so... *different*. It means seeing cool sights while selling her art at galleries along the way. And most of all it means almost three months alone with Noah Hutchins, the hot, smart, soul-battered guy who's never judged her. Echo and Noah share everything—except the one thing Echo's just not ready for.

But when the source of Echo's constant nightmares comes back into her life, she has to make some tough decisions about what she really wants—even as foster kid Noah's search for his last remaining relatives forces them both to confront some serious truths about life, love and themselves.

Praise for
Katie McGarry
bestselling author of

PUSHING THE LIMITS

'The love story of the year' —*Teen Now*

'A real page-turner' —*Mizz*

'A romance with a difference' —*Bliss*

'McGarry details the sexy highs, the devastating lows
and the real work it takes to build true love.'
—Jennifer Echols

'A riveting and emotional ride'
—Simone Elkeles

'Highly recommend to fans of hard-hitting, edgy,
contemporary and to anyone who loves a smouldering,
sexy, consuming love story to boot!'
—*Jess Hearts Books* blog

'McGarry is definitely a YA author to keep an eye out for.'
—*ChooseYA* blog

Also available
PUSHING THE LIMITS
CROSSING THE LINE (eBook novella)
DARE YOU TO
CRASH INTO YOU
TAKE ME ON

Find out more about Katie McGarry at www.miraink.co.uk
and join the conversation on Twitter @MIRAInk or on
Facebook at www.facebook.com/MIRAInk

BREAKING THE RULES

Katie McGarry

Published in Great Britain 2015
MIRA Ink, an imprint of Harlequin (UK) Limited,
Eton House, 18-24 Paradise Road,
Richmond, Surrey, TW9 1SR

© 2014 Katie McGarry

ISBN: 978-1-848-45357-9
eBook ISBN: 978-1-474-00860-0

47-0115

Harlequin (UK) Limited's policy is to use papers that are natural, renewable and recyclable products and made from wood grown in sustainable forests. The logging and manufacturing processes conform to the legal environmental regulations of the country of origin.

Printed and bound by
CPI Group (UK) Ltd, Croydon, CR0 4YY

Katie McGarry

was a teenager during the age of grunge and boy bands and remembers those years as the best and worst of her life. She is a lover of music, happy endings and reality television and is a secret University of Kentucky basketball fan. She is also the author of *Pushing the Limits, Dare You To, Crash Into You, Take Me On* and the novella *Crossing the Line*.

Katie would love to hear from her readers. Contact her via her website, katielmcgarry.com, follow her on Twitter @KatieMcGarry, or become a fan on Facebook and Goodreads.

NOAH

Echo shifts, and the cold rush of air against my skin causes my eyes to flash open. The Colorado State Park Ranger for the Great Sand Dunes wasn't kidding when he said temperatures drop overnight. I stretch the muscles in my back then turn onto my side in order to touch Echo again. My palm melts into the curve of her waist.

She's curled in with her back to me, and she's tugged the blanket tight to her neck. Her tank top no longer provides protection against the elements. Last night was hot, in more ways than I can count, and the cover wasn't required for any of our activities—neither for the sleeping nor the kissing. Without a doubt, this has been the best damned summer of my life.

Outside the tent, birds chirp, and off in the distance an engine sputters to life. Gravel cracks as a car leaves the campground. Echo releases a contented sigh. She's gorgeous in her sleep. Her red curls flow over her shoulder, and a few strands cover her face.

We've got one week before we have to return to Kentucky. College orientation is starting, and my place of employment, the Malt and Burger, will reopen after being closed for renovations. I'll no longer be a burger-flipper. Instead, I've entered management, where I'll be teaching other assholes how to flip burgers. Who'd have thought I'd be the responsible type?

My hand wades through the mess of clothes near Echo's head, and I dig out my cell. Seven in the morning.

Good and damn.

Good—Echo slept through the night again without a nightmare and damn, she needs to wake up. I've got a promise to keep to a nine-year-old.

I lean down and press my lips to Echo's shoulder while my finger teases the strap of her tank. A disgruntled groan slips from her throat, and I chuckle as she half-heartedly swats at my hand. "Go away. I'm sleeping."

My nose brushes the hair away from her ear. Her sweet scent overwhelms my senses, and my mouth waters. I'm about to trash my intention of seducing her awake and replace it with plain seducing, but there's one lesson I learned quickly at the start of our road trip: Echo's not a morning person.

I gently nip her earlobe. While mornings aren't her thing, she's definitely a night girl. "I promised Jacob I'd video chat with him today. You wanted to shop for a new dress, and we have one more stop before we hit Denver."

Jacob—my younger brother.

I spent the past three years of my life plotting and scheming to gain custody of him and our youngest brother, Tyler. This spring, after experiencing one of those life-altering moments you see in the movies, I walked away from the custody battle and gave my brothers the life I could never provide. I shattered the fucked-up remains of my heart in the process. But Echo, being a damned magical siren, gathered the pieces and has slowly sewn them together.

"I take it back," Echo mumbles into the pillow. She fails at pulling the cover over her head when I pinch the blanket with my fingers to keep it in place. "I don't want a new dress for Denver. You take the keys and go chat with Jacob."

Echo's been invited to an art showing, and this one has her on edge. If I had to guess why, I'd say she's tired of the same pretentious jerks acting like they know everything. I've been over this nonsense since our second week, but Echo's into it, and I'm into Echo. "We need to map out the rest of our trip so I can call ahead and get shifts. I need cash if you want to stay in a hotel again."

I worked at the Malt and Burger for two years in Louisville, and thanks to their employee travel program, I can take swing shifts at sister stores throughout the nation. Gas and food on this trip hasn't been cheap, and then I sent a chunk of money to my best friend, Isaiah, for a deposit on an apartment.

"I've got money." Echo nestles in like it's three in the morning instead of seven, and damn if she doesn't look sexy doing it.

Even with the slump she's hit this past month, Echo did well earlier this summer by selling her paintings at galleries. I agree she could finance us, but the only thing I have left is my pride, and I'll eat shit before anyone rips that from me.

"I'm earning my way," I say. "If you don't come with me today, we'll end up going through Kansas again."

She wrinkles her nose but has yet to open her eyes. "It's a large country, Noah. We can live without seeing Kansas again."

"If you wake up and come with me, we'll have plenty of time to plan a new route."

"Know what I haven't had plenty of in two years? Sleep. Now—shhhh. I'm nightmare-less, and you're ruining my streak."

Echo's been nightmare-less for seven days. It's a big milestone, for both of us. "Echo…"

"Please," she whispers in this sensual Southern drawl full of the cracked grogginess that drives me crazy. "Pretty please?"

Everything inside me softens. Hands down, this girl owns me. I gave up caring this past spring how fucked I am because of it. "Five minutes."

"An hour."

"Ten minutes, and we'll stay in a hotel tonight." We're visiting Colorado Springs for the next two days before we drive to Denver. It's our last sightseeing trip before going home. Until this point, I've been adamant we camp.

Accepting her silence as consent to the deal, I hook an arm around her and draw her into my body. Echo flips, resting her head on my bare chest, and I don't miss the unrepentant smirk. Her breath tickles my skin, and the thought of seducing her creeps back into my brain. I shove the impulse away. I made a deal and I'm a man of my word.

With the soft sound of her even breaths and her body molded to mine, my eyelids grow heavy. I battle the urge to sleep along with her. This summer has brought a sense of peace I haven't experienced since I was fourteen, since the night before my parents died.

A herd of footsteps race past the tent, and seconds later a small kid's voice yells, "Hey, wait up."

I force my eyes open. "Come on, baby. It's time."

"You're mean, Noah."

The blanket falls off her arm as I slide a finger down her shoulder. Goose bumps form along her skin at my touch. She may be cranky, but she's responding.

"A deal's a deal," I remind her.

"I changed my mind. I'd rather sleep." With her eyes still shut, she hunts for the cover, but I kick it off. She presses her lips together. "I'm serious. You're the meanest person I know."

I kiss her neck then blow on the skin, pleased with the smile she's fighting.

"Does that feel mean?" I ask.

"Horribly." She giggles. "It's torture."

Echo rolls onto her back, tossing her arms over her head, and flutters her emerald eyes open. Her red hair sprawls over the array of pillows, clothes and blankets. My heart warms when I spot the spark in her eye.

I love her. More than I thought I was capable of, and I would sacrifice my life for her happiness.

She sucks in a breath when I caress her face. It's a slow movement, one that memorizes her skin. We've been traveling since graduation in June, visiting art galleries, exploring the country and each other. But there are some places that we haven't been, and while I'm fine with waiting until Echo's ready, there's that span of time when she looks at me and I kiss her lips where I wonder: Will this be our first time?

Echo's phone rings. She blinks repeatedly then bolts upright. "Crap."

It's a miracle her cell has power. She's had a bad habit this summer of not plugging it in.

Echo tosses my shirt at me before grabbing her cell. "I forgot to call Dad last night, and he's going to be ticked." She drops her voice so she can mimic his pissed-off tone. "'I thought you were going to be responsible, Echo. You said you'd call every other day by seven.'" She returns to her normal voice. "Just crap. Will you please put your shirt on?"

"Your dad can't see I'm shirtless." Because she'll go red-faced and stutter if I'm not fully clothed while they talk, I slip the shirt on and unzip the tent. "Don't forget to tell him I've been respectful."

I glance over my shoulder to see her answering smile freeze. The cell continues to ring, and Echo holds it in her hand, staring at the screen. Her face is void of color, and her body begins to tremble.

"Baby?"

Nothing.

I edge closer and run my hand through her hair. "Echo."

The cell stops ringing, and Echo turns her head in a movement so slow that it's painful to watch. The eyes that were full of life moments before are now wide and terrified. "It was my mom."

Echo

Alexander, my baby brother, cries in the background.

"Is he all right?" I ask.

"Yes," my father says on the other end of the line. "Just hungry. Can you hold on? Ashley needs his blanket."

"Sure." I listen as Dad thumps up the stairs of our house.

Alamosa is a small town in southern Colorado and the closest thing to civilization near the Great Sand Dunes. With that said, it was still a tortuous, caffeine-free, thirty-minute ride to coffee. Noah, being, well...awesome, waits in the winding line for my latte while I sit at the sidewalk table and chairs.

He glances over his shoulder at me again. His shaggy hair covers his eyes so I have a hard time deciphering his emotions. Noah was quiet, unusually pensive, during the drive in, and that bothers me.

Two girls in line admire Noah, and I don't blame them. He's undeniably hot: tall, dark brown hair, chocolate-brown eyes and cut in all the right places. The jeans and black T-shirt he wears definitely amplify that. Plus, he has swagger.

As one of the girls drops her purse, he's got a little more swagger than I'd like as he helps her collect her items.

"I'm back," says Dad.

"Okay."

It's like watching a horror film in slow motion. She tucks her hair behind her ears, gives him a hesitant smile and speaks. The girl is pretty—very pretty. I run my hand over the scars on my left arm. Sometimes I don't understand why Noah's with me. Especially when I'm so...

"You're quiet today," Dad says. "Are you okay?"

Noah answers the girl then motions at me with his chin. Both girls turn, and their faces fall. Noah waves. I wave back. Butterflies tumble in my stomach when he flashes his wicked grin.

"Echo?" Dad prods.

"I'm fine." I blink three times, and Noah raises an eyebrow.

"Lying?" he mouths.

I throw a mock glare at Noah, and his shoulders move with a chuckle as he refocuses on the counter.

I haven't told Dad that Mom called because I don't know how I feel about it, so I'm hardly ready to listen to his opinion. There's no absolving Mom in Dad's mind, and I'm not sure that's fair. I forgave him for his part of the night that changed my life, so shouldn't I at least try to forgive Mom? Nausea rolls through me, and I fight a dry heave. Okay—shouldn't I at least consider trying to forgive Mom?

"How's Ashley?" My stepmom, and an excellent change of subject.

A year ago she was my wicked stepmother from Oz. Now she's my stepmom who means well, but doesn't know when to stop. Like when I ask her thoughts on an outfit, and I'm not really searching for complete and utter honesty, and she drones on for twenty minutes about how I should wear something that flatters my figure because, let's be honest, God blessed me in the top area, but fell short on the hip portion...yeah, that's how Ashley talks.

"She's good. Alexander still wakes up at night so she's having a rough time functioning during the day. I'm worried that she's sleep deprived."

"Uh-huh." Try two years of insomnia, then we can discuss tired.

"Where are you heading next?" he asks.

"We're going to stay in Colorado Springs for the next two nights, then we'll head to Denver. Noah and I are visiting a gallery there. This one is huge. I hear people have been trying to get an invite into this show for weeks."

"That's good."

That's good. I roll my eyes. The men in my life don't understand the biggest part of me. Sometimes Noah shows the same disappointing amount of enthusiasm.

"I assume Noah's treating you well," Dad says, like he's one hundred percent on board with me being on this road trip with—how did he refer to Noah before I left Louisville? Oh, yeah, as a guy I barely knew, that is if I really paused and thought this through. Which, according to him, he doesn't believe I did, but hey, I'm here and Dad's in Louisville. I won this round.

"He's treating me great." My dad and Noah have an unsteady relationship. Dad respects Noah for seeing beyond my scars and for being there for me during an awful period this past spring, but he's still wary.

On the outside, Noah can still come across as the rough

foster-care kid, and what parent would be thrilled with his daughter taking off for an entire summer with a guy half her school is terrified of? The day before Noah and I left, Dad sat me down and talked to me for a long time about how "this is a phase in your life" and not to do anything I would "regret" and that if I ever needed him, to call.

"Echo…"

Warning flags. The use of my name along with any dramatic pause by my father means bad, bad—very bad—news. *I accidentally forgot your favorite stuffed animal at the hotel…your mother is bipolar…your brother, Aires, is being deployed to Afghanistan.* Bad news.

"I'm considering selling the house."

"Oh." I slump back in my seat, half relieved to discover that the plague hasn't been intentionally released into the world, but then a sickening sensation strikes. *"Oh."*

"I've considered it for years," he continues. "But it was your home, and I didn't want to take something else away from you after you'd lost so much."

Like how I'd lost Aires when he died in Afghanistan, or how I'd lost my mind after a visit with my mother went horribly wrong at the end of my sophomore year of high school.

That type of lost.

"But now that you've graduated and are moving on, I thought Ashley and I could start somewhere…" He cuts himself off.

"New," I finish for him.

There's a crackling silence on the line, and Dad releases a heavy sigh. "Yes."

He's not replacing me. He's not shoving me away. Yes,

Dad has a new wife and a new baby, but I'm not being thrown out of this family. I'm part of it. I've talked this over with my therapist, Mrs. Collins, again and again, but the nagging doubt still slices through me like a ragged knife.

"What are your thoughts on my selling the house?" he asks.

I'll miss sitting in the garage and watching Aires's ghost work on his car as he counseled me through my high school life crises. I'll miss staring at the constellations my mother painted on the ceiling of my room. I'll miss the happy memories. That house has been one of the few constants in my life.

A knot in my throat keeps me from saying those things. My world's changing again, and sometimes I hate change. "Mom called this morning."

The hydrogen bomb I dropped alters the entire conversation.

I ram my thumb on the icon for Off and toss my cell onto the table. Blood swooshes in my veins, and each throb in my temple ticks me off more. Obviously, Dad and I were never meant to see eye to eye.

With his legs kicked out onto the sidewalk and his fingers laced across his stomach, Noah regards me from across the table. "Vexed?"

"Vexed? Did we enter medieval times?"

"It means mad," he says.

"I know what it means. Why are you using it?"

He shrugs casually. "It was an ACT word. Figured if I had to learn the shit I might as well use it."

I giggle in spite of myself then stop when dread weighs down my entire body. "Yeah, I'm vexed."

Noah edges my ignored latte toward me. I pick it up and attempt to disappear by pulling my legs along with me onto the seat. "Dad doesn't get it."

He says nothing and glowers at the mountains in the distance. Noah overheard most of the conversation between me and Dad, at least my side of it. I drink, and the latte is like little shards of heaven in my mouth. A part of me relaxes with the introduction of caffeine into my system.

"What if I told you I don't get it, either?"

With the coffee still poised at my mouth, I have to force the swallow. "What?"

"I don't get why you're interested in talking to your mom. What she did...it's not forgivable."

My forehead wrinkles as I set the cup on the table. "I never said I've forgiven her. I told Dad that maybe I should answer if she calls again. Maybe I should listen to the voice mail instead of deleting it. She's my mom."

"You talked to her before and didn't get anywhere."

"But maybe I should talk to her because...because..." Because...I don't know, but I do know that there's a hollowness inside me. This dull ache that screams that something's missing. I felt this before—after I lost Aires and before I recovered my memories.

I believed that the cure would be this summer. That leaving home and spending time with Noah would heal the wound.

"I *did* get someplace the last time Mom and I talked. I remembered what happened that night, and I learned that she's on her meds again, and that she's being responsible about her condition. You don't understand what life's been like for her."

"She tried to kill you." He says it as if he's telling me something new—something I don't agonize over every single time I look in the mirror.

"Really?" I thrust my scarred arms into the air. "Guess I forgot."

Noah swears and glances away. Two guys our age walk past, gawk at my scars then stare at each other. Ashamed, I lower my arms to my lap and close my eyes when I hear the whispered "freak."

The table slams into my knees, and metal cracks against the sidewalk. My eyes flash open to find Noah's chair flipped backward. I'm trapped by the table, and I press my hands against it, desperate for escape.

Noah grabs the nearest guy, twists the material of his shirt near his neck and pounds him into the wall. "Say it again, asshole. Say it to my fucking face."

The table screeches against the sidewalk as I push it away and scramble to my feet. "Noah! No!"

The guy trembles in Noah's grasp and his friend, thankfully, isn't much help as he gapes at a distance. If this had happened to Noah and Noah's best friend, Isaiah, had been here, it would have been a bloodbath. But then again, Noah would never disrespect a girl.

I place my hand on Noah's biceps. His eyes flicker to mine and soften the moment our gazes connect.

"Let him go."

It takes a second, but Noah releases his white-knuckle grip, though not without an extra shove. He refocuses on the guy then jerks his head in my direction. "Apologize."

My lips flatten, and I wish I could disappear. One minute here. Another gone. Into thin air. No longer freaking existing.

The guy's eyes linger on my arms, and it's not too different from the way Noah stared at me the first time he saw my scars this past January when I'd fallen on the ice. Except back then, I was hiding them from the world. This spring, I gave up trying to care what the world thought, but moments like this...I have to admit I care.

"I'm sorry," the guy whispers.

"It's okay." But it's not. He called me a freak. I heard it, and so did Noah. Once an insult like that has been released, there's no way to take it back. It becomes one more cut on my soul.

Noah slides away and the guy runs off, his friend trailing close behind. Around us, people have stopped what they were doing to focus on me and Noah. What's worse is that when they reanimate, they lower their voices and talk to one another as their eyes zero in on my scars.

My foot taps the sidewalk. Somehow I thought graduation was going to be the end of this torment. That the moment I walked across the stage, all the demons that haunted me during high school would somehow be exorcised.

I can handle the questioning looks and sometimes the appalled shock, but the words still hurt. Even if they're whispered. Especially if they're whispered. I wonder if I'll ever fit in.

Noah reaches over and touches my cheek, but I lean back, not allowing him the opportunity to seek redemption. Noah should have let the taunt go, but he didn't. He drew more attention to my scars. He made more people stare, made me more of a spectacle than I already am. Instead of two guys thinking I'm a freak, an entire crowd of people thinks the same thing. For the first time since we left Kentucky, Noah did something that made me feel worse.

NOAH

My younger brother Jacob inherited my father's eyes and my mother's smile. I normally love the familiar sight on the computer screen, but today it slowly strangles me from the inside out. If my parents had survived the fire that claimed their lives three years ago, today, July twenty-seventh, would have been their nineteenth wedding anniversary.

It doesn't help that I've pissed off Echo.

I glance out the window of the coffee shop. Echo sits on the hood of her Honda Civic and burns a hole into the sidewalk with her glare. It's hot out there and cool in here, and that shows the intensity of Echo's anger. She'd rather roast in the sun and inhale gasoline fumes than be with me in an air-conditioned building that smells like ground coffee beans.

If I were a great guy, I'd be out there instead of in here chatting with my younger brother, but I suck at the boyfriend thing. If I went out there, I'd succeed in ticking her off more.

I lower the picture of me and Echo at the Great Sand Dunes, and Jacob remains transfixed like the photo is still there. "Mountains of sand in Colorado?" he asks.

"This is in southern Colorado," I answer. "The forests

are north. You'd like it here, Jay Bird. Enormous dunes of sand right next to towering mountains."

I don't know if he would or wouldn't like it, but I pretend that I do. These Skype visits and phone calls have been a summer-long reintroduction to each other. Until last week, I didn't know that he was allergic to peanuts. Until last month, he didn't know that I have a long scar that snakes up my biceps and down my back.

His eyes got big and moist when I explained I got it by protecting him and our youngest brother, Tyler, from falling debris when our home burned down at the end of my freshman year of high school. The same fire that killed our parents.

I saved him from the play-by-play of how I hauled Tyler and Jacob through the choking smoke and fire. They didn't see much as I had swaddled them in blankets and half pushed, half carried them out of the house, using my body as a shield.

I also left out how I failed him and our parents—a secret only a few that were at the scene know. Some hero I'd be to him if he knew the truth.

Jacob stares at his picture at the bottom of the screen when he talks. "Did you know that there's an entire planet of sand in *Return of the Jedi*?"

"Yeah."

Jacob leans closer to the computer, and his baseball cap hits the monitor. I chuckle and in the background, his adoptive mother, Carrie, whispers for him to take the hat off. "Dad and I watched the whole trilogy last weekend. It was super awesome, Noah. I think *you* would have liked *that*."

The jacked-up social services system in Kentucky kept

me away from Jacob and Tyler for over two years when I was labeled a discipline case. It happened after I hit an adult because he beat his son, then no one backed my side of the story.

"You're right. I like it." I clear my throat. "I first watched it with *our* dad."

It no longer feels like someone's yanking my balls through my ass when he refers to Carrie and Joe as his parents. The pain's been downgraded to a railroad spike being shoved into my eye every ten seconds. The adoption became official last month. Now and forever, Carrie and Joe will be Jacob and Tyler's mom and dad.

I'm okay with it. What I'm not okay with is being alone—being the one without a family. Echo's the lone string that's held me together since I decided to walk from the custody battle, and sometimes I'm afraid she'll get tired of my shit and snap.

"When are you coming home? I want you to see me play." Jacob had a baseball game today, and his team won. He had a double, a single and one home run. I missed each and every play. Not just today, but for the whole summer. "Mom said I only have a few games left."

"I'm heading back east after Echo's last gallery appointment."

"Hasn't she seen enough art galleries? Paintings look the same, right?"

I laugh, and Carrie reprimands Jacob in the background. "Sometimes," I answer.

"Try to come soon, okay?"

Now washing dishes on the other side of the kitchen, Carrie says, "The last game is in two weeks." Jacob parrots the message, then the two of them have a sidebar on whether or not he has a make-up game.

I relax back in my seat and let them talk. Jacob's nine and thinks he's right. Carrie has a patience with him I'm not sure I would have possessed.

Echo slides off the hood, and her hips have this easy sway as she walks to the back passenger door. Damn, she's gorgeous—red, curly hair flowing over her shoulders, a pair of cut-offs hugging her ass and a blue spaghetti-strap tank dipped low enough to show cleavage.

My fingers twitch with the need to touch. I'm going to have to pull some major groveling to gain forgiveness. If I were smart, I'd find a way to say sorry without opening my mouth. Never fails that half the time I try to apologize, it comes out wrong.

It also doesn't help that I'm not sorry for throwing the asshole against the wall and twenty bucks I don't own says that's what she longs to hear.

"So maybe my last game is in two weeks," says Jacob, drawing me back to him. "But you need to see me play."

Echo's had a rough tail end of the summer when it comes to selling her paintings, and she's contemplated adding more appointments on the way home, which could prevent me from seeing Jacob's game. I rub at the tension forming in my neck, hating being torn between two people I love. "I'll try."

"Awesome!"

"Tell Tyler I'll be home soon and that I love him." I already told him earlier, but I want Tyler to hear it as many times as possible from as many people as he can. He's five, and because of the foster care system that kept us apart, he doesn't have a decent grasp of who I am.

"I will." Jacob says goodbye and I do the same.

As I'm about to end the connection, Carrie's blond ponytail swings into view. "Noah."

My finger freezes over the touch pad of Echo's laptop. Carrie and I have despised each other for three years and when I stopped pursuing custody of my brothers, we called a truce. I don't hate her anymore, but it doesn't mean I want to chat with her. "Yeah?"

Carrie scans the room around her then settles into the seat Jacob abandoned. "Are you really in Colorado?"

Unsure where the hell this is going, I scratch at the stubble on my face. "Yeah."

Lines clutter Carrie's forehead, and she releases a long breath. "I'm not sure I'm doing the right thing. Joe thinks it's wrong. He says that you're doing well and that we should let the state handle this, but when it comes to you we've made too many wrong choices. I'm afraid this will get lost in the system and, besides, you're an adult and you should decide."

"Decide what?"

"About your mother's family," Carrie says.

"What about them?" My mother told me she was an only child and that her parents had died before my birth. This past spring, Carrie's husband, Joe, informed me that was a lie. At night, when Echo's tucked close to me asleep, my mind wanders with thoughts I don't dare entertain during the day. I have living blood relatives. Ones I could meet.

"They live in Vail."

It's a town north of here. "And?"

"They emailed us, asking if they could see Jacob and Tyler."

"So?" Though my fist tightens under the table. Mom's family didn't try for custody of me when Carrie and Joe asked them to sign away their rights to Jacob and Tyler for the adoption. I may not have admitted it to a single soul, but the idea that I was forced into foster care when I had living blood relatives makes me feel like trash thrown to the curb.

"They also asked to see you."

Her words land like a blow to the gut. "Little late, don't you think?"

Carrie picks up a napkin ring and rolls it between her hands before setting it back down. Her anxiety twists the coil within me.

"Let me forward you the email. They say..." She trails off, and her cheeks puff out when she exhales. "They say that when we contacted them two years ago about adopting Jacob and Tyler, they thought we were asking to adopt you, too. There's been a misunderstanding. They thought we were taking care of you."

Fuck. Me.

Noah sits inside, and I sit outside. It's not unusual for me to give him space while he talks with his brothers, but what is unusual is the silence between us before he went in. I've got nothing to say to him, and he obviously has nothing to say to me.

My hand flies over the page and what typically erases the unease and melts the apprehension doesn't smooth away anything. My grip tightens on the chalk, and each swipe across the paper becomes more clipped and less thought out until the markings represent disoriented lines on a page and not an image or a picture or anything.

I toss the sketch pad and the chalk onto the table and rub at the wetness forming in my eyes. Freak. The guy called me a freak, and that's what I am.

Noah and I are heading back home, and the nightmares I thought I was running from lurk behind every corner and coffee shop in America. In less than a month, Noah and I will start college, and I'll have a roommate in the dorms and new classes, and a ball of dread knots in my stomach. This summer was supposed to change me, and nothing has changed.

NOAH

Back at the parking lot of the campsite, Echo sets her sketchbook into the passenger side of the car and riffles through her duffel bag of clothes. She hasn't spoken to me since the incident at the café. It's not the first time Echo's been pissed at me, but somehow this anger feels different—weighted.

I drop the packed tent next to the open trunk and lean my hip against the car, praying Echo will at least make fleeting eye contact. It's not like her to go this long without acknowledging me. I've been hoping she'd talk—give me an idea of what direction to take.

If she said, "I hate you," then I can say, "I'm an asshole, so you should, but I love you." If she said that she's mad at me then I can respond that she should be, but it doesn't matter because I love her. But she gives me nothing. Silence.

Echo tosses the duffel bag in the backseat and rummages through another. With her clothes stacked to the side, Echo withdraws a light white button-up sweater. She jams the clothes back in and closes the car door.

Fuck. Plain and simple fuck.

It's nine in the morning and close to eighty degrees. She's covering her scars again.

As Echo walks down a trail leading to the campground

and the dunes, she slips the sweater over her arms and draws the sleeves over her fingers. I haven't seen her do that since March. And Echo wonders why I don't think she should talk to her psychotic mother. One phone call along with the wrong words from a stupid-ass bastard and she spirals.

The memory of the way her face paled out when I told the bastard to apologize circles my brain. Echo has a habit of making me feel like a dick, and this is one of those moments, but damn it, I went after that guy for her.

Screw it. We'll get on the road, and she'll calm down after some distance. I pick the tent up and try to cram it into the small space I left for it in the trunk. When it won't fit, I push harder, and the sound of material ripping causes a rip within me. Possibly my sanity. "Shit!"

I slam the trunk with a thunderous bang. For two months, Echo and I didn't worry about our messed-up lives in Kentucky. She didn't focus on her mom or dad or her newfound memories or the scars on her arms, and I didn't think twice about how in June I turned eighteen.

Eighteen. Out of foster care, out on the streets, pack your shit, get out of my fucking house, eighteen.

Soon Echo and I will be heading home and back to our problems.

Once Carrie sends the email, I'll have one more problem to add to this list: deciding whether or not to read it and what the hell to do with the message.

My head falls back, and I focus on the crystal-blue sky overhead. I blow out a rush of air then inhale slowly. Mrs. Collins told me to do that whenever I was hit with the urge to tell her where to shove her annoying questions. I'd never admit it, but sometimes, as in now, it works.

I need to go after Echo, but I've got no clue what to say. Desperate for help, I pull out my cell, scroll to a familiar number and press Call. Two rings and I smile at hearing the voice of my best friend and foster brother on the other end. "Aren't you supposed to be in the middle of nowhere?"

"S'up, Isaiah. What's going on there?"

"Watching Beth's back...as much as she'll let me. Right now she's picking up her pay at the Dollar Store."

I met Isaiah and Beth over a year ago when social services placed me into a new foster home—the same home as Isaiah. He had been placed at Beth's aunt and uncle's house years ago and because of Beth's messed-up home life, she often crashed there with us.

"Watching her back how?" I ask.

"Some shit's going down with her mom."

"How bad?" Beth's mom is a nightmare, plus her mom's boyfriend makes serial killers look like cuddly puppies.

"Bad." The short answer creates chills. "But Beth doesn't know, and keeping her in the dark is becoming complicated."

"Should you keep her in the dark?"

Isaiah pauses. "It's Beth. If she knew what her mom is mixed up in, she'd try to fix it, and then she'd end up in trouble that *I* couldn't fix."

This is the kind of guy Isaiah is: loyal to the end and a fixer. Even if the person he loves doesn't want to be helped.

"Yeah. I get it." There's not much I wouldn't do for Beth. She's the closest thing I have to a sister. "We'll get Beth to move out with us. The more distance she puts between her and her mom, the better."

"Thanks, man. So why are you calling?"

My gaze roams back to the path. "I fucked up with Echo."

"When don't you fuck up with Echo?"

My best friend's a comedian. "A guy called her a freak, and I threw him against a wall."

"Good for you."

"She's pissed. Won't even look at me."

"Why?"

Exactly. "I love her, but I never said I understood her."

"Have you said you're sorry?"

"No, and I'm not sorry." Not in the least.

"Try it. Who knows, it could help."

"It could."

"And people say you're smart."

"Fuck you." I let sincerity into my voice.

"Right back at you. When are you coming home?"

I study the mountains looming on the horizon. "I don't know. I thought we'd be heading back later this week, but some shit's come up."

"Shit?"

"Shit."

"Got it." That's Isaiah. He doesn't need to know details to sympathize.

"Did you put the money down on the apartment?" I made a promise to Isaiah that I wouldn't leave him behind in foster care. Even though the state would pay for me to live in the dorms, there's no way I can leave my non-blood brother behind, so we decided to move out together, even though he'll only be a senior in high school this fall.

"We move in September first."

I exhale. One less situation to worry about.

"I got a favor to ask," says Isaiah.

"Shoot."

"If you're going to be gone for another few weeks..." Isaiah's not a guy who hesitates, nor is he the kind that asks for favors. He'd rather break off his arm and sell it than ask for help. "I'd like to bring Beth out. A guy owes me, and I can get one-way bus tickets cheap. Watching Beth with her mom is like watching a ticking time bomb without a pair of pliers to clip the wires."

"Is Beth going to be on board with this?" Beth doesn't like being away from her mom.

"She owes me, and she knows it, but it doesn't mean she won't bitch." A long pause. "The shit Beth's mom's into...I need to get Beth out of town for a few days. Change her perspective. Then maybe she'll stop going over to her mom's so much."

That would take a damn miracle. Regardless of that I say, "Come on out."

I should discuss it with Echo first—hell, I still need to talk to her about my mother's family. Beth and Echo can be oil and water. It's tough for Beth to trust people, and she's given Echo a rough time from the get-go. I'm sure Echo's going to be thrilled to hear we'll have guests, but the decision needs to be made and made now.

If Echo's anything, she's understanding. We'll enjoy Colorado Springs then get to Denver. I'll take her out to a nice dinner after the showing then tell her everything. She's got too much on her plate at the moment to deal with my baggage.

"We'll be in Colorado Springs for the next two days.

Denver for a night after that." And screw me. "Maybe Vail will be on the list."

"I've gotta go. Beth's walking out."

Isaiah hangs up, and a tug to return home grows. I've got Isaiah, Beth and my brothers waiting for me. Plus, Echo will be at my side. I'm not alone—I'm not.

Echo's red curls bounce as she drags the cooler up the path. With her eyes fixed on the car, she lifts the cooler, tosses it into the backseat, slams the back door shut then slides into the front passenger seat and yanks *that* door shut with pissed-off pizzazz.

We've got a couple of hours in the car together, and my girl has a hell of a temper. This should be an interesting ride.

Echo

Colorado Springs is, according to the guy who tried initiating small talk a few seconds ago outside the hotel, unseasonably hot. Hot enough that I'm shocked that people don't melt the moment they step into the sunlight. The sweater doesn't help.

I push off the hood of my Honda Civic, twist my hair off my neck and duck into the shadow of a towering fir tree. The stark contrast between Alamosa and Colorado Springs is beyond amazing: desert and flat to green with mountains rising in the distance. The urge to paint and draw overwhelms me as the sights and colors here are a feast for my artistic palate.

I could have joined Noah in the hotel lobby, but then he'd believe he was winning, and he's so not. We haven't talked since the café, and he's dead wrong if he thinks I'm caving. I don't care how many wicked smiles he flashes in my direction or how many times he "mistakenly" brushes his hand against my cheek or thigh. He can make my head spin and my blood run hot, but I'm strong enough to resist his every temptation.

I haven't gone this long without kissing Noah since this spring when we broke up for a couple of weeks. I shiver despite the heat. That was one of the darkest periods of my life and, unfortunately, I'm well versed in dark.

Noah exits the lobby, and I'm hypnotized by his confident strut. Even in the heat, he wears jeans and a black T-shirt and never breaks a sweat. Not impervious to hot weather, I blow a couple of curls away from my face.

"You wouldn't be so hot if you took off your sweater," he says.

My fingers clutch the ends of the material.

Noah rests a hand on my hip and chuckles when I pull away. "You're going to have to talk to me sometime."

I will not crumble. He started this fight, not me. Going around and bullying guys because they called me a name...it's not okay, especially when it attracts attention to me and leads people to wonder if what they said is true.

He holds up one key card and with a slip of his fingers reveals two. I extend my palm and waggle my fingers for my key, but Noah only grins as he lowers his hand and walks past. Arrogant, conceited, smoking, full of himself...

Without looking back, Noah strolls into the side entrance. I've got two options: liquefy from the heat and dissolve into the pavement or follow Noah. I actually weigh the choices. I really, really don't like admitting he has the upper hand because Noah is a sore winner.

A bead of sweat drips from my scalp and onto my neck. We do sleep in the same bed, and I could smother Noah with a pillow later tonight or toss his pants and boxers onto the front lawn of the hotel. Except the last one would make him smile and me blush.

With an exaggerated sigh, I yank open the door and spot Noah down the hall sliding the key card into a slot. The cool hotel hallway reeks of chlorine, and the farther

I walk in the direction of our room, the sound of splashing and children shouting in delight grows.

Noah enters the room and disappears. My agitation reaches a new level as tension builds between my muscles. Is this how he's going to be? Ignoring me? Not even waiting? My skin tightens until I feel paper-thin and ready to rip.

My hand stings when it pounds into the cracked open door, and a cold blast hits me as the air conditioner roars to life. "Do you seriously think you have the right to treat me this way after what you did this morning?"

All the air rushes out of my body. Roses cover the full-size bed closest to the door. The long-stemmed kind. Noah bought me flowers...for the first time...ever. Despite the anger and hurt from earlier, every romantic notion inside me squeals with excitement.

"I'm not sorry for defending you." Noah leans against the wall next to the bed with his arms crossed over his chest. "But I am sorry for hurting you, so talk to me, Echo. Or yell. Anything but the silence."

The door clicks shut behind me, and I become hyper-aware. I'm alone with Noah. It's not the first time, but whenever we enter a room with a bed, in complete isolation, the same strange sensation hums along my body, like a tuning fork being struck.

Speechless, I ease over to the bed and rub the silky petals between my fingers.

This isn't a swanky room. In fact, it's modest with two beds that share the same thin multicolored comforter. A two-hundred-pound television sits on a dresser, and the corner contains a particle-board table and chairs.

The air from the conditioner has a musty, this-room-is-older-than-me scent. Heck, this hotel could be older than my dad. But as I stare at the roses, it's as if the bareness of the room fades, and I'm the princess entering her castle. Noah always has the ability to turn reality into fantasy.

I pick up one of the long stems, and the smooth petals caress my lips as I bring it to my nose. Noah's kisses always start off soft and gentle. If I face him, would Noah notice the vein pulsing wildly in my neck? If so, he'd know I was imagining him and his kisses and right now, I'm not sure I want to be kissed.

The fragrance of the rose isn't overwhelming. It's mild and sweet and perfect, and it must have driven Noah crazy to buy them.

"Come on, baby, you're killing me here."

"This had to be expensive."

I risk a glance at him and catch his eyes before he lowers them. "You're worth it."

Noah finds spending money difficult, and I try my best to understand. Until this summer, I never thought about purchasing my morning latte. Then I noticed Noah avoiding breakfast or skipping lunch or dinner. He's fended for himself for so long that he's constantly scared of losing what he's earned, and his pride won't allow me to pay for his meals. I practically had to arm wrestle him into letting me pay halves on the hotel rooms, which is why we camp, often, at my suggestion.

I lay the rose back on the bed. "I love you."

He pushes off the wall and snags a belt loop on both sides of my hips, tugging me into him. "You didn't say you've forgiven me."

The heat of his body surrounding me in the midst of the cold room creates a fluttering in my bloodstream. It's impossible to hold a steady thought when he's this close. "So you agree that throwing people into walls isn't okay?"

"It is when someone fucks with you."

I attempt to step back, but Noah halts the escape. "I mean it. No one treats you like shit. At least when I'm around. That's nonnegotiable."

"You embarrassed me."

"He hurt you."

"You hurt me," I snap, and this time he allows the release. I shake my head trying to expel the memory and the ache building in my chest. "When you told him to apologize and the way he looked at my arms..."

This pain, it was supposed to be over. None of this was supposed to carry out of high school and into normal life.

Noah brushes his fingers along my sweater-covered arm. "You have nothing to be embarrassed about."

I close my eyes at his intimate touch. It's a slow movement, not one meant to seduce. It's one to show how much he loves me, and I flatten my lips, fighting the urge to cry. Noah nudges me toward him and if it wasn't for his hold, I'd drop like a house of cards.

I fall into him, and Noah wraps me in his arms. "It's okay, baby. We're okay."

I cling tighter to him, because it doesn't feel okay. For the past two months, life was good and easy and everything I dreamed it could be. Despite my efforts, the muscles at the corner of my mouth tremble. I wanted to be done with tears and with whispered comments thrown in my direction like knives and with this overwhelming sense that I'm less and that I'll never belong.

"I thought I was past this." Past caring what people thought. Past people caring about the scars on my arms.

Like a diploma somehow gave the world and myself a magical maturity.

"You are."

"I'm not." I've been living in a delusional bubble. The world hasn't changed, and neither have I.

"You are. It's the day." Meaning like everyone else, he blames my mom. "Just a bad day."

Noah kisses the top of my head before cradling me to his chest. I love the sensation of my cheek against him, the protective shelter of his arm around my waist and the sound of his steady heart. If I could live here for the rest of my life, I could be happy. But at some point, he'll have to let go, and then I'll be back where I started: alone.

"What if this is all I'll ever be? What if this is only a small taste of what's waiting for me at home?" I whisper. Chilling adrenaline drips into my body at the rawness of the statement. This week we'll no longer be heading away, but going back. "What if I'll always be the person on the outside? The person who doesn't belong."

"You belong, Echo," he says against my temple. "Right here with me."

NOAH

Rays of the late-evening's summer sun stream through the crack of the curtains. I lay on the bed with Echo curled tight next to me and my arms locked around her. Our shoes are still on and so are our clothes. The roses are bunched together on top of the bedside table.

We've lain like this for an hour, maybe two. We've been quiet the whole time, but sometimes we both say more within a silence than we can in hours of words.

She needs me. I need her. I never knew what peace there was in being wanted, but I hate how today has gone. I hate how one phone call and one asshole's comment have caused her to withdraw. I hate how I fear and long for one email.

The email. I should tell Echo about Vail and Isaiah and Beth. Denver. I'll wait until after the gallery in Denver.

I sweep my fingers along Echo's arm to the tip of her fingers to wake her in case she's drifted to sleep. She swipes her thumb across my hand in response.

Parts of me stir with her touch. Echo has no idea how sexy she is and how I dream night after night of completely showing her how much I worship her body.

I tug at the ends of her sweater near her wrist, and her fingers twist up in defense. Nope. Not having it. First chance I get, I'm throwing every long-sleeved item in the trash and burning it with a single match and a gallon of gas. She'll be pissed, but I won't watch her backtrack.

Ignoring her hold, I pull at the material, easing the sleeve down.

"Noah," she whispers in reprimand.

"You've never complained when I've tried to undress you before."

Echo readjusts so she can see me, and for the first time since this morning, those eyes dance. "Yes, I have."

"When?"

"The last day of school."

"So you've complained once." When I led her to the nook of the abandoned hallway in the basement near my locker. I only meant to sneak in for a kiss during lunch, but things got hot and heavy and well...sue me. "I didn't buy a yearbook, so I was memory-making."

Her mouth gapes. "They would have kept us from participating in graduation if we got caught."

"Walking across stages is overrated."

"Is not." She lightly kicks my shin. "It was awesome, and you know it. Did you forget the dressing room at the mall?"

Forget? I have wet dreams involving that day. "That's not my fault. You asked how you looked in those jeans."

"Good would have sufficed. Attempting to take them off wasn't necessary."

"They did look good. Good enough that I wanted to touch, and then I wanted to touch more."

Echo laughs, and the sound warms my heart. "They have security cameras. People go to jail over stuff like that."

I roll onto my side and drape my leg over hers. "I had

you covered from sight. Very covered." Backed her up against the wall and covered her body with every inch of mine.

That siren smile that I love so much crosses her face. Her fingers reach up and trace the line of my jaw. "You are the most impossible person I know."

"Damn straight."

"That's not always a good thing. Sometimes you make life more complicated than it needs to be."

"Never said I was going to be easy."

"I know," she says as her smile fades. "I never said I was going to be easy, either. In fact, I promised the opposite."

"I like you just the way you are."

My fingers tease the end of her sweater again, but this time Echo doesn't stop me as I edge the material off her arm. In fact, she leans forward so I can slip the entire sweater off and toss it to the floor where it belongs.

I skim the length of her arm, specifically the longest scar from top to bottom. "Why, Echo?"

"Why what?"

"Why hide them again?"

She's silent, and we won't leave this bed until she answers.

It's hard to imagine her lying in a pool of her own blood. It drives me crazy that I almost lost her before I had the chance to meet her. I'm schooled in loss and understand its permanence.

Just the thought of losing Echo creates an anger bordering on fear. It's a dangerous combination, and I hate her mother for causing such suffering and pain.

Echo's breathing hitches when I slide my thumb along a smaller scar. She likes that spot. I've memorized it. A centimeter below the crook of her elbow. Her skin is sensitive there, and when I kiss it, Echo normally falls apart and nearly shatters.

I gently press my lips behind her ear, and Echo nudges closer to me. "Why, Echo?"

"Because."

I nip at her earlobe, and she shivers. "Because why?"

Her shoulder moves under my body. A half shrug maybe. "It makes me feel better."

Fuck that. "Why?"

A kiss on her neck. A long one. A lingering one. God damn, Echo tastes so good. Her skin is soft and tempting. But I want answers.

"Because sometimes I want to blend in."

I raise my head and stare straight into her eyes, spotting the plain honesty. What she doesn't understand is that she could never blend in. Blazing red hair. Bright emerald eyes. The most beautiful girl in the world. She'd turn heads regardless of a sweater.

As I open my mouth to respond, my phone rings.

Echo

Noah drops his forehead to my shoulder and groans. Good God, I completely understand. My body pulsates like a five-alarm fire. I kiss his collarbone and rub my hand along his spine, in regret...in apology. His phone rings a third time. "You should answer."

"Fuck." He presses his lips against my neck before drawing away and yanking his phone out of his back pocket. "Yeah."

Noah's eyes meet mine, and I tilt my head in question. I exhale when he subtly shakes a no, telling me the call is benign.

"Yeah," he says again then flashes a smile promising lots of naughtiness. "I understand."

Noah cups my waist and swipes his finger underneath the material of my shirt. My mouth pops open. No way. There is no way he means to explore while he's on the phone. His hand begins to travel for my bra. Holy freaking crap. I bat at his arm and mouth. "No."

"Why?" he mouths back, but his grin grows.

"Because," I yell-whisper.

Noah lowers his arm away from my bra and instead snakes it around my waist, gathering me to his side. He nuzzles my hair before saying into his cell, "I'll be there in a few minutes. Thanks."

He ends the call and slides his phone back into his jeans. "Tell me I'm forgiven."

"Who was that?" I ask.

In lightning-fast movements, Noah rolls us both, and his heavy weight pins me against the mattress. "Say I'm forgiven."

"For what?" My brain goes blank. Noah's on top of me, and subconsciously my legs hook around his. Through his jeans and my jean shorts there are parts of him that are sweetly touching parts of me.

We haven't made love yet. I think of it. I dream of it. Sometimes I wake up so on edge that I worry I'll explode, but when it comes to *it*, I haven't found the courage to cross the line. And Noah's always patient...so patient. Even when he has to resort to cold showers or really, really long hot ones.

I don't ask what he's doing in there, but I kinda can guess, and that only makes me feel epically worse.

"For upsetting you this morning," he answers. "Tell me I'm forgiven."

I nod because I love him, and I can't imagine not forgiving him. "Just don't do it again."

Noah rests his forehead against mine and closes his eyes as if I handed him a death row pardon. "I love you, Echo."

The pterodactyls that only he can create lift their wings and soar in my stomach. I love those words out his mouth. Almost as much as I love his hands on my body and the way his eyes devour me. Almost as much as I love him.

He kisses my lips and before I can repeat the same to him, he's off the bed. "I've got to roll. The last Malt and

Burger jacked up my hours in the system, and they want me to go into a local one and fix it."

I sit up on the bed and bite the inside of my lip to keep from throwing a fit like a toddler. "How long?"

"An hour. Maybe longer." Noah places one of the room keys on the dresser next to the television. "By the way, I want to take you out to dinner in Denver to celebrate. Someplace nice."

"Celebrate what?"

"For when you blow those pretentious assholes away with your paintings."

I smile, amazed by the roses, by his faith in me and by the fact that he's absolutely fantastic. "Thanks."

Noah gently pulls one of the curls. "Damn, baby, don't look at me like that."

"Like what?"

"Like you want me to kiss you."

But I do want him to kiss me. Instead, I shove at his wall of a chest, and he winks at me before he grabs the keys to the car and walks out the door. The air conditioner kicks off, and I lean against the headboard, staring at Noah's roses on the bedside table. I pick one up, inhale the sweet scent and wonder, when it comes to *it*, why I'm waiting.

NOAH

Time sheets from two weeks ago hang on the overpinned bulletin board, and balls of wadded paper overflow from the trash. I'm not feeling that this Malt and Burger is organized. In the cramped back office, I reenter my time from last week then roll back my chair to give space for the manager to approve it.

"The guy at the store down south said you're a great worker. That you're fast and keep your grill clean." The manager, Jim, according to his name tag, wears pants that are too long and not in the girl-catching way.

I nod at his statement. I'm good at what I do, but being a fry cook isn't my die-hard aspiration for a career. My goal's to be a man that Echo will be proud to walk down the street with. What I am now won't be enough to keep her for life.

He leans over, and his tie hits the screen. "Want to take a few shifts here?"

"Not staying in Colorado Springs long enough. Thinking about heading to Vail. Any stores there?"

"Yeah. I know the manager there and could give him a call if you want." Jim minimizes the screen.

Personal recs make getting in easier. "I need to check an email to see if Vail is an option." I motion at the screen with my chin. "Mind if I use this?"

"Go ahead."

One of his employees calls his name, and the two have a conversation at the door of his office. With a few clicks I'm into my personal email account, and my gut coils like a damn snake. Carrie sent the email.

I run my hand over my head then hover the cursor over her name. This could change everything.

Echo

There's nothing like the rush of being chased by the great Noah Hutchins.

Yesterday, we stayed the night in a hotel room. Tonight, we're at a campground outside Colorado Springs, but I don't mind it. Especially since the two of us have left behind the problems we ran into in Alamosa and have returned to complete and utter freedom.

The bark of the huge tree I hide behind is rough on my back, and I slowly slide against it as I chance a glance behind me. The fading evening light dances in the thick forest and reveals the green on the trees and the dirt of the ground, but what I see deceives me. If only by sense, I know Noah is close.

Twice he has almost caught me and twice I've eluded his grasp. Both times, if Noah wanted, he could have trapped me, but like me, he loves this game.

It's like I've merged into my namesake: the true Echo, the wood nymph my mother loved in stories. But I'm Echo before the nightmare that created her myth—a girl I've never understood before this summer, a girl that Noah helped bring to life. I'm playful, and I'm free.

Two words no one would have ever associated with me.

A twig snaps, and I jerk back behind the trunk. My pulse speeds up as I fold into myself. A few feet in front of me is a clearing full of wildflowers—white, yellow and purple. My fingers twitch. For two months, I've stopped and drawn anything I craved for as long as I've desired. I'm spoiled, and while the field before me is beauty that deserves to be immortalized on paper, there's a game that I plan on winning.

I inhale through my nose, and the scent of pine fills my lungs. This national forest has become our playground. It's awe-inspiring and magical, and I almost believe that we've been transported to another realm...another time. No worries. No past. Just us. As if we've stepped out of the black-and-white and into the brilliant and majestic Land of Oz.

I hold my breath and strain to listen past the late-day birds singing in the branches above. The fine hair on the back of my neck rises as if Noah has appeared behind me and deliciously blown over my skin. I close my eyes. He's so near I can imagine his body wrapped around mine.

Noah is wily and good at seeking, but I'm crafty and better at hiding. I edge to the side again and in painfully slow movements look behind me and...

"Gotcha."

I scream. Loudly. My heart ramming through my chest. Birds' wings beat together as dozens of them take to the sky. The moment I spot the laughter in Noah's chocolate-brown eyes, my scream quickly morphs into a fit of giggles. He reaches for me, but I stumble back from the solid arm attempting to sneak around my back.

"You're not getting away this time." Noah's deep voice vibrates down to my soul.

Noah's arm slides one way and in a maneuver so slick it

seems choreographed, I slip to the side, once again barely dodging his grasp.

"You're too slow," I taunt as I gain traction and sprint for the field of untamed wildflowers. The white-and-yellow daisies brush against my legs as I push forward. My skirt swishes against my thighs, and I love how the smooth material grazes my skin. Clean air fills my lungs, and my blood beats manically in my veins. Never in my life have I felt so alive. So high that I'm soaring.

"I'm letting you win," he calls out.

"You are not." I slow and pivot to watch as he struts behind me. The tall grass and flowers reach his jean-covered legs. For once, his dark hair doesn't hide his eyes, and I love the spark of naughtiness in them. "You're sore that you're losing."

He flashes the type of grin that encourages tingles. "You're becoming cocky, Echo."

I laugh, and the sound causes his smile to widen. Even though he's slow in his approach, his wide gait closes the distance between us faster than I'd like. I steadily walk backward, unable to tear my eyes off the fluid way he moves. "Now, now. Out of the two of us, we both know you own that title."

"Own it, wear it, I am it. I've never claimed differently."

Nope, he never has. Noah is exactly who I see. A few months away from Kentucky, away from home, the rough foster kid is evolving into a man.

"Hey, Echo." Noah gestures with his chin that he has something important to say, and I stall, watching as his gaze falls to my midriff. "Your tank rode up."

I peer down and in a heartbeat realize my mistake when grass rustles and Noah grabs my waist. In a dizzying circle, my arms wrap around his neck and somehow we both end up on the ground. Me on top. Noah on the bottom. As always, Noah becomes my safe place to land.

With a wink, Noah rolls us, reversing our positions, but I don't complain. I dream of his body over me. The heavy sensation is familiar and addictive. Noah skims his nose along the side of my neck, and the pleasing tickle causes me to suck in air.

"I won," he whispers against my skin.

I find myself in a waking dream as I savor his caresses. "Did not."

Noah presses a kiss to that sensitive spot behind my ear. A stream of warmth floods my body. Longing for more, I twist to expose my neck.

"Did, too." His hands roam, sliding to my side. I melt and tense at the same time. We're in the wide open, but I can't stop the way my body molds to his. My fingers bunch the material of his shirt as I play with the idea of removing it. We're far from the walking trail, far from the campsite. How many people, besides Noah and me, allow themselves to wander to the point of being lost?

"You said you could find me in five minutes," I say softly. "That was longer than five minutes."

"Echo," he says as he raises his head. His fingers begin this little dance. Moving up then slowly down. Each down is slightly lower and promises very wicked things.

"Yes?"

"I've got you beneath me and not a person in sight. That's winning."

A peacefulness unfurls within me. I have to agree. That is winning.

I scan our surroundings, and a snippet of concern enters my brain. "Are we forest-ranger-can-find-us lost or one-of-us-better-know-how-to-start-a-fire-with-twigs lost?"

Noah shifts to the side, leaving one leg and arm draped over me. "Look to the left."

I do, and a nervous shock causes me to jump. The path. That's the path. How did I not notice? Oh, God, did an entire AARP tour group shuffle past, watching me and Noah make out, and I was clueless? "Are there other people?"

"Relax. There's no one around. You ran in circles most of the time."

And here I thought I had been running straight. Guess I'm not as crafty as I thought. "One of these days we really will get lost if we keep straying from the path."

"Paths are overrated. Besides, I'll never let you get so far in front of me that I can't catch you."

Warm fuzzies engulf me. Noah said he'll always be around. "Promise?"

"Promise. I've got no interest in letting you out of my sight."

I pluck a daisy off a stem. Because, at times, I playfully test how far I can push Noah, I stick the flower behind his ear. He raises an eyebrow. I grin.

"I like it here," I tell him. "This has been my favorite stop so far."

Noah yanks the flower from behind his ear and loops it through on one of my red curls. "Want to sleep here tonight?"

"We are." I motion with my thumb in the direction of the campsite. "Remember that tent that took us forever to put up?"

"No, I mean sleep in the field. I can grab some blankets, and we can stay here."

"Walk all the way back to the campground then walk all the way back here?" Honestly, that prospect doesn't bother me, but it sounds like a fantastic excuse.

"You can stay here, and I'll get everything."

Crap. He foiled my plot. "So we'd sleep in the open? Like alongside bugs and other things that have more legs than us crawling on me?" Or worse, things that don't have legs and hiss and bite and have venom.

Or big things with four legs and fur. The overgrown carnivore with hair and teeth will scare me then eat me. In the end, the whole thing will be tragic.

Noah scratches the stubble on his jaw in an attempt to hide a smirk. "Yeah. The open."

I inch forward, and Noah removes his leg and arm to allow me to sit up. Bending my knees beneath me and smoothing out my skirt, I survey the area. Risk-taking. Not my strong suit. I took a huge risk this past spring when I broke into school to keep Noah from getting arrested, but since that breakthrough moment, I've remained fairly calm.

My goal this summer was to change—to not be the Echo Emerson that started her senior year twelve months ago. I want to be someone different when I go to college orientation.

Footsteps crack against the ground, and Noah and I turn to observe three shirtless guys and one bikini top-clad girl walk off the path and hike in our direction. Most of them carry beach towels over their shoulders.

"Where are they going?" I ask.

"Beats me," answers Noah, but he offers his hand to me

as he stands. This I understand about Noah: he doesn't like being caught in a defenseless position. I let him help me up, and I brush the dirt off the back of my skirt.

"I can help you with that," says Noah with a gleam in his eye.

"You just want to touch my butt."

"Damn straight I do. I can't help it if you have a beautiful ass."

My lips curve up with the compliment, and as I go to continue the banter, Noah's muscles stiffen. He angles his body to block me from the group. He may appear relaxed to everyone else with his thumbs hitched in his jean pockets, but he's one second away from taking any one of them out.

While there's a part of me that sort of likes the princess-locked-in-the-turret-with-a-knight-sworn-to-protect-her vibe, another part wonders when this protective streak is going to land either Noah or me or both of us in a heap of trouble.

"S'up," Noah says when one of the guys nods at us.

"Nothing much." The guy with surfer-blond hair tangles his fingers with the hand of the girl in the bikini top and cutoffs. "You guys camping here?"

"Yeah," answers Noah. "You?"

"Yep. Been coming here since I was a kid. I'm Dean." Dean introduces everyone else.

"Noah. This is my girl, Echo."

Everyone says something in greeting, and they all gawk at the scars on my arms. I clutch my arms close to my body, and Noah shifts so that he's the main attraction. "Where you guys heading?"

Dean points beyond us. "There's a gorge over that

ridge. It's a fantastic jump into cold water. Great way to end a day. You guys want to come along?"

Noah assesses me over his shoulder, and I detect that I'm-always-game-for-the-insane tilt of his mouth. He'll bow out if I ask, but I'm game. "Sure."

Dean leads the way through the woods, and Noah motions for me to walk in front of him as he hangs back to walk with two of the guys. That's the kind of person Noah honestly is—the type that will literally watch my back.

Dean's girl is easy to talk with, which is sort of nice. After a conversation weighing the pros and cons of camping in sandals, I say, "I didn't know there was a gorge here. It wasn't on the visitor maps."

"It's not on a map." Dean turns in front of us to walk backward. "It used to be when I was a kid. People would come through here and swim in the gorge, but then one guy out of a hundred thousand jumps the wrong way and bam—he's paralyzed. They shut the whole area down. It's a damn shame. Entire generations will grow up thinking they can't do anything fun because others are afraid of getting sued."

Sure enough, the trees give way to a small rocky clearing, and my breath catches when I step out onto the towering drop. To my right, a stream pretends it's rapids with white foam as it barrels out of the woods and falls over the cliff.

Below, gray rocks jut from the ground. The crystal-blue water reflects the green trees that protrude from the rocks and surround the area like a canopy. It's gorgeous, but standing three feet from the edge, I'm paralyzed by the force of gravity trying to drag me over the cliff.

I agree with the posted sign threatening prosecution

if anyone trespasses or jumps. This gorge is beautiful, but dangerous.

With a hand on my uneasy stomach, I ease back as everyone else races forward, and I bump into something warm and solid. Noah wraps an arm around me and rests his hand on my hip bone. "You okay?"

The girl shimmies out of her cutoffs, and the guys toss their towels to the rocks below.

"Yep." I blink three times.

Without warning, Dean launches himself over the cliff, and my lungs squeeze. I grab on to Noah's hand so I can brave a peek and pray like crazy that Dean's not plastered on the rocks below. A wave shoots up when Dean hits the water, and his friends whoop and yell.

Taking longer than I prefer, Dean resurfaces and gestures for everyone else to jump, and like dominoes, they do. One right after the other. All of them without a sense of self-preservation. Without thought. Without fear.

"Want to do it?" Noah asks.

"What? Either crack my head open on a rock or drown? No, thanks."

Noah leans over the ledge, and I wrench out of his hold because there is no freaking way I'm getting any closer. Noah chuckles. "Way too uptight, Echo."

"You can call it uptight all you want, but I call it not being suicidal. I have a four-inch-thick file in my therapist's office, and I can guarantee not once does the word *suicidal* appear. *Depressed? Withdrawn? Freak of nature?* Sure. But not *suicidal*."

"I'm sure the guy before Mrs. Collins used the word *sociopath* in my file, so jumping's my style."

"But Mrs. Collins is the reigning therapist now, and

we go with what she writes and neither one of us are suicidal!"

Noah laughs, and I can't help but smile with him. Only the two of us can joke about such subjects. "You're the one that said you wanted to take more risks. Look, we'll do it together."

A little twinge of guilt along with happy warmth funnels through my cells. I can see it play out. Noah taking my smaller hand in his. Him leading the way. The rush of falling together and the splash of cold water at the bottom.

I have no doubt that I won't regret it. It'll possibly be the most exhilarating experience I've ever had, and Noah does look extraordinarily sexy wet. I bite my bottom lip and peer over the edge like it's going to reach up and snatch me.

"What do you see when you look down?" asks Noah.

"You sound way too much like Mrs. Collins, and that's not a compliment."

"Answer the question."

I should be poetic and mention the green trees and the white foam floating atop the blue water and the purple wildflowers blowing in the breeze, but honestly all I see are... "Rocks. Lots of sharp, kill-me-by-impaling rocks."

Noah stands right on the edge so that his toes are off the side, and dirt crumbles near his feet and plummets to the death trap below. A pang of fear grips my chest, and I reach out to him. "You should step back."

Because he'll fall and then the one person I desperately need will die...like Aires. "I'm serious. Just step back. Okay?"

"Know what I see?" Noah says as if I hadn't spoken.

You continuing this sick, twisted replay of my life? I love and trust someone, then they die a horrible, violent death? "I'll sleep in the field. That's risk-taking. As in there are probably venomous spiders and snakes and rabid raccoons. That's a lot more death-defying than this."

"Water. I see water, Echo. A large pool of water."

Our gazes meet, and his dark brown eyes are so soft that my belly tightens and flips. But there's also an ache there. Something I don't quite comprehend. "What else do you see?"

Noah breaks our connection and stares out into the glorious ravine. "A missed opportunity."

I lower my head as the nausea strikes hard and fast. "I can't do it." But I want to. I wish to be a risk-taker, but this overpowering fear has me rooted to the ground.

Because God can occasionally be merciful, Noah steps away from the cliff. "All right. We'll leave suicide off the to-do list for the night. Instead of jumping off cliffs, how about we sleep in the open?"

I want to be a risk-taker. I want to change. A silent mantra said over and over again. Sucking in a deep breath, I accept the death sentence if only because I stupidly offered it earlier. "Okay. We'll sleep in the field."

Noah chuckles. "Are you sure?"

"Nope, but I'm willing to do it anyway." Forced smile. Very, very forced.

Noah yells down a goodbye, and they shout goodbyes back. We stroll back in comfortable silence, and I discover another con of wearing sandals when the leather strap rubs the skin beneath it raw. Returning to the field where Noah caught me a while ago, I pause and pull the sandal off my foot.

Noah narrows his eyes at it then surveys me. "Why don't you stay here and I'll bring what we need back."

"I'll be okay. It's not even a blister yet."

"Let me do this," says Noah. "Sit down and relax."

Noah wades through the field toward the path. He has swagger when he walks and powerful shoulders. With him, I'm hardly ever afraid. Noah possesses the ability to scare my monsters away, at least the ones that haunt me while I'm awake. For a brief few days, he's also scared away the demons that torture me in my sleep.

It's not until Noah reaches the path that I notice how fast we've lost light. There are more shadows in the forest than there is light from above. While night isn't my favorite, I've never really been spooked by the dark, but there's a nagging sensation pricking at me. An unease in the way this feels like a memory in slow motion.

Aires left this way—in the shadows. When his leave from the Marines ended, my brother said his goodbyes to everyone the night before and asked us to sleep in since he had an early-morning flight. He requested that we let him depart without a fuss. My father and Ashley agreed to it, but I never did.

I woke earlier than Aires. With a light jacket and in my pajama pants and shirt, I sat on the front porch steps waiting for that last moment with my older brother, my best friend. The sole person in the universe who kept me sane in a house full of chaos.

The humidity of the night left a dew on the ground and on the bushes. The curls I had straightened the night before reappeared within minutes. The porch light flipped on, the front door opened and, dressed in fatigues, Aires paused when he saw me.

With his lips thinned out, he closed the door behind him and motioned for me to stand. I did, and I was still small next to his massive frame. He resembled our father with his brown hair and height. I favored our mother.

"You don't listen," he said.

"I don't like it," I answered. "That you're leaving when the sun's not even up. It feels…" Unlucky. Wrong. "Early."

He offered a sympathetic half smile. "It's a Marine thing."

"Are you happy?" I asked. "Being a Marine?"

"I love the traveling," he admits, and I hear what he doesn't say. Aires couldn't live here anymore. Because Mom and Dad couldn't speak to each other without raising the decibel level to earsplitting, Aires became the go-between as he always tried to bring peace. That part of his personality sentenced him to a life of presenting each of their arguments to the other like a courier pigeon.

Before he had signed the papers to join the Marines, he confessed to me that he felt trapped.

Aires peered over my shoulder and down the street. Like he had asked, the cab waited at the corner. He didn't want the headlights or the idling car to wake any of us. "I've got to go."

I threw myself at him. So hard and fast that he rocked on his feet. He dropped his duffel bag and hugged me in return. "I'll be back soon."

Hot wetness burned my eyes and I swallowed, hoping it would help me form a sentence or a word, but all I could do was squeeze him tighter.

"I'm coming back home," he said. "I promise. There are too many important things here for me not to."

Because I was pathetic, I craved to hear him say the words. "Like what?"

"Well...my car's here." His 1965 Corvette. He found it in a scrap yard, and it had become the love of his life as he pieced it back together. "I'm not going anywhere until my baby is working."

I released him and rolled my eyes, even though I heard the tease in his voice. "Of course. Love the car more than your sister."

He grinned. "Priorities. Be good, Echo."

Aires started down the driveway and into the shadows. My heart beat faster as he merged into one more dark image in the unforgiving night.

"I love you," I yelled out.

"Back at you." His voice seemed too distant, too far away. Then the night became too black and my brother was gone.

Gone.

And Noah is fading into a shadow. It's like a steel knife lodges into my throat. I can't lose him. Not the person that I love. Not again. I jump to my feet and run through the field as if my life, as if Noah's life depends on it. "Noah!"

He keeps going, and this frantic panic pummels my bloodstream. *Don't lose sight of him. Don't.* "Noah!"

On the edge of light, Noah stops and pivots to me. His face falls as he notices my arms pumping, the air puffing out of my mouth.

"What's wrong?"

He grabs on to me when I skid to a halt, and I try to bend over to breathe again.

"You're trembling." Noah rubs his fingers over my hands. "Damn it, tell me what happened."

My mouth dries out, and I shake my head because the words solidify into concrete. I search for a way past the block. The last time I saw Aires was three years ago this month. Goose bumps rise on my arms, and a shiver snakes up my spine. Three years. Oh, God, I've been without him for three years.

"Echo," he urges.

I could tell him. He'd probably understand. Noah lost his parents.

"I...just..." Huge, shaky breath. "I need to go with you."

Noah's eyes narrow with worry, but he nods as he tucks me under his shoulder. "Okay."

He surveys the field as if he could catch sight of the ghosts tormenting me, but in order to do that, he'd have to crawl into my brain, and I'd never want that. My thoughts are a terrifying place to visit.

"We're staying in the tent tonight," he says.

My stomach sinks. "Noah—"

He presses a hand to the small of my back and urges me to the campground. "Another time. Another night. But not this one."

If Aires had left at another time or on another day, if Noah had chosen another time to return home the night of the fire or another day to go on that date, would the worst moments in our lives have happened?

Even worse? There's a dark part of me that's grateful for the way life has turned out because without any of that, I wouldn't have the man walking beside me.

Hurt rages like a flash flood, and I edge closer to Noah, hoping his strength can keep this new demon away. "Okay. Another time. Another day."

I try to pull myself to the present. Tomorrow will be a new destination. A new adventure. But my past beckons to me, this time in the form of guilt.

NOAH

Echo was silent on the way back to camp and has remained that way as I gather everything we need to start a fire. Dark fell fast over the campground because of the thick clouds hanging overhead. Unfortunately, clouds aren't the only thing dangling over us.

It's been a long time since I've lost Echo to her mind. Possibly since the first week after we took to the road, and I can't say I've missed it.

Sitting on a blanket next to our tent, she becomes a shell of the girl I love. Overall, she looks the same—same beautiful green eyes and red silky hair. Today she wears a white lace tank that shows a hint of the gifts God gave her and because I'm a lucky man, a skirt that ends mid-thigh.

But in the light of the neighboring campfire, Echo's green eyes possess the life of a dollar-store plastic doll, and she's paler than normal, making her freckles stick out.

In the span of a minute, something flipped in Echo's brain. Only her brother and her mother have the power to haunt her. I'd like to serve them both with eviction notices from her mind.

I drop the milk jugs I filled with water harder than I meant, and Echo switches her focus from the pine needles on the ground to me. Her brother's ghost doesn't bother me as much as her mother's. Aires died, and I understand that type of pain, but I still hate to see Echo anything but happy.

A breeze blows through the thick forest surrounding the campground, and a group of children runs past us on their way to the bathrooms. A few feet over, a boy around my youngest brother's age plays with a toy fighter jet. Complete with the appropriate noises for war.

I wish he'd shut the hell up. Echo's brother died in Afghanistan.

Since I entered foster care at the end of my freshman year, I've never been the boyfriend type, but Echo deserves the best. I scratch the back of my neck and try to do that making her feel better shit. "You okay?"

She nods. "Just thinking about Aires."

Good. I still don't handle her mother baggage well and after our fight at the Sand Dunes, I'm not eager to revisit those issues. "Want to talk about it?"

"Not really."

Echo never does, and because she respects my privacy when it comes to the loss of my parents, I back off. She returns her attention to the ground near her feet, and I pop my neck to the side. We've only got a few days left on the trip, and this isn't how I want it to end. "Tell me Aires's myth."

Echo's psychotic mother named them both after Greek myths. Last winter, Echo told me the myth associated with her name while she kicked my ass in pool. Maybe sharing a happy story will brighten her mood.

Her forehead wrinkles. "I've told you that story."

I crouch and pile two logs then thread smaller sticks for kindling under them. "No, you haven't."

"Yes," she says with a bite. "I have."

That was out of left field. I check Echo from the corner of my eye, and my girl is glaring at me like she caught me groping a gaggle of cheerleaders. "You haven't."

"I would tell you that story. You don't remember me telling you. That would mean that I don't discuss Aires, and I do!"

That's it right there—she doesn't. "You hardly mention Aires. And before you say something smart back, think who you're talking to. I mean what I say at all times. Don't mess with my word. If I say you haven't told the story, then you haven't."

"Like you're Mr. I-Share-Everything when it comes to your family?"

"Mind retracting the claws?" I say in a low tone. "Because I don't feel like bleeding." Or feeling threatened.

Echo blinks, and the anger drains from her face. "I am so sorry—"

A high-pitched shriek cuts her off and pierces my soul. I heard that type of scream before, and it's not one I've wanted to hear again. My entire body whips toward the sound, and I convulse at the sight of the toy airplane in the bonfire in front of the neighboring tent. The kid that was shooting down pretend targets seconds before is now crying and shaking as a small flame licks up his pants.

Tyler.

Jacob.

My brothers.

I snatch a blanket off the ground and in six strides I tackle the child. My heart pounds as I smack at the flame. The smell of burned flesh rushes through my mind, and the roar of flames lapping against walls fills my ears.

"Noah!" a voice that's familiar, but doesn't belong in this nightmare, calls to me. "Noah, you put out the flame!"

Soft fingers grasp my biceps, and it's as if I'm yanked from a long, dark tunnel. I turn my head, and the girl I love, the girl that owns my heart, stares at me as if I've lost my mind.

"Let him go," she says. "The flames are out."

I look down, and a small child with black hair and blacker eyes gapes at me. My hands hold his blanket-covered leg. I lift my arms, and Echo removes the blanket, revealing singed, now threadbare, jeans. The skin beneath is only slightly red. Not even a real burn.

I suck in air and smell smoke. No burned flesh. I fall back onto my ass and run my clammy hand over my forehead to catch the small beads of sweat. The sights. The smells. I'd been reliving the damned memory of the night my parents died.

"Oh, thank God!" A woman appears at the boy's side. He sits up at her touch and begins to weep. Jacob wept like that after I dragged him out the house. So did Tyler. I couldn't cry. No matter how I felt like I'd been torn open again and again, I couldn't cry.

"What happened?" she asks.

"His plane fell in the fire." Echo points to the melting toy in the thick of the fire. "We didn't see it, but he must have tried to get it. Noah yanked him out and put out the flames."

"Thank you," says a voice beside me. It's a man. Black hair. Black eyes. The damn bastard is probably his dad. "We walked over to say hi to friends camping with us. My son knows better than to play near the fire—"

I'm on my feet and in his face before he can finish. "He's a child! What the fuck is wrong with you that you'd leave him alone near an open flame? People get hurt this way! They die!"

"Noah!" Echo shoves an arm in front of me and uses her body as a shield between me and the bastard who should have his parental rights revoked. "It's okay."

"Okay!" I explode. "It's not fucking okay. That kid could have died!"

Echo pushes at my chest, attempting to walk me backward. "You're scaring him!"

"Good!" The bastard needs a kick in the ass.

"The child!" she chides. "You're scaring the child!"

It's as if she dumped a bucket of cold water over my face. The child is clinging plastic-wrap tight to his mom, his body shaking. A park ranger is applying something to the wound. Another one is talking into a cell phone, and I hear words like *ambulance not needed*.

The undertone of voices and movement from the campground has come to a lull as everyone scrutinizes the boy. Echo scans the area then links her fingers with mine. "You did great, Noah, but let's leave them alone, okay?"

"Is everything fine here?" The park ranger moves the phone away from his mouth and jerks his chin from me to the dad, who's continually combing his trembling hands over his head.

"Yeah," I say, and secure my grip on Echo. Without another word, I lead her back to our tent and unzip it, motioning for her to get inside. I join her and in a second, zip the door up, wishing it could block out the entire world.

Echo clicks on a lantern and makes herself smaller

as she tucks her legs beneath her. "Are you okay?" She drums her fingers to that silent rhythm.

Fuck me. Wasn't that the question I asked her a few minutes ago? I rub my eyes. No. I'm not okay. I'm the furthest thing from it.

Three months ago, I held Echo's hand in a hospital and watched her battle for her sanity. I promised her and myself that I'd become the man she deserves. The man who'd be strong enough to get past my shit in order to take care of her. I let Echo down once, just like I let my parents down the night of the fire.

The guilt of that night, of how I failed, has left a deep, dark stain on my soul. Echo's dealt with enough of my crap since we met, and she's had a hard time sorting through her stuff since she retrieved her memories.

I can't unload my fucked-up problems onto her. The truth would drive her to realize that she shouldn't be with a punk like me, and she'd finally walk. "I'm tired."

Her fingers tap faster on her thigh. "It's still early. Maybe we should go do something—"

"I'm tired," I cut her off. I'm being rough, I know it, but I can't deal with anything right now. I lie down and turn away from her. "And you said you wanted to get into Denver early so you can prepare for the show."

Echo's silent, and after a few strained minutes, she clicks off the lantern and settles beside me. Because the girl has always been a damned miracle, she slowly edges near me and places a cool hand on my shoulder.

"I know what it's like to lose someone," she whispers.

Her words cut deep. She may get the loss, but she doesn't understand feeling responsible for them dying.

Echo presses her lips to my shoulder blade, and I close my eyes.

"Aires..." She falters. "Aires was a ram sent by Zeus to save someone."

My eyebrows furrow together as I move to face her. Her body is nothing more than a shadow in the night. I can't see her features, but I can hear the pain.

"I..." she continues in a taut voice that rips out my heart. "I don't want to talk about it anymore."

She doesn't have to. I find Echo's hand and guide her until she tangles her body with mine.

"We're okay," I lie. It feels like it did when they lowered my parents' caskets into the ground. It feels like it did when Echo broke up with me a few months back. It feels like it did when I decided that my brothers were better off without me.

Echo slides an arm around my chest and holds on like I'm preventing her from falling off a cliff. My girl sometimes mentions God. Some days she believes in him. Other days she's not sure he exists. I don't think much one way or another because if there is one, he doesn't believe in me.

With that said, I toss up a silent prayer that all this hurt, all this guilt, will be gone in the morning. Not for my sake, but for Echo's.

She deserves happiness.

Echo

"I'm two hours late calling my father, my boyfriend looks like he's ready to step in front of an oncoming freight train to cure his boredom, I'm terrified someone will mention my mother and no, I don't like the use of the gold against the greens in the painting."

It's how I'd love to respond to the curator tipping her empty champagne glass at the floor-to-ceiling painting in front of us, but admitting such things will hurt the fragile reputation I've established for myself this summer in the art community. Instead, I blink three times and say, "It's beautiful."

I glance over at Noah to see if he caught my tell of lying. He bet me that I couldn't keep from either lying or blinking if I did lie for the entire night. Thankfully, he's absorbed in a six foot carving of an upright prairie dog that has headphones stuck to his ears. If I lose, I'll be listening to his music for the entire car ride home from Colorado. There's only so much heavy metal a girl can take before sticking nails into her ears.

In a white button-down shirt with the sleeves rolled up, jeans and black combat boots, Noah shakes his head to himself before downing the champagne in his hand. Absorbed was an overstatement. Prisoners being water tortured are possibly having a better time.

Noah stops the waiter with a glare and switches his empty glass for a full one. He's been scaring the crap out of this guy all night and at this rate, Noah may get us both kicked out, which may not be bad.

"I heard you tried to secure an appointment with Clayton Teal so he could see your paintings." The curator's hair is black, just like I imagine her soul must be, yet I force the fake grin higher on my face.

"I did." And he rejected me, or rather the assistant to his assistant rejected me. I can't sneeze this summer without someone gossiping about it. I swear this is worse than high school. It's been months since graduating from what I thought was the worst place on earth, and I've descended into a new type of hell.

"Little lofty, don't you believe?"

"I sold several paintings this spring and—"

She actually *tsks* me. *Tsks.* Who does that? "And you don't think your mother had anything to do with those sales?"

My head flinches back like I've been slapped, and the wicked witch across from me sips her champagne in a poor attempt to mask her glee.

"Well?" she prods.

I tuck my red curls behind my ear. "My work speaks for itself."

"I'm sure it does." She gives me the judgmental once-over, and her eyes linger on the scars on my forearms. The black sleeveless dress shrinks against my skin. I've only had the courage to show my arms since last April, and sometimes, as in now, that courage dwindles.

In high school, no one knew how the white, red and raised marks had come to be on my arms, and for a long period of time, neither did I. My mind repressed the night of the accident between me and my mother. But with the help of my therapist, Mrs. Collins, I remember that night.

As I've traveled west this summer, visiting art galleries, I've discovered a few people in my mother's circle are aware of how I had fallen through her stained-glass window when I had tried to prevent her from committing suicide.

Unfortunately, I've also met a few people who loathe my mother and prefer to slather their displeasure with her like a poisoned moisturizer onto my face.

"She contacted people, you know?" she says. "Telling them that you were traveling this summer like a poor peddler and that she'd be grateful if they showed you some support."

It appears this woman belongs to the I-hate-your-mother camp, and the sole reason I've been asked to this art showing is for retribution for some unknown crime committed by my mother. A person, by the way, I no longer have contact with. "Would you have been one of those people she called?"

She smiles in the I-drown-kittens-for-fun sort of way. "Your mother knows better than to call me."

"That's nice to know." I half hope my mother dropped a house on her sister and that she's next.

The curator angles away from me as if our conversation is already done, yet she continues to speak. "A piece of advice, if I may?"

If it'll encourage her to pour water over herself so that she'll melt, I'm all for advice. "Sure."

"There's no skipping ahead. Everyone has to pay their

dues and you, my dear, the daughter of the great Cassie Emerson, are no exception. Using your mother's name, no matter how many people are misguided into believing her work is brilliant, is no substitute for actual talent. I'm taking this meeting with you tomorrow because I promised a friend of mine from Missouri that I would if he agreed to feature some of my paintings. Do us both a favor and don't show."

I know the man she refers to. He was one of the last to buy a painting from me and since that day in June, I've hit a dry spell. The smile I've faked most of the night finally wanes, and Noah notices as he sets his glass on the outstretched prairie dog's hand.

I had two goals for this summer. Number one: to explore my relationship with Noah, and that has proven more complicated than I would have ever imagined. Number two was to affirm to myself and the art world that I'm a force of nature—someone separate from my mother. Regardless of what my father believes, that I'm capable of making a living with canvas and paint and that I have enough talent to survive in an unforgiving world.

The curator turns to walk away, but my question stops her. "If you detest me so much, then why invite me tonight?"

"Because," she says, and her eyes flicker to my scars again. "I wanted to see for myself if the rumors were true. If Cassie really did try to kill her daughter."

Wetness stings my eyes, and I stiffen. I wish for Noah's indifferent attitude or one of his non-blood sister Beth's witty comebacks. Instead, I have nothing, but this witch didn't completely break me. She was the first to look away then leave.

The corners of my mouth tremble as I attempt to smile. Realizing that faking happiness is completely out of the realm of reality, I let the frown win. But I'll go to hell before I cry in front of this woman. I release a shaky breath and will the tears away.

A waiter passes and in one smooth motion I grab a glass of champagne off his tray and hurry for the door. My heart picks up pace, and my throat constricts. This isn't how the summer was supposed to go. I was supposed to evolve into someone else...someone better.

I slide past a couple gesturing at a painting, and the glass nearly slips from my hand when I ram into a wall of solid flesh. "What's going on, Echo?"

"Nothing." Something. Everything. I pivot away from Noah, not wanting him to see how each seam of my fragile sanity is unraveling one excruciating thread at a time in rapid succession.

Noah's hand cups my waist, and his chest heats my back as he steps into me. "Doesn't look like nothing."

I briefly close my eyes when his warm breath fans over my neck, and his voice purrs against my skin. It's a pleasing tickle. Peace in the middle of torture.

"Look at me, baby." When I look up, Noah's beside me, and his chocolate-brown eyes search mine. "Tell me what you need."

"To get out of here." The words are so honest that they rub my soul raw.

Noah places a hand on the small of my back and in seconds we're out the front door and into the damp night. Drops of water cling to the branches and leaves of the trees. Moisture hangs in the air. Each intake of oxygen is full of the scent of wet grass. While inside experiencing my own hurricane, it rained outside.

She contacted people, you know? I didn't know. I had no idea, and the thought that any of my success belongs to Mom kills me. A literal stabbing of my heart, shredding it to pieces.

Resting the champagne glass I've now stolen onto the hood of the car, I tear into the small purse dangling from my wrist and power on my phone. The same words greet me: one new message.

Not listening to my father or Noah or anyone, I kept it. Last April, I thought I could sever my mother from my life—that after one meeting with her, I could move on, but she's still here, surrounding me, haunting me, like shrapnel embedded too deep to retrieve.

Noah slowly rounds on me as if I'm teetering on the edge of a bridge, ready to jump. As I meet his eyes, I realize he's not far off. "She called people. She told them to buy my stuff."

He assesses the phone then refocuses on me. "Your mom?"

I nod.

"Who'd she call?"

"The galleries..." I trail off when the door to the gallery opens and laughter drifts into the night. My mind jumps around, searching for another answer, hoping for a plausible solution other than that I've been handed the truth.

But maybe Mom didn't call. Maybe this woman is wrong. Maybe the curator is mean and she's evil and before I can think it through, my thumb is over the button. The phone springs to life. Numbers dial. Little lines grow with the cell phone reception. The phone rings loudly once.

Noah bolts forward. "What the fuck do you—"

"Echo?" The desperate sound of my mother's voice shatters past the confusion and slams the fear of God into my veins. The phone tumbles from my hands and crashes to the ground.

The phone beeps—the call lost—and Noah stands open-mouthed over the cell as if I murdered someone. "What the hell, Echo?"

"I..." The rest of my statement, my train of thought, catches in my throat. I called her. I knot my fingers into my hair and pull, creating pain. Oh, my God, I called her. I initiated contact, and now the door is open...

Cotton-mouthed, I whisper, "What have I done?"

Noah scrubs both of his hands over his face. "I don't know."

"This is bad."

He steps forward. "It's not. You hung up. She'll assume it was a mistake."

The phone rings. Each shrill into the night is like a knife slicing through me, and the panic building in my chest becomes this pressure that's difficult to contain—a pulse that's hard to resist. *Answer, answer, answer!*

"Think about this, Echo."

My eyes snap to Noah's. "I need to know."

"She's not going to give you the answers you want."

"What if she did call the galleries? What if my success was a pity offering from her?"

"Echo—"

Closer than him, more desperate than him, I swipe the phone off the ground before he can move, but the phone stops ringing. My hands shake, and this desperation claws at me as I run a hand over my neck, searching for whatever is constricting my ability to breathe. "I could call her back."

With both hands in the air like he's handling a kidnapping negotiation, Noah edges in my direction. "You could, but let's discuss it first."

My fingers clutch the phone. "If she did this I need to know. I need to know if she asked people to buy those paintings from me."

"What if she did? Why does it matter?"

"Because if she did, I'm a failure!"

He halts, and his eyebrows furrow together. "That's bullshit."

"But it's true."

"It's not. Nothing good happens when you talk to your mom. What makes this different? What she says to you, what she's done—it fucks with you!"

"She's my mom!"

"And I'm the one holding you in the middle of the night when you can't decipher what's real and what's a dream. She's not here. I am. Not her!"

Anger explodes up from my toes and spirals out of my body. "You don't understand! It's more than the paintings. It's more! She's my mom. You don't understand what it's like to be torn between wanting to hate someone and wanting them in your life, then hating them all over again!"

"Fuck that, because I do. My mom's family contacted me. They want to meet me. The goddamned people she ran from want me in their fucked-up lives."

NOAH

Echo and I stare at each other, and I suck in air to get my breathing under control. Her eyes are too wide, and my heart's pounding too fast. It's not how I meant to tell her, but it's out, and I can't take it back. The edges of my sight are blurry. I've drunk too much, but I'm glad the truth is out.

"What did you say?" she asks.

I yank the folded email out of my back pocket and offer it to her. Echo reaches for the paper like she's seconds from handling a ticking time bomb. She unfolds it, and I slump against her car. Rainwater pooled on the hood, and it soaks through the bottom of my jeans. Damn this entire week to hell.

Too many emotions collide in my brain, and I rake both hands through my hair to ward off any spinning. The alcohol was supposed to help, not hurt.

"It's not that long, so quit stalling." The email is short, to the point, and every misspelling informs me that the shit I'm in is deep.

Ms. Peterson,
We no the adoption is compleet, but we'd like to see the boys for a visit. My Sarah wood have wanted that. If not

the younger ones, then Noah. He'd be a teen by now. Let him decide.

Diana Perry

The paper crackles as Echo folds it again, and her heels click against the blacktop. Her sweet scent surrounds me followed by the butterfly touch of her fingers on my wrist. "Noah."

She lowers her hand to my thigh and damn if fire doesn't lick up my leg. Even when I'm drunk, my body responds to her. My legs automatically drop open, and the tension melts as she eases herself closer. Her fingers caress my face and with gentle pressure, she edges my chin up. I lose myself in those green eyes.

"What are you going to do?" she asks.

I wind my arms around her waist and slide one hand down her spine. Echo's my solid, my base, my foundation. She has no idea that the single fear that keeps me up at night is knowing one day she'll discover she doesn't need me like I need her.

"Noah," she whispers again. Echo's always been a siren, calling me to her even when I don't want to be captured. "Please talk to me."

Her lips brush the corner of my mouth, and my fingers fist into her hair. Echo's warm and soft. I shouldn't kiss her now. I shouldn't crave to kiss her now, but damn, she owns me.

"Talk to me," she murmurs. "I can't help if you don't talk to me."

As she sweeps my hair away from my eyes, I hear myself say, "They're in Vail."

Her head nods against mine in understanding. "We've got time before we have to be back."

"Mom ran from them."

"You don't know that." She pulls back to look at me, but my grip on her hips keeps her near. "There could be a million reasons why your mom left."

"Carrie and Joe said that Mom's family is bad news."

"Carrie and Joe said that you shouldn't have been around your brothers. They were wrong then. They can be wrong now."

The same thought has circled in my brain since Carrie broke the news. "What if they're right?"

"What if they're wrong? And if they are right, what if your mom's family did screw up? Maybe they deserve a second chance."

My eyes flash to hers, and my blood goes ice-cold. "Are we talking about my situation or yours?"

She tilts her head. "They may not be so different."

"Fuck that. There's no comparison."

"You're drunk, Noah."

"I am."

Her foot taps against the ground, and she does that thing where she glares off in the distance. It's not hard to read she's silently tearing me a new ass, but has enough grace to leave the internals internal. One of these days, she'll snap.

She's torn into me before, and the last time she did, she left me. My stomach plummets as I wonder if she'll walk again.

Reaching behind me, Echo lifts the glass of champagne she brought with her from the gallery. "Well, there's good news. It looks like we'll be free tomorrow. The curator and I decided it would be best if we no longer share breathing space...or continents."

Echo presses the glass to her lips, but I lift it from her hand. I've had a few of those tonight. More than a few. Enough that walking a straight line could be a problem.

My girl throws me a hardened expression that could send me six feet deep. "Damn, Echo. I'm not stealing your firstborn. I'm the drunk one, remember?"

She releases a sigh that steals the oxygen from my lungs, and she moves so that her back rests against me. I mold myself around her and nuzzle my nose in her hair. Echo inclines her head to the glass now in my possession. "How many of those have you had?"

I drink half the champagne while eyeing the prairie dog again through the gallery window. Champagne's not my style, but free alcohol is free alcohol. "Not enough to understand that."

"It's a prairie dog," she answers.

"With headphones."

"It's a commentary on how we are destroying nature."

"That's wood, right?" I ask.

Echo rolls her eyes, and I smirk. She hates it when I do this.

"Yes, the artist cut down a tree, used a chainsaw that required gas, and the whole process defeats the purpose."

"Chainsaw?" These bastards are strange.

"Yes."

I finish out the glass. "As I said, not enough."

A couple exits the gallery, and they're way too loud and way too full of themselves to peer in our direction. While

I could give a shit about everyone inside, Echo cares, and the longing in her eyes as she watches them hurts me.

"Want to talk about the stuck-up bitch in there?" I ask.

"Nope."

Good. Odds are I'd say things that would make Echo cry. "Then let's get the fuck out of here."

Echo

Noah and I slept deeply, we slept long, and then we held each other for longer than we should have. Now, check-out is looming.

Cross-legged on the middle of the bed, I cradle my cell and stare at three messages: one new voice mail, one missed call, one new text. Each one from my mom. There's a pressure inside me—this overwhelming craving to please my mother, to gain her approval—that prevents me from deleting them. The memories don't help...both the good and the bad.

Mom said she's on her meds. She said that she's in control of her life. If that's true, is she mimicking my father's parenting style by attempting to dominate my life?

Noah steps out of the bathroom fully dressed, and his hair, still wet from his earlier shower, hangs over his eyes, leaving me unable to read his mood.

"Did you call her?" he asks.

"No." I pause. "But what if I did?"

Noah shrugs then leans his back against the wall. "Then you did. I don't claim to understand, but I promised you back in the spring that I'd stand by you. I'm a man of my word."

He is. He always has been. "But you don't agree that I should call her."

"Not my decision to make."

I shift, uncomfortable that Noah's not completely on my side. "I'd like to know you support me."

"I support you."

"But you don't approve."

"You need to stop looking for people's approval, Echo. That's only going to lead to hurt."

My spine straightens. "I didn't ask for a lecture."

"You asked me to be okay with you contacting the person that tried to kill you. Forgive me for not setting off fireworks. You want to call her, call her. You want to see her, then do it. I'll hold your hand every step of the way, but I don't have to like seeing her in your life."

His words sting, but they're honest. The phone slides in my clammy hands. "I won't call her today."

"Because that's your decision," Noah says. "Not because you're trying to please me."

We're silent for a bit before he continues, "I called the Malt and Burger in Vail. They can fit me into the schedule this week. If I want in, they can give me the walk-through of the restaurant this evening."

A sickening ache causes me to drop a hand to my stomach. A week. We were supposed to travel back to Kentucky today. We were going to take another route so that I could try new galleries. But Noah has this need to find his mom's family. He desires a place to belong.

Just like me.

If he wants to search for them, I can't be the person standing in the way. "You should ask them to schedule you."

"What if my mom's family is bad news? Why would I want them in my life?"

"I don't know." It's a great question. One I deal with daily. Maybe if we go, Noah will finally understand my struggle with my mother. "Let's do this. Let's go to Vail."

Noah cuts his gaze from the floor to me. "This means you'll be giving up visiting galleries on the way back."

It will. Granting him this can cost me my dreams, but I've had enough time, and I guess I've failed. "There are probably galleries in Vail." Hopefully.

"We'll stay in a hotel the whole time. I'll pay."

"Noah..." My voice cracks. "No. I'm fine with the tent or I can help pay—"

"Let me do this," he says, and the sadness in his tone causes me to nod.

"So we're still heading west," I say.

"West," he responds.

NOAH

My head pulses with the same speed as the cursor on the computer at the Vail Malt and Burger. Champagne hangovers suck.

"Clock in as soon as you walk in, and clock out the moment your shift is done and this is where you put your orders, you hear me?" The manager of the Malt and Burger is in the process of explaining to me the way "his" restaurant runs. He's a six-two, two-hundred-and fifty-pound black man who, like the other managers throughout the summer, thinks he's the only one that uses the system of sticking the paper orders over the grill. Two words: *corporate policy*.

"Got it," I answer.

"You hear me?" he asks with a wide white grin. "It doesn't leave the grill until it hits one hundred and sixty degrees."

"Yeah, I hear you." Food poisoning's a bitch.

He slaps my back and if I wasn't solid, the hit might have crushed me. "Good. Called around about you. Hear you're a good man. We get a lot of travel employees through here, and you aren't the only fresh face working this week. I expect you to pull your weight and not miss a beat, hear me? Otherwise, I'll put you out."

Loud and clear, and it's going to be a long week if he says that phrase as much as he has in the past thirty minutes.

"So we'll see you tomorrow?" He uses a red bandanna to wipe the sweat off his brow.

"Tomorrow."

We shake hands, and I let myself out the back when the drive-through worker yells that the headset shorted. Vail's cooler than Denver, but not by much and because of that, I walk in the shadows of the alley.

"You were too serious-looking in there, you know? Surely a year can't change someone that much."

I glance behind me and notice a girl with short black hair and wearing a Malt and Burger waitress T-shirt leaning against the brick wall next to the Dumpster. A cigarette dangles from her hand and as she lifts it to her mouth, the ton of bracelets on her wrist clanks together.

"Do you know me?" I ask.

She releases smoke into the air. The sweet scent catches up and for the first time in months, the impulse for a hit becomes an itch under my skin. The chick's smoking pot.

"I know you, Noah Hutchins. I know you very well."

I scratch my chin as a dim memory forces its way to the surface: pot, beer, her naked body and the backseat of my car. Shit.

"Mia," I mumble. She introduced me to the employee travel program. Last fall, she trekked across the country working for different stores, and for two weeks while she had stopped in Kentucky, we traveled down each other's pants.

"You remember my name. I'm touched." She extends the joint to me. "Our last encounter started this way, too, which works for me. I just got off shift and if I remember correctly you had a killer backseat."

I shove my hands in my pockets. "I don't have my car."

"You don't?"

"We took my girlfriend's."

She chuckles then takes another hit. Mia's silent as she holds the smoke, then studies me while she blows it out. "Never thought of you as boyfriend material. Pegged you to be like me."

"Guess you pegged me wrong."

"Guess I did." Mia smashes the small remains of the joint between her fingers, and it disintegrates as it falls to the ground. "Did you move here or are you visiting?"

"Visiting for the week."

"What a coincidence—so am I." She releases the same sly grin she gave me moments before going down on me last year. Twenty bucks the girl knows what she's doing now just like she knew exactly what she was doing then. "Tell me about your girl."

Standing here and reminiscing with someone I spent hours exploring in a haze isn't the best way to be true to Echo. "I've gotta go."

"You were badass, Noah, but you were never a dick. This is just a conversation between two old friends."

She's wrong about me, and sometimes Echo is, too. I am a dick, and I especially was when I was doing her. "We're not friends."

There's a pessimistic tilt to her lips. "Touché, but we did enjoy the hell out of each other's bodies. We will be working together, and as I said about the whole dick thing—it meant you had a slight conscience. So let me guess, you found the good girl who redeemed you."

I rub the back of my neck. This is one of the things I hated about sleeping around. Occasionally, a girl had the stones to call me out on my shit and they'd be right.

Two minutes of conversation. I can give it to this girl if it'll wipe the slate clean. "Yeah, but it's more like she found me."

She nods like I said more than I did. "So how redeemed has she made you? College route now?"

The hairs on my body rise like I've got a sniper trained to me. "Yeah."

"When was the last time you hung out with anyone not her and partied? You know, be eighteen and not ninety?"

Before the two of us got serious. "What's it matter?"

She toes a piece of green broken glass. "Matters more than you think. You'll need to bring your girl in to let me meet the competition."

"There's no competition," I say.

"Oh, Noah." She pushes off the wall and walks backward for the opposite street. "Life is only about competition."

I watch what I used to be leave. This is going to be a great conversation with Echo: You know how I decided to stay here for a week, ruining your chances to meet with other galleries before we head home? Great news: I fucked one of the waitresses, and she wants to meet you.

My cell vibrates, and I pull it out of my pocket, hoping to see a text from Echo. My eyebrows draw together when I spot Isaiah's name: Where you at?

Me: Vail

Isaiah: Staying?

Me: Fir Tree Inn Room 132

Isaiah: See you by morning.

"Damn." I forgot to tell Echo about Isaiah and Beth.

Echo

Nestled at the bottom of a mountain, Vail is possibly the most beautiful town I've ever visited. The cobblestone streets with tidy buildings transport me into a cute little Swiss mountain village. Each store I pass screams expensive and boasts if you break it, you buy it. Well, the ice cream shop doesn't boast that, but it would be cool if it did.

Staying in the hotel with Mom's messages on my phone became torture, and walking alone isn't the needed distraction.

A couple exits a store, and they laugh and hold hands. They're beautiful together—wearing the same type of clothes and smile. They look like they've materialized out of a J. Crew catalog and chat over their shared love of some vase.

Noah and I would never have that conversation.

Feeling suddenly insecure and underdressed in my cut-offs and blue T-shirt, I tuck my free-flowing curls behind my ears and cross my sweater-covered arms over my chest as I wander past a line of galleries. I've visited lots of galleries over the summer, and judging by the quality of art in the windows, none of them have been this high-end. In any of these places, my work wouldn't be fit to display in the bathroom. If what the curator in Denver said was true, my paintings are probably inhabiting a Dumpster.

Noah wouldn't say it, but he harbors guilt for changing our plans. He won't after I gush over the number of galleries in Vail. This side trip could be life-altering. Maybe I do have one last shot at proving myself before going home.

My pack dangles from my shoulder. I brought a sketchbook and chalk in case inspiration hits. Lots of inspiring views around me, but the art...wow. Talk about feeling less.

A beautiful painting of the night sky hangs in the window of a gallery and catches my attention. It's not the lines or the choice of coloring that draws me to it. It's the constellation, and I become completely lost.

"What do you think?"

"Excuse me?" I glance to my right, and a guy with a mop of sandy-brown hair sporting a pair of jeans and T-shirt stands next to me. He's older than me. Easily thirtysomething, I guess. To be honest, people sort of blend in between twenty-five and forty.

He raises a bag in his hand. "I've walked by a couple of times, and you've been here staring. So I'm thinking you must like it."

I blink, not realizing I had been entranced for so long. "It's good," I answer, because it is. "I like the shading here." Then motion to where the blacks and blues merge. "It gives it a nice Impressionist feel."

With the bag on his wrist, he shoves his hands into his pockets and appraises me as if I should have more to say, which I don't.

"Is there a problem?" I ask.

"You don't like the painting."

I hike a brow. "I like the painting."

"No." The reusable grocery bag crackles. "You don't. There's a look people have when they like something, and you don't have that light."

Not caring for the interrogation, I break the news. "It's wrong."

His head jerks back. "What?"

"It's wrong," I repeat and gesture to the middle of the constellation. "It's missing a star."

"It's art. There's only what the artist intended."

"True, but I don't think that's the case here."

"Why?"

I motion with my finger where the star should be. "Because if I meant to leave the star out, I would have made this area a shade darker. Just enough that you could only see it if you were searching. I also would have left a small indication that something so important, something so critical to your soul has disappeared. The sole reason a constellation exists is because it's a sum of its parts. To lose one of those parts...it's painful and irreversible."

He's silent for a moment as he focuses on the area I pointed out. "Maybe you're wrong on the constellation."

"My brother's name was Aires. I couldn't forget that constellation if I tried." A heavy weight slams into my chest. I've gone too long without remembering my brother. I used to think about him several times a day, and now I haven't thought of him since last night. I miss him, and what does it mean that he's not haunting my every thought? Am I forgetting him?

With a sigh that actually causes me pain, the man stalks into the gallery, lifts the painting off the easel and carries it into the back. If I was Noah, I'd drop the f-bomb right now, but I'm not, so a simple crap will suffice. I broke a cardinal rule: keep your mouth shut until you know who the gallery owner and the artist are because they can be hiding in the Trojan horse of a tourist with reusable shopping bags.

So much for the idea of making connections in Vail.

I stand there, staring at the empty slot, wondering if there's any way to salvage this, like: "I didn't mean it" or "I smoked crack before I traipsed over here" or "I've been kidnapped and a bomb's been strapped to my chest, and if I don't trash other people's paintings, a bus on the highway will explode."

Yeah, I don't think he'll buy it.

I turn and begin the long walk of shame back to the hotel. My cell vibrates. I pull it out of my pocket and frown the moment I spot the name of my therapist, Mrs. Collins. It's like the woman is hardwired to me.

Her: What are your thoughts on moving our Skype visit to tomorrow?

I stop dead in the middle of the cobblestone street, and I rush out an apology when a couple has to separate their hands to move around me. Me: My father told you, didn't he?

Her: Told me what? :)

Me: That my mom called! And the drill sergeant control freak finally returns. My father lasted two months longer than I thought he would before interfering with my therapy. Me: I thought he was giving me space!

Time. Too much time. Maybe she's moved on with her life instead of stalking mine. Right as I slip my phone into my pocket, it vibrates again. Her: He wasn't the one to tell me.

My chin drops to my throat. Noah is a dead man.

* * *

Sitting on the floor of the hotel room, I stare at a blank pad of drawing paper and rub my temples. Oh, God, what have I done? It seemed like a great idea at the time. In fact, it seemed like the most brilliant idea in the course of human history, but I was mad. So mad and Noah is going to freak.

Freak.

Noah's never been truly angry at me. Aggravated? Yes. Ticked at me? Yep. Strongly annoyed? Heck, yeah. Infuriated? No.

The handle on the door rattles, and a half second later there's a click when Noah's key card unlocks the door. I press my hand to my stomach, hoping it will prevent the contents of lunch from making a reappearance.

He steps in and smiles the moment he spots me. It's a horrible, horrible, sweet smile. The type that says he loves me beyond belief. His hair partly covers his dark eyes, and when his face widens with the grin, I can spot the sexy, rough stubble of a five o'clock shadow on his cheeks.

Oh, hot Hades in a snowstorm, he's happy. I wish I could crawl under the bed and die.

"You okay?" he asks as he heads to his suitcase on the extra double bed. He's a foot from me, and he's going to want fifty football fields between us when he opens that bag.

When I don't answer, he continues, "We're going to splurge tonight and eat at a restaurant. I meant to take you out in Denver after the showing, but..."

But Denver was the fifth level of hell.

He begins to unzip his suitcase, and I blow out air to stop a dry heave. "Noah," I say to try to interrupt him, but he doesn't hear my quiet declaration because he realized he had opened the wrong part.

"A nice restaurant. I know my shirt from last night needs to be washed, but I've got another nice shirt in here somewhere. Your choice of where to eat and don't worry about the money. You deserve something nice."

"No, I don't." I really, really don't.

His hands pause on the zipper as he glances at me, and my heart thrashes once against my rib cage. He is going to go nuclear with a hundred percent chance of radiation fallout.

"I want to do this," he says. "Besides, we need to talk."

The crackling of the zipper starts again. I jump to my feet and charge Noah like a linebacker in the Super Bowl, only I weigh a hundred and twenty and barely cause Noah's hair to blow in the breeze. "Stop!"

I wrench his hands off his suitcase, and Noah grabs on to my fingers. "What are you doing?"

"I am so sorry." My foot taps against the floor, and I shiver because this is so freaking bad. "I'm sorry. But you texted Mrs. Collins, and you told her that my mom called and then she texted me and I was so angry because that's something my dad would have done, and I don't want to be dating my dad. I mean, he's a control freak and you're not, so why would you contact her? And I was so angry that I did this and now I wish I didn't do this, and I'm sorry."

His dark eyes dart around my face. "Mrs. Collins told you that I texted her?"

"She told me that you told her." A flash of anger and hurt strikes me like a lightning bolt, and I yank my hands away, remembering why I've done this. "How could you?

It's my decision if I want to talk to Mrs. Collins about my mom. Not yours."

"I didn't tell her," he says.

"But if you didn't..." Blood rushes out of my head, leaving me light-headed. I suck in a breath of air, but it stays in my mouth. "...and my dad didn't..."

"Baby, you need to sit down."

Little lights appear in my vision, and for a second, I think they're pretty. A high-pitched ringing drowns out all other sounds...all other sounds but one.

"Fuck!"

NOAH

With my knuckles, I rub the back of my head and when I inhale, the air contains a full dose of chlorine. I chuckle because what the fuck else is there to do?

"I am *so* sorry." Echo stands beside me with her arms wrapped tight around her waist and stares at me with the most pathetic puppy dog eyes. After she realized that her mother, not me, had contacted Mrs. Collins, Echo hyperventilated. Scared the shit out of me, but after I sat her down and gave her some water, she returned to breathing normally.

Can't exactly be mad at someone when you're happy they're okay, plus this...well...Echo's got balls. "My boxer shorts are in the filter."

She slams her eyes shut, and I extend an arm around her shoulders, drawing her closer to me. "It's all good, baby. No harm, no foul...assuming management hasn't figured it out, otherwise we'll be staying in the tent tonight."

Every article of clothing I own is floating at the top of or has sunk to the bottom of a small indoor rectangular pool. Our voices carry in the closed-in room, and because one thing today is going right, it's completely empty except for us.

She groans and drops her forehead into my chest. "I

threw your clothes in the pool and hot tub. You have got to be angry."

Hot tub. Hadn't caught that one yet. Sure enough, my button-down shirt drifts at the top. "Damn."

"I'm so sorry," she mumbles again into the fabric of my lone dry shirt. "Are you mad?"

Am I mad? I step back from Echo and pop my neck to the right. I'm not happy, but am I mad? The filter ejects a pair of my socks. Son of a bitch.

I bend my knees, and in a swift motion sweep Echo off her feet and toss her into the pool. Water splashes up and soaks part of my shirt and jeans, but at this point, I don't care.

I crouch by the edge and watch as Echo kicks up from the bottom. Her red hair wildly fans out in the water, and as she breaks through to the surface, it slicks back against her head. She coughs, then drags in her first gulp of air. Damn if my siren doesn't look sexy all wet and disheveled.

"Feel better?" she half chokes out.

"I'm not mad," I respond.

"You forgot to add anymore."

"My bad. Anymore."

Echo laughs, and I smile along with her before releasing a long breath. The past couple of days have been like dragging Echo through glass in the middle of a firefight. If I'd known throwing her in a pool would erase the tension, I would have done it earlier. Guess there's something to be said for baptism.

With some effort, Echo slides off her shoes and throws them onto the concrete. Then she peels off the sweater, also lobbing that to the side. I make a mental note to steal it when she's not looking.

"I really am sorry." She treads water in the middle of the pool, and I hate the shadow that crosses her face. "I didn't stop to think that my mom would contact Mrs. Collins. I'm so used to Mom being gone, you know? It's just…I don't know." She slaps the water with her hand. "Crap, Noah. I don't know about any of this."

"I get it."

"Do you?" It's there in her expression, the same desperation that mirrors the craziness clawing at my insides.

"Yeah, I do."

"I'm sorry," she says again. There's a white silence in the closed-in room, and it makes her apology seem solemn. "For this. For all of it."

"Me, too." The water ripples around Echo as she stays afloat, and it eventually reaches the wall next to me. "Time to start bobbing for jeans."

Her mouth squishes to the side and the contents of my stomach bottom out. "What?"

"I can't open my eyes under water."

"You're kidding."

Tiny voice. "No."

Fuck me. I straighten, pull the shirt over my head and kick off my shoes and socks.

"What about your jeans?" Echo asks. "It's just us and I'm cool with you swimming around in your boxers. You need at least one dry outfit."

I glance at my jeans and they hang right at my hips. "It wasn't a boxer type of day."

Echo sinks and when she resurfaces, it's only with her

eyes then slowly up to her chin. "One of these days you are going to get us into a ton of trouble."

"Baby, so far the trouble's been on you. Breaking into guidance counselors' offices—"

"That was you!"

"—tossing clothes into the pool."

She splashes me as she kicks back.

I shake my head to get the water out of my hair. "You're paying for that one, princess."

"You have to catch me first," she taunts as she grabs at a floating blob. My favorite black T-shirt smacks onto the concrete with a wet flop.

"Little full of yourself tonight, aren't you?"

I love the light in her eyes. "I was the three-year-straight swimming champ."

That I didn't know. "So was I. Mine in the Y from third to fifth grade. What's your story?"

Echo's grin widens. "Backyard baby pool against Lila. Reigning preschool champ."

"You've got me quaking in my boots."

She goes under for the balled socks in the three foot section, and I eye the deep end. A pile of blue jeans covers the drain. Wonder how many quarters it will take to dry all of this. Doesn't matter. The answer doesn't get my clothes onto land. Like my dad taught me, I raise my hands over my head and dive in.

Dripping from head to toe and shivering so much that my brain rattles, Noah and I scurry down the hallway, each of us carrying a hundred-pound load of completely soaked clothes. Okay, only I scurry. Noah more or less struts, and I tote fifty pounds while Noah shoulders the rest.

My hands shake so badly that I miss the slot for the key card twice and breathe a sigh of relief when the door clicks open. The air conditioner I had turned down earlier in the day has officially become my worst enemy as goose bumps creep up my arm to my neck.

"Damn, Echo. Freezing meat?"

"I was hot."

Noah dumps his clothes into a lump on the floor and readjusts the thermostat from arctic winter to what will eventually be tropical heat.

"Really?" I ask. "We've got to sleep in here."

"Win the lottery?"

Good point. Even if our clothes weren't drenched with pool water, hotel dryers cost a fortune to get clothes to somewhat damp. "So what's the plan?"

"Lay them out flat and bring on the room heat. That is, after a shower."

I drop my own bundle of clothes at the mere mention of a shower. Heat against my skin, soaking past my muscles to my bones. I've never yearned for anything more in my life. A cold bead of water escapes from my scalp, glides down my face and onto my chest. My teeth rattle, and Noah assesses me at the sound. "Let's go before you turn hypothermic."

"You're letting me go first?"

"Do you think I'd make you wait?" Noah walks into the bathroom and I follow, rubbing my hands against my arms. He opens the shower curtain and leans over to turn on the water.

Good God, he's gorgeous. Noah's jeans ride low, low enough that if he hadn't told me, I'd still know he wasn't wearing boxers. Every single one of his glorious abs are exposed, and I even spot some of the smooth skin beneath the ripped-out muscles that lead to very private areas.

Warmth curls in my belly. A warmth I wish would spread through the rest of me. Water splashes against the tub, and my eyes widen when Noah flicks the button of his jeans through the hole.

"What are you doing?" I ask.

Noah's lips slowly form into that wicked grin I'm way too familiar with. Oh, crap. Just crap. "I'm cold, Echo, and so are you. A hot shower sounds nice, doesn't it?"

I nod, too frightened I'll squeak instead of speak. Noah and I have messed around, a lot. We've kissed and touched and shed clothes in moments where things became as hot as an inferno, but there's always been a discreet air surrounding us.

Certain things stayed on when other things came off. Hands would wander below instead of a complete unveiling. And the times that we pushed beyond our normal boundaries and our blood rushed too hot for too long...there would be a blanket and one night, his black leather jacket.

After that delicious night, I will never smell leather again without blushing.

But now, this, standing in the middle of a hotel bathroom, Noah is suggesting that we strip ourselves of everything and huddle together behind a shower curtain and...well...bathe. That's just...intimate.

"I..."

And Noah unzips his jeans. I spin on my heel, and my reflection in the mirror confirms the shock exploding in my body. My green eyes are too bright against my pale skin, and my drenched hair molds to my head and cheeks. Goose pimples outline my skin, and my body quakes.

Because they're wet, Noah's jeans are a bit stubborn sliding down, but he's successful, and in the mirror I'm drawn to his naked body. I love the raw power of his shoulder blades and the curve of his back that trails lower to his...my mouth dries out...oh, crap...his butt is...how do I describe something so exquisite?

Everything about Noah is sexy, and as he bends to pull the jeans off his foot—

"If you get in the shower with me, Echo, you'd get a better look and you'd warm up."

"I should get...my pj's...so that they're in here...when we...finish." Or something.

"Finish?" he repeats with a tease. "I'm all about finishing."

Internally screaming, I half turn and throw myself

into what I believe is the doorway and instead ram into the corner of the wall. "Ow!"

My hands fly up to my bang line to cover the now possibly dented and crushed area of my skull. I am the most impaired person on the face of the planet.

"Echo?" Noah's concern leaks into his voice, but I wave him off—without peeking.

"Go. I'm fine. I'm just...go."

Instead, a warm hand settles on my shoulder, and my fingers slip down to hide my entire face. At least my cheeks are now hot. "You're naked, Noah."

"Yeah. I am. Nothing you haven't seen before—now let me see how bad it is."

"I'm fine."

"You cracked your head, and I want to look."

"I haven't."

"Haven't what?"

"Seen you." The words are muffled through my fingers. "Down there. All the way. I've...avoided it."

Water continues to pour into the tub, and I distantly wonder if the drain is open, otherwise we'll flood the room. Noah brushes his thumb against my neck. "But you've—"

"I know," I cut him off. I've touched him, but no need to get all conversational about it.

"And you haven't—"

"No." I really, really don't want to discuss this or hear him say out loud what I've done or haven't done because it's like pointing out that I overplucked one eyebrow or that my bangs are uneven or, I don't know, it's embarrassing!

"Have you ever seen a guy's—"

Oh. My. God. "Yes."

"You have?"

Crap and I wish I would melt into a puddle on the floor. "No."

Noah's hands ease down my arms, then he folds me into him. His front heating my back. He dips his head to my ear and whispers. "Lower your hands."

"Nuh-uh." My mind chants, *can't make me*, followed by, *la, la, la*.

"Baby, I've got no problem turning you around, propping you up on the sink and kissing you until you look at me."

And he wins. I drop my hands and catch his eyes in the mirror.

"It's okay," he says.

"I'm..." What am I? Damaged? Idiotic? Twelve and playing spin the bottle? "I wish I wasn't like this."

"I like how you are just fine." He kisses the side of my neck, and my knees literally go weak with the warmth of his lips against my cold skin. "You take a shower. I'll lay my clothes out to dry then take one after."

He releases me, and I snag his hand. "No. Wait. I want to do this."

"Echo—"

"No!" I spin and come close to stomping my foot. I crave this, and I'm done with him excusing my stupid fears because that's all they are—stupid.

I methodically stare straight into Noah's eyes because I'll probably go into anaphylactic shock or seize if I outright gawk lower. The normally smooth patch of skin between Noah's eyebrows wrinkles as he checks out the pounding spot on my forehead. I tremble when his fingers lightly trace the area, but this time, it's not because I'm cold.

"Well?" I ask to fill the silence because the running water creates this weird vacuum effect. "Am I dying?" The answer is yes. I'm dying of embarrassment.

Noah cups my face with both hands, kisses my wound, and something inside me gives. A thawing of frozen muscles. His lips skim lower—a kiss to the end of my nose—then he tips my face up, and he gently presses his mouth to mine.

It's a slow kiss. One that causes my heart to stop, and when it starts again, it doesn't resume at a normal pace. It's the type that washes away my fears and where I automatically tilt my head in a silent plea for more.

His tongue slides against my lips, and I part them. Every inch of me springs to life. Each caress of his hand on my back, along the sides of my waist, near my thighs, stokes a fire that, over the past two months, has been rising in intensity.

Noah rests both of his hands below my butt, and before I can move closer to him, he lifts me and props me onto the sink. I suck in a breath and pop open my eyes. Noah smiles at me in a way that makes me fall in love with him all over again.

"You said you'd only do that if I didn't lower my hands and look at you," I tease.

"What can I say? After I spoke the words, it was a done deal. I'm all about making my fantasies realities with you, Echo."

I giggle, and Noah grows serious as he grazes his thumb against my cheek. "Are you sure about the shower?"

No. "Yes." I blink three times.

Noah chuckles. "Right."

"What if I want to be sure?"

NOAH

Echo captures my hand in a death grip. "I mean it. I want to do this."

And I want her to, but fuck me, I'll only do it if she's a hundred percent positive. I've coaxed too many girls into situations they regretted. As much as I liked the high of making out, I hated the fallout when they realized they gave me too much. I loathed the hollow expression as the reality hit that what was lost could never be returned, and they wasted it on me.

I love Echo, and I will never hurt her because she's not ready for more. "We can wait."

"I'm tired of waiting," she rushes out, and I freeze. She's never said anything like that before. Echo claws at the neck of the wet shirt clinging to her body. "I'm tired of being me. This trip was supposed to change that. I was supposed to become more, and two months later I'm still stammering like a stupid child, and we're going home next week and it's all going to be the same. Me. You. Mom. Dad. Everything."

Okay. This conversation has detoured far from showers, and her body convulses with another fit of shakes. If we continue to hang out in the bathroom, my dick's going to break off from frostbite, and Echo's going to resemble a sheet of ice.

"Echo..." I don't know what the hell to do. I'm screwed any way I go.

"I want to do this," she repeats.

"Okay."

"Okay," she says again.

Yet nothing speeds up. "I'll get in the shower first, then you go in and if you change your mind at any time, I'll get out."

"Okay," she mumbles under her breath.

I stare at her. She stares at the ceiling.

"Clothes need to come off." Then I reassess the situation. "Or not. You can shower fully dressed, and I'd be okay with that." Not exactly every man's dream, but if it helps Echo...

Echo's lips slant up. "Do you hate me?"

"No." I slip my fingers underneath the hem of her shirt. "I can help you if you'd like."

She finally meets my gaze, and I love the spark in her eyes. "I'm sure that would be such an imposition."

"We all have our crosses to bear."

Echo raises her arms, and parts of me jerk to life as I lift the material from her skin and slide it over her head. I briefly close my eyes to stop the groan: black lace bra. The one that's see-through. Echo could wear this bra every day for the rest of my life, and I'd fall to my knees in praise.

"Let me guess," she says. "You look."

"Not look. Memorize." I grab hold of her hips and drag her off the vanity and into me. "You've got a beautiful body. A guy would have to be dead not to look. Matching underwear?"

"What is it with guys and matching underwear?"

"I'm a simple man. Too many things going on at one time can be distracting."

She laughs, and the sound warms my heart.

"You seem insanely focused."

"Didn't answer about the underwear," I say, because she's deciding on clothes going forward. I won't seduce her into this, though I'm fighting the instinct.

Echo lowers her hands, and I'm hypnotized by the way she undoes the button to her jeans and the crackling of the zipper. Damn, the girl never lets me down. "You match."

"Because I know you like it," she says quietly.

"We're doing this one step at a time." I knot my fingers into her hair and take her bottom lip between both of mine. Her sweet scent overwhelms me and when Echo brushes her tongue across my lips, every single cell sizzles.

If I don't start reciting baseball stats, we won't reach the tub. I step away and open the shower curtain. "Just a shower. If you want me to stay on the opposite side, I will. I won't kiss. I won't touch."

Echo flashes that siren smile. "What if I want to kiss you?"

"You're trying to kill me, aren't you?"

She giggles. I step in then close the curtain as she eases her jeans past her underwear. If Echo kisses me, touches me, shit, looks at me the right way, I'll lose my fucking mind.

I raise the knob, the water stops cascading from the faucet, whines in the pipes then sprays out of the showerhead. With a fast switch to the right, I turn off the hot water and lower my head, permitting the freezing water to pummel my urges. When the rings of the curtain jingle against the rod, I glance over my shoulder and turn the warm water back on. Damn, she's beautiful.

Echo

Noah devours me with his eyes as he peers over his shoulder. There's a wildness in them that creates a jolt of hysteria and excitement.

My arms twitch with the need to cover myself, but I keep them straight to my sides. According to Noah, he's seen all of me before, but what if it hasn't been all of me, but parts of me at different times and maybe I was sort of shadowed?

I rub at the scars on my left arm as Noah wipes the droplets from his face. Noah's a sight with the water darkening the bangs hanging over his eyes. His skin glistens, and the beads highlight each curve and cut of his muscles.

"You're beautiful." He offers me his hand. With a deep breath I accept and step in.

I link my fingers with Noah's and cling to him as if I'd fall apart if he let go. He draws me closer to him and turns so that hot water hits me instead of him. Very intimate areas of me press against him, and I blow out a long stream of air to prevent myself from hyperventilating again.

Warm water rolls down my shoulders, over my breasts and sneaks into the impossibly minuscule crevices between me and Noah. As it flows between us, I swear the water becomes hotter. Noah shifts, and his body glides easily with mine. The lack of friction births a strange sensation—a sensitivity, an awareness...a hunger.

I lick my lips and taste clean water. Noah watches the movement, his eyes growing darker by the second. My thumb swipes across his wrist, and his pulse pushes past his veins and skin. Standing so near, can Noah feel my heart beating?

Noah holds my gaze, and I silently thank him for giving me a good excuse to not look down. Because I want to look down, but I don't want to look down, and if I look down I want to look down without Noah knowing I'm looking down.

He squeezes my hand. "Do you want me to let go?"

I shake my head then discover the courage to speak. "No."

With his other hand, Noah frees a tendril of hair sticking to my cheek. As if the brush against my skin is a lightning rod, energy zaps from my head to my toes.

"I want to kiss you," he murmurs.

I've lost the ability to breathe. "I want you to kiss me."

Noah releases my hand and as he leans forward, I inch back and find myself against the cold wall. It's a strange tingle in my body, to be warmed on one side and cold on another. As Noah presses against me, the wall starts to absorb my heat, and I'm suddenly toasty.

I take in Noah's heady scent. It's a mesmerizing smell, one that causes my mouth to water and my muscles to relax. As if sensing my give, Noah wraps an arm around my waist and cups my face with his other hand.

I *feel* Noah. In a different way than I ever had before, and I wait for the panic or the insecurity, but none of it shows. As I stare into Noah's eyes, I only sense peace, as if this moment is natural and is meant to happen.

"I love you." So much that sometimes it hurts.

Noah tilts his head down, and his nose skims against mine. "You're my whole world, Echo. Someday, when you're ready, I'll show you how much."

Small drops of water trail down our faces, and it's like little teasing fingers. I run my hands up his back, exploring. When they tangle into his hair, I whisper against his lips, "Maybe soon."

Maybe now.

NOAH

Echo's different, and as I take her lips with mine, every ounce of my being responds to the change. She holds me closer, melts farther in and she's lost her hesitancy. Her hands are everywhere, and mine behave the same. I can't touch enough of her fast enough, and the urge for more drives me to press my body against hers. The flames are consuming both of us, pushing us to transform into a blazing wildfire.

My tongue slips between her lips, and Echo arches into me. I bite back a growl, terrified of scaring her. My hands tangle in her hair and skim along her wet body, enjoying each sensual curve.

The kiss is wild, passionate and deep. Kissing Echo has always been steaming, but this is beyond. As if a dam's been breached, and the pent-up attraction floods out.

Echo gasps for air, and my mouth brushes down her cheek to her neck—nipping, kissing, devouring. She tilts her neck to the side, granting me access, inviting me to explore more...explore lower.

"Noah," she says in the way I've dreamed of since the night I backed her against a wall outside of Mike Blair's house in January. My name falling from her lips has been a major part of every erotic dream.

She glances up at me from below her eyelashes, and

my world stalls into slow motion. There's a depth in her eyes that's never been there before—a slow sexiness, an expectation. With the shower angled at her body, running down her beautiful curves, steam rising into the air, Echo's red hair reshapes into ringlets.

I slide my hands down her arms until I link our fingers together. "I need you to be sure."

Her chest moves as she inhales deeply. A bit of the tentativeness I'm used to with Echo returns as her fingers tighten around mine. "I think I am."

I want her. More than I've ever desired anyone. Need is a damn pulse in my body, and I can barely breathe with trying to keep myself under control. Image after image of taking Echo, right here, right now, becomes a virus in my mind. "Not think, Echo. You've got to know."

Echo places a hand on my chest and nudges me back. I'm cautious, watching her stare at my stomach. She's thinking, weighing, and I need to give her space. A rush of air escapes her lips, her arms fall to her sides, and my damn little siren switches her focus and looks down.

My lips edge up as her eyes widen. "No," she whispers.

"No what?"

"There is no freaking way *that* will fit."

Echo

The smugness radiating from Noah is nauseating. He wears this infuriating grin that encourages me to smack him upside the head, but the guilt from throwing his clothes into the pool prevents me from tackling him.

With a towel wrapped around his waist, he lays out his clothes on the floor, on the table and over the chairs. Basically anywhere there's an open spot. The cross tattooed on his biceps stretches as he hooks a hanger holding his dress shirt onto the heater vent near the ceiling.

I *saw* Noah tonight...all of him, and he was gorgeous. I mean, I knew what to expect as I'm not a nun. We have biology books at school, and I've had sex ed, but it was different, standing there, *seeing* him...and then I went and said the most epically tragic thing ever: *There is no freaking way that will fit.*

Sitting on the bed in a tank top and pair of boy shorts, I press my hands over my blazing cheeks. Saying that was like handing a match and a can of gasoline to a pyromaniac. "I didn't mean it that way."

Noah chuckles. "Yes, you did."

"No, I didn't. I meant that...you know...there's a limited space and you just appeared...and it's not what I meant." Stop digging the hole. It's already too deep for daylight.

Will this ever cease being so uncomfortably weird and

agonizing and strangely glorious? I like the glorious part. The rush of discovering something new, but I wish I could leave uncomfortable and agonizing behind.

Noah glances at me from over his shoulder. "So you saying I'm not abnormally large?"

"Yes." That sounded bad. "No." Somehow that sounded worse. "I'm sure you're normal."

The stubble on his face moves as he smiles. Noah places his hand near the knot on the towel hanging at his waist. "Would you like to have another look?"

My mouth goes dry, and I fumble with my hair pick before combing it through my curls. I'm doing my best for casual though casual seems impossible. I saw *Noah* tonight. "No, I think I'm good."

"Regret skipping the conditioner?" Noah asks.

Yep. "I didn't need it. Using too much can cause buildup."

Not true at all. There are certain things needed to survive in life: water, food, conditioner. For the millionth time, the pick catches on a tangle, and I consider scissors. Lots of girls cut their hair short before college. Why shouldn't I be one of them?

"Could have stayed in longer," Noah says. "The hot water didn't run out as fast as you thought it would."

"Well...you know...it had been running for a while, and what type of guests would we be if we drained the water tank?"

"Uh-huh." The bed dips as Noah sits beside me, and I don't miss how the towel slides up his leg. Oh, God, I'm obsessed now.

"So you bolting had nothing to do with me being naked?" he asks in this I-know-everything tone, and I sort of want to wipe that smirk off his face. As I peek at him, I realize I could kiss it off.

I think of the shower and his wet body and the comforter on the bed becomes suddenly fascinating. "Not at all."

I try the tangle again with both hands. The pick combs through the top then snags at the middle. Hard. The teeth scrape my skin, but when I attempt to pull it out, it yanks my hair, threatening to rip it out by the roots.

"Need help?" Noah asks.

"No."

"That's a ginormous knot."

"I've got it." Yet as I drag the pick through, it becomes totally ensnared, making everything worse, making me flush, making me want to... "Screw it!"

My hands slam down on the bed, and I sit there, utterly humiliated with a plastic growth now embedded in my hair. At least people will have something new to tease me about.

The heater kicks on, and I groan. The room teeters on sauna status. Noah shifts, and my shoulders slump when a tug on my hair causes my head to fall back. It's as if he believes he can untangle the mess that is my life.

"It's useless," I tell Noah as the tugging on my hair inches increasingly close to yanking. "You're right. I rushed out of the shower because you were naked, and I needed conditioner. Now I'm forever screwed."

"Not forever, baby," he says gently.

My eyes stupidly burn, and the weight of the last few days covers me like a shroud. "It feels like forever."

He says nothing, and I'm very okay with that. Sometimes I prefer silence. My hair drifts right and left and up and down as Noah tries to repair the twisted damage.

"What if I can't measure up?" I ask, and the pressure on my head pauses. The question even startles me.

"What?"

With Noah behind me, balancing a lock of my hair with one hand and the wedged-in pick with the other, I'm literally stuck, and I fight the urge to dash to the opposite side of the room...or the country. "Nothing."

"Talk, Echo."

I link my fingers together and unlink them. Noah grants me a moment of silence as he continues to extricate the tangle. As each stroke works through larger sections of my hair, I sense my reprieve coming to an end. He won't let this go, and I'm not sure I want him to.

I drop my mouth open to tell him the truth then lose my courage. "I messed up my only hope at making a contact with an art gallery in Vail."

"How's that?" Noah pauses to use his fingers against the knot. "Showed them your art and they felt inferior?"

I giggle before sighing. I wish. I'll be going home a failure—as someone not capable of succeeding on my own with my art. At least not without my mother's help, and that isn't an option. "No, I wasn't thinking straight. There was a painting of the constellation Aires that was wrong and after everything that happened...the owner came out...and he asked what I thought and...I messed up."

"How'd he take it?"

"Not good."

"Not good like I need to talk to him or not good that you're scared you hurt his feelings?"

"Second one, and since when do you have talks with people?"

"I'll rephrase. If he yelled at you, I need to shove my foot up his ass." My head jerks back, but then the pick swipes clean through my hair. "Got it."

"Thanks."

I wait for him to hand me the pick back, but he continues to brush the rest of my hair. No one's done anything like that for me before, and the act makes my skin joyously sensitive.

After a few minutes, he places the pick on the nightstand and settles back against the pillows. I turn and watch as he messes his hand through his hair. I like it damp. It's a tad bit darker and gives him this hint of wildness.

"I don't want you scared of me, Echo."

"I'm not."

"You are."

I think of the first night we made out in the basement of his foster parents' house. He told me he didn't want me to be scared of him. I told him I wasn't, but I was. I was frightened by the sensations caused by his touch. Months later and I'm still terrified. Noah's right. I'm no different.

I move so that I face him, but stay safely near the end of the bed. "I'm scared."

Noah scratches his chin with his knuckles and shakes his hair over his eyes. "Me, too."

"What?" Maybe we aren't discussing the same thing.

"I'm scared."

"Of what?" He's Noah Hutchins. They guy who has done it backward, sideways and forward. "I mean you've done *this*, and I haven't. I can't even get myself together enough to handle looking at your—" I wave both hands frantically in the air "—*stuff*."

"Stuff?"

Oh, my God. "Noah, if there was something sharp nearby, I'd slam it into my brain so I wouldn't have to have this conversation. So can you stop pointing out my inability to say...stop pointing out my inabilities."

"Fine. We'll do this your way." Noah stretches out his legs and offers me his hand. "But we're talking."

Talking. We're going to do this. We are going to talk about *it*. We've discussed this before...the night I was willing to do *it* with him, but we didn't do *it*, we did other things, and since then he's been patient.

Still sitting cross-legged, I edge closer to him and bring his hand into my lap so that I can hold it in both of mine. My knee rubs against his thigh, and I like how the hair on his legs tickles my skin.

Noah frowns and tips his chin, indicating that I should come closer, but I can't. I need distance so I can curl into a ball and die if the conversation becomes too much. That would be harder to do being tucked next to Noah.

"What are you scared of?" I ask.

Noah slides his ring finger along mine, and a small amount of liquid heat flows into my veins. "Hurting you."

Fantastic. "So you are abnormally large."

Noah laughs, and I blush so hard that I could roast marshmallows off my cheeks. He squeezes my fingers until I finally meet his gaze. "While I don't go around checking out the competition, I'd say I'm normal."

New, refreshing air fills my lungs. Good. That's good. I think. "Lila said her first time hurt."

"I'll try not to hurt you, but a lot of it's going to depend on how into it you are."

Kill me. Please tell me we aren't discussing what I believe we're discussing. "Got it."

Yet he keeps going. "Because if you aren't sure this is what you want to do and you say yes, it's going to be difficult because you won't be—"

"I said I got it," I snap, and throw him a glare that says I'll happily cut his *stuff* off if he doesn't shut up.

"I've got condoms that are lu—"

"No." I slam my hands over my face. "You have them. I know you have them. I do not need to know their specific function and attributes."

Noah brushes his thumb against the inside of my wrist before he wraps his fingers around my hand. He pulls until my shield gives. "It's okay. I'm fine continuing with what we're doing."

My foot rocks frantically on the bed. "But I want to."

Noah's grim as he watches my foot. "If it's this difficult for you to talk about sex—"

"Because I'm embarrassed!" I yell. "I'm embarrassed because you know everything, and I know nothing, and I hate that no matter what I do, I won't be good enough."

Noah sits up, and when I try to duck out of reach, he advances like a tiger and flips me so that I'm lying flat on the bed. He presses his palms onto the comforter on both sides of my head, and his dark eyes bore into mine. My heart pounds wildly and, because I can't help myself, I reach up and touch his face, sliding my fingers over the rough shadow of his jaw.

Noah leans into my touch, and I love that I have that

effect on him. I lick my lips, half hoping he kisses me—half wondering what would happen if he did.

"Echo, kissing you for the rest of my life would be good enough, and you need to get these fucked-up thoughts out of your brain. I'm scared of making love to you because you're too good for me. I'm terrified that after I share this with you, you'll realize the mistake, and I can't take that. Not from you."

My eyebrows furrow. "Mistake?"

Noah slams his eyes shut then rolls away. Now I'm the one up after him, clinging to his hand before he can bolt off the bed. "What do you mean that I'll think it was a mistake?"

"Let me go." A thunderhead creeps onto his face as he stands next to the bed.

"No." I wind my other hand around his wrist. "We're talking about this."

"I'm going to put some of these clothes in the dryer." He reaches for the only pair of jeans that are halfway dry. I let go of him, grab them then shove them underneath my bottom.

Noah pinches the bridge of his nose. "I'll go naked, Echo."

I'm sure he would. "I looked at your penis today so you can talk to me about this."

Noah's eyes widen as they jump to me.

"Yep, I said it." *That's right, world, I'm capable of a sexual conversation.*

We're silent and I toe his T-shirt on the ground that has a skull and crossbones on the back. "You're good enough for me. In fact, you're the best for me."

"You don't get it. There were girls…"

It's hard to keep from cringing, and I hate that he notices. I love him so much, and it's difficult to imagine him intimate with anyone else.

Noah swears softly. "This is how I don't want to hurt you."

I don't want to hurt, either, especially over this. "We went to school together and despite my lack of popularity, I still had ears and heard the gossip. This is old news, so keep going."

It helps that every girl we're discussing is thousands of miles away in Kentucky.

"I warned them up front what I was and what it would be. I was a game to some girls, and I was fine being played. Others regretted it. Those girls, afterward, I'd see how they'd look at me at school. I think most of them thought after we had sex, I'd fall in love and when I didn't—they regretted it. I hated the expression on their faces, but I swear to you, I gave them the out."

"Like you give me the out?" I hedge. Noah never pushes me. Ever.

"I need you to be sure." Noah meets my eyes. "I want it to be different with us. I don't want you to view me as some sort of prize you scored or as the asshole that used you. I don't want to lose the way you look at me—like I'm something...someone. I've survived a lot, but I don't think I can survive if you regretted it. It would kill me if you looked at me any different than you do now."

There are moments when your heart breaks and melts at the same time. When there's so much love flooding your soul that you're drowning in the tide. This is that moment with Noah. "I could never look at you differently."

Noah stares at the floor, and his voice gets strained. "I hope not."

The direction of the conversation bothers me. More than I would have thought it would. "Don't you trust how I feel? What I say?"

Noah's that soft place I fall. He makes me laugh. I can talk to him for hours, plus he makes every area of my body hot and drives it close to the brink of insanity. I love him. He loves me. Why am I hesitant to make love to Noah? What is it that I don't trust?

"Someday, Echo, you're going to wake up and realize that you're more than me. That everyone you know is right. That I'm a phase that'll die out. Someday I won't be the man you want to walk down the street with."

A slow, agonizing burn tortures my stomach as I replay his last statement. "You don't trust me?"

A long heavy silence. I might as well be suffocating.

"Probably as much as you trust me." He clears his throat. "Which is more than I trust anyone else in my life."

I am suffocating, and that sting in my chest is the lack of air. It's creating a strange numbness throughout my mind and limbs. "I guess that's good."

But is it enough to help us last beyond a few months of living in a bubble?

"Do you ever think..." I cut myself off while focusing on a framed print of fir trees on the wall.

"Do I ever think what?"

"Are you scared that we're going to be heading home soon? Back to everything that threatens to pull us apart?" This summer was supposed to change me, and it hasn't. I'm returning the same person as when I left.

Noah nods, and his agreement smarts more than it should.

"What does that mean for us?" I ask.

Noah releases a long breath and crosses his arms over his chest.

My fingers shake as I shove my hair away from my face. "Did we leave Kentucky because we didn't believe we'd last if we stayed?"

"I don't know." Noah kneads his eyes and when he lowers his hands he repeats, "I don't know."

NOAH

Flames lick along the stairwell, blocking the only way up, and it's the coughing from the living room that keeps me from charging the bedrooms. Smoke smothers my eyesight...my ability to breathe.

It's dark. Too dark to see, but a burst of color from something electrical exploding in the kitchen creates a flash that illuminates my brothers on the floor. Jacob lying over a lifeless Tyler.

"Jacob!" I shout, and he lifts his head.

"Noah!" He hacks so hard that I'm afraid he's choking—dying. Fear grips me like it never has before. They're dying. My family is dying.

My lungs constrict and burn. I cough then crouch to move along the floor. Jacob launches himself at me. My heart beats again with the feel of tiny arms around my neck and the sight of Tyler's chest fighting upward for air.

Sweat beads on my brow. The heat threatens to melt my skin. "Where's Mom and Dad?"

"Upstairs."

Upstairs. Nausea rolls through my stomach. My brothers out first. Then my parents. Maybe they escaped through the back. Out the window, down the tree. But this paralyzing panic eats the logic. They'd never leave without Jacob and Tyler. Never.

Behind me, the flames dance closer to the door. Protect

them—*a screaming mantra in my brain. I grab two blankets off the floor, wrap my brothers up and race for the exit.*

Two steps to go for the foyer and there's a crack from above. In pure instinct, I turn my body and huddle Tyler and Jacob close to my chest. A rush of hot air, embers flying around and pain slams into my shoulder. I yell out as fire feeds off my shirt, and I dart through a wall of flames for the door. Jesus Christ, I'm on fire.

My eyes shoot open, and my body jolts. There's a pounding through my bloodstream, and my heart's a damn freight train. I'm not a nightmare type of guy. Never have been, but sometimes, my mind replays my past.

It's a nightmare that reminds me that I failed, and as I inhale, I remember the promise that I swore to Echo the night she recovered her memory...I won't fail her... never again.

I glance over at the clock. It's still early. Echo's locked in my arms, and I'm surprised she didn't wake when I squeezed the life out of her. She let me hold her as she slept, and it was my sole comfort in a long, torturous night. Our last words hanging over me like a guillotine.

Echo shifts, and her bottom presses into me. I take advantage and draw her closer. Her tank rides up, and I rest my palm against the heat of her stomach. I lived too long in cold isolation before Echo stumbled into my life, bringing her warmth and love. When we drove out of Louisville, we seemed indestructible.

I need us to be indestructible. I can't return to cold and alone. Things are complicated. No doubt. But we'll battle through this. We have to. Giving up is not an option.

"Me and you," I whisper, hoping my words will sink

into her subconscious, beyond where she overthinks. "It's how it's supposed to be."

Echo's hand glides over mine, and she links our fingers together. "You like disturbing my sleep, don't you?"

I kiss her shoulder, permitting my lips to linger on her soft skin. Guess I did wake her. "Just keeping things straight between us."

"In my sleep?" Damn, I love that groggy voice.

"You argue less that way."

Her body shakes with silent giggles. "I don't argue."

"That sounded like an argument."

"You're impossible." Echo eases to her back. Her smile fades, and I hate that last night still weighs on her. "It all seems overwhelming. Like everything is stacked against us."

"It's not so bad other than your dad would prefer for you to get over your juvenile delinquent phase and our friends hate each other."

The smile doesn't reappear like I'd hoped. Guess telling the truth as a joke didn't work.

"Being together, Noah, it's hard and you know it. We keep each other honest. It would be so much easier to slink back into our old lives."

Very easy. Return to living day to day, not giving a shit one way or another about anything or anyone. Not killing myself over a future in college and a damn degree. But if I chose simple, I wouldn't have Echo.

She forces me to question myself—why I do whatever I do. Before her, I couldn't have cared less about college or a job that went somewhere or a future. But Echo deserves a man she'd be proud of, and the Malt and Burger isn't good enough.

That same pride she has in her eyes when she walks down the street with me now, I want her to have walking down the street with me in ten years. If I stay as I am, she won't remain proud.

I brush a finger slowly along Echo's arm, tracing the smooth skin between her scars. She covered her arms in public again, and my shoulders stiffen. Am I busting my ass to move forward while Echo is falling back into her old life? Before I can ask, Echo opens her mouth. "Will we be okay when we go home?"

"We've been through too much for something like this to get us down."

The knots coiled in my gut relax when that siren smile appears on her face. "So we have to stay together because we've walked hand in hand through hell?"

"Don't overanalyze the rules, baby. Just follow them."

Echo laughs out loud. "Since when have you followed any rules?"

"Since always. They happen to be mine."

"The ones you make up don't count."

"They do." I slip my hand along her side. "Like the one that says that I have to kiss you if we're in bed together."

Echo raises a brow. "That's a rule?"

"Fuck it, Echo. I'd kiss you if you were sunbathing on nails. A bed's a hell of a lot more comfortable."

She stares up at me from beneath dark eyelashes. "You are so bad."

"Damn straight." Right as I go to kiss Echo, someone knocks on the door. Damn it all to hell. "Go away!"

"Be nice! It's probably housekeeping." Echo shoves at my chest and while she doesn't have enough strength to push me away, I drop back like a domino, and she hops out of bed.

"Be right there," she calls out, then she lowers her voice to address me. "We're lucky we didn't get kicked out last night over the clothes."

"We?" I repeat. "I'm not the one clogging hotel filters with boxer shorts."

She pins me with a glare. I turn onto my side and prop my head up on my hand, deciding to enjoy the show of Echo hot as hell and strutting across the room. Spaghetti-strapped tank top and boy shorts that show a hint of her ass. On second thought... "You may want a robe if you're going to open that door."

Hell, a shirt would help.

"I'm going to crack it open to tell them that we're still sleeping."

"We're eighteen and in a hotel. Did you want them to laugh?"

Her face turns red, and she shushes me.

Damn, she's going to answer the door like that. I roll off the bed and grab a pair of jeans. "Let me. My luck it'll be the maintenance guy, then he'll be stalking you for the rest of the trip."

Echo sticks her tongue out at me, but steps back to let me by. "Be nice."

My lips tilt up as I rub my thumb against her cheek. "I'm always nice."

"At least button your pants."

With a chuckle, I open the door wide enough to see who it is, but not enough that wandering eyes can drink in Echo's gorgeous legs and ass. My muscles grow rigid when I spot a guy my height, a smaller build and a few years older slouching in front of my room.

"What do you want?" I growl.

His eyes morph into two ovals. "Sorry, I thought this room belonged to a red-headed girl. Is this her room?"

He checks out the room number beside the door, and I broaden my stance. "What makes you think she's here?"

The guy winces. "I followed her."

A tremor runs through my body, and I have to keep from grabbing his throat and shoving him into the wall. *Keep talking, asshole.* I won't have Echo pissed at me when I take a swing at this guy. I'll allow him to bury himself first. "What do you want with her?"

"Noah," Echo whispers behind me and touches my bare back. "Did he say he followed me?"

The guy pulls his hands out of his sagging jeans. "I know this is strange, but I want to talk to her."

"Noah?" Echo inches as if she's going to peek out, and I slide in front of the door, holding the handle to keep her safely inside. This guy's going to need a hell of a right hook to get to her.

"You need to go," I say.

He rams both fists into his hair, and he's got dark circles under his eyes like he hasn't slept. "Look, I know this is insane—"

"You're right—you're fucking crazy. Guys knocking on hotel rooms of girls without being asked is sick." I jerk my thumb for him to leave. "Serial killers belong at the next exit."

"You don't understand." He steps in my direction and in response I step into the hallway, letting the door hit me. The asshole retreats. "I *need* to talk to her."

"You got two seconds to go before I rip your fucking heart out and shove it down your throat."

He throws his hands in the air. "Tell her that she was right on the painting, and that I didn't know that the star was supposed to be there. I wasn't trying to stalk her. I was trying to catch up, but she entered the hotel before I could. I saw the room she went in, and it didn't feel right at the time to knock so I went home, but I couldn't stop thinking about the painting so I came back and—"

"I said go!"

"Noah!"

My fingers curl into fists. Damn it, why couldn't Echo stay in the room? Behind me, Echo edges around the corner of the door. I should crush the damn guy for the way he ogles my girl's chest like he's a starved cartoon character who's seeing meat for the first time in weeks. "What?"

"That's him," she says in a soft voice. "That's the gallery owner."

This means she'll want to talk to him. Fucking great. My eyes bore into his. "You hurt her and you'll deal with me. Period."

Echo

His name is Hunter, and he's the owner of not one but three galleries. While that's amazingly cool, Noah is amazingly hot, and not in the sexy way. As Noah stalks back through the door and Hunter walks down the hallway to the exit, I desperately search for the right words to explain why I did what I just did—why I agreed to meet with Hunter.

Noah pulls a shirt over his head and pushes his arms through the holes with so much force it could rip the material. I lean against the door, and it clicks shut behind me. "What he said made sense."

He shoots me a glare that could freeze lava. "Sense? He fucking followed you, Echo, then turned up on your doorstep at nine in the morning. He thought you were alone."

True. He obviously wasn't prepared to find Noah fuming at the door, but I understood that look in Hunter's eye. The feeling that something you've worked on for so long isn't right, and that if you don't fix it you'll go insane.

That painting means something to him, and art means something to me.

"You heard what he said. He tried to catch up with me after we talked, but when he saw me enter the room he

thought he should wait until this morning. He just wants
to discuss the painting. I get that."

"I get that he was staring at your tits."

A shockwave of anger bounces throughout my cells.
Don't kill the boy you love. "I had my arms crossed over my
chest. I was wearing a sweater yesterday so he was probably staring at my scars. Exactly like you did when you
first saw them. It's what people do!"

Noah clasps his fingers to the back of his neck as if that
will keep him from throttling me. "Tits. Not your goddamned scars. You're the one that obsesses over them,
not the rest of the world. Trust me, he wants to talk to
you because he liked what he saw, and I don't care for it."

My mouth pops open, and all the air rushes out, leaving me speechless. Shocked, hurt, pissed, just freaking
frustrated. "You...that was..."

"What? It was what, Echo?"

"Sometimes people like to discuss things. Sometimes
people might see me as a person with talent! He didn't
see the scars yesterday so it was a shock today. He showed
not because of my—" and I wildly gesture at my top area
"—stuff. He and I had an actual conversation, and he
showed here because he wanted to have another conversation involving art! Not everyone is interested in sex!"

A muscle in Noah's jaw ticks, and a small part of me
immediately regrets the words, but there's no way I'm
taking them back. Not until he apologizes to me.

"Tell me that you didn't mean what you said to him,"
says Noah. "Tell me that you were trying to get him to
leave without me having to intervene and that you have
no intention of meeting with a guy that *stalked* you."

There's a pleading expression on Noah's face—his forehead wrinkled, his dark eyes a bit shadowed. I've only seen that type of desperation when Noah used to mention his need to be with his brothers, and it slightly kills a part of my soul that he's wearing it for me.

Even worse? That he's wearing it for me, and I can't grant him what he craves. Not without compromising my dreams. "He owns three galleries, and I've heard of him before from multiple people. He can open doors for me. I believe him when he says he wants to talk. I'm going to meet with him."

Noah throws out his arms. "He's psychotic!"

"I'm meeting him at a coffee shop! It'll be a little obvious to the staff if he tries to chop me into pieces!"

"We'll find another gallery. Someone else!"

"No!" I scream.

"Why?" he yells back.

"Because!" My voice breaks. "Because I understand what it's like when someone sees something in your work. Not just the beauty, but the message. I saw something in his painting, and he knows it. He wants to improve it, and I want to help. I need this. I need to belong to something bigger than me. Something..." My eyes flash to my arms. "Something more than me."

Noah pivots away, and nausea hits my stomach. This is all we've done for days now—fight. We're at odds with each other, and I hate it. I want us to go back to one week ago, two weeks ago, any time after graduation and before this—free from the world, free from arguing. "I don't like fighting with you."

"Neither do I," he says so quietly that I'm not sure if he said it.

Someone knocks on the door, and I lower my head.

How can we repair us when we keep pressing Rewind on the same parts of the same tired movie?

The knock becomes persistent, and when Noah says nothing, I open the door. I blink with the first glimpse and blink again because there is no way this is happening. Black T-shirt, ripped jeans, a backpack hanging on one shoulder, and her long black hair tumbles over the strap of the pack as she looks over my outfit. It's Noah's sister by choice, Beth, and my every nightmare come true.

A wide grin spreads across her face that spells eight layers of trouble for me. "I'm assuming your outfit means that Isaiah and I are interrupting this morning's extra-curricular activities. If so, hurry it up. I need to use the bathroom."

NOAH

Dressed and sitting on the edge of the bed, Echo shoves her feet into her sneakers and yanks at the shoelaces as she ties them. I told Beth and Isaiah that we needed a few minutes then slammed the door on any comment from Beth. Anything I do or say at this point doesn't matter because I'm fucked. "I meant to tell you."

"Yet you didn't."

As I said, fucked.

"How long have you known they were coming?" she asks as she strangles the laces of her right shoe.

I pick up the last of the clothes that I had laid out to dry, hoping to buy myself time. The truth isn't going to help. "Since the morning we left the sand dunes."

Echo tosses her hands into the air. "Oh, so you've only known a few days. Then my bad, why should I be angry? Tell me, is Rico coming? Maybe Antonio? Did we need to reserve adjoining rooms for your foster parents?"

Echo grabs her keys, and my heart pounds hard once, threatening to tear out of my chest. "Where are you going?"

She turns her head so quickly that her curls bounce. "To meet with Hunter."

"Echo—"

"Coffee shop, Noah, not the Bates Motel, and I highly

suggest keeping your opinions to yourself. If you're lucky, I'll come back."

She jerks open the door, bangs it shut and leaves me alone in the room. I'm so deep in this damn hole that it feels like walls of dirt have collapsed and are smothering me. I reopen the door and a quick scan of the hallway informs me that Echo's long gone.

Relaxing on the floor with their legs stretched out, Isaiah and Beth stare at me. Beth pops open her mouth, and I hold up my hand. "Not in the mood."

Beth shrugs and returns to folding a brochure on mountain climbing into a paper airplane, but my best friend continues to study me. When a guy a year younger with more tattoos on his arms than he has skin gives the pity look, it's bad.

"I'm sorry, man," he says. "Look, we can go."

"Fuck that." Beth sends the badly constructed plane into the air. "You dragged my ass here, and you can't make me get on another shit-ton bus if your life depended on it."

"The phrase is if *my* life depended on it," says Isaiah.

"Your life's worth more. In fact," she says, winking, "we should consider getting an insurance policy on you. Isn't that what fancy, rich people do?"

"We ain't rich," he answers.

"I decided that since we're here in Colorado, we are rich. Noah—" she snaps her fingers "—fill my room with bottled water."

Isaiah smiles. "Gone dry?"

"Please, Isaiah. Have some class. We can't drink before noon. That isn't what fancy, rich people do. They wait until twelve-oh-five."

The two of them never stop. "In or out, but I'm done listening."

They stand, and Isaiah pats my back as he enters the room. "Seriously, we'll go."

I close the door behind me and sag onto the bed where I held Echo less than an hour ago. "We were fighting before you showed. I'll talk to her. Straighten it out."

Beth and Isaiah share one of those glances that say they see an oncoming train on the track I'm tied to, and they aren't sure whether or not to tell me I'm on the verge of being creamed. "Me and Echo are fine."

"Whatever." Beth collapses onto the other bed and kicks off her shoes. Against the white pillowcases, she's too pale. "How about you guys shut the fuck up and let me sleep."

"You okay?" I ask.

"Trash can in puking distance may not be a bad idea and before you ask, jackass, I'm sober, thanks to Isaiah. I swear, Echo has totally destroyed the two of you with her squeaky-clean attitude. My goal in life is to get that girl—" Beth covers her face with both her hands then moans like she's in pain "—stoned. If I was stoned right now, I wouldn't feel like this."

I lift my head, going on high alert. Isaiah disappears into the bathroom, and the sink turns on. What the hell? He returns and places a towel next to Beth on the edge of the bed, a wet washcloth to her forehead and a trash can on the floor. "Sleep, Beth."

Isaiah eases onto the other side of the bed, careful not to touch her as he lies down. Beth doesn't shrink away from Isaiah, and she wouldn't. He's her closest friend, and though she won't admit it, she hates being alone.

Beth appears small curled up, and that's because she is. She couldn't reach five-five if she tiptoed in heels. She's also thin. Unless she's at her Aunt Shirley's—my foster home—food can be a rarity, and Shirley isn't conscientious about stocking the fridge.

Isaiah and I stay silent and after a few minutes, Beth flinches in her sleep. Isaiah surveys Beth then whispers to me, "Turns out if Beth's in a moving vehicle for over two hours, she pukes. She didn't sleep during the trip."

Which means Isaiah didn't, either. He's always searching for the threat that follows Beth. "Did you know she'd get sick?"

"Beth didn't know it. When has she been in a car longer than thirty minutes?"

Her life has been limited...and so has Isaiah's. "This your first time out of state?"

"Since entering foster care." Isaiah rubs his red eyes. "Can't shake the vibe I'm a criminal on the lam."

"Felt like that, too, when Echo and I crossed the state line. You and I have had so many social workers up our asses, I thought the cops would pull Echo and me over as soon as we crossed the bridge into Indiana. Then I realized no one gives a shit."

"True." Isaiah chuckles then falls somber. "It's good to see you, man. It's been...not right without you."

"Same here." He's my brother, not by blood, but in the way it counts. We've stood strong on the streets together. There's nothing I wouldn't do for him or Beth.

"What's going on with you and Echo?"

Fuck if I know. "Can't get our shit together."

"You'll work it out. Have to."

"Have to?"

"One of us has to get a happy ending." His gaze drops to the sleeping girl beside him.

"Yeah." Yeah. "Some days I don't know why Echo's with me. What she gets out of it. A messed-up kid from foster care with jacked odds of giving her a future. I'm a real prize."

"She looks happy to me when she's beside you."

I laugh bitterly. "She looked real happy when she left."

"She looked hurt. Hurt means she cares. It's indifference that should scare you. The same look foster parents give you when you come and go."

I can't live like this anymore. Jumping around from place to place, knowing no one cares. Echo keeps me grounded. Gives me roots. "You think happy endings happen to people like us?"

He scratches the top of his shaved head and settles back on a pillow. He'll be out in seconds. "Who the fuck knows."

I snatch Echo's laptop. The urge is to rush the coffee shop, but with the mood Echo left in, she'd probably pour boiling coffee down my pants. Instead, I'll find a dark corner in the hotel and dig for info on my blood family. "Shut down, bro. I'll be heading to work later, and I have a feeling that Echo will be AWOL."

Isaiah extends his hand, and we share a short shake. "Tell Echo I'm not freeloading. I'll cover me and Beth."

"It's all good." But as I walk out the door, I'm drowning in worry.

Echo

I should have brought pepper spray.

Noah bought me some the day before he started his shift at the St. Louis Malt and Burger. Even though the campsite we stayed at was so family friendly it bordered on annoying, and despite the fact that I planned to call on art galleries, Noah felt uneasy with me being alone.

He also tried to teach me how to throw a punch, but all I ended up doing was accidentally kneeing him in the crotch. As he held on to the trunk of the car, half bent over, he didn't see the humor, but I giggled.

The memory causes me to pause outside the coffee shop. After the past few days, thinking of such a light-hearted time with Noah honestly stings. If going home is the problem, maybe we should stay away forever.

A part of me floats—maybe we should.

At a back table of the coffee shop, Hunter looks up from a sketch pad and spots me. In seconds, he moves from startled to relieved, then waves.

"Not the Bates Motel." I enter and inhale the rich scent of ground coffee beans.

It's a quaint shop with seven older-than-me round wooden tables and just as worn wooden seats. What I like are the raw sketches tacked onto the walls, creating a wallpaper of art in progress. I feel like a missionary Jesuit priest walking into St. Peter's Basilica and a bit like a child skipping into Disney World—small, high and enlightened.

Near the front, two girls with their heads huddled together whisper intently, and midway through the shop, a guy has his legs propped up on a chair as he sketches with charcoal. Behind the counter, a cute girl with blond hair slicked into a ponytail sits on a stool and reads a worn paperback with yellow pages. She gives me a cursory glance and when she notices Hunter stand, she returns to the words on the page.

"Now, that look," says Hunter, "is what I like. That means you like my shop."

"Your shop?"

In a dark blue button-down short-sleeve shirt and too-baggy-for-him jeans, Hunter flashes an I'm-a-proud-daddy smile. "Opened it four years ago on my twenty-fifth birthday."

In other words, he's much older than me, still sort of young, and is business savvy.

I smirk. No reason to make his life easy just because he's an artist and established. Though I won't admit it to Noah, the guy did creep me out this morning. "Is that your way of getting me to share?"

He laughs. "Maybe."

And I'm smart enough to not answer, for now. "Let's discuss the painting."

"Fair enough. Coffee?"

I'd love coffee, but for the moment, it's best not to accept drinks. "I'm fine. Thanks."

He motions for us to sit, and when I do I become enthralled with the sketch of a baby cuddling near a delicate shoulder.

"It's for my sister," he says. "She had her first child last month."

"It's good," I respond. Very good.

"What's your name?" he asks.

I comb my fingers through my hair, wishing I did accept his offer for a drink so I'd have something to fiddle with. Hunter Gray is a name I've heard several times this summer. He's some sort of an artistic genius that exploded into the art scene a couple of years ago. Some people at shows mocked him for his success and his indifferent attitude to the art community, and some people called him courageous and gushed about him like he was a rock star. With all that was said, nobody ever trashed his work. It was wildly understood that he is exceptional.

And I told him one of his paintings was wrong. "I'm sorry."

His sandy-blond hair is a little like Noah's in the front, but unlike Noah's, it's long everywhere else. The waves lick his shoulders. "That's your name?"

Just crap, he had asked me a question and I spazzed. "No, it's Echo." Leaving off the Emerson because I'm not giddy about involving my mom.

He falls back into his seat, causing the wood to squeak. "That's definitely better than I'm sorry. And the pissed naked guy at your hotel room would be your brother?"

"My boyfriend—Noah." And he had jeans on.

"Figured. The beautiful girls seem to have those."

There's a muttered "Humph" from behind the counter, and while I assess the girl, Hunter keeps his eyes on me. Rushed by the sensation of being on display, I slip my hand along the scars of my left arm. I should have worn the sweater, but I was so mad at Noah that I forgot.

"So...the painting?" I say, circling the conversation back around.

He leans forward and picks up the pencil he'd been drawing with. "Let's discuss it, Echo with no last name and who must be old enough to travel with her boyfriend. Tell me which would you do—paint in the star, or do what you said and make the area where it's missing darker?"

Not caring for how he stares at me like I'm announcing the cure for cancer, I grab a napkin out of the dispenser and fold the edges. "What did you intend for it to be?"

"To be the full constellation, but when I tried to fix it last night, I couldn't. I kept hearing your voice yapping about constellations and how they represent the sum of their parts. But what struck me was when you mentioned a darkness because something is missing from your soul. I realized at three in the morning that I wanted the painting to be that and more."

My mouth squishes to the side. "Then make that area darker."

"I can't." This guy never tears his gaze away.

"Why not?"

"Because it wasn't my idea." He flicks the pencil, and it bounces onto the floor. So he has a conscience and wants permission to use my suggestion. I didn't know people like that existed.

I toss the napkin in his direction. "I'm officially giving the idea to you. Paint as many dark spots as you want, and I'll never claim that we had the conversation."

"What do you do? Paint? Draw? Sculpt?"

"Um..."

"You're an artist. I can tell. What's your medium of choice?"

"Painting," I answer immediately. "I love to sketch. I've grown fond of charcoal over the past two years."

"Are you studying someplace?"

How to explain to an art guru that I scheduled business courses along with the art? "I start college in the fall."

Smugness radiates with the grin. "Eighteen?"

I blow out a breath in affirmation. Dang it, he got me.

"Who are some of your favorite artists? Dead and alive."

I watch his body language with every artist I mention. Some surprise him, some he nods at and because I'm just crazy enough to play with fire, I drop one final name. "Cassie Emerson."

He lifts his chin. "Cassie Emerson?"

I brush away pretend crumbs on the table. "Do you know her?"

"Not personally, but I like her work. How she thinks. Screw it. She's an artistic genius, who hasn't received the recognition that she should. Just surprised you know who she is."

Yeah, well, she sort of gave birth to me and then attempted to kill me a couple of years ago, and now she's searching for forgiveness. "I'm familiar with her."

"That's amazing that you're a fan of her work. We've got some of the same tastes in artists." He focuses on the table as he loses himself in thought.

A high like being drunk runs through my veins. Hunter doesn't know who I am. Noah will lose his mind, but this is my opportunity to prove that I have talent without anyone else, especially my mom, interfering. "I don't have them with me, but I have some sketchbooks and paintings. Maybe one day I could—"

Hunter's phone pings. He pulls it out and scrolls through it with an arrogance that reminds me of my father. "I want you to paint the constellation Aires for me."

Air catches in my throat, and I choke. "But...I can't... you haven't even seen..."

"I won't pay you, but if I like what I see, I'll take a look at the rest of your work, and then we'll go from there. Deal?"

"But it's Aires."

"Yeah, that's what I said. Aires."

My lungs collapse, and I clutch the table, hoping to stay upright. It's my brother's constellation. It belongs to him and to visit there...to touch that part...to enter past locked doors...I close my eyes, thinking of him dying. What it must have been like for him, what it was like for me to hear of his death.

I open my eyes, and Hunter stands there waiting for an answer, totally unaware of the chaos inside me. Panic builds in intensity, and I swallow to bury the pain—to bury it so deep that the misery never escapes...that it never touches the surface. "I can't."

"Echo—" Hunter motions to my white-knuckled fingers "—whatever is going on there, that's why I want you to paint it. It's why you had the guts to say to me what you did. I want that emotion in the painting."

"I said it because I didn't know who you were."

"You said it because it was true, and I miss hearing the truth." Hunter scribbles on one of the napkins then slides it to me. "Here's the address to my studio in case you forgot where it is. It's above the gallery, and there's usually someone else there besides me so you can tell your boyfriend to chill. If you show tomorrow, then I have my answer."

Without another word, Hunter leaves the shop. The girl behind the counter studies me as if she's experiencing a vision. "Now that has never happened before."

NOAH

The hotel has a "business center" that's comprised of a long folding table, a chair with more rips than leather and a shoddy wireless connection. In between moments of connectivity, I found nothing on a Diana Perry of Vail, Colorado. In this day and age, it seems damned impossible to not have a digital footprint.

Diana Perry—my grandmother. A small part of me withers. Mom left her family and kept them a secret. They have to be bad, but is awful better than being alone?

I lean back in the seat and check the clock on the bottom of the screen. My shift starts soon, and I'm nowhere near where I'd thought I'd be. I could email the lady, but it's not what I want. This one has to be on my terms, no one else's, and I definitely need space.

I stare the monitor down like it's a drunk guy waiting to take a swing. There's another way to discover info on Diana Perry, but it's an option that'll kill my pride. Rubbing the lines forming on my forehead, I type the email before I can talk myself out of it. Only a few sentences because God knows we hated each other when she was paid to be my social worker.

Keesha,
Is it true that my mother's family is looking for me? If so, I want their phone number and address.
Noah

I click Send immediately. I'll deal with any regret later.

"What are you doing?"

My body freezes at the sound of Echo's soft voice. With her arms wrapped around herself, she rests a hip against the door frame of the closet-size room.

"Looking for stuff on my mom's parents."

"Have you found anything?"

I should tell Echo I emailed Keesha, but I can't. I fucking can't. I don't know how the hell I feel about contacting Keesha, and if I tell Echo that I sent the message, she'll ask about my emotions. When I say nothing because I can't sort through the chaos in my mind, she'll get hurt because she thinks I'm not talking to her. Silence at times is better than words.

I close down my email account and switch back to my last Google search. "Not a thing."

Echo's shoes tap against the tile floor as she nears me, and I breathe for the first time in hours. As if sensing I'm seconds from implosion, she eases her hands onto my shoulders and kneads at the tension that has formed knots. "We'll find them."

We'll—as in the two of us. Shit, she always has the right words. Echo's thumb slides to the spot below my shoulder blades, and my muscles melt under her touch. My shoulders roll forward, and Echo deepens the massage. "You're tight."

"I'm fine." Better now that she's here, and we aren't

attempting to verbally kill each other. I peek over my shoulder. "Does this mean I'm forgiven?"

She presses too hard on a sore spot. I flinch. She smiles. "Is that your way of apologizing?"

"It is if it means it'll work."

Echo slaps my back, and I chuckle. I turn in the chair and grab onto her hips, bringing her closer to me. I drop my legs open, and she glides in, tangling her hands into my hair. I look up and see those green eyes drinking me in, something that never fails to take my breath away.

I ease my hand to that sweet spot below her gorgeous ass. She pulls my hair in reprimand while also sighing with my caress. Beneath my jeans, I spring to life, and I stumble upon the problem of having Beth and Isaiah in tow. "Close the door, and we'll declare this make-up official."

"We have a room," she whispers.

Had. I take her hand and guide her onto my lap. I love how Echo molds her body around mine: head on my shoulder, her hair teasing my neck, her arms winding around my chest. I hug her and revel in her warmth.

"When do you have to work?" Her breath tickles my skin, making the fine hairs on my neck stand at attention.

I inch my fingers under her shirt. "I've got time."

"I said we have a room." Echo places an openmouthed kiss below my ear, and my grip on her tightens.

I groan, and my head hits the back of the chair. Reality is my and Echo's greatest threat. "Beth's sick."

Echo raises her head and damn if there isn't concern for a girl that's treated her like shit. "Does she need a doctor?"

"No, she's carsick from the ride. She's green around the gills, but nothing sleep won't cure."

Echo lays her temple against my shoulder again, and I glance at the open door. We could lock it and there's plenty of room in this chair.

"No way, Noah," she says, disrupting my fantasies.

"Never said a word."

"Your mouth isn't the only part that talks."

"Can't help what you do to me." I readjust Echo, shifting her away from the part of my body currently running its mouth, and draw my hand through her curls.

Her foot bounces against my leg. Something has her worked up. "What's going on?"

"I need to talk to you about some stuff."

Yeah. A long conversation needs to be had—my shit included. "Then talk."

"Hunter asked me to paint a picture for him."

Hunter needs his face rearranged. "Did you accept?"

"No, but I haven't declined." She pauses, and the rhythm of her foot picks up speed. "What if I need you to trust me on this?"

Why doesn't she ask me to rip out my own jugular?

"I mean it, Noah. I need you to support me."

Outside the office, a group of children sprint down the hallway and from the sounds of their squeals, they're heading for the pool. Seconds behind, a woman laughs as a man calls for them to wait. I had that type of family once. A mom and a dad who took me on trips where we stayed in hotels and swam in pools. At one time, life felt simple—without complication. Exactly what Echo and I are searching for now.

"I'll stand by you," I say.

She nods, but focuses on her still-moving foot. Fuck this. We aren't going back to any of this crap. Not today. "No more worrying. This is home base, Echo. Just us."

"Okay," she mumbles against my shoulder. "Did I ever tell you that Dad took Aires and me on vacation a few times? Sometimes with Mom, then without, then with Ashley."

"Did you throw Aires's clothes in the pool?"

Echo giggles then sighs. "He also would have tossed me in."

She stretches her arm toward the keyboard of her laptop. I swivel the chair so that she can reach. With a brush to the pad, the monitor turns on. "Have you considered searching for your mom by her maiden name? Sarah Perry?"

"Thought about it." But I haven't. There's this heaviness inside me, an ache, preventing me from typing my mother's name. A name that belonged to her before my father. A past she never alluded to. "Let's sleep in the tent tonight."

She scans my face, weighing the change of subject.

"I'll do everything," I coax. "Pitch the tent, put out the blankets, make dinner and repack. Plus, Beth and Isaiah need sleep." More important, I need time with Echo.

Her nose wrinkles, not believing me. "So all I have to do is sit. No lugging the cooler, no opening a can of beans...nothing."

"Nothing," I repeat. "Except make out with me."

She's still examining me. I can sense her energy extending out to touch mine as she tries to gauge how close to insanity I am as I delve into my mother's past.

Come on, Echo. Let this go.

A shadow crosses her face. "Hunter asked me to paint the constellation Aires."

My heart beats once in pain for her. Jesus, it's like the two of us can't catch a break. I cup her face with my hand, and Echo leans into me as if she needs my strength. She's been strong for too long. Even with the summer reprieve, can either of us survive more reminders of our hurts?

"Don't do it if it bothers you."

"But this could be it, Noah. My chance to prove that I have talent beyond my mom."

"You don't need him to prove anything."

Neither one of us blinks as she thinks over my words.

"I mean it, Echo, you don't need him to—"

"I'll sleep in the tent," Echo says, cutting me off.

I stiffen at her sharp reprimand, but hear the words underneath. She let my shit go, and I need to let her shit go. Camping isn't her favorite, and she's giving me what I asked for when I promised her a week in a hotel. "Then I'll pick you up after work."

Echo

Noah left the hotel's business office hours ago. With my computer in my lap, I permit the seat to cradle me with my back against one arm of the chair and my legs dangling over the other. I have several windows on the computer open. Noah's mother the subject of all of them. They're sites Noah will want to see, I think, even if they lead to dead ends.

"S'up, Echo." Isaiah strolls into the room and rubs his hand over his shaved head as if to wake himself.

"Hey." I perk up at the sight of Noah's best friend. Even with his tattoo-covered arms and the double row of hoop earrings in both ears, Isaiah's definitely one of the good guys. "How are you?"

"I'm all good." Isaiah flips a metal folding chair around and straddles it. "You?"

"Good." And because it's polite to ask... "How's Beth?"

"Still sleeping. Whatcha working on?"

I readjust my legs so that my feet touch the ground and I'm straight in the chair. "Stuff for Noah."

Isaiah's eyebrows shoot up, and I weigh whether or not I should tell him what type of stuff. Noah can be private. Isaiah and Beth are, too. Hanging out with them is like tangoing through a minefield of secrets, and I never have any idea which secrets the other person knows. I go with safe. "How was your trip?"

The left side of his mouth tips up. "Nicely played. Trip sucked. Look, I told Noah and now I'm telling you—Beth and I will split. Last thing I want is to bring trouble."

I'd rather play leap frog in traffic with a porcupine than engage in small talk with Beth for the week, but I like Isaiah and love Noah. Beth is part of their package deal. "It's okay. Noah and I have had a rough couple of days, and he failed to mention your plans, but we'll work it out. He and I are going to sleep in the tent tonight, anyhow."

Isaiah shakes his head, and I lean forward to catch his attention. "Noah needs the tent tonight, and I need to give it to him. It doesn't have nearly as much to do with you and Beth as you think."

He pulls on the bottom earring of the double row. "You sure?"

"Yes."

"I'm paying for me and Beth. All the way." Even though, like it is for Noah, money is hard for Isaiah to come across. He'll pay because Isaiah also possesses Noah's stubborn pride.

"We'll figure it out when the time comes," I answer.

"Cool. Don't hang in here because Beth and I are crashing, otherwise I'll be mad." He hitches his thumb over his shoulder. "Vending machines?"

"We have drinks and food in the cooler."

"Vending machines," he repeats.

Yep, same infuriating pride. "Around the corner."

Isaiah stands, and my fingers lightly slide over the keyboard. A bit of panic seeps into my bloodstream as I contemplate what I've been doing since Noah left for work. If anyone understands Noah, it would be Isaiah. "Isaiah?"

He pauses at the door.

"I...I found pictures of Noah's mom...when she was a teenager. Do you think I should show him?"

Isaiah sucks in a deep breath, and the tiger tattooed on his arm appears to ripple as he shoves his hands in his pockets. "Does he know you're hunting around in his business?"

"I suggested he search the internet for her earlier and... Noah shut down. But it's his mom. He may want to see them."

He leans his head back until it softly bangs against the corner of the door frame. His gray eyes stare at the ceiling like he's envisioning something else, somewhere else. "What's he looking for?"

"I thought maybe he'd like pictures of his parents." I blink three times.

"You'd suck at poker. What's he looking for?"

My fingers tap the arm of the chair. "I don't think I should be the one who tells you—"

"Is he looking for his mom's blood relatives? The ones that his foster parents said are still alive?"

My eyes meet his. Dang it.

"I know, Echo. At least I know that they're alive. He's searching for them, isn't he?"

I'm tiptoeing on thin ice with Noah and his trust issues. My fingers stop the rhythmic tapping and go for persistent. "Don't make me say something I'll regret."

Silence. Long enough that it becomes heavy. Isaiah pops his head to the right then to the left, as if he's literally releasing steam from an engine on the brink of explosion. "I need to know."

"Why?"

"Because I need to know the path I'm on. If Noah has family, and that's the direction he's heading, I need to know. You're loyal to him and that's what I love about you, but I need to know if Noah's leaving."

"Leaving?" His words land a punch to my gut. "Do you think Noah's going to drop you for them? All Noah's talked about is the apartment you're getting together after we return to Kentucky. He loves you and Beth."

Plus Noah promised he'd never leave either Isaiah or Beth behind. His loyalty belongs to them because they're his family.

"I've seen patterns like this before, and you have, too." Isaiah's eyes pierce me and I shift, uncomfortable. It's like he detects something that he shouldn't. A part of my soul that I hide. "We have a lot more in common than either of us would admit."

A pattern that Isaiah has seen and so have I...

Heat creeps along my neckline as I brush a curl away. I don't know the specifics, but Isaiah's parents abandoned him. Mine are still physically present, but when it counted, they both left me, as well. "Noah won't leave us."

"You and me, we've grown up with nightmares for moms, but Noah had something once. He had a real family. He gravitates to us because his life fell apart, too, but if he finds what he had before..." Isaiah shrugs. "People leave...it happens."

Sometimes life happens...it's what my father said when he tried to explain why he divorced my mother, why he married Ashley, why he left me behind. He's selling the house. He had a new baby...

"Noah wouldn't do that to you, to us," I say. "He considers you a brother, and he loves me. He has Beth and his brothers. I'm going to start school in the fall, and so is he. We're his family. He's going to be where he belongs."

Noah won't be my father or my mother. He'll put me first because he promised. I wasn't Noah's priority when he was seeking custody of his brothers, but he's placed me first since then. Noah keeps his promises—always.

My computer beeps, signaling a Skype call. Just what I freaking need—Mrs. Collins poking in my life. I look at Isaiah, and he's disappeared. Fantastic—guilt. Isaiah's that type of guy who I'd rather burn my entire set of sweaters than upset.

Biting my bottom lip, I push Accept, and in a slicked-back ponytail, a black Nirvana T-shirt and her Labrador retriever smile, my therapist pops onto the screen. "Hi, Echo."

It's hard to focus when I'm hoping Isaiah will reappear and admit he didn't mean what he said. He's forever encouraging and strong, and what just happened was a side of Isaiah I've never experienced before. Possibly a side Noah has never seen, either. A powerful urge screams to chase after him, but if I did, what would I say?

"Echo?" The smile and her sunny disposition wash away as she falls into serious therapist much sooner than normal. "Are you okay?"

Six months ago, I would have blocked Mrs. Collins and repressed the turmoil inside me. But then I realized that she was the one person who cared. The one person who could help. "No. I'm not okay."

NOAH

I wipe the sweat forming on my forehead then flip the six frying patties. For the past two hours, the orders have poured in nonstop, and the heat radiating from the grill has me wondering if most of the girls I screwed got their wish and I did die and was sentenced straight to hell.

In a swift motion, I slip the toasted buns off the grill, throw the patties on them and slide them down the counter to the chick working on the toppings and sides. I turn to the left, searching for more tickets and release a breath. No more orders.

"Take a break, Noah," the shift manager calls out as he rings up a line of people. "We'll have another wave in a half hour."

Without a word, I dump the mandatory apron and go out the back door for the alley. The early-evening air feels good against my skin and, to cool down, I whip the bandanna off.

"Shit, Noah, it's like you want a repeat of our summer in Kentucky."

Fuck me. The door behind me snaps shut, and I remember one second too late that the door locks from the inside and that the only way back in is through the front. I'm stuck with Mia.

In a white shirt buttoned low enough that it highlights the two assets she's most proud of and a black skirt that barely covers her ass, Mia leans against the graffiti-covered brick wall. One quick inhale confirms that this time she smokes a cigarette.

Mia twists her hips to show off more of her outfit. "You like? I get great tips in this."

"I hear there's a Hooters in Denver."

She only smiles. "Have sex with me. Right now. My car's around the corner."

Jesus, to think what attracted me to her was her direct style and noncommittal attitude. I didn't realize that she sucked the soul out of then ate whatever she fucked. "Told you. I'm taken."

With one final drag off the cigarette, Mia drops it to the ground then grinds it out with her foot. "That only makes me want you more. The first time, it was because you had that bad-boy persona. Now you've got that reformed bad-boy thing and I want to..." She curls her fingers in the air and lowers her gaze to the zipper of my pants.

"I'm not playing, Mia."

I walk past her for the street, and Mia calls out, "You're eighteen, right?"

The two of us never talked age last year. She was out of high school, and I wasn't. "Yeah."

"And the human race has evolved to the point that we easily live to be in our nineties."

"Got a point?"

She assesses me, boots first then slowly up until she meets my eyes. "I've thought about you a lot since we talked."

That's what I get for talking. "Shouldn't think of me at all."

Mia ignores my comment. "I've done what you've done—graduated and played house with the good guy. It doesn't last long. The summer. Maybe a few months into fall, but the good ones lose interest. Redemption becomes boring or maybe we become boring once we're redeemed. There's only two ways this can go—she'll hurt you now or later."

My body locks up. If this was a guy, I'd knock his head off. "You don't know shit about me and Echo."

Mia loses the confidence that pushes out eight feet in front of her and suddenly, she looks smaller than Beth. "Have you started fighting yet? Like no matter what the conversation is, you can't be on the same page?"

It's likes she's crawled into my brain, and I don't like it. "How about you shut up?"

"Want to know the next stage?"

I don't, but I do. I rub my neck, ignoring the urge to tug at my shirt as my ability to breathe constricts.

"Soon she'll find something that interests her and her alone. That special thing they were born to do and when they find it—they come alive. That's when they meet the real people they're supposed to be with. Suddenly, people like you and me, the rebellious one that was cool to be with six month ago? We morph into a strangling chain around their neck. Listen to what I'm saying. We're a phase. That's all we'll ever be to people like them."

I'm shaking my head, but I don't have words. Mia's verbalizing my worst fears. Like she's reading my fucking mind and foreseeing my damned future.

"I'm getting my shit together. I'm going to be the man she wants." Yet it isn't lost on me that Mia and I are the ones standing in the back alley next to a Dumpster overflowing with trash. It's where we met last year. It's where we've met again and somehow, I'm more comfortable here than when I stand beside Echo at a gallery.

"I was going to become the girl he wanted," she says. "But there's no way people like you and me can move quick enough. Have you fallen back onto a bad habit and you got that look of utter disappointment? Sort of like they watched you kick a puppy?"

The expression Echo had when I threw the guy against the wall. The small apprehensive glances at the galleries when it's clear I don't belong.

"You were my rebound for my Echo," she continues. "You helped me remember that it's better to be in control. We're the same type of person, Noah."

"Why do you care?" I spit out.

She shrugs. "Because I wish I would have cut my relationship with him off earlier. I wish I could have walked away with my pride intact. You helped me once, and here we are meeting again. I don't believe in coincidence. The reason I ended up in the middle of nowhere Colorado is to be the rebound for you."

"You're wrong," I tell her, and begin toward the light of the main street.

A lighter clicks behind me. "I hope I am."

Echo

Two seconds after I answered Mrs. Collins's Skype call, I closed the door to the hotel's business center, granting me the illusion of privacy.

"Is that it?" Mrs. Collins asks. I told her everything: how my sales plummeted, my mother calling, the conversation with the Wicked Witch gallery owner and me and Noah fighting. To cover that I'm lying, I hide my face in my hands when I answer, "Yes."

I like Mrs. Collins, but I can't look at her again if we share an analytical discussion regarding my sex life or, lack thereof, with Noah.

When I spread my fingers and peek at Mrs. Collins, her eyes have narrowed into slits. "That's not everything."

I lower my hands onto my lap. "Can't it be enough?"

"I get the sense that there's something else going on..."

She leaves her statement hanging as if it will bother me that something has been left unsaid, which, *phsh*, won't work. I mean, just because the words just dangle in the air like a thousand pounds of rock doesn't mean that I have to say something to close out the sentence. My knee bounces, and it causes the table to vibrate.

I'm not falling for it. Not at all... "Do you think Noah's going to leave me?"

Aw, heck...my chin drops to my throat. Why did I ask

that? I raise my head, hoping for a positive outcome to my slip. Mrs. Collins is good at putting things in perspective—good at making me discover things that are right in front of me.

What I prayed for doesn't materialize as I meet her sad blue eyes. "I'm not a fortune teller, Echo."

"It would be cool if you were." I give her a weak grin, and she offers a genuine smile back.

"What makes you think Noah's going to break up with you?"

I shrug, and Mrs. Collins leans forward so that her face encompasses the entire screen. "Tell me the first thing that pops into your mind. What makes you think Noah is going to leave you?"

I hate this game, but unfortunately, it's effective. "I don't know."

"What do you eat at the movies?"

"Popcorn."

"What color are you wearing?"

I glance down. "Blue."

"What's your middle name?"

"Cassandra."

"Why do you think Noah's going to leave you?"

"Because my mom did." I honest to God groan after I answer. I'm so stinking pathetic.

"Why else?"

Evidently ripping out my heart and setting it on fire isn't enough. Oh, sorry, it's Mrs. Collins so no, she demands so much more—like my soul.

"Come on, Echo. Besides your mom, why do you think Noah's going to leave you?"

"My dad left me." Though not like Mom. He divorced

Mom, married someone new and has begun a life that can continue fine without me. On top of that, my father ignored my desperate call to him for help the night I ended up with the scars. The night I almost died.

"Who else?" she says in a soft voice. "You know it's safe to talk about it here."

My lower lip trembles and I suck in a breath, trying to keep it all in: the words, the pain, the grief.

"Who else, Echo?" Mrs. Collins repeats as a lullaby.

"Aires left me," I whisper.

She moves her camera so that the angle of her is less sharp horror film and more soft light. "We've been working together close to eight months and did you know that you rarely mention Aires?"

My head snaps up, and a wave of anger shouts at me to throw something at the screen. "Yes, I do."

"Aires must have been a big part of your life, correct?"

There's this ache deep within. Like millions of paper cuts. The type that happen quickly then continue to throb for days. Except this throb has lasted years, and each morning when I wake and think of Aires, it's like someone pours alcohol over the open wound again and again. "I don't want to talk about Aires."

She nods as she scribbles into a file. I hate it when she does that. It's like she's tallying how many times those words have dripped out of my mouth.

"What about Noah?" I ask, trying to get the conversation back on course.

Mrs. Collins places the pen over the file and clasps her hands over it. "Let's pause for a moment and see where our conversation has taken us. You're afraid Noah's going to leave you, yes?"

I bob my head in indifference because it feels like I'm cheating on Noah by even discussing this. "I guess."

"You already feel like other people have left you."

"My mom and dad," I say for her.

"You also mentioned Aires."

I pick at a fingernail instead of answering. "I asked about Noah."

"Echo, I wonder if there are things we aren't addressing. I wonder what you would say if I asked what Aires and Noah have in common."

My eyes flash to hers. Noah walked into darkness, and it reminded me of Aires.

It's like there are a thousand voices in my head and none of them belong to me. "I don't want to talk anymore."

With one click of the button, Mrs. Collins disappears.

NOAH

With his legs kicked out on the bed, Isaiah relaxes with his back against the headboard. Beth rests her head against his shoulder and is absorbed in a movie they found on one of the five cable stations. She's not as green as before, but dark circles mar the skin underneath her eyes, plus she hasn't bitched yet. She must still feel like shit.

I returned thirty minutes ago to discover Echo missing. I showered, shaved and when I reemerged from the bathroom a half pound of cooking grease lighter, Echo stood near the window, peeking out the curtains. The moment I walked out we packed, in coordinated silence, what we'd need for the night. I zip up my pack and I say, "You ready, baby?"

"I need a few minutes."

Echo disappears into the bathroom, and Isaiah and I share a glance. "Give me a hand?"

Beth shifts to free Isaiah, and he grabs my stuff as I shoulder Echo's. The moment we're in the hallway and safely away, I jack my thumb toward the room. "Beth going to live?"

"Yeah. She said she feels like she's still moving. I sure as shit hope she's not sick. I don't know if states take another state's free insurance."

"Give her until tomorrow, and then we'll figure it out."

I shove the door open with my back, and the heat of the day permeates from the concrete. The sun's low in the west, and the blue horizon starts to merge into that pink that Echo loves. We've got maybe an hour and a half before sundown. Not much time to set up camp, especially since I promised I'd do it on my own.

With the push of a button on Echo's key chain, her trunk pops open, and Isaiah and I set the stuff in. "Is Echo okay?" I ask.

Isaiah pulls on his bottom earring before squeezing the last bag into a cramped spot. "She didn't say anything when she came in. I saw her a while ago, though. She was hanging out in some room with her computer."

"Yeah." That's where I left her.

"Look, bro. We were talking then that Mrs. Collins contacted Echo..."

"I got it," I tell him so he doesn't have to explain. Part of me is relieved to hear Mrs. Collins is the reason for Echo being withdrawn and not me. "Echo can get that way after they talk." It can also mean night terrors.

"I'm not sure that's what got her—"

"Isaiah, Beth's asking for you," Echo says the moment she exits the hotel.

He warily eyes Echo, and my mouth turns down when I notice her mirror Isaiah's dark expression. What the hell? Isaiah offers his hand to me. "Have a great time."

I accept the short shake. "We'll catch up tomorrow."

"S'all good," he says then strides over to Echo, who's hanging by the hotel entrance.

I pretend not to watch as I rearrange the cooler. Since Echo and I became the real deal after I gave up my brothers, the two of them have become tight. Not as tight as me and him and not as tight as him and Beth, but there's an understanding between them. Nothing romantic, just a sense of acceptance on a different level.

He lowers his voice and mumbles something to her. Echo nods and offers him a half smile. She whispers back, but knowing Echo well enough I can read her lips. "It's okay. I'm sorry if I upset you."

"It's my shit," he answers in a normal tone and places his hand over his heart like he's swearing a promise. "Not yours. Won't happen again."

She holds out her arms to offer a hug. He looks over his shoulder at me, and I slightly tip my chin in approval. It's a quick hug, one like I'd give my brothers, and Isaiah says something to Echo that makes her laugh as they both walk away.

"You and Isaiah okay?" I close the trunk after he enters the hotel.

"Yes."

It's like dragging concrete through mud. "Are you going to tell me what's up?"

She folds her hands over her chest and holds her elbows like she's cold. "If you want me to, but I think it's better left behind."

Neither of them would do me wrong. Few things can press Isaiah's buttons, and it's the same type of button that can propel Echo over the edge. "You guys talk about moms?"

She nods.

"Then I get it."

"Does that bother you?" she asks. "That we talked and that we hugged?"

I lock my finger around her belt loop and bring her closer to me. "The opposite. It feels good to know I have a family."

Echo

In the fading evening sun, my hand rushes against the page as I attempt to capture the way the long grass of the field dances in the light breeze. I love the colors here: the deep green of the grass, the dark blue of the water cutting through the meadow, the still barely snowcapped purplish mountains looming in the distance.

What cements this picturesque scene is the sky. Behind me to the east, the black-blue of night races me to the end, threatening to cover the way the oranges and pinks and reds of the sunset bleed together. The scent of pine is thick here. So thick the smell is probably being absorbed by the page, and I hope it is. I want to remember this moment—forever.

My eyes narrow as I try to defeat the night, but like always, time runs out, and I'm on the losing end. No longer able to see, I drop the oil crayon and fall back onto my elbows on the ground.

To my right, there's a click, and the area brightens as the rest of the world falls dark. The lantern Noah and I purchased back in April for this trip flickers before remaining lit. Sitting next to it, Noah's sexy as heck as he watches me from beyond the hair that hides his eyes.

"Hi," I say, like I'm a shy child caught peeking around the corner.

"Hey," he replies.

"How long have you been there?"

"Awhile."

I tuck my hair behind my ear and busy myself with slipping the oil pastels back into their allotted slots of the container. "You could have told me that you were done with the campsite."

"Could've," he says. "But then I wouldn't have been able to watch you."

My cheeks burn and when I don't respond, Noah inches close enough to caress my cheek. "I love it when you do that."

"What?" I ask a little breathlessly. His fingers brush against my skin, causing goose bumps on my arms.

"Look at me like the first time you told me you loved me."

The heat rising off my face intensifies. Noah cups my jaw and skims his thumb against my skin one more time. I swallow, thinking of his lips touching mine.

"Are you hungry?" he asks.

My stomach growls as if it recognized the question, and Noah's mouth tilts into this slow, seductive smile. Those mutant pterodactyls that Noah spawned when we began the game of flirting months ago spread their wings and fly. This is what I miss about us—the simplicity in the chaos.

Noah stands and offers me his hand. I gather my sketchbook and pastels and when my hand is firmly in his, he lifts the lantern and leads me from the field to the campground.

We hold hands on the dirt path, our fingers entwined. The long grass lazily grazes along my thighs. Noah doesn't hold hands often. In fact, it was one of the few rules I understood, and it's not lost on me how special this moment is. It's like the roses. Noah's showing me his love.

Because of that, I concentrate on the rough sensation of his skin against mine. The heat between our palms. How his larger and stronger fingers grasping mine make me feel smaller, extremely feminine and protected.

Near the entrance of the campsite are two camper trailers, and on the far left, closer to the bathroom facilities, are a few more tents. Noah set us up as far from everyone as humanly possible, designing our own little world.

With one firm squeeze, Noah releases my fingers and leaves me and the lantern at a blanket he laid out next to the tent. He quickly goes to work lighting the campfire. Without a doubt, the fire has been my favorite part of camping. I love the fluttering light, the scent of the smoke, the way I lose myself while admiring the flames.

At the start of our trip, I asked Noah if the campfires bothered him, and he told me no. He said they reminded him of all the times his parents took him camping. Still, a part of me wonders what he really sees when he looks into the fire.

"There's some food in the cooler," Noah says. "Hope you don't mind, but I already ate."

"Not at all." Noah's familiar with my odd artistic moods and learned he could be waiting for hours until I officially wake to reality. I root through the cooler and smile when I find a ham and cheese deli sandwich on wheat drenched with honey mustard. "You're spoiling me."

"Damn, baby, I've got to step up my game if ham's a spoil."

I tear off a corner of the sandwich. "It's the thought, not the ham."

Noah clicks the lighter, and flint sparks against metal. He places the glowing flame near the wood. He doesn't say anything, but I spot the satisfied glint in his eye.

Inside the tent, Noah has created a cozy layer of blankets and pillows—illustrating how he's polished the fine art of presentation. I turn to tease him, but Noah quickly averts his focus to the kindling. I could grow accustomed to being wooed by the great Noah Hutchins.

With the fire crackling toward a slow roar, Noah slides next to me, and I pop the last bite of my favorite fast dinner into my mouth, licking the last drops of honey mustard off my fingers. Right as I go to lick my ring finger, Noah snags my wrist, and my breath catches in my throat.

Noah opens his mouth and draws my finger in, his tongue moving against my skin in a way that causes a warm tingle in my belly. It's a pressure and a pull and a sensation I crave to melt into. His eyes lock with mine, and it's like I'm hypnotized—powerless over him, but I love being here...I love being under his spell.

Noah lets my finger go and when he does, I can barely breathe. He reaches over and brushes his thumb near the corner of my mouth. "You have some sauce..." Another brush. "Right there."

My mouth slightly drops open, and Noah keeps his hand at my face. All thought starts and stops and races. I should kiss Noah's hand like he did mine, but I freeze, wondering if that's what he wants or if he'd laugh if I did.

His hand glides down my face, lingers on my neck then moves on to my shoulder. I'm split between being disappointed in avoiding what could have been a moment, and enjoying Noah's touch.

"Come here," he says, and he leans back against the cooler and leads me so that I'm resting between his legs. I settle in and lay my back against his chest as he wraps his arms around me. I inhale his dark scent, and I have the overwhelming feeling of coming home.

NOAH

Echo releases a slow breath and for the first time since I've known her, she sets her gaze on the stars. There's a million of them in the sky. Each stop across the country has been a perfect spot to observe them, but Echo always chose to stare straight ahead at the flames. Because of that, warm, cold or boiling hot, I've created a fire.

As she peers at the sight she avoids, I comb my fingers through her curls. "What do you see when you look up?"

Echo adds another protective layer around herself by tucking her hands under my arms. "Aires."

I focus on the stars. Bright and dim lights dot a black sky. It's disorganized chaos to me, but Echo recognizes patterns and pictures in the confusion. I wish I could view the world through her eyes. I might be less jaded then. "Where's his constellation at?"

"It's a December constellation for the northern hemisphere."

"Then why Aires?" This is a tricky conversation with Echo. The stars above, they're a deep root in her life—like how Spanish is a bond between me and my mother and architecture is between me and my dad. There are times that I talk to my friends Rico and Antonio in their first language, and a knife slashes through my gut and, as I prepare to study architecture this fall, I sometimes feel as if someone has punched me in the throat.

While I like the bonds that link me to my parents, there are times the gift of the memories serves as a curse. But Echo has been distant the past few days, and I need her to give me this. I need her trust.

Echo

Noah rubs his smooth jaw against my cheek and when he eases back, he nips the tip of my ear. Heat spreads down my neck, through my body and makes me very aware of me and Noah and where this night could lead...

"Tell me, Echo," he coaxes. "Why do you think of Aires when you look at the stars?"

I clear my throat and fight the haze of seduction, remembering we were discussing Aires. My head falls back on his shoulder so I can lazily scan the sky. Hercules stretches across the horizon as well as Draco the Dragon. What would it be like to look up and see nothing but random stars...to be ignorant of the stories involving not only heaven, but hell?

Cuddled in Noah's arms, I try to find words to explain. "Mom was the one who taught us the night sky, but Aires was the one who brought it to life. He loved the myths far more than I did and he was a better storyteller than Mom. We'd lie out for hours during the summer or huddled up under blankets during the winter, and Aires would tell me the same stories Mom had told me, but when he talked, I couldn't get enough."

Like the last summer I saw Aires...I stepped out of my old boyfriend Luke's car, and the humidity of the night smacked me like a truck. The garage door was open, and

Dad's car was missing. My stomach had sunk with the sight. Mr. Overprotective, Mr. I'll-Be-Upset-if-Any-Boy-Brings-You-Home-a-Minute-Late had left, and there are times when a girl returns from a bad date and she wants her dad.

Just to know somebody cared...to know that somebody loved me...to know I was needed.

I shoved my hands into the pockets of my jean skirt and shuffled toward the house. Luke's engine growled as he peeled away from the curb. I could have been hours late, and Dad wouldn't have known.

"I'm not sure he's the one for you." Aires appeared from the open garage and wiped the grease off his hands with a blue rag. Home from the Marines for a short break, Aires once again was messing with his Corvette.

I glanced down at myself, searching for the outward sign that Luke and I had been fighting again. He had cheapened a romantic evening by pressuring me to do *it* and...well...I said no. "Did Dad take Ashley out again?"

With Aires home, Mom had been around more, and Ashley didn't like the reminder that we had been a family before she weaseled into our lives.

"Nice abrupt change in subject and yes, Dad took Ashley out." Aires threw the rag into the garage. "Do I need to beat the hell out of Luke?"

"Everything's fine—"

"Echo." Aires cut me off and gestured at his cheek while he stared at mine. "Tear tracks. They taught us to be observant at basic."

My lips turned down, and moisture pricked the corners of my eyes. "It's complicated."

"Doesn't have to be complicated all the time. Sometimes it can be simple."

The world felt heavy, and it seemed like I was the only one shouldering the burden. "I don't think simple exists."

"It does." Aires inclined his head to the backyard. "Hear there's going to be a meteor shower tonight. Want to watch with me?"

Spend the remainder of the night with my brother after my moronic boyfriend broke my heart? I couldn't imagine anything better. "Are you going to tell your stupid stories again?"

Mom's stories, but told with so much more flare and zest.

He smiled as he pulled me into a fake headlock. "Don't hate, Echo. Don't hate."

The fire snaps, and it jolts me from the memory, causing me to jump. A burning ember launches into the air and becomes one more light in the night sky. Noah's arms tighten around me, and his thighs exert pressure against mine. It's as if he thinks he can squeeze away the pain.

"Sorry," I whisper.

"It's all good, baby. Sometimes we don't choose the memories, but they choose us."

That's the one thing we understand—becoming lost.

"I'm tired of living in the past." I'm tired of it dictating my future.

"Mrs. Collins likes going there," Noah mutters.

She does, but it's because it's where Noah and I seem to wallow. "Can we pretend for tonight that we don't have pasts?"

I warily glance at Noah, and he's mirroring the same look. "What does that mean?"

It means it's exhausting being the daughter, the sister, the girl with the scars… "I'm so defined by everyone else's actions that…that I don't know. I'm Echo, right? And you're Noah."

Raised eyebrow on Noah's part. "Uh-huh."

The chains strangling me unlock, and I practically float. I'm heading in the right direction, even though Noah's convinced that I've bought a plane ticket to crazy.

"So I like to paint, and you like architecture, and let's pretend that none of that has anything to do with our pasts. Like…we're together because I love you and you love me and there is no other worry in the world."

Noah gives me an amused grin. "You want us to pretend we're who we are now. I need to define role-playing for you. If we're going there, I've got a few ideas."

A strange adrenaline rush of embarrassment and lust overheats my body. "Not role-playing."

His shoulders shake as he laughs. I lightly smack his arm and settle back into his chest. "You're impossible."

"Damn straight." Noah runs a finger down my arm. "Seriously, I get it. No more heavy stuff for tonight. I can deal with that."

That's exactly it, yet not. I scan the camp, and beyond the fires in the distance only total blackness exists. But when the sun shines in the morning, it'll be a wonderland of sights: the mountains covered in green trees, the flowers creating a palette an artist would die for. Lying in that field today, I forgot my problems, and it felt amazing.

Frogs and crickets perform a symphony, and the smell of the pine wood burning in the flames tickles my nose. Noah and I are a thousand miles away from every push and pull and worry of the real world.

"I wish life could be like this forever," I say. "We'd be okay then. We'd forever be okay."

Noah kisses the bend of my neck, and I sharply inhale with the divine sensation.

"I could build you a house," he whispers. "I thought about it while I watched you paint."

I suck in the corner of my bottom lip. Is he saying this because he's simply playing along with the idea that we're unattached to anyone or anything but each other for the night? "Where?"

He points to where the mountains lie. "Up there. I can see you sitting on our front porch, completely entranced with the land below. You'd have all the inspiration you'd need and never have to leave our home."

Our home. A thrill circles in my chest. "So I stay home and you..." I drop the statement, curious how he'd answer.

"Stay home with you." Oh, God, his deep voice vibrates down to my soul.

"One of us has to make money. I'm assuming houses on mountains, especially those in national forests, are pricey."

With a pop, more embers fly into the sky, and the fire begins to fade. Noah releases me, and cold air rushes to my back. He edges close to the fire and uses a long stick to stir the flames. "Didn't you know? You bank millions off your paintings, and I run my architecture firm from home."

My smile spreads from ear to ear, and I love how Noah's chocolate-brown eyes dance when he peers at me from over his shoulder. I'm especially in love with the game we're playing. It makes life, as Aires had told me, seem less complicated.

"Will we have pets?" I bite back the question regarding kids. While this might be a fun fantasy, imagining being responsible for something like *that* is terrifying.

"Sure." Noah stays near the fire on one bent knee and occasionally pokes it to keep the dwindling flames alive. "I had a dog once."

"What type?"

"A mix of some sort. Part Lab, part something smaller than Lab. Its paws were too big for its body, so it skidded across the kitchen floor."

"Is that what you want?"

"If we're going to live alone on a mountain, we need a guard dog. A German shepherd. Something like that."

"Guard dog?" Not what I had in mind for the fantasy. "We need something cute and cuddly." I squish my fingers in the air as if I have the little puff ball in my hands. "It can sleep in our bed."

"No fucking way, Echo. I'm not sharing my bed with a dog."

There's something indescribably titillating about Noah taking this theoretical glimpse into our future so seriously. While I couldn't care less if a dog sleeps in the bed I'd share with Noah, I can't help but tease him. "But it'll be our baby. We can't let it stay on the cold floor."

"I'll buy it a pillow," he says way too slowly.

I giggle and scoot to the end of the blanket to be near him. Placing my toes behind the heel of my other foot, I kick off my shoes, one after another. Then I peel off my socks and nudge Noah's butt with my toes.

Noah eyes my foot then flashes a wicked grin. "Trying to tell me something, baby?"

I shrug. Maybe. "So we'll have a front porch?"

"Wraparound." Noah falls back to sit beside me and grabs my bare feet to put on his lap. "With a porch swing facing the west so we can watch the sunset every night."

I blink and survey Noah as if it's the first time I've seen him. He's in the same clothes as when we left: black T-shirt, jeans, black boots. The bottom of the cross tattooed on his biceps peeks out from under his sleeve. The firelight dances across his face, and his hair hangs over his eyes. Noah's just as beautiful as the time I sat next to him in the school's main office all those months ago, but the words he just said—those aren't from the boy that asked me to smoke pot with him the night of Michael Blair's party.

Noah traces the small bones on the top of my foot, and I'm amazed how the simple touch races up my veins to private areas.

"Um." *Clear thoughts, clear thoughts.* "One story? Two?"

"One and a half." He won't meet my eyes, and I'm okay with it. He's permitting me into his typically guarded thoughts. "Rustic cabin style, but with all the amenities. Wide-open floor plan. Living room, large kitchen, stairs up the side that go to the loft that'll hold our bedroom."

"You've really mulled this over, haven't you?"

Noah continues to draw his fingers along the top of my toes and stays silent. The fire cracks, and only a dim flame remains. He exhales as if he's jumping off a cliff. "I've already drawn the plans."

NOAH

Echo tilts her head, and her red curls tumble over her shoulder. I love how she looks in the firelight. The flickering flames create a soft glow around her and highlight her green eyes. "You drew plans for a house for me?"

I have a hard time meeting her gaze, so I stare at the red center of the fire. "Yeah."

"When did you do it?"

I meant to give it to her as a graduation present, but chickened out. "Few weeks ago."

Echo's feet rock in my lap. "That's..."

Pathetic. Stupid.

"...the best thing anyone has ever done for me."

My eyes snap to hers, and the peaceful smile playing on her lips is all I need. "It's just a floor plan."

Echo slides her feet off my lap and sits up on her knees next to me. "Do you have it with you?"

Tell her no. "Yeah."

I shove a stick at the hot coals at the bottom of the fire, and they dissolve into white ash. A few months back, Echo drew pictures of my parents and she was desperate to stop me when I flipped the page to see what she had done. I thought she was acting stupid for trying to steal the sketch pad from me, but now I understand her anxiety.

"Can I see it?" she asks.

I toss the stick into the flames as the fire is done for the night. "It's in my pack. Back pocket in a folder."

Echo jumps to her feet. "Are you coming?"

"Let me put this out, and I'll join you in a few." Because if she hates it, I'll notice, and that would break my fucking heart.

"I can help," she says.

"I promised you wouldn't do a thing."

She angles her body in the direction of the restroom. "It's not a big deal. I can tote some water from—"

"Gave my word, and you're going to let me keep it."

Echo rolls her eyes and ignores my statement as she reaches for an empty water jug. She asked for it. In a swift motion, I bend over and ease her over my shoulder. Echo squeals as her feet dangle near my chest. I unzip the netting of the tent and slip Echo in. Her curls cover her face, and the sound of her laughter soothes my weary soul.

"Stay put."

Her laughter continues to dance over my skin. "And if I don't?"

There's a seductive tease in her voice that causes me to drop my head and moan. I glance over my shoulder, and Echo's giving me that hooded look. Fuck me. "Then I'll be forced to kiss you into compliance."

Her eyes fall to my lips. "Good luck with that."

Moments like this are how I learned early in the trip to keep two jugs of water nearby. Without responding, I leave the tent and pour water over the dying flames. I then kick enough dirt over it that archeologists won't be able to find the remains. I've got issues with unattended fires.

Echo zips up the inside flap, which means she's getting

ready for bed. A click and the inside of the tent glows like a hot-air balloon. I strain to hear her unzip my pack, but I've got no clue if she's opened it or not.

I stand near the fire pit, occasionally kicking more dirt over it to satisfy that itch beneath my skin.

Echo wanted to pretend that we had no past for the night, and I tell her that I dream of our future. That drawing could freak her out. It could cause her to realize that I'm not playing about the two of us, because I'm not. I need her in my life.

Content the fire's out, I enter the tent and my breath catches in my throat. Echo sits in the middle of the blankets and pillows. She's in a black tank top, lace bra and a pair of boy shorts. I've seen her in less, I've seen her in more, but it's the first time I've been greeted this way this early. It's not lost on me, that she's chosen tonight.

In her hands are the plans I designed for our house, and I swear to God there are tears in her eyes.

Her lower lip trembles. "You really aren't going to leave me, are you?"

Noah hesitates at the entrance, and his eyes widen. Oh, heck, wrong thing to say. Exact wrong thing to say. In my possession is the most beautiful gift anyone has ever given me, and I'm pushing him.

Oh, holy freaking crap. I'm pushing Noah Hutchins.

Noah Hutchins.

The guy who doesn't do commitments. The guy who doesn't fall in love. The guy that somehow broke both those rules and ended up with me, and now I'm being pathetic and saying things like... "I mean, you know, this is a house and you drew it out on a piece of paper, and it looks great and stuff."

My palms disintegrate from dry to clammy and I worry I'll smear the pencil marks if I hold the design much longer, but at the same time, I crave to never let go.

Noah zips up the flap, and the two of us are very, very alone. The same tingle from when we enter a hotel room skips through my veins and I shiver.

"Are you cold?" he asks.

I shake my head, but that doesn't prevent Noah from joining me on top of the mound of blankets, sleeping bags and pillows, and laying an arm around my shoulder. His fingertips slightly graze the bare skin of my shoulder, and

I become hyperaware: of him, of his touch, of the paper on the verge of bending in my hands.

"You like it?" he asks quietly.

"Yeah," I barely breathe out and stare at the squares on the page again. It's a layout. More math than art, but in my mind I can see what his logic attempts to tell me. Twelve feet one way, ten feet another, and he's created a room with indentations that indicate outcrops for floor-to-ceiling windows. "A lot."

Noah slips the paper from my grasp and places it on top of his pack. My foot begins to sway against the blankets in my own silent, internal rhythm. That feeling that everything is twisted and messed up and that I've somehow lost control, and that I'm on the verge of losing everything worthwhile in my life...all of that builds inside me.

"Echo," Noah says in that deep voice I've only heard him use with me. Unable to stop myself, I turn to him. That's the type of voice someone uses when they're calling you home.

Noah tilts his head, a sign indicating he's going to tell the truth. Knowing that the truth more often hurts than helps, I have to fight to keep from closing my eyes. My heart picks up speed. He's pausing, and if Noah Hutchins does anything it's full throttle and without fear.

"Echo...I will never leave you."

The tears that had formed when I looked at Noah's vision of our future threaten to return, and I rapidly blink. "Being with you, it's the only time when the noises stop. When the chaos ends." Being with him, loving him...is simple. "I love you."

***

My fingers shake as I reach for the bottom of my tank. I've never undressed in front of Noah before. He's taken my clothes off, sometimes with a little assistance on my part. Noah has always been the confident one, and I've always been more than happy to let him set our course.

But not tonight. Not now. Not when he's opened himself up and showed me that this trip isn't just about me or just about him, but about us. With a deep breath, I gather the material of my tank over my head, and my curls bounce against the bare skin of my shoulders and back.

Noah freezes, sort of like he went into shock. The right side of my mouth twitches. *Mark the date, world. I stunned the great Noah Hutchins.*

His eyes spark as his gaze dips to my cleavage, and this gives me courage. I shift forward and slip my hands under his shirt, brushing my fingers against the muscles of his abdomen. Noah sharply inhales and, in seconds, his shirt is off and thrown into the corner of the tent.

I love his naked chest, and I decide to play. Biting my bottom lip, hoping to contain the smile, I nudge Noah's shoulder, indicating for him to lie down. He flashes his wicked grin and reclines back, except he snags his hand around my wrist and tugs me with him.

I laugh as I come face-to-face with him. My body on top of his and when I wiggle, I close my eyes, liking the pleasure of intimate parts touching. My hips squirm and with the movement, Noah immediately kisses my lips while knotting his fingers in my hair.

There's no subtlety in our kiss. All of the passion, all of the longing, all of the emotion rush out of us like water hurtling toward a cliff. It's fast and raw and out of control. My mouth opens, and Noah consumes every part of me. He turns his head and with a strong grip on my hair, he urges me to tilt mine so that he can kiss me more deeply.

I immediately comply, and Noah moans. The sound causes my blood to pump faster. Unable to resist, I move my hips against him again, but this time it's methodical, it's in a rhythm. Noah releases my hair, and it falls around us—a silky rain covering us both.

He lowers one hand and squeezes my hip. The other cups my bottom, coaxing me to continue. His fingers tease right along the hem of my underwear, and a burst of warmth spirals through me.

The world becomes hazy. Thought no longer exists. Just his lips. Just the heat of his body. The feelings of pleasure and urges and this desperate need for faster flows in my veins. It's like I'm roasting—clinging to a flame, and I long to be burned.

Noah runs his fingers along my spine, and instantly my bra loosens around my shoulders. It's a tickling stroke as he eases one strap and then the other off my arm. He rolls us, and I gasp for air when Noah frees the last bit of material separating our chests.

His lips leave my mouth and begin their descent down. My fingers tangle in his hair, letting him know that I'm lost in his exploration. Lost in this moment. Lost in this love we share.

I could do this forever and never stop.

Noah nips my belly button, and I giggle and flinch with the sensation, but it doesn't halt his barrage of kisses. He maneuvers his mouth to the side of my stomach and rubs the sensitive spot he just kissed, taking away the tickle, and transforms it into this massage that makes me suck in my breath and curl my toes.

"Noah," I whisper as my hips rock without my consent. Our gazes lock. Lust and love darken his chocolate-brown eyes.

There are many places we can go. Many ways we can do this and over the past couple of months, we've explored, and reexplored, and developed new twists on old ways to bring ourselves to that glorious high. As my heart beats frantically, I know that this is the night that it's new. This is the night I make love to Noah Hutchins.

"Can you..." I whisper, then trail off. My entire body seems to quiver with my pulse. I swallow and try again. "Can you..."

Read my mind. Oh, God, I'd give anything if he could read my mind. Noah tucks a curl behind my ear as his eyes desperately search for what I can't communicate. "What, Echo?"

With the words stuck in my throat, my fingers trace down and undo the button of his jeans. Noah's eyes snap to mine while I slowly pull on the zipper. My hands wander to the part of him that I hope will help him decipher my desires.

Noah shuts his eyes and shifts closer to me. Within seconds he reopens them, and it's like looking upon a deep lake. His lips brush against mine in a tender way. In a way Noah's never kissed me before, like he's saying the words I love you over and over again, but there's no sound. Just his heart. Just his soul.

My thumb hooks around his jeans and begins to edge them off. Noah caresses my face, and I lean into his touch.

"Are you sure?" he asks.

"Never been more sure of anything." And I mean it. There's this calm, this knowing, this understanding that was never present before. I said no for years hoping that I would know when I was ready, and I smile, satisfied that I truly did wait for the right moment.

Noah slowly takes my bottom lip between his then releases it. One kiss along my jawline. Another on my neck. Pleasing goose bumps spread across my skin. With one last glance at me, Noah rolls away while reaching for his pack.

My heart thunders with the crackle of a package ripping open. I'm doing this. I'm going to make love with Noah Hutchins.

He shrugs off his jeans, and I become aware of my underwear when I notice that today wasn't a boxer shorts type of day for him.

With his bare butt to me, Noah pauses to do what he has to do so we don't create other little Noahs and Echos. I'm on the pill, but we agreed to be overcautious.

Unfortunately, all the need, all the desire that had been building to an explosion is replaced by the coolness of the night air pricking at my skin and the millions of fears whispering in my mind. What if it hurts? What if I don't like it? What if Noah doesn't like doing it with me? What if I do it wrong? What if…

Then Noah finishes and eases his body next to mine. The cold fades away and so do the questions. He settles beside me. An arm and a leg drape over me as he kisses my shoulder. "Any time you want to stop, we can. Just say the word."

"I want this." So much that I ache.

His fingers begin this slow dance, lingering in areas,

exploring. Noah skims under my breast, along my stomach, down my legs, to the inside of my thighs, then to a place that causes my back to arch. With kisses that make me drunk and touches that send me soaring, Noah eases off my underwear.

My breath comes out faster, and my hold on him tightens and right when the world is going to fracture into a million pieces, Noah covers my body with his, and I sense *Noah* in areas that he's never been before. Like inside me, yet not. He's warm and solid.

Noah brushes his mouth against mine and caresses my face as he distributes his weight to his elbows. "Are you sure?"

"Yes," I whisper with the need to shout. I'm right on the verge of exploding, and I want this release.

He kisses a trail to my ear. "I love you, Echo Emerson."

"I love you—" And Noah slips in. My breath catches in my throat, and my arms choke his neck, my fingers yank his hair. We both lie completely still, and my eyes squeeze shut with the burning pain.

Noah strokes my hair and presses his lips near my temple. "It's all right, Echo. We're all right."

Moisture forms in my eyes, and Noah kisses a path up my cheek. I open them, and he stares down at me. His body shakes as if he's trying desperately to stay motionless. "Are you with me, baby?"

I swallow then nod.

"We can stop." He rests his forehead on mine, and his pulse visibly pumps in his neck.

I'm holding my breath, and I hesitantly suck air through my nose then release it through my mouth. The pain isn't as sharp anymore, and I gather my courage to continue. "I'm okay."

When I'm able to breathe normally, Noah moves. It's slow, and it doesn't hurt as much. He closes his eyes like he's concentrating, and when he opens his eyes, he gives me a small grin. "Try to relax."

"I am." I'm not.

"You're drawing blood."

Oh, crap. My nails are embedded in his back, and my fingers strangle his hair. I loosen my grip, and the horror makes me anxious and a bit hysterical. For the love of all things holy, I honest to God giggle. My cheeks flush with the sound, but the shyness and embarrassment fade when Noah chuckles with me.

It's like my entire body sighs with relief. All of the tension melts away, and having Noah inside me no longer aches.

Noah skims a hand down the side of my body and when he reaches the curve of my butt, he nudges himself *farther* up. Only a slight discomfort this time and in the dark private areas in my mind, I liked it more than I hated it.

The thought causes warmth to return to my lower sections, and I'm able to kiss Noah back when he reclaims my lips.

"You're so beautiful," he murmurs.

I internally hold my breath. "Am I doing it right?"

A glint sparks in his eyes. "You're perfect."

And I smile.

Another kiss to my lips; another nudge forward. "Keep relaxing for me."

Instead of concentrating on relaxing, I focus on the

heat of his body against mine, his spicy scent and how the light of the camping lantern strikes the few gold pieces in his dark hair. And I especially fixate on how when Noah shifts up, it creates addictive sensations in certain areas that I really, really...I mean really like.

As Noah moves again, his grip on me tightens yet he possesses the same amount of gentleness. Like I'm precious glass he's afraid of breaking.

He drops his head, and I kiss his shoulder while wrapping my feet around his. A rough sound leaves his throat, and a thrill sweeps through me that I have the ability to twist him inside out.

"Jesus Christ, Echo." His fingers dig into my shoulders. "I don't want to hurt you."

"It's okay," I whisper into his ear, and squeeze my body to his.

Noah holds his breath and with a few final sharp pushes, he shudders. He breathes hard and fast, and my body completely absorbs his weight as he gains his bearings.

"I love you," he whispers. And he says it again. And again. Then each uttering of the statement is followed by his lips pressing against my body.

There's a split second when he rolls away, takes care of certain business, but then he's quick returning to me. "Are you sore?"

"Kind of, but not as bad as I thought I'd be." I skim my fingers along his face. "I love you."

So much. And giving him this, it feels like a forever sort of thing.

My body is in this strange teetering state. There's a surge of adrenaline that I made it to the other side unscathed. Then there's a stream of desire still crying out to be released. A huge part of me acknowledges that I'm nowhere ready to do that again...yet.

Noah grabs a blanket, covers us both and adjusts the pillows so that I'm completely surrounded. As I snuggle next to him, Noah's fingers trace up the inside of my thigh and when my eyes roll back in pleasure, he kisses my lips and appears to begin again.

"Not again," I beg, though I'm loving his touch. "Not yet."

"Not again," he says. "Just for you."

Noah kisses and touches and declares his love through intimate whispers, and he becomes a man determined to finish what I had started.

NOAH

Echo flinches in her sleep, and my eyes snap open. She's been restless with her arms flung over her head and the blanket bunched between her legs. Little lines form in the space between her brows, and she sucks in a sharp intake of air.

A flash of panic rips through me. No. Not tonight. Not after we made love. A night terror isn't the memory I want her to have. It's not the memory I want to carry.

I wrap an arm around her, and my fingers slide against the wide scar on her back. Anger ripples along my muscles. I've touched her scars hundreds of times, but after what we've shared, the emotion evolves into a monster.

I know how much I love Echo. After what we've done… my heart aches…I fucking worship her now. How the hell could someone that claimed to love her do this? Leave her scarred? Mentally…physically.

Echo's body jolts as if she was zapped by electricity. I lean down and kiss her neck. "Echo."

"Please," she begs, still lost in her dream. "Don't do this."

It's hard to pull her out of the world she's stuck in once she's there. The dream becomes alive and vicious and grows tentacles that cling to her and drag her deep. When

I talk, she talks back, but not to me. Never to me. It's to her mother, and each time it makes me hate the bitch more.

Echo's face is cool to the touch, even though sweat beads along the roots of her hair. I peel back a curl smothered to her cheek. "Baby, I need you to wake up."

Before the screaming starts, because those shrieks tear out a part of my soul. It's like watching her die, and I'm behind a glass wall, unable to save the girl I love.

She jerks her head back and forth. Large, hot tears pool in the corners of her eyes then spill down her face. Fuck me. Just fuck me.

"Echo." The desperation increases in my voice, grows in my body. "Don't do this. Wake up. Come on, wake up."

Her arms fly out to shield her face, and I can see how the glass slashed across her arms. How a scar on her right arm begins then ends as a scar on her left. I've considered showing her because I don't think she's noticed the pattern. Her two arms create a whole picture of the nightmare she experienced.

I grab on to her wrists, pull them away from her face and kiss her lips, lips that can't kiss me back. "Please, wake up. I'm right here."

I take in her bottom lip, and it's hard to do when her body trembles and her arms shake for freedom. As I move away, Echo briefly stills. My heart pounds hard once. She heard me. "It's a bad dream, Echo. It's not real."

Her arms relax as she stops fighting, and when I link my fingers with hers, she holds me back. Behind her closed lids, her eyes dart. She still belongs to the dream, but for the first time, I'm in there with her. I lower my forehead to hers. "Come back to me, baby."

Echo turns to the sound of my voice, and her eyelids

flutter open. A few more drops fall down her face, and her body jerks as she realizes that she's awake. I've held her enough times throughout this summer to know that even though she's rejoined reality, the demons will continue to scream at her from the back of her mind.

Her body quakes as Echo tries to prevent the sobs, and she throws her hands over her face. "It wasn't supposed to happen tonight."

Like I have so many times, I scoop her up, tucking the sheet around her, and cradle her in my lap. Echo buries her head in the crook of my shoulder as she releases the pain, the frustration, the hurt.

"It's okay," I tell her. "We're going to be okay."

"She was there, and there was blood, and I couldn't stop it." Echo wraps her arms tighter around my neck, and I draw her closer, wishing I could steal the nightmares that torment her.

"You're safe." I shut my eyes and attempt to kill the anger at her mother. How the hell does Echo turn it off? How can she wake like this, totally shattered, then hours later contemplate talking to her, listening to the bitch's messages? "I swear to you, you're safe."

And as far as I'm concerned, Echo's going to stay that way.

I comb my fingers through her hair, massage her back and make that shushing noise that calms her. When her sobs are less intense, I begin to sing. More whisper than song. Right in her ear. The same song as the night we first kissed.

Echo relaxes in my arms, and I sing it through, one more time. A little for her, but more for me. I don't know how to protect her from the demons in her mind. How do I fight something that can't be seen?

When I finish, there's silence. I strain to hear anything, but the land around us says nothing. No cars, no planes, no jacked-up people yelling into the night.

"I'm tired of living in the past," Echo whispers. "I don't want to go back."

"Then no more past," I answer. "Only the future. We're going to get our degrees, we're going to get married and we'll never look back."

"We were fine after graduation and before the sand dunes. Before we talked about heading home. Everything was perfect."

My neck stiffens. "Tonight was perfect."

Echo raises her head, and it's damn hard to meet her eyes. If I spot regret there, I'll lose my shit. I blink when I notice the smile playing at her lips and how she shyly glances away.

Fuck me. Heaven in the middle of hell, but how else would Echo and I do this? She fell asleep after and so did I—tangled in each other's arms. This is it. This is the moment of truth of the after and so far, I like what I see.

Her cheeks flood red, and when she takes in our lack of clothes, her eyes widen. "Oh."

I choke down a laugh. Hoping to help her modesty, I lay her down, draw up a cover and prop my head on my fist. "You okay?"

"I heard you in my dream telling me to come back. No one else has been there before."

Damn straight she heard me. "See, we're kicking your past's ass already."

The right side of Echo's mouth strains up but then tugs down. "Was *it* okay for you?"

We've moved away from night terrors. "Perfect."

"I'm not good at it."

"Echo..." I sigh. There's no right way to explain this. "What happened tonight was special because I did it with you."

She messes with the cuticles of her nails. Damn it, I can't get the girl to stop thinking. I wish I could crawl into her mind and hear what she's mulling over, but then again, it's probably better if I remain ignorant.

"It's sort of weird," she says.

I place my hands over hers to stop her assault on her nails. "What's weird?"

She shrugs, not able to meet my gaze. "I'm not a virgin anymore."

Pain strikes my chest. *Don't regret it. Please don't.* "Are you okay with that?"

"Yeah." Echo's green eyes drift to mine. "It's...I...uh... read this article once that said when you have sex with someone it releases these chemicals in your brain, and it makes you more attached."

Could explain my fresh need to kill her mom. "Okay."

"And I already loved you..."

I run a hand over my face. Is this the buildup before she pushes me over the edge? "Yeah?"

Echo fidgets with the end of the blanket. "Well...my virginity was mine to give. I mean, how many times have I heard over and over again that there's only one shot at this. That there's no take backs. That once I give it, it's gone."

And now she regrets it. I rub my eyes as I don't like the

wetness in them. I don't like the way my muscles tense. I fucking love her and would stand in front of a god-damned train to protect her, and she regrets the best damned night of my life.

"I guess I'm saying," she continues, "now that it doesn't belong to me anymore...well...I'm glad I gave it to you. So in a weird way, my virginity is yours now. That's something you'll always have and...I sort of like the idea that it belongs to you."

My head shoots up, and my heart stops beating. "What did you say?"

She bites her bottom lip. "If I'm going to be closer to someone, I'm glad it's you. I'm glad you're the one I gave this part of myself to."

My mouth pops open, but no words escape. The burning wetness that was there because I thought she was going to break my heart still hovers in my eyes, but now it's there because entire parts of me are being reborn. Parts of my soul that I thought would be dead forever.

"It's heavy if you think about it." She yawns. It's an hour before dawn, too early for either of us to be awake.

"How?" I don't care about the heaviness. I'll take it if this is how it feels to be loved by her. I gather Echo into my arms, and she rests her head on my pillow.

"Like it gives you a power."

"What type of power is that?" My eyelids close.

She yawns again and her words are slurred through her exhaustion. "So now that I gave you this special gift, isn't your job to take care of it?"

Taking care of her—I can do that. "I'm going to spend my whole life making you happy."

"You better." Echo jerks then resettles.

She does this—falls asleep then floats into barely awake. There's a brief few seconds where I can ask her anything, and the truth tumbles out of her mouth. I'm a dick for taking advantage of it, but I never claimed to be the good guy. "What will make you happy, Echo?"

"You," she mumbles groggily.

Not enough. "What else? What will make you happy?"

"Staying here." Her voice trails off toward the end. "I don't want to go home. Ever."

The smile on my face fades as I stare at Echo now asleep in my arms. I think of what she said when she calmed down from her night terror: *I'm tired of living in the past...I don't want to go back... We were fine after graduation and before the sand dunes. Before we talked about heading back. Everything was perfect.*

She tried to tell me, several ways, but I assumed something else and cut her off. It's like someone's rammed a knife into my gut.

Fuck me—I took her virginity, knowing what it meant to her, and in return I promised her happiness, a home, a life, a future. How the hell could I swear promises to her when in the end, I've never understood what she craves out of life.

I made love to Noah Hutchins, and the entire world has continued on as normal. It seems like I should be granted the time to soak this in, to sort out the emotions and excitement and fears, but like always the world doesn't spin in my favor.

The green trees of the forest merge into a collage as Noah flies past them in his hunt back to Vail. He works tonight and, in theory, I should be working, as well. That is, if I decide to paint the constellation Aires.

Noah's quieter than normal. Not that he's all conversational the majority of the time, but I catch him staring at me when he thinks I'm not paying attention. Like now, as I sit in the passenger side of my Honda Civic and scroll aimlessly through my phone, he keeps peeking at me. Real intense, as if he's scared I'm going to go *Alien* and freak.

The night terror I had last night wasn't my worst, but I'm devastated it happened. My mind has converted into an insecure seesaw, and I'm over being on the ride. But as much as I try to concentrate on a solid path, the questions continue to multiply.

For instance, now that he's conquered me, like Beth's continually suggesting, will Noah move on? And if that's not the case, am I the same person to him as before we made love, and does he like what he now sees?

Because to be truthful, deep underneath my skin, in the light of morning, Noah appears different to me. Not in a bad way, but just...changed.

Experience has told me that change normally is the absence of good, and this causes the sensation of ants crawling around in my stomach. My foot drums against the floor, and Noah raises an eyebrow. "You okay?"

"Yes." Absolutely not. My entire world is in flux again, and it's like grasping on to a slippery rock next to a waterfall. I can't get a good grip, but at the same time I wouldn't mind the fall into the deep pool below. It's all so beautiful yet terrifying.

"You sure?"

"Yeah." But this frantic panic gains traction...am I different to him and if so, what does that mean for us?

It's funny how, until waking next to him this morning, I never noticed the small scar above his eyebrow, and how there's this spicy sweetness to his dark scent. Over the past couple of months, I've memorized Noah's smell, but now it seems to be everywhere, all the time, and I clutch it like it's a blanket. It reminds me of him pulling me close and declaring his love.

I bite my tongue, wishing I could utter the words, *I love you more now, and it scares me. Please, please, please never leave.* That's all Noah must dream about. Making love to a girl who goes pathetic in the morning.

"There's something going on, Echo. So tell me what."

I give an exaggerated sigh and dig out the least wretched of my worries. "Will people know?"

"Know what?"

I glance him over and get a little thrill with how the muscles in his arms ripple as he readjusts his hold on the wheel.

"That we...you know..." Say it. "Made love?"

He rubs his mouth to hide the smirk forming there, but I smack his arm because I saw it.

"You're not making me feel better," I say as a tease, but I'm as serious as a death sentence.

Noah chuckles. "You're way too uptight, baby. If you act like this, then yeah, Isaiah and Beth will spot it a mile away."

My head hits the back of the seat. Freaking fantastic. I'm so utterly screwed.

"But it doesn't matter how you act."

"Why?"

His eyes devour me. "Because they'll know it the moment they see me."

A silly grin spreads across my face as I might like where this is heading. "Why's that?"

"From the moment we finished last night, I wanted to do it again. My fingers hurt because I want to touch you so bad. I can't stop the itch to explore your skin and to kiss you and..." His fingers actually flex on the wheel. "No one's going to miss that I'm continually three seconds from yanking you behind a closed door and stripping you naked."

That one declaration causes those mutant pterodactyls to raise their heads and grow restless, stretching their wings in preparation for flight. While the fantasy he wove is fantastically cool and amazing, it makes me hot and flustered to think he wants me bad enough to actually do something like that...in public...

"Will we do it all the time now?" And as soon as the question leaves my mouth, I'm swamped in the land of lame. "I mean, I know that wasn't a one-time deal, but is that what we'll do forever? Like now that we've accomplished actually doing it, is that what we'll do night after night or will we do other things?"

And I'm rambling. Horribly so. *Oh, God, kill me. Now. Send a bolt of lightning from the sky and strike me dead.*

"Because it was special." Because I have this horrid deficiency where I feel the need to explain why I'm a freak of nature. "And while it was special and awesome, I'm not sure how awesome it will be every single night. Because...well..." It hurt.

Noah laughs, but his laughter dies when he notices I'm not laughing with him.

"Hey," he says. But I can't look at him because of this sickening weight in my stomach. Noah laughed at me. I opened up, just a little, and he laughed.

"Echo." Noah switches the hand he's driving with then reaches over and grabs on to the fingers resting in my lap, but I jerk them away. "Look at me."

But I can't. "I wasn't joking. This is still new and it still scares me and...forget it."

"I'm the dick. I keep telling you to talk then I cut you off. I thought you were kidding."

Anger courses through me like a rocket launch. "Do I look like I'm kidding?"

"No." He alternates his focus between me and the road. "You look fucking pissed."

I don't know why, but I giggle. So much so, that I smack a hand over my mouth to stop it from coming, but the giggles continue. "Do I look that bad?"

Noah opens his mouth, closes it then smashes his lips together in a fine line as if examining his thoughts. "Not anymore. What's going on in your head?"

I trace the outline of my phone as the whiplash emotions settle. "I don't want us to change. What we did was huge, and I want us to be okay."

Noah seeks my hand again, but this time I let him take it. He lifts my fingers to his lips and kisses my knuckles. "We're okay. I swear."

NOAH

Echo stays silent when I ease into a spot at the hotel and shut off the engine. She gave me a special part of her last night, and I almost fucked it up. First my parents then my brothers. Echo's the lone piece of my soul worth holding on to.

"I'm sorry," she whispers.

I will never understand her. "For what?"

"For being me." Echo drops the statement and exits the car. What the hell?

I follow her out then join her when she leans against the side of the car.

"I thought after we took this trip," she continues, "that I'd somehow be stronger and more confident—I thought this summer was going to change me, but I only have two thousand more questions instead of any answers."

I rest my hands on her shoulders and stare straight into her eyes. "Do you regret it?"

She blinks, shocked at the question. "What?"

"Do you regret making love to me?"

Lines form on her forehead as she squints. "No. I...I..."

Not reading her mind is torture. "What?"

"I want things to be simple...and for us to be okay... and...and to know that after all this, you still love me."

Bang—the sound of the weight of the world sliding off

my shoulders. Is that it? Is that all that bothers her? I gather Echo into me like a man pardoned from death row. "I love you. We won't change. I promise."

It's when she relaxes in my arms that I find the peace I had last night when we were together. She craves simple, and all the two of us have ever known is complicated.

I'm a man of word, and I'm determined to keep this promise. If I'm doing this whole relationship thing then it's time I figure out how to put her needs first. Damn me to hell that this plan includes eating my pride. "What are your plans for today?"

"Laundry," she mumbles into my chest. "I've noticed your lack of boxer short wearing."

"Easy access, baby."

A muffled *humph* on her end. "I've already told you that the dressing room was a one-time deal."

"Stop messing with my fantasies. What else are you doing today?"

"I need to call my dad."

"What else?"

Echo's shoulders turn rock-solid, and she shifts. She's terrified of starting another fight. For the past couple of days we've been unbalanced. I can't allow it, not anymore. Not after last night. "You should try the painting."

She rises onto her toes. "For real?"

For that look? "Yeah. Knock this Hunter asshole dead."

Literally, and then I'll kick him while he's down for shits and giggles.

"He's giving me a shot. He's not an ass. I swear, he's a good guy."

Hole. I said asshole. He stalked her then stared at her tits in front of me. Open a dictionary and that would be the ghetto translation of asshole. "All the same, I'm dropping you off and picking you up. If I text, you text back. If I call, you answer. Otherwise, I'm showing. At least for today. I want to confirm the guy's not a serial killer who's decided to create a living doll out of you."

"Are you going to beat your chest next and toss me over your shoulder before killing something with your bare hands for dinner?"

I love that she throws shit back at me without batting an eye. "I'll even start the fire to cook it up."

Her head falls back. "Oh. My. God."

"Just for today. Push me on this, Echo, and I'll redefine caveman for you. No one fucks around with you. Got it?"

No one. I once failed the two most important people in my life, and I won't fail her. Period.

"You're impossible."

Which means I won. "Damn straight."

"Fine, but you have to play nice with Hunter." Schooled on how to seal a deal, she stretches for a kiss. Echo's going for a quick peck, but I'll be damned if that's all I get. My fingers weave in her hair, and I immediately crush my lips to hers, sweeping my tongue into her mouth, a move that drives her wild.

Echo goes weak as if her knees gave, but she draws enough strength to heighten the kiss. The entire world fades, leaving only her fingers tracing my neck. She presses her body so tightly to mine that I can feel the soft weight of her breasts against my chest. Our lips greedily dance in time, and my exploration of her body begins.

My hand cups the curve of her ass, and flashes of her naked body under mine from last night rip through my brain. Her warmth surrounds me, and a rough sound leaves my throat. I want Echo, and I want Echo now.

"Get a room," Beth says.

Echo jerks away, and I immediately rest my fingers around the nape of her neck to keep her close and to silently tell Beth to back off.

Beth stands with her arms crossed over her chest near the hood of the car, scowling at the move. "For real. You. Her. Walls."

"I had a room," I say. "But someone took it."

"That's something you should have considered before you told Isaiah to drag my ass to everybody-loves-nature middle of nowhere."

"Don't you have somewhere to be?" As in not here.

"That's the problem—no, I don't."

I scratch my forehead. She's right. She doesn't. Not for a week.

Beth looks Echo over like she's a mannequin in a store. "I need a bathing suit."

"We're not the same size," replies Echo. My girl is taller—by half a foot.

"I'll stuff the top with tissues if you're that concerned, but it still doesn't remove my need of a bathing suit. There's a hot tub, and I'm going in. Unless you help me out, clothing is becoming optional, and I'm telling hotel management that it was your idea."

Echo beelines for the hotel entrance. "I've got a couple you can try on."

Beth follows her and heads in, but Echo hesitates. "You're coming, right?"

I shove my hands in my pockets. Once I walk through that door, regardless of whether or not we're in Kentucky, with Beth and Isaiah staying with us, Echo and I will be back to our reality.

That's good and it's bad, and I'm determined to make it work. "Yeah. I am."

Noah scans the outside of the gallery like he's a Special Forces soldier on the prowl behind enemy lines. We're in the same quaint little village as I was before with the cobblestone streets and cute Swiss-type buildings, but Noah acts as if we're dodging hostile fire.

We left Beth and Isaiah at the hotel, her in the possession of one of my bikinis, while Noah and I headed over to Hunter's gallery. Noah's shift starts soon, but he's determined to walk me in like a kindergartener on her first day.

"You said you were fine with this," I say.

"I am," he bites out.

"Noah...please no throwing this guy against the wall, okay?"

His jaw ticks. "Let's get this done."

Noah opens the door for me and nods for me to enter. This is one of those places where you draw your arms and legs in to make yourself smaller. The paintings are so detailed, so magnificent that they have to be worth more than my life and Noah's put together. Cherubs are carved into the white molding, and crystal chandeliers hang from above. While I meander through, wide-eyed and reverent, Noah struts in with the grace of a bull in a glass factory.

"Echo! Good to see you!" Hunter calls from the back of the store. He waves his hand for me to follow and disappears behind a wall of beads.

"That would be where he keeps his torture chamber," Noah mutters. "Do you think he snaps before and after pictures of his prey?"

"Shhhh."

He does, but shoulders past me to take the lead. Behind the beads, a dimly lit staircase winds up, and Hunter's footsteps echo from above. With a sigh that almost passes as a groan, Noah starts the climb, and I trail after.

Light beckons us forward. When we reach the top, I crane my neck to glance around Noah and release an excited breath. It's raw. It's floorboards. It's the spikes of roofing nails protruding from the ceiling, and it's lit by hundreds of tiny Christmas tree lights. Windows run along the back wall, and canvases sit every few feet waiting for their owners to return. Each painting is in various stages, but I can see the genius in each one.

In the corner, Hunter places a blank canvas on an empty easel. "This is yours. Everything you need is right here at your fingertips, and if you can't find it, tell me and I'll get it for you."

Like a magnetic pull, I'm attracted to the canvas. A million butterflies crash within me when I spot the new paints and brushes. Never used. Never opened. All ready for me to crack the seals and explore. This is a holy moment.

"I'm Noah."

I practically vault for the ceiling with the sound of Noah's voice behind me, and guilt creeps into my soul. I got so entrenched in what was in front of me that I forgot introductions. Nearly killing me, I pivot away from the easel and clear my throat. "Hunter, this is my boyfriend, Noah. Noah, this is Hunter."

Noah offers his hand, and the two guys shake for a really, really long time as they stare each other down. I shift footing, and they finally let go. Noah crosses his arms over his chest and seems to be made of stone while Hunter regards Noah with as much interest as I would garbage.

This meeting is going well.

"There are lots of easels here. Does that mean there will be other people?" asks Noah.

"Are you asking if I'm going to be alone with Echo?" Hunter retorts. I swallow a sigh. The meaning behind Noah's question is whether or not Hunter prefers to torture his victims before or after he ties them up.

When Noah doesn't respond, Hunter barely moves his hands in an I-don't-know-fashion. "I don't hover over my artists. There are plenty of them, and they come and go as they please."

Crap, Noah's going to love this. I spin on my heel and grab Noah's hand. "I don't want you to be late. I'm sure other people will show soon."

I also eye meld, brain express, beg for psychic abilities to remind Noah that this was *his* idea, regardless of the fact that I was going to do it anyway, and that he *agreed* to play nice.

"Where do you work?" Hunter asks, but it's obvious from the T-shirt that Noah's spending time at the Malt and Burger.

"I start college in the fall," Noah answers, and this

surge of pride skips through me. I've never heard Noah answer like that before.

"Noah's going to be an architect," I add.

"Flipping burgers is the backup plan?" Hunter asks, and my stomach drops.

My mouth pops open because I should say something to defend Noah, but he beats me to it. "I like humble. Keeps me in my place."

Hunter snorts a half laugh. Maybe working with him is a bad idea.

Noah ignores Hunter and looks down at me. "You okay here?"

"Yeah." I think.

Noah frames my face and gently kisses my lips. "I'll be back soon, baby."

A part of me melts when I spot that wicked glint in his eyes that tells me that I'm officially naked in his mind. I bite my lip as he releases me.

"I love you," I say.

Noah flashes me a pirate smile and disappears down the stairs.

"Bad-boy phase?" Hunter asks after Noah's footsteps fade.

I wrinkle my forehead and return to the canvas. "He's not a phase, and he's not that bad. You freaked him out by showing at our hotel room."

"Did I scare you?"

Something in his voice causes me to whip my head in his direction. Hunter appears casual with his hip cocked against a table that contains multiple bowls of fruit. He's dressed up in a pressed pair of jeans and a black button-down shirt with the sleeves rolled up. But his question feels weighted.

"No, you didn't scare me." Yeah, he did a little, but I have one last chance to prove my talent outside my mother's influence, and I'm not going to blow it again by telling the truth.

"Good." Hunter straightens. "Do you need a picture of the Aires constellation?"

Not when it's engraved as scar tissue on my soul. "I know it by heart."

Amid the sensation of bliss comes a wave of disorientation. Dizzy, I shut my eyes and sink to the stool next to the canvas. Aires. *I miss you. So much that part of me always feels like I'm dying a painful death.*

"What are you going to start with?" Hunter asks and my eyes reopen.

"The horizon." Because that's safe. Light still exists in the horizon. I combine the red and yellow to create the hue I desire then focus on last night's sunset and the memory of Noah's strong arms holding me.

NOAH

Lucky for me, the Malt and Burger is packed again, giving me little time to focus on Echo with that cocky bastard. The noise from the crowded restaurant reaches a new decibel of loud, and the heat from the grill causes sweat to form along the roots of my hair.

I toss on two more patties and squeeze the hell out of two already frying. Wish it was Hunter I was throttling. The reason I didn't tear out of that art attic with Echo over my shoulder was that damn light shining from her face when she saw the blank canvas and paint.

I don't claim to understand her obsession with art, but I understand Echo. If I don't grant her the space she needs to play with her passion, she could run from me.

Mia sashays up and bends over to rest her arms on the counter, exposing what she thinks I want to see. "There's going to be a field party tomorrow night at the fry cook's place. Drinking, drugging, a little casual sex."

I flip a patty and slam my spatula on it. The grease pouring out sizzles. "I told you—"

Her laughter cuts me off. "That you're going to get your heart ripped out very soon because you can't read the signs of a bad-boy phase going downhill. Yeah, I know. You told me. That doesn't mean that I can't find other mice to play with in the meantime. So here's another bullet point to add to your growing number of check-list items. Did your boring person once enjoy being at a good party and now wants to stay home and watch *Wheel of Fortune*?"

The answer is, I don't know. I watched Echo throw a few beers back before graduation. Fuck, one of the first times I screwed with her was at a party where she was drunk off her ass. But after we left Kentucky, parties haven't come up. "Not your business."

I slide the patty off the grill, lay it on the bun and shove the plate in her direction. "Someone pays you to deliver this, don't they?"

She only winks. "Party, tomorrow night, nine o'clock. Ask your girl and find the answer."

My muscles lock up when I think of Echo at those gallery shows this summer. She glided through the parties as if she belonged, as if she was finally in her element, and I stood out like that damn beaver with the headphones.

This morning, Echo said she was terrified that we were going to change, but what if the problem is that she has and I haven't? If I ask my girl to a party, would she say yes or no? Does she still belong in my world?

I rub the tension out of my shoulder. Fuck it. It's a party. Not a verdict from the jury. Mia's good at messing with my mind, and I've got to stop letting her.

I glance at the clock then at the neighboring grill. The other cook is already filling orders. It's fifteen minutes past the end of my shift, and I'm done. I yank the bandanna off, and my hair falls into my eyes.

"I'm out," I shout at the manager.

"Noah!" he responds from the register. A line of people

shift impatiently as they wait for him to ring them out. "Just a few more minutes."

A few more minutes with Mia may cost me my sanity. "I've got to pick my girl up." I clock out then bolt for the alley door.

The evening air cools the sweat crawling along my neck, and I lean against the brick wall to gain my bearings. A car honks from the main street at the end of the alley. Real life isn't what's happening in that fast-food joint. The real world is out here. It was last night under the stars and holding Echo in my arms.

We made love. Echo never would have made love to me if she wasn't going to stick it through. Me and Echo. We're good.

"We're good," I say to myself, and push off the wall. It's time to find my girl and prove it.

Echo

Crouching on my knees, I brush the red paint along the curvature, and heat licks along my skin. Images flash in my mind, so hauntingly real, so utterly divine. It's like Noah's fingers are gliding against my body. His hands are rough from the wear and tear of his normal day, but they are also gentle. So gentle that with a simple touch he can easily coax my body to respond to him, and then those encounters of *being* with Noah leak into my dreams.

My mind is racing—so fast that my hand can hardly keep up. A stroke here, a smudge there, a blending of lines here to show how Noah and I were separate then merged into one. My eyes dart over the painting, searching for the next color, the next shadow, the next way to bring the canvas to life.

A curl swings into my eyesight, and my cheek becomes wet as I impatiently wipe it away. My fingers are slick, and a drop rolls from my hand onto my arm. It doesn't bother me, but the slickness of the brush does. I readjust my grip yet the brush falls from my hands and rolls on the floor until it stops at bare feet.

Bare feet.

I'm not alone.

Fear rages through my veins, and I jump back. My heart gallops as if I was on a dead run, and my hand flies to my chest as if I could catch it. I assess the room filled with people, attempting to find the threat.

Filled? Maybe not filled, but full. My mouth dries out. Yeah, there was nobody here before. Hunter was here, but left, then it was empty and I was alone and now it's full...almost filled...and every eye is gawking at me.

"Nine hours." My head whips to the right, toward the sound of Hunter's voice. "You haven't moved from that canvas for nine hours. Not to think. Not to use the bathroom. Not to eat. Your hand moved like you were a machine. I've never seen a thing like it."

I smooth out my clothes as if that would save me from this weird attention and try to maintain eye contact with Hunter. No threat. There is no threat. Deep breaths, Echo. Stop acting like a sideshow freak.

But still, there's a room full of people—watching me. Not only are they sitting on the floor, they're also lounging on stools or standing against the wall, but they're all staring at me as if I'm twirling flaming batons.

"I get this way sometimes," I explain, then clear my throat as a girl leans over to whisper in another girl's ear. They share a glinted look then smile. Blood rushes to my pressure points. They're probably disgusted by my scars. "I...uh...get lost in the painting."

"Does it happen every time you paint?" asks Hunter.

"I usually get pulled out pretty quick." By the school bell or Dad or Noah.

"But you didn't answer my question." Hunter weaves through the mass of bodies. His loafers click against the wooden subflooring. Most of the people in the room are young. My age or twenties. Over to the left there are several women with gray in their hair. For kicks there appears to be one or two token older men. "Is this what happens to you when you paint? Do you always become... hypnotized?"

Yes. And only my art teacher and Noah know. It's something that's private because...because I'm scared what it means at times. If I lose myself in a painting, what does that imply for my sanity?

Layers of paint cover my hands, and I fist my fingers, understanding that my face might be caked in color, as well. Great. I literally have an audience.

When Hunter reaches me, I ask my own question instead of answering his. "Who..." And I motion to... everyone else. Flustered as I am, "who" will work fine as a question.

"Echo..." A grin spreads across Hunter's face. Dang. He's definitely handsome. That is if I were into guys ten years older than me. "...this is everyone. Everyone, this is Echo."

The greetings blow in like a storm gale. Most are hi's and hellos along with a few what's ups. All of them from friendly faces.

"Hi," I shyly say back then whisper to Hunter, "Not what I meant."

"I know. Some of them work for me, some study under me full-time and some are taking classes at various universities around the world and are spending the summer with me for credit hours. Summers can mean a full house."

"And winters," adds someone from the back.

"I was trying not to scare her," Hunter responds. "Everyone go find something to do and stop staring at the new girl."

Why couldn't Noah see any of this? I pick up the paint brush and begin to clean it. "So I'm not the only person you chase after to paint?"

He laughs. "Actually, you are. Everyone else had to go through a rigorous application process. Paperwork, essays, major portfolio critiques. There are a limited number of spots in my program."

I angle my back to him as I set the brush down. "Is there an open spot?"

"Not until next year."

Dang it. Long internal sigh. Because I'm in theory a big girl, I confront him again. "So why allow me to do this?"

"Trial by fire," he answers. "I wanted to see what you would create if I pushed you, and if you could handle the stress of doing it under pressure."

"Why?"

His eyes turn deadly serious. "Because I expect a lot from my artists. My program is in top demand, and I want to see if you have talent I can work with. With that said, consider yourself special."

Hunter inclines his head to my canvas and even I suck in a breath when I notice the horizon before me. I've returned to my Impressionist roots. Peace drifts into my soul. When I began painting again after the incident with my mother, I developed an abstract style, and I thought I lost my original love.

It's nowhere near done. There are so many colors and shadows and problems to be fixed, but a part of me warms at the sight. It's the sunset and field that belonged to me and Noah. It's the eve of the night that we made love.

"You've got talent," Hunter says.

A smile bursts onto my face. He said it. Hunter Gray said that I have talent. Wow. Just wow.

"But there's a problem. A big one I'm not sure I can forgive."

My entire being plummets to the point that I'm convinced I've been incinerated, and my ashes have been thrown to the ground. "I just started. I know it needs work."

He owns the same hard expression my dad wears when he's disappointed in me. I shrink from Hunter, reminding me of how I always shrank from my father.

"I asked for the Aires constellation. Not a sunset. Are you capable of doing what you're told or are you only capable of painting one picture? Lots of artists can do that—paint or draw one solid image over and over again. I want more."

"I have tons of paintings and drawings I can show you."

He silences me with his hand, and I consider ripping it off. "I want the Aires constellation. That was our agreement. Are you doing it or not?"

My foot taps the floor. This summer I've craved to hear that I possess talent, to know that I have a shot at a career with my art and I've reached the goal. Hunter said that I have talent. While part of me considers telling him where to shove his silencing hand gestures, another part of me desires his approval. What forces my foot to move faster is that I don't understand why.

"What do I get out of it?" I ask. It's a bold question for me, and my palms grow cold and clammy.

Hunter snorts, but when I say nothing, he actually smirks. "You're serious."

Nervous adrenaline courses through me, and I have to

swallow to keep air flowing through my windpipe. Noah has told me how Isaiah hustles people for favors or car parts and that the most important rule in making any deal is to have expectations on the table up front.

I've never hustled before, but I never thought I'd be the girl who made love to Noah Hutchins. There's a first time for everything. "If I showed here with my paintings and drawings, I would have hoped that you'd offer to show something of mine in your gallery."

A pause for his reaction. "Why can't that be the same agreement here? You paint me Aires and if I like it, I'll hang it in my gallery."

"I'll paint you Aires, but it won't be finished before I go home. I'll have to finish it in Kentucky then send it to you. Look at my paintings now, and if you like what you see, hang one of them in the meantime."

"When do you leave?"

"In a few days."

Hunter assesses the canvas before him. "If you paint this fast, you'll be close enough to done before you go."

I'm shaking my head before he finishes. "I can't paint Aires that fast."

"You can."

"But I won't."

He doesn't blink and neither do I.

"I've got plenty of people hoping for a shot and none of them are demanding a thing from me. Why should I do this for you?"

This will either work or I'm nailing my coffin shut. "You're the one that said I was special, not me."

Hunter laughs so loudly that people look up from their canvases. "Bring in your five best paintings and drawings tomorrow, but I want the Aires constellation on the next canvas. Got it?"

I clap like a small child at the circus. "Yes. You won't regret it. I'll get as much done as I can before I leave."

Someone calls Hunter's name, and he walks away, ending our conversation. My phone vibrates in my back pocket and the cup of joy inside me overflows with Noah's text: On my way.

Me: I'll be waiting.

NOAH

Echo keeps the canvas angled toward her, and she swivels it from side to side as I fish the key card out of my wallet. She's had a silly smile on her face the entire ride back from the gallery and while I'm not fond of Hunter, I miss seeing that type of light in her eyes.

"Are you going to let me see it?" I ask.

"Once we're inside."

The door clicks, releasing the lock, and when I push it open, the voice of an announcer mentioning a two-one count carries out of the room and into the hall. Echo wrinkles her nose, possibly having forgotten about our guests. "Or not."

"You want me to put it back in the car?"

"It needs to dry. I should have left it at the gallery, but I was too excited for you to see it."

And neither Echo nor I were eager for me to visit the gallery so she brought it to me. I hold the door open for her and Echo heads in.

"S'up, Echo," Isaiah calls. His heavy combat boots hang off the side of the bed. When I come into view, he tips his chin at me. "Noah."

"Hi, Isaiah! Hey, Beth."

Beth lies on the bed next to Isaiah in the opposite direction. In her tank top and with her black hair falling over one shoulder, Beth is sprawled on her stomach with her feet bent in the air and her chin resting on her folded hands. She's completely absorbed in the game. When Beth says nothing in return, Echo tries again. "Who's winning?"

"I don't have a fucking clue nor do I fucking care."

Echo's head ticks back.

"Back off, Beth." I cross the room, drop a kiss on the curve of Echo's neck and whisper in her ear, "She'd rip me to pieces, too, right now. She's a bitch when the Yankees play."

Her eyebrows rise. "Is she a Red Sox fan?"

Isaiah chuckles and we both throw him a glare, but he doesn't notice as he's absorbed in a car manual.

"Beth hates baseball."

Echo's eyes dart from Beth to the television to me then she waves her hand in the air for an explanation.

"She watches," I explain. "Yankees only. It's what she does and there are some things we don't question about each other."

"Just the Yankees?" Echo whispers.

"Just the Yankees," I repeat.

"And she hates baseball?"

"With a passion."

"That's..." Echo says in a hushed tone. "That's messed up."

"We're all fucked up in this room, princess," says Beth. "Get used to it."

"Did you fall into some paint, Echo?" Isaiah asks, changing the subject.

Echo's shoulder slumps as she pivots toward the mirror. She groans as she touches her cheek and forehead that are more red and pink than skin. "Dang it. Why am I such a mess?"

"I think it's sexy as hell," I say.

"I think I'm going to barf," Beth mocks my tone.

Death radiates from the look I send her way. Enough that it should melt her. "Ever sleep in a tent, Beth?"

Beth focuses on the screen while raising her middle finger in my direction.

"Screw it." Echo turns away from the mirror. "I need a shower."

I smile, Echo blushes, then I laugh. Damn me for inviting Isaiah and Beth to share our room.

"Anyhow." An excited glint strikes Echo's eyes. "Are you ready? I hope you like it. It's sort of...for you. But it's not done, okay? I mean, something like this would actually take a while to perfect, so I guess I'm saying—"

"Echo."

"Yeah?"

"It's all good."

"Okay." Her fingers drum nervously over the top of the canvas before she repeats, "Okay."

"I'm assuming that's not the constellation Aires?"

"No. I'll have to start on that tomorrow." With a deep inhale, Echo pulls out a chair from the table and rests the painting on the arms and leans it against the back so it will stay upright.

Air rushes out of my body, and I sink onto our bed. It's the same damned shock as when she drew my parents this past spring. There's awe and joy and this ache that hits deep in my gut. I bend forward and rest my joint hands on my knees and stare at the sight in front of me.

Fuck me, my eyes burn. I shut them, attempting to get

my shit together. It's a painting. Only a painting. I reopen them, and it's the same disorientation as a right hook to the head. It's more than a painting, and that's the reason my throat swells.

Last night meant as much to me as it did to her and she painted it, capturing it in a way unique to Echo. She's right, it's not done. It's a skeleton compared to her other work, but I see enough to know what she desires, what she plans to design. Up close all those colors would look like chaos, but when viewed as a whole it creates this beautiful picture. In the end, that's the best way to describe me and Echo, our relationship. Our love.

The bed dips as Echo eases onto it, settles behind me and props her chin on my shoulder. Her signature scent that reminds me of walking into a bakery becomes an invisible blanket surrounding me. "What do you think?"

"It's us," I whisper, and knots form in my stomach. Echo always finds a way to blow my mind. She tenses behind me and I continue, "It's where we spent last night."

"It is." Echo relaxes, and her fingers curl around my biceps. "Do you like it?"

Struggling for composure, I place my hand over hers and pause. "It's..."

I'm not Echo. I don't have words for what happens inside me. If I did, I'd fail at describing this. I shift to rest my forehead against hers. "I don't deserve you."

"That's my statement," she says so only I can hear. "I wish we were alone again."

I press my lips to hers, slide my hand through her hair and watch as the curls bounce back into place. "Me, too."

If we were alone, I'd take it slow, worshipping every inch of her body. I'd work like hell for it to be her night—

the night she enjoys the actual act of making love. And if it didn't happen tonight, then I'd dedicate every night to that single pursuit.

Echo edges closer, and our lips move slowly as we both try to fight the build. There's other people in the room. Other people.

Isaiah clears his throat. "Let's take a walk, Beth."

"Walks are overrated." Odds are the Yankees are winning, and Beth's oblivious to the world, meaning she's in the dark about the heat radiating from Echo and me.

Echo's hand drifts from my arm, applies pressure to my chest and places a few inches between us. She lets out a long gush of air. I understand her frustration. My body is wound tight.

"I'm going to take a shower." Echo slips off the bed. After she's done, I'll probably take a long, cold one.

Echo gathers her actual pj's, not her tank and underwear, and I glance at the clock. It's late, and if Echo painted that much she didn't eat lunch or dinner. I may not be able to spend the rest of the night bringing to life my fantasies, but I can do the small things that cause her to smile.

I grab her keys off the dresser. "Chicken sandwich or Chinese?"

"I'll make a ham sandwich."

"Nonnegotiable. You choose or I will."

Echo kisses my cheek, and the caress burns past my skin and into my blood. "Chinese."

She disappears behind the bathroom door, and my eyes catch Echo's laptop. There's a reason why I dragged Echo to Vail and it's time I man up and face my mother's past.

Echo

There's something intimate about emerging from the bathroom fresh from a shower and in the clothes I intend to sleep in for the night so I can crawl into bed with someone. With Noah, I've actually reveled in that moment of entering the room. Especially when I've worn way less than this. His already deep brown eyes will darken, and a shadow of lust will cross his face.

After my scars, I thought no one would want or love me again. Noah's proved me wrong.

With that being said, I brushed my hair five times in my attempt to build the courage to walk out the bathroom door. With Beth and Isaiah waiting on the other side, I find myself as nervous as the first night Noah and I spent alone.

Taking a deep breath, I leave, and the cooler air of the bedroom rushes my skin. Goose bumps form, and I rub my arms. Isaiah and Beth sit on the bed and munch on a shared container of pepper steak.

"Stop bogarting the rice." Isaiah moves some of the pile from Beth's side of the container, and she darts her fork as if to stab him, but he quickly snatches his hand back.

"You got the egg roll," exclaims Beth. "I get the rice. That's how stuff works between us, so stop messing with the system."

"You ate half the egg roll, so I get half the rice."

I roll my eyes and ignore them. The scent of sweet-and-sour chicken drifts in the air and the Styrofoam container sits on the table with a plastic fork and bottled water, but Noah is missing.

"He dropped off the food then left with your laptop," says Isaiah, reading my mind. Which means Noah's in the business center.

"Thanks." I glance down at my outfit: a T-shirt that slightly shows my midriff and gray drawstring pants. It's not glamorous, but it'll do for the hotel hallways. I grab my dinner and set out to find Noah.

NOAH

With Echo's food left for her in the hotel room, I drop into the chair in the business center and watch as her laptop springs to life. Anxiety snakes within me, and I think of Echo and her tapping foot. At least she has a way to release the pressure.

Echo's Skype account appears with that annoying whooping sound, and as I minimize that window her email pops up. I notice a few unread messages: one from her dad, one from Lila, another from Mrs. Collins. I log Echo out and sign myself in, holding my breath as the account I hardly use loads.

I click on the lone new email from Keesha, and I briefly cover my eyes at the first sentence

Noah,
Yes, your mother's family has contacted me, and they would like to meet with you, but...

There's always a *but*. I skim through the rest of the email, most of it legal shit that'll protect her ass if I sue or they sue, but at the end of the message is a Vail address.

Even though she closes with *if you ever need anything, please feel free to contact me* bullshit, there's an unsaid "you're on your own." A slow pulse throbs in my brain, and I massage my temples to ward off a headache. This situation is no good.

I'm a few miles from my only living blood relatives, and a part of me feels compelled to meet them. Another part of me feels the compulsion to leave a hundred miles between us. Then yet another jacked-up part wants to charge their door and ask them what the fuck they did to my mother that she would bolt from them and never mention a word to me of their existence.

Echo's computer beeps, and a direct message conversation box through Skype appears in the right-hand corner.

L. Collins: I'll make an assumption that yesterday was a computer glitch. I'm up if you'd like to chat.

She thinks Echo's on. I kick my legs out and lean back in my seat. The lady is a damn nutcase, but my mind ticks back to the hundreds of times she cornered me. In the end, she helped shed light on things that I didn't know how to tackle.

Another beep.

L. Collins: Echo?

I switch windows and push the button that says call. A computerized melody plays for two seconds, and I cross my arms over my chest as she accepts. With her blond hair pulled back in a ponytail and a Grateful Dead T-shirt, Mrs. Collins finishes hole-punching a stack of papers. "I was surprised to see you on so late. I would have thought you and Noah would be out."

"I hear you've been fucking with my girl."

My lips twitch with how fast Mrs. Collins's eyes snap up to see me coming through her screen. Without missing a beat, she masks her shock. "Language, Noah."

"I graduated."

"From high school, yes, but those rules that are put in place in school are meant to help you learn how to function out of it. So..." She rests her chin on her linked fingers. "This is a nice surprise. How has your summer gone?"

"I asked about Echo."

"You did, but if you remember correctly, I won't discuss Echo with you, but you're more than welcome to tell me how things are going with her." She practically bounces in her chair. "In fact, I'd love it. Dish all the details."

I snort. "I don't dish."

"Neither of you ever do. So what's up?"

Less than a minute and she's already digging. Six months ago, I would have stormed out of her office and slammed her door, but it's the familiar that puts me at ease. "Not much."

"In all seriousness, is Echo okay?" she asks.

I answer because Mrs. Collins cares more for Echo than her own parents do. "She's good."

Mrs. Collins kneads her red eyes. It's ten here so it's one there.

"Up a little late, aren't you?" I ask.

"I keep strange hours." She flashes a weak smile. "What's going on with you?"

"I'm eighteen now."

"Happy belated birthday, but that doesn't answer my question."

"The state dropped me from your program the day I walked across the stage. Can't afford your overpriced fees."

"Consider this a conversation between two people who know each other."

I toe the legs of the table. I contacted her. I'm the one that's forcing open this door. "My mom's family is looking for me."

Not an ounce of surprise, and I swear under my breath. "You already know."

She frowns as a yes.

"How?"

Her head moves to the side, and I answer for her. "Jacob."

Mrs. Collins still works with my younger brother on his night terrors. He harbors guilt because he's the one that lit the candle that started the fire that killed our parents. Because of this, she'd be privy to anything regarding him, including if my mother's parents requested to meet him.

"Why didn't you tell me?"

Mrs. Collins blows out a long stream of air then bends out of view. A zipper rasps, then paper crackles and she reappears on the screen. She holds a dollar in her hand. "You see this?"

"Yeah."

"You gave it to me."

I raise an eyebrow.

"You left it on my desk on the last day, remember?"

Barely. "That's because you bought me a Coke."

"No, the Coke was a gift, but you did give me this dollar because..."

She drifts off, and her eyes are begging me for something. I've got no clue as to what that something is so I repeat her last statement to see where that gets me. "I gave you the dollar."

Mrs. Collins nods like I gave her the correct answer for final Jeopardy. "Yes! You gave me a dollar because you knew that you would possibly be asking for…"

She circles her hand for me to finish. Aw, fuck me. I suck at charades. "Your help?"

"Yes! Exactly! So that means that you're asking me to be your therapist again?"

Got it. "I left payment for you so you can be my therapist again. So, yeah, I'm asking."

"I accept! Yes, Noah, your mother's family is trying to find you."

"And you couldn't tell me because you're Jacob's therapist, not mine."

"But I'm yours now, so we can talk."

"I'm in Vail, and I have their address."

Mrs. Collins slumps back in her chair like I announced I detonated a nuclear bomb in a day care. "Who told you about your mom's parents?"

"Carrie." I pause. "I got the address from Keesha."

"Have you visited them?"

"Not yet."

She picks up a pen and taps it against the table. "How does the idea of meeting your mother's family make you feel?"

"How much do you know about them?"

"Enough."

"More than me?"

"Probably."

Conversations with her have always been like playing an intense poker match, but usually she's on the fact-finding mission, not me. "Are you going to download what you know, or am I going to continue to waste my time?"

She halfheartedly grins. "If that's all you wanted to know, you could have asked Carrie or Joe or Keesha. All three of them know more than me. In fact, you have your mother's family's address in your hands. Who better to ask than the source?"

I readjust, and the chair squeaks beneath me.

"But you didn't do that. You called me. What's going on, Noah?"

There's a shifting inside me. Years of self-preservation fighting against the new trust formed with the head shrink. I scrub my face with my hands, hoping it will help win the war, but it's still hard as hell to open my mouth.

"My mom ran away from them. At least that's what Carrie and Joe said. And she never brought them up to me. In fact, she said they were dead, and she was an only child."

"So your mother lied to you."

"She didn't," I snap.

"She didn't?"

She did, and I feel fucking betrayed. A strangled sound leaves my throat, and I lean forward. I feel betrayed and angry and pissed. "My mother never lied to me."

Never lied and never downplayed. Not when one of our dogs died. Not when Grandma was diagnosed with stage-four cancer and then when Papa died of a broken heart six months after she passed. Never did my mother try to make a situation less than what it was.

Hurt is a part of life, Noah, she said to me when she held my hand at the hospital the last time I saw my grandmother. *I'm not doing you any favors by shielding you from it. Besides, it's always better to be honest.*

"Tell me about your mom," Mrs. Collins says when the silence must irritate her.

"She talked to me in Spanish." Even when it pissed me off. She was a Spanish professor, and she was determined that I'd be as fluent as she was. "And she laughed a lot."

My throat swells, and grief pulls at me. "She'd poke her head into my bedroom at night and tell me she loved me." When I was younger, I used to say it back. Then somewhere along the way, I stopped.

I could throttle the guy I was then. My mother was there, in my room, night after night, and I never said the words back. Fuck me.

What's worse, Mom told me she loved me before I left that night and told me to wake her when I got in. The opportunity was there. I could have opened my damned mouth and told her what I can't tell her now. But I didn't. Instead, I failed her. I failed her in the worst way possible.

I clear my throat and tug at the collar of my shirt as too much heat has built up around me. Fuck this. Just fuck this. "Do you know if it's true? Did Mom's family misunderstand? Did they think that Carrie and Joe were adopting me, too?"

Did they think I was being taken care of, or did they purposely leave me to rot in foster care? That coil forever ready to spring inside me twists one more time, and it's like I'm racing toward an explosion.

"Noah, why does it matter now?"

"It does."

"Why?"

I scoot to the edge of my chair and have to force myself not to fly out of it. "Because! What if they wanted me? What if someone fucking wanted me, and the system screwed it up?"

The door to the business center clicks open, and Echo hesitates when she spots me, then Mrs. Collins, on the screen. Faster than a jackrabbit, Echo spins to leave, and I swivel the chair to catch her. "Don't go."

The relief of seeing Echo makes me feel like a man teetering on the edge of hell only to be brought back to life. With the dinner I bought her in her hands, Echo's eyes flicker between me and her computer screen. "I can come back."

"Echo," Mrs. Collins says, and my girl's shoulders roll forward like she got caught shoplifting.

"Yes?"

"We still have a Skype appointment next week, correct?"

"Yep."

"Good. Do you mind giving me and Noah a few more minutes alone?"

The urge is to tell Mrs. Collins to fuck off. Instead, I nod, and Echo caresses my biceps in support before she leaves. When the door is shut, I turn back to Mrs. Collins. "You know I'm done, right?"

She points a finger at me. "Just a little more time."

"One minute."

"It's okay to be mad at your mom."

She's wrong. "I'm not mad at her."

I can't be. That would be unforgiveable. Besides, if anyone had the right to be mad, it'd be Mom. She should be fucking pissed at me.

"We'll discuss this next time."

"There won't be a next time."

"Yes, there will." She waves away my statement. "You paid me in advance. My departing thoughts are a word of caution."

That gains my undivided attention.

"I understand your need to connect with surviving blood relatives, but before you do, I think it would be wise for you to understand why you're reaching out to people your mother never mentioned. Maybe consider the options as to why your mom didn't tell you about her family. Maybe think of what your expectations are before you reach out to them."

"I don't expect anything from them."

"I have a feeling you do, but don't realize it."

"Is what Carrie and Joe said true? Are they awful human beings?"

"I don't know the answer to that. I only know what Carrie and Joe have told me."

Every single conversation and fight I've had with Echo about her mom crashes into my mind. The irony of the next question isn't lost on me. "Is it possible they've changed?"

"People do change, but you know I don't have the ability to answer that question as it pertains to your mother's family."

"If they had known that I was in the system, do you think they would have taken me?"

A shadow spreads over her face—she knows more than she's telling.

"What?" I push.

"Keesha swears to me that your mother's family understood the situation. She admits that the state made a mistake when they initially didn't search for surviving blood relatives—"

I shake my head, cutting her off. "I told them everyone was dead. Why would they have looked? But when Carrie and Joe started filing for adoption two years ago, and they searched to confirm there weren't blood relatives, did Mom's family think I was also being adopted? Is it possible that the system screwed up?"

"Mistakes can be made," she admits. "But Keesha is good at her job. Even you know this. Noah...I've seen some of the paper trails between Carrie and Joe and your mother's family. I don't see how there could have been a mistake."

Talking to Mrs. Collins was supposed to help, not mess me up more. "Then why are they reaching out to me now? Why would they lie?"

"I don't know, and because of that, please be careful. Please keep me involved in this."

I somewhat tip my head. Not really an agreement. Not really a dismissal.

"Answer me one more thing," she presses. "If you do, I think it will help you understand what you're looking for."

I toss my hands in the air in a why-the-hell-not.

"Give me the first thing you'd want from your mother if she were here."

My eyes flash to Mrs. Collins, and my insides wither and die.

"Tell me," she coaxes.

My stomach acids churn. "Redemption."

Mrs. Collins blinks. "Redemption?"

"Redemption." And this session is done. "I've gotta go."

"This conversation isn't over."

Yeah, it is. I end the call and slouch back in the seat and run my hand over my hair. Echo asked me for simple and damn if my life doesn't keep getting complicated.

Closing the computer and swiping it up, I shove away from the desk and poke my head into the hallway. Looking sexy as hell with her damp hair and wearing a pair of drawstring pants plus a shirt that fits snugly across her breasts, Echo leans against the wall across from me.

"You okay?" she asks.

"Yeah. Are you?"

"Yeah," she parrots. "Do you want to talk about it?"

No. "Do you want to tell me why Mrs. Collins is stalking you from yesterday?"

"Not particularly." Echo holds up the Styrofoam container. "Dinner?"

"Let's go."

Echo

Because the streetlamps illuminate the hotel parking lot like noon at the equator, the stars aren't visible, and I'm perfectly fine with avoiding the constellations tonight. Noah and I sit on the hood of my Honda Civic and share the sweet-and-sour chicken. Noah would have grabbed food at work, but I picked Chinese because that's one of his favorites to eat...mine, too. It's the simple things that we have in common that create warm fuzzies.

The container rests on our joint knees, and I like the closeness of the meal. We've been quiet, but this type of familiar quiet is a gift. We're synchronized, and I love it.

Noah likes to combine the pineapple with his chicken so I push the last pineapple chunk in his direction. I pop another bite of chicken into my mouth then twist the fork to him.

"You better watch it." Noah hands me the rest of the egg roll while taking the fork. Like I predicted, he goes for his preferred combo. "You'll get my cooties."

I choke on the egg roll, and Noah pats my back as I cough down my dinner. He cracks open the water and offers it to me. The cool liquid helps, and I hand it back to him when I can properly breathe. "Did you say *cooties*?"

Noah chuckles. "Yeah."

"*Cooties* seems like too tame of a word for you."

He winks and scoops another forkful. "I like to keep you guessing."

"Well, it's too late. I already have your cooties."

Noah finishes chewing and peers at me. "There's a party tomorrow night. We should go."

I study the egg roll like it can read my fortune. Let's see: drunk guys, me with scars on my arms and a high Beth. Sounds like a freaking fantastic time. Why didn't I think of it earlier? "I don't know. Where's it going to be?"

"Around. Someone from work is throwing it. We should go. It's been a while since we've let loose."

"Let loose?" I repeat. "Did you block out how drunk you were the night of the beaver with headphones?"

"I got drunk to block out the beaver with headphones. Not to have a good time."

Noah rarely asks for anything, and he's probably itching to do something fun since Isaiah's in town. "You, Beth and Isaiah should go. I'll stay in." I wiggle my bare toes and fake a smile. "My feet are in desperate need of a home pedi, and that's sort of weird to do with a boyfriend around."

Noah scratches the spot above his eyebrow. "I want you to go."

"Why?"

"Because it'll be fun, and I want you there."

I shrug, feeling a little peer-pressured and not appreciating it. "I'm not a big party fan."

"One of the first times we talked was at a party, and you were drunk."

I grin at the memory of me spilling my private thoughts to the great Noah Hutchins on the back patio of Michael Blair's house. "That proves my point. Lila blackmailed me into that party, and I was drunk out of self-preservation with a little desperation thrown in for good measure. It was either the party or having dinner with my father and Ashley. I chose the party."

"You drank at the party at my foster parents' house."

What is this, the Spanish Inquisition for underage drinking? Losing my appetite, I toss the rest of the egg roll into the container. "One beer and it took me three hours to finish it. I spent most of the time drawing, talking to Antonio, then making out with you in the basement. In case you noticed, I'm not stopping you from going. I'm encouraging you."

"That's not the point." Noah stabs his fork into the chicken, slides off the car then throws the container into a nearby garbage can. "I want to spend time with you at a party. Don't you want to spend time with me?"

"Sure. I love it when drunk guys make fun of my scars, and then you get pissed off and punch them in the jaw. Which will be great because Isaiah will be here, and if you hit someone and that someone hits you back, Isaiah's going to kill them. Yeah, that sounds like a fabulous time. I don't know why we don't do it every single stinking night. Before we go, can you tell me how much bail is in Colorado, because otherwise I'll have to call my father to wire the money to get the two of you out of prison."

Noah throws his arms out. "Is that how you see me, Echo? Most likely to spend time in prison?"

"No! I don't, but I do know that you lose your temper when someone hurts me, and what's frustrating is that I don't even know why we're fighting, so do you mind telling me what your problem is?"

Noah places his hands on his hips and lowers his head. "Nothing. Just forget it."

Yeah, because I can force amnesia. "If it means that much to you, I'll go."

He glances up at me from behind the hair covering his eyes. "You'll go?"

"Yeah." Though I don't understand why the heck this is so important to him. "I'll go."

Noah collapses back on the hood of the car and, honest to God, looks relieved. "Thank you. It's crazy, but I want you there with me."

"I like being with you." And boys think girls are confusing. "I didn't mean to upset you."

"You didn't. Come here." Noah widens his stance, and I cozy up next to him between his legs and settle my head on his chest. We stand like that for a while, and I lose myself in the soothing and addictive beat of his heart.

Noah pulls at my curls, and a tingle reaches my toes. "Do you believe your mom's going to change? Is that why you think about letting her into your life?"

The chicken in my stomach begins to crawl back up, and Noah's fingers creep onto the nape of my neck and start a slow massage.

"I don't know," I answer. "I guess. She could be a good mom. Like I told Mrs. Collins, she was never the cooking or baking type, but she was awesome at doing fun stuff with me. Mom used to let me play dress-up with her clothes and makeup. As I got older, she used to talk to me about art."

"Is that what you miss? Having someone who understands your art?"

I replay being in that room full of people who love art

so much that they forgot their own canvases to watch me work. As much as it freaked me out, it was insanely cool.

"Maybe. I...my mom..." How do I explain it? "She's my mom. See...Mom being selfish...always making everything about her...that wasn't the bipolar. That was just her. I get that now more than I got it before. Meeting her at the cemetery, hearing what she had to say, knowing that she was finally taking care of herself and she still couldn't say she was sorry..."

The words catch in my throat, and breathing becomes difficult.

There's this need inside me, this desperation to say out loud that one frantic and dark truth that no one knows. The one thing I internally beg for day and night. "I want to forgive her, but how can I forgive her when she can't admit that she's sorry?"

Noah's massage increases when my muscles tense. I wait for him to get mad because I'm considering cutting my mom slack, but the rebuttal segment of the conversation never solidifies.

"Why do you want to forgive her?" he asks in a soothing tone, and a part of me is a bit startled that he's not angry.

Why do I want to forgive Mom? "Dad loves me, but he has Ashley and Alexander. Aires...is gone." My voice breaks, so I let any thought of him drift away with the cool breeze blowing across the parking lot. "Mom seems to be trying. It's messed up that she asked her friends to buy my paintings, but..."

My hand touches my throat in an attempt to ease the strangling sensation. "I'm tired of the blackness inside me—this goo that sludges in my veins. I'm tired of being angry. I'm tired of being heavy. Letting the past go, it's got to be easier, right?"

I peek up at him, wary of Noah's reaction.

"I'm the wrong person to ask," he says. "Me and the past aren't friends."

My forehead wrinkles, and a burst of worry overtakes me. What demons did Mrs. Collins dredge up?

"I've tried to let go of the past," I tell him. "But it's like running laps and being shocked I finish where I started."

A car rips into the parking lot, and the beams of the headlights flash over us as they turn toward the main entrance of the hotel.

"If your mom said she was sorry, you'd forgive her," Noah says as a statement.

As the prospect of actually forgiving her sinks in, I snuggle closer to Noah. The newly found memories of my mother lying beside me while blood flowed from the cuts on my arms torture my mind. Noah tightens his hold as if he could squeeze out the nightmares.

"I think I want to forgive her," I answer. "But I'm scared to."

"Why?"

"Because she's selfish. Mom has always done what she wants, never thinking about anyone else. It's like after I saw her in the cemetery, my entire view of the life we shared together got distorted. If I forgive her, doesn't that imply I'll have a relationship with her again? And if that happens, does that mean I have to trust her again? Does that mean I have to put up with her selfish crap because she said she was sorry? But if I don't forgive her, will I always be bitter? I'm exhausted of being bitter."

I'm sick of feeling alone.

I've got Noah, but will we work? Are we a forever type of thing?

An invisible vise clenches around my heart, and I can't comprehend anything associated with Noah leaving. He drew me plans for a house—our house. We made love. This is forever now. Noah would have never made love to me if we weren't a forever thing, but there's this doubt. This lingering doubt that Mrs. Collins said I'm not facing.

My mom is blood family, and family is that segment of my life that's supposed to stick with me. If that's the logic I should follow, shouldn't I be wavering toward having more family in my life rather than less?

If I'm going to continue to be so starkly honest, raw to the point that the truth rubs like sandpaper against my soul, then I'll admit the last fear. "Is having bad family better than having no family?"

Noah dips his head so that his cheek is against mine, practically shielding me from the world with his entire body.

"I don't know, Echo," he whispers. "I don't know."

NOAH

Through the rim of light outlining the drapes of the hotel's window, I can decipher Isaiah as he rolls to a sitting position and places his feet on the floor. Like he does most mornings, he pops his neck to the side—a release of the pressure that builds inside him day after day.

Echo flips in her sleep, and I shift along with her. For the first time on our trip, she took sleeping pills, and she slept like the dead. The stillness of her body throughout the night would jerk me awake. Each time a wave of horror thundered through me, thinking that she had left.

Is having bad family better than having no family? Echo's question has circled my mind. I asked about her mom in an attempt to understand my mom's family, but I only upset Echo.

I'm a goddamned selfish bastard.

Swamped in guilt, I press the balls of my hands onto my forehead. Echo said her mom was selfish, but I'm just as bad. I never once thought about Echo sleeping in a room with two other people and the fear she must possess over having a night terror in front of them. Echo hates relying on the pills, and I drove her to them.

Just fuck me.

The dim light from the clock radio shines against Isaiah's double row of earrings, and he jacks his thumb in the direction of the bathroom. We've been living together in cramped quarters for over a year and have memorized each other's rhythms. "You want the shower?"

"It's yours," I mumble. "I'm going to grab Echo some coffee. You want anything?"

Beth launches a pillow at me, and I catch it in midair before it can hit Echo. "For you two to shut up and go back to bed."

"We're good," Isaiah answers, ignoring Beth. Like a predator in the jungle, he moves across the hotel room, not making a sound. My best friend can be easygoing on the outside, but he's damn lethal if pushed.

Light seeps from under the closed door of the bathroom, and Isaiah starts the shower.

I throw the pillow back at Beth and smile when it smacks her head. "One day, Noah, I'm going to kick your ass."

"Bring it, Beth," I mutter, knowing she can hear the tease in my voice.

I glance down, startled to find Echo staring up at me. Her hands are tucked under her cheek and from the soft glow of light, I detect an unfamiliar glaze in her eyes.

"Go back to sleep." I caress her cheek, hoping she'll shut her eyes with the downward motion. "You don't have anywhere to be."

Echo's eyes drift closed but then snap back open. This is why she doesn't like the pills. She said it's hard for her to wake up and stay awake. "Don't leave me here alone."

I chuckle then lean down to brush my lips to hers. Echo responds, but not with the fierceness I'm used to. Her kiss is soft and groggy, and she's damn sexy as she wraps her body once again around mine to settle into another round of sleep.

A part of me goes hard as steel while other parts soften. It's been over twenty-four hours since I loved Echo properly, and my body is begging to do it again. Under the covers, I stroke my hand along her spine and continue until my palm curves around her ass. The waiting to be physical again is creating a friction between us that's close to becoming electric.

"You are so bad," she whispers, more asleep than awake.

"I'm just getting started, baby."

"I'm gagging over here," says Beth.

"I hear showers help," Echo says to me, with a soft laugh that plays over my skin. "Cold ones."

Damn, I'm being ganged up on. "Beth and Isaiah are only with us for a few more days, Echo, and then you're mine."

That siren smile I love so much briefly graces her lips, but then her eyes twitch beneath her closed lids, her breathing becomes rhythmic and her forehead relaxes. She's fallen into a dream. Not a nightmare. A normal, every night dream.

Grateful, I say a prayer to the God that had forsaken me years ago and kiss the top of Echo's head. Normal isn't something Echo and I take for granted.

When I'm sure she's out again, I untangle myself, throw on a shirt and shoes and grab her car keys. Isaiah opens the door to the bathroom, and steam pours out. He sports a pair of jeans and no shirt.

"Wear some clothes around my girl."

Isaiah digs through his duffel bag. "Why? She already

knows I'm the better-looking one. Echo chose you because you've got that smooth mouth."

Jackass. "I'm heading. Watch over her, all right?"

"S'all good."

I open the door and look over Echo's sleeping form.
Is having bad family better than having no family? Guess it's
time to figure it out.

Echo

I woke to an empty bed and to Beth and Isaiah playing travel chess.

Chess.

At first I thought I was dreaming, and that the Mad Hatter was going to magically appear and whisk me away to Wonderland while we chased large white bunnies, but then Beth called Isaiah an asshole for the move he made, and I knew I was awake.

I dressed leisurely, hoping Noah would return. I called him once. Sent a text. It was weird enough that Noah left without saying something to me and weirder to have to wait for a response with an audience. When there was no reply, I headed to the art gallery.

There's a low hum in the attic studio, and it reminds me of art class in high school, including the girls whispering as they peer at me.

With my cell resting on the easel in case Noah checks in, I sit on a stool and study the blank canvas. Painting or drawing something has never been an issue before, but the oomph needed to paint the Aires constellation escapes me. Not one inkling of where to start or what shades I'd like to use. Not. One. Thought.

Oh, dear God in heaven, I'm experiencing writer's block.

As if they can hear my internal screaming, the two girls who can't be much older than me once again whisper to one another then gawk.

My fingers form into a fist. Really? Just really? "Is there a problem?"

Some of the "low hum" in the room dies off as I channel my inner Beth. Guess I am affected by who I hang with. Who would have thought those guidance counselors had it right?

They both stare at anyone other than me, and one starts to pick at the strands of her paintbrush. Strand girl, the one with hair so black it looks blue, plucks at the brush as if she's sifting out the split ends. "We...uh... we're wondering...um..."

My right hand slips over the scars of my left arm. I freaking hate my life at times. "How I got my scars?"

Her eyes widen. "No. God, no. We were wondering if you were going to go into that trance again. It was amazing to watch you paint and...well...we liked watching."

"Oh." Oh. My cheeks burn. At least I just didn't make a fool of myself. My gaze falls to the blank canvas. "I'm blocked."

"That happens to me a lot," says the girl with brown hair. She closes the gap between us and extends her hand. A thick mark runs vertically up her forearm. "I'm Meredith."

Two years ago, I wouldn't have been able to stop myself from gaping at the scar on her arm and conjuring up the story of how it got there. But now I welcome the bright blue eyes that are full of life. "I'm Echo."

Meredith and her friend Brigit asked me to lunch and I have to admit, I haven't been this excited over a meal in a long time. Who asks me out to lunch? No one. No one asks me to share food with them, and these two girls did.

My happy moment consists of peanut butter sand-wiches from the coffee shop while lounging on a park bench across from Hunter's gallery, but I swear this is the best meal of my life.

"I heard that you're here with your boyfriend," says Meredith.

Even though I'm giddy, I'm still super-nervous that I'll say the wrong thing and screw this up. "Yeah. His name is Noah."

"FYI," says Brigit. "Hunter isn't fond of boyfriends. He says that guys our age are unsupportive."

I pause midbite. "Noah's supportive."

"According to Hunter," Meredith adds, "boys our age *pretend* to be supportive. Anyhow, I'm thinking that I'm past the unsupportive boy stage. I turned twenty-one last month."

Twenty-one. Even though it's not that far, it feels far away from eighteen. "How long have you been studying under Hunter?"

Meredith and Brigit share a glance, then Meredith clears her throat. "I've been trying to get into some sort of program with Hunter since I was eighteen, but this is the first time I've been accepted for anything. It was only for the summer program, but I just learned that I've been accepted into the year-long program starting in the fall."

She's grinning from ear to ear, and I can't help but smile with her. I like Meredith. For the past hour she's been kind and gentle, and she hasn't once stared at my scars.

The happiness fades from her face, and she begins to

shred her sandwich. "I gave up a lot coming to Colorado. My parents don't understand my obsession with art. They informed me that if I quit college to come out here, then I wasn't welcome back home. When Hunter told me last week that I got the year program..."

Meredith sort of chokes then puts a hand to her mouth. "It was a happy day, but when I told my parents that I was dropping out of school..." She smiles genuinely at me even though tears glitter in her eyes. "It was a happy day regardless. How many of us get to follow our dreams?"

That's a good question. Not many of us do.

NOAH

A couple of months ago I sat on a park bench and watched from a distance as my brothers played so I could spy on their home life. It appears my stalking days aren't over, except this time I can't hide at some fancy park. I have no idea who I'm searching for, and odds are I wouldn't know my answer if it smacked me in the face.

But across the street from the empty church parking lot where I parked Echo's car is a house that can't hold more than a bedroom and a bathroom. The gutter hangs off the house, and one of the two windows in the front is X'd over with gray tape. The once concrete stairs have crumbled into a pile of rock, and an old plastic milk crate serves as the new and improved step. A front yard of three-foot grass is a barricade warding off whatever moron would want to approach the door. This place screams halfway house for the criminally insane.

A sickness slowly devours me. The longer I stare, the more my thoughts distort. If my mom grew up here, I understand why she ran and why she ran far.

Regardless of that, the question remains, is bad family better than no family? I belonged once, and I won't bullshit that I don't miss the feeling.

A couple walks past on the sidewalk, and I pretend to

fiddle with the radio to convince them I'm doing anything other than stalking.

Two taps on the window, and my stomach drops. I glance out and a fucking priest in the whole black outfit and white collar waves at me to roll down my window. For a brief moment, I consider talking in Spanish, but my luck, the asshole could also speak it.

I turn the ignition one notch to power the windows and roll them down. "Yeah?"

"Can I help you?" He's middle-aged nosy, brown hair with a few gray strands in the sideburns, with a master's degree in condescending looks.

"No."

"You've been here awhile."

"I have." One of the first rules I learned in foster care is I don't owe anyone an explanation at any time. I save that shit for the people-pleasers.

"Are you broke down?"

"No."

He assesses the car, searching for the mobile meth lab a punk like me with Kentucky plates should have. "Are you lost?"

Hell, yeah, I am. "I'm good."

"I stepped outside and saw you here earlier and just noticed you're still here now." He cranes his head toward the massive church. It's old-school basilica-style. We took a family vacation once, road-tripping those big bastards. "I work there."

"No shit."

The priest actually smiles then rubs his nose with his thumb. "Why are you interested in the Perrys?"

Hearing him say my mother's maiden name so casually is like having my nuts ripped open. "Don't know what you're talking about."

"The Perrys aren't here."

I power the engine to fight asking where they are or when they'll be back. "Let me guess, you're the neighborhood block watch. Even pick up the mail while everyone's gone and take out the trash."

"No. I happen to notice when my parents are gone. They're visiting friends on the other side of the state."

My head snaps in his direction, and he taps the roof of the car again. "It's time you move along."

I rev the engine and throw the car into reverse, but this deep need keeps me from hitting the gas. He steps back to allow me room to leave.

"When you're done with the attitude," he says, "and ready to talk, you know where my office is."

"What makes you think we have anything to say to each other?"

He smiles, and my heart stops. Jesus Christ, that's my mom's smile. "Kentucky plates, an email sent against my advice and my sister's eyes. We have plenty to discuss."

My mouth drops open, and he's not done. "And Noah, don't try to approach my parents on your own. There's a reason why Sarah ran and why I followed in her footsteps. Talk to me before you cross that bridge."

The priest...my uncle...walks away. I rake my hands through my hair and glance down, wondering where the fuck the blood is because I just got shot.

Echo

My canvas reminds me of my brain back when I repressed the memories of the night of the incident with my mom: color around the edges and a blank hole in the middle. I've got mere days to impress Hunter, and a blank canvas will not help my plight.

When I try to imagine painting the stars that comprise Aires, I freeze up, but the sky surrounding it, I can do.

"So you are human." Hunter walks up beside me, and I can't help but smile at his words. "I was worried I had an art-superwoman on my hands, and that the government would come and perform tests on you."

"I'm very human." Using my wrist, I wipe my hair from my forehead, but sigh when I lower it and spot dark blue streaking against my skin. I wave my hand. "Very, very human."

Hunter doesn't laugh at me; instead, he dips his head to the side as he looks at what I've done so far. "It's more of a blue-black than a black sky. Why?"

I busy myself by cleaning my brushes. "Just feels blue to me." Like a bruise. A big, fat, swelling bruise that's so raw and painful that it's close to black, but it's still smack-a-baseball-bat-on-the-baby-toe blue.

"I like it. It has a soulful aura." His eyes dart around the canvas. "You continue to surprise me."

At his feet, like if he moved a fraction of an inch he'd kick it, is the sample of my paintings and drawings he asked to see. My foot taps the floor. I don't want to be all... *please, please, please look at my paintings and love them.* I'd rather he remember and me be all...*oh, I totally forgot that you agreed to see a sample of my work. Silly me. I'm so happy to be in this moment that I forgot.*

His attention strays from me when someone says his name, which means my fantasy isn't going to happen so it's time to step outside of my shell again and be forceful. "I brought the samples of my work."

That drew back Hunter's focus. "Let's see it."

I grab my bag and that would be when Noah's ringtone sings from my cell. Part of me relaxes with relief. Another part arches my back like a cat about to attack a dog twice its size. He left this morning without a word, and has been AWOL for hours. Hours. And the moment Hunter shows interest in my work, Noah finally calls.

Hunter glances at the phone, and of course, Noah's face and name blare from the screen. "Should you answer so that he doesn't assume I've forced you drink the Kool-Aid?"

Ah, talk about seriously awkward and uncomfortable to the point I wish I would disappear. The ringtone enters supersonic. I did promise Noah I'd answer, and he did promise to go ape insane if I didn't while I was with Hunter, but in theory that was for the first day. Besides, Noah doesn't know that I'm here since he left.

"No, Noah's cool with everything." I'm willing Noah to be cool. "So what do you want to see first, the paintings or the drawings?"

The phone thankfully stops ringing.

"Paintings."

"Echo," says Meredith. "Do you want to grab some coffee?"

I blink, repeatedly, like I lied, but I'm not having the reaction over me. She has to be lying. Besides Lila, a failed few dates with an ex and then Noah, I can't think of the last person who asked to go anywhere or do anything with me in public in years, and now she's done it twice.

Asking me out twice...I've made a friend. I open my mouth to scream yes, but Hunter shifts beside me.

I point at Hunter, who's moved past patient and has opened my portfolio. Don't freak—just because he's currently appraising my work, and my entire art career is on the line, is no reason to panic. Oh, the emotion spectrum. Pure joy to utter fear. "Can I have a rain check?"

Meredith's cheeks pale as her gaze falls to Hunter then jumps back to me. She mouths, "Sorry," realizing what she wandered into.

Portfolio viewing. It's like waiting to hear the verdict in a death sentence trial.

"Rain check," she whispers, and her friend Brigit snatches Meredith's arm and pulls her across the attic. Both of them give me a thumbs-up before they disappear down the stairs.

Wow. Freaking wow.

In slow motion, I pivot toward Hunter and flinch when I notice him assessing me and not my work. Crap. I missed his expression. The important one. Not the words—the obligatory "It's good." The facial one. The one Hunter spotted in me when I first saw his painting. Eyes never lie.

"You fit in here, Echo."

The smile that I didn't even know was on my face fades. A weird heaviness rolls into me like a fog. It's not a bad sensation, but the type I experience when Noah rests an arm around my shoulder when we're walking down the street, or when he places a hand on the small of my back when he guides me through a crowded room. It's like a large cape drawn around me, making me feel safe and wanted. Making me feel included.

I stagger back. My legs hit the stool, and I lower myself down onto it. Scanning the room, I see people from every walk of life. All of them different, all of them their own unique palette of paint.

What's amazing is that I belong.

Me.

Echo Emerson.

The girl who didn't belong anywhere. The girl nobody wanted.

A wetness burns my eyes, and I have to quickly rub them to hide my emotional meltdown, but my hands tremble.

I belong—scars and all.

"Does that mean you like my work?"

"You have a lot to learn."

My eyes flash to his as my stomach tightens into a ball. This has to be the cruelest joke. To tell me I belong then rip the hope out from underneath me.

"But you have raw talent that I could never teach. So yes, I like your work."

Flutters in my chest, flying high in the sky. I have talent. I'm going to succeed on my own. I'm off the stool and hugging Hunter. The moment his hands touch my back and press me closer, I jerk. But even with that, Hunter runs his hand along my spine.

No one should ever hold me this close. No one should touch me like this. Not someone who isn't Noah.

"I'm sorry." I push away, wondering if I've given a wrong sign. "I shouldn't have—"

"Echo?" The question in Noah's voice slashes like a knife to my heart.

My hair hits my face as I turn to him. "Hunter likes my work."

Noah's brown eyes flicker between me and Hunter. "That's good." But he doesn't say it like he's happy. He says it like I hurt him.

I suck in air and hope Noah will understand. "Hunter just saw my paintings, my drawings, and he likes them and I got excited."

Please hear what I'm saying. He sees my potential. He sees my talent. All of it without my mother's influence. For the first time in my life, I'm standing on my own.

The room's gone quiet, and Noah notices how everyone watches us. He shakes his hair over his eyes, and he hauntingly reminds me of the boy I first met months ago. Not the boy who shares his soul with me, but the one that made fun of my name. The one who, when I refused to give him back his leather jacket in public, said horrible things and made me cry.

Two nights ago, Noah held me in his arms and loved me like no one has ever loved me. Right now the man to my right has the possibility of making my dreams come true. Why does it seem that any way I choose, I'm going to break someone's heart?

Mine or Noah's or both.

NOAH

From behind Echo, the bastard smiles and, fuck me, Echo's pleading with me to let this go. But she doesn't see what I see. She didn't notice that asshole's face when she wrapped her arms around him. Like she handed him a gift, and he was hell-bent on opening it as fast as he could. My fingers curl as he mockingly raises his eyebrows. The bastard acts like he's calling my bluff.

It's no bluff, you damned snake. It's no bluff at all.

Echo shuffles her feet as if she can't decide who she should be more concerned over. "Noah?"

I release a stream of air through my mouth, attempting to rein in my temper. Losing it here, it's what he wants. It's Echo's nightmare. "I was stopping by to see if you needed anything."

And to fill you in on my mom's family. Then the conversation will detour to how I walked in to see her tackling another guy—a guy I already have issues with.

"I..." She glances behind her, and the bastard's smile vanishes before she can spot it. "Well, Hunter was looking at my work, and we were talking about how he liked it and—"

"It's all right, Echo," says Hunter in a sugar-sweet way that causes me to want to punch his face. "Since you aren't officially a part of The Attic, we haven't discussed how there are boundaries between your professional life and your personal life. And even if we did have the conversation, you didn't ask your boyfriend to rush in and cause a scene."

My spine straightens, and I cross my arms over my chest. A scene? I'll throw him through the fucking window, then we can discuss a scene.

"Maybe you and your boyfriend should take this outside?" Hunter says to her. "And after you clean up what's going on here, we can discuss whether you can focus on a career in art."

Echo's cheeks flare red, and she drops her gaze. I briefly close my eyes. She's embarrassed—over me.

Hunter leaves and heads down the stairs. Motion around us, a shifting of feet on the loft flooring, and Echo hugs herself as if the action could make her small enough to disappear. "Let's go."

She avoids eye contact as she passes me and doesn't permit her arm to graze mine. Nor does she look back to see if I follow.

Pain pricks my chest. The worst type of letting go isn't the kicking or the screaming, because at least then there's enough emotion left to fight. No, the worst type is the silent acceptance. The quietness of the release. That's when the person realizes they no longer give a damn.

Echo

Unable to walk past Hunter's office, I exit at the bottom of the stairs. The large metal door clicks shut behind me, and the warm Colorado sun kisses the bare skin of my arms. The loading dock reflects me, inside and out: not much to look at and empty.

Two girls accepted me, one of the best artists in North America likes my work and whether he meant to or not, my boyfriend embarrassed me.

Crap.

Just crap.

Behind me the door squeaks open. It's Noah. I can sense him, taste him. Like he's been absorbed into my pores. Like he's embedded into my being.

The urge is to run to him, to embrace him, to have his arms shelter me like they have so many times this summer, but this constant push and pull will never end if I do.

Footsteps against the loading dock and the sound of material rustling. Noah's shoving his hands into the pockets of his jeans. I've seen him do it a million times, and I can picture him clearly in my mind: his jeans riding low against his hips, his body cocked to one side, his biceps straining as he tries to look relaxed, when on the inside he's anything but.

"You once hugged me like that," Noah says.

Moisture fills my eyes, and I blink it back. There's no accusation in his voice. No anger. Just hurt.

"I brought Isaiah to work on your brother's car to impress you. You were dating that ape Luke again, and each time I saw you with him, it got under my skin. When Isaiah told you that he could get it running and you hugged me..." Noah trails off, and I close my eyes, permitting the sweet memory of that day in the garage to caress my skin.

"I didn't understand it at the time, but I loved you then. I fell for you the moment you called me out in the guidance counselor's office, and I've been yours since."

I love you. Words that Noah doesn't throw around. I turn, and Noah's exactly how I imagined—strong and handsome as ever.

"Now that's an apology," I whisper.

His lips tug up then fall back down. "I'm learning."

"I wasn't hugging him like I hugged you. Today was stupid. An impulse. That day in the garage, Noah...you meant something to me then, too. Hunter's giving me a chance with my art. That's all. I mean, he's ten years older than me. He's not even interested in me that way."

Evidently not in agreement, Noah straightens his arms as if he's creating fists in the pockets of his jeans. "Is he going to buy your work? Hang it in his gallery?"

"I don't know. That's when you interrupted."

Noah stares at the ground, and I hate the tension building in our silence. Please, please, please let us be okay.

"Jacob's last game is next weekend, and he wanted me to come. We could leave tonight, swing through Texas on our way home. Last week, you mentioned a gallery in Dallas then another one someplace in Oklahoma. We could visit those and not be rushed for orientation."

My mouth pops open as I try to sort and categorize. Going home and his brothers and galleries in Texas and... "You said you wanted to go to a party tonight."

"It's a party. We can skip it."

What the heck? "You made a federal case about it. You *wanted* to go. You're the one that *wanted* to be here in Vail."

Noah rubs the back of his head. "You *wanted* to start home a few days ago. You *wanted* to visit those other galleries. I'm telling you we can do it."

"I don't understand. Hunter was seconds away from making my dreams come true, and now you want to go home?" It's like the earth has vanished beneath my feet and I'm falling, forever falling. "Besides, we came here for you. What about finding your mother's family?"

Noah pales out, and I flinch as if punched. I've never seen him like this before. Not even when he told me that he gave up custody of his brothers. "Noah? What's wrong?"

His forehead wrinkles, and he kicks at the concrete. "Are you happy here?"

My arms drop to my sides as I hunt for something to grasp. The world is shifting and not in a good way. It's the dizzying kind. The distorting kind. I don't like the heaviness in his words. "What are you asking?"

I search Noah's eyes. There's a stark honesty and an ache radiating from them. His hurt literally rips my heart wide open.

"I'm asking if you're happy here. I'm asking..." Noah clears his throat, and he tears his gaze away. "There's a lot of people here so I'm guessing this is some sort of school, and I'm saying I want you to be happy."

My pulse pounds at every pressure point, and Noah

has to sense it. Even though Noah hasn't moved, it's like he's fading...into the shadows...into the darkness...to realms that I fear. "Where is this coming from? Why did you leave so early today? Why didn't you answer when I called? Explain to me what's going on, because you're scaring me."

"I discovered some info on my mom's family," Noah answers.

His words hang in the air, and I'm terrified to breathe. "And?"

"Just God fucking with me again." His shoulders slump forward.

I internally kick myself. Noah walked in and caught me hugging Hunter—a man he doesn't trust—while Noah was bleeding.

I touch the top of Noah's shoulder, and the connection jolts both of us. He withdraws. A prick of rejection begs me to lash out, but I ignore the emotion. I risk a second attempt, and this time Noah stays still when I glide a hand along his arm and step into the shelter of his body.

Come on, Noah. I'm trying here. A part of me melts when Noah finally loops a loose arm around me. Can't complain. It's contact. I rest my head on his shoulder, and he leans his body into mine. He's not really holding me. It's more like I'm keeping him upright, and I'm okay being his rock. Whatever happened today had to cut him deep.

Understanding that there are some pains that are too hard to verbalize when they're fresh, I offer the out...for now. "Later, then?"

"Later." A pause. "Forget what I said about leaving. We'll go when you're ready. Stay the whole week."

"Give me a few days, okay? Let me see what I can do

on this Aires painting, then we'll go. We'll skip Texas, and you can be home in time to watch Jacob play. I swear."

Noah gently kisses my forehead. "Okay."

But it doesn't feel okay. Noah's hurt, and I don't know how to ease his suffering. "Do you have to work today?"

"Yeah. A few hours this afternoon."

"When you're done you should round up Beth and Isaiah, and then we'll go to the party." Maybe that'll help.

Noah twirls a curl around his finger and yanks. "How about I send Isaiah and Beth and we spend time alone in the room."

"You have a one-track mind, Noah Hutchins."

I had hoped for his patented wicked smile that promises trouble, but I only receive a slight tilt of his mouth. "When it comes to you, I do. Go back to work, baby. I'll see you in a couple hours."

Noah walks away, and I have the same hollow devastation in my stomach as when I watched Aires leave all those years ago.

NOAH

My need to attend the party tonight was about me listening to Mia and trying to prove that Echo and I are solid. After this morning with the priest and after that moment with Echo, a beer isn't a bad idea. Hell, three may not do the job.

Like Mia said, Echo's finding where she belongs, and it's not with me. My problem—I don't know how the hell to be man enough to let her go. Loving her like I do, I don't know how I can keep her.

I pull Echo's keys out of my front pocket and swear under my breath when I reach the street. The damn bastard's standing in front of his gallery. I spin on my heels. I'll walk the entire perimeter of this small town twice before I pass him. Echo wants her shot, and I want her happy.

"Noah," he calls, and I freeze on the sidewalk. The right thing to do would be to ignore him. There's nothing good to be said between us. "It's Noah, right?"

With my thumbs hitched in my pocket so I won't knock his ass out, I face him. "What do you want?"

"Echo."

I step closer and damn if he doesn't flinch. "Last I checked she makes her own decisions, and she's chosen to be with me."

"For now," he states. Echo said he's ten years older, and he has that belated frat-boy look going on. I'm sure he's used to getting exactly what he desires. "I've seen this many times. Lots of girls come here fresh from high school or a year removed, still thinking that high school love is forever, but it isn't."

"Did you know her older brother was younger than you?"

He laughs, but it doesn't touch his eyes. "I'm interested in her talent. That's another issue with high school boys. They think the reason anything happens is because of sex. Someday you'll discover there's more in life, but for now stop jeopardizing Echo's chance at a career."

There we're on the same page. "You leave me alone, I'll leave you alone. In fact, I'll stay thirty feet away from this place if it'll make her life easier."

Asshole shakes his head like I'm a damn toddler caught in the finger paints in preschool. "I see how she looks at you. How she reacts around you. Echo will follow you before she follows her dreams. Don't ruin this."

My head falls back, and I attempt to remain calm. "I want Echo happy."

"If you mean that, keep walking and don't look back. I've lost brilliant artists before because they're stuck on a fling that fizzles before it starts. Chances like the one I'm about to offer her happen once in a lifetime."

My world stops then collides into itself. The opportunity he's about to offer her...

"Look me in the eye and tell me that you're interested in her talent."

He accepts the challenge and goes for full-fledged eye contact. "She's possibly one of the most talented young women I've come across. She's green, is sloppy in some areas, but her work has soul."

It's there, the truth. He believes in Echo and possesses the answers to her dream.

"Now tell me you aren't interested in getting into her pants."

"She fits here. Seamlessly. Have you seen that happen anywhere else?"

He's struck blood, and it's hard to mask the wound. "I didn't ask you that. I asked if in that fucked-up head of yours, you've undressed my girl."

The dickhead avoids looking at me and angles his body in the direction of his gallery. I've got my answer. "Don't screw with Echo unless you're interested in her art."

"I am interested in her art. If you care for her, you'll let her stay where she belongs. This is her world. Ask yourself if she honestly belongs in yours."

In the world I live in now, Echo doesn't belong. I know it, he knows it, and it's a matter of time before Echo figures it out.

With the keys digging into my hand, I force one foot in front of the other. I promised Echo simple; I promised her we'd never change; I promised to take care of the gift she gave to me, and I've got no fucking clue how to keep any of those promises.

I sit on a stool and tap the paint brush repeatedly against my face. I'll regret it later, but somehow it helps me think. It encourages me to see beyond the canvas and beyond what's in the front of my mind. Somehow I go deeper and sneak past locked doors, delve into secrets and play in the blackness. The colors, the lines, the shades—it's all there in the darkness, but there's a wall preventing me from placing the brush to canvas.

"That's not enough room for nine stars." Hunter eases beside me and draws me out of my haze.

Standing with a stretch, I scan the room. Except for another girl packing up her things, the attic has emptied out. "Does everyone keep bankers' hours?"

"They have keys," he says. "They enter through the back and come and go as they please. You should know that inspiration can't be dictated by a schedule."

So true.

"You didn't answer about the room and the number of stars."

I didn't. "I have all the room I need."

His eyes narrow into slits. "Are you creating a smaller scale of the constellation? Is the entire focal point going to be the blank sky surrounding it?"

"No," I answer, then raise an eyebrow as I consider it. I

like the idea. Having something small in the middle and the main focus being the nothing surrounding it, but it's too late to do that with this painting and he knows it, hence why he's being a jerk. The entire space on the outside is wrong for such an idea.

"Then there's not enough room for nine stars."

For the love of God. I slam my paint brush down with a snap that vibrates across the room. "And that would be where you made your original mistake when you painted Aires."

Oh, crap. Hunter turns a strange shade of purple when he's angry. "You said I forgot a star and I had eight."

"Yes, you forgot a star and yes, you had eight," I rush out. Desperate, my head whips around like a cartoon character's. Not locating what I need, I dip my finger into the blue and drop three dots onto my arm. "Technically, Aires can have more than four stars, but the root of it is four. Only four."

I gesture to the blank stretch of skin between the dots. "And you just didn't forget one star. You forgot the biggest and brightest. You forgot the important one."

He forgot Hamal, but an aching tug on my heart prevents me from speaking the name.

Hunter rests his fingers over his closed mouth and stares at my arm like it's Michelangelo's David. My heart beats hard twice. I painted on my arm—I forgot about my scars, and I'm drawing attention to them...

"That's why you didn't think I purposely left out the star," Hunter says as if paint on extremely scarred arms is normal. "Why you said if I had meant for it to be missing I would have somehow let that missing piece be known."

I wince. *Freak of nature!* "I promise this whole speaking-out thing is unusual for me."

"I hope it's not," he says. "It's what I like about you. You've got fire, Echo. Don't apologize for it."

I've got fire. My lips lift a little. "Noah's the one that's lit it."

"Fire is there or it's not. If anything, he probably showed you where to look. Don't give him any more credit than that." He cuts off any response by directing me to the canvas. "Tell me, are you painting four or three?"

It's like he poured a bucket of water over my blaze. "I don't know."

"You've got plenty of time to figure it out. I'm not asking you to finish it in days."

"I only have days," I mutter, though I guess I could finish it from home, but the only reason I'm doing this is to impress him. I'd rather have the people of Munchkinland toss me into a tornado than do this painting for kicks.

"That's where you're wrong."

I dare to peek at him from the corner of my eye. Hunter picks up the stool and places it next to me. A nonverbal for me to sit, and I do. He remains standing, and my knees bounce.

"The other people in this program have spent months of their lives filling out applications and gathering portfolios for the opportunity I'm presenting to you."

I check over my shoulder, and there's no one there. Oh, heck, he's talking to me.

"Study under me for the next year, Echo. We're on a break, which is why it's so disorganized at the moment, but in two weeks, I start teaching classes again."

My pulse thuds in my ears. "I have a scholarship to college."

"You'll have a scholarship here. Most of my students do, but it's a barter system. You'll work in the coffee shop and the gallery twenty hours a week in exchange for studying under me. Most of the students find apartments together. If you still need extra money, I'll pay you for anything you work over the twenty hours."

My eyes dart in front of me, but I'm not finding what I'm looking for. Hunter Gray just asked me to study under him. The room shakes, though it's more my hands than the floor. The best artist in the country believes in my work enough that he invited me to study under him.

"On top of that," he continues. "If you can get this painting in decent shape before next week, I want to show it at the Denver Art Festival under my work-in-progress section along with those ten sketches of hands you've done."

I snap out of my stupor. "That was in my sketchbook." *And I haven't shown you that.*

He points to the floor where I had left my sketchbook for anyone to peruse. How would he respond if he knew those are Noah's hands? Drawn while he slept beside me. Drawn after he had caressed me so tenderly in the night.

"What do you say, Echo?"

What do I say? "Yes."

A huge smile brightens his face. "Good."

Hunter pulls out a key from his back pocket and lays it on the easel. "This is yours. Come and go as you please. I'm assuming you'll need to return home and collect some stuff, but I expect you back here by the start of session in two weeks."

Go home...then return here... Noah...my stomach plummets. "I mean, no. I mean...I mean..." This would mean being separated from Noah. "I mean I can't..."

"You're saying no?"

"No," I rush out. "I mean, I don't know." I rake my hand through my hair, pulling at the roots. What's wrong with me? "I need time to think."

"What's there to think about? You're going to college for art, right? Is their program better than studying underneath me?"

"No," I admit weakly. "But..." But Noah won't be here. There's no doubt he'll go home. The state's paying for his education. His entire world—his brothers are back there. There's no way he'd cut off ties and leave his home to be with me.

"But what?"

"My father..." I whisper. But my father is moving. Moving forward, moving out, moving on. Our relationship works better via phone than it ever did in person. "I...told him I would try business classes as well as art because I was good at it...the business stuff as well as the art."

"Business?"

My neck cracks to the side. I'm so exhausted having to explain this. "It's not just my father's idea, I believe it's a good move, too—"

"It's a brilliant move."

That stalls all train of thought. "Excuse me?"

Hunter grabs a stool and sits across from me, and this rattles me more than him standing over me like a kid called into the principal's office. It's like he values me as an equal.

"This is where most artists run into problems—the

making money part. We can paint anything we want, anytime we want, but it changes when we attempt to make money. Art is art and will always be art, but I also like eating. You, Echo—" he leans forward and his leg brushes mine "—are a genius for thinking ahead."

Mouth completely open. "What?"

"When does college orientation start?"

"Two weeks."

"Where are you studying?"

"The University of Louisville."

He blanches like he tasted sour wine. I know, I know. Not the Mecca of art, but they have a great program. He taps his finger to his face in a persistent pattern as he assesses me in this slow, agonizing way that makes me self-conscious. I'm clothed, right?

His hand lands on my knee, and my body goes rigid under his touch. "I'm going to work on this, but in the meantime, you need to get the painting of Aires in decent shape for the showing."

Hunter hops off the stool and is across the room before I can process anything that happened. He touched me. He's offering me the world. He's changing the game. Forget that...he touched me.

"Wait!"

Hunter glances at me over his shoulder. "What?"

What? "Really? That's all you have to say. You offered me the chance of a lifetime, and I may or may not have accepted it, and you tell me you're going to work on something?"

"That sums it up."

Because I can't control it, I smash my foot to the floor like a toddler. "Am I studying under you now?"

"That's up to you, but what I'll work on is that business class angle."

I throw my hands out now, more confused.

"Only worry about that painting. We'll discuss the details of you studying under me later." Ending the conversation, Hunter waves his hand in the air as a goodbye then disappears down the stairs.

I release a long breath, and my palm scrubs the spot on my knee where his hand briefly made contact as if that will erase the sensation of someone other than Noah touching me. Going two years with hardly any physical contact leaves me uneasy when someone does offer such an intimate gesture. It's especially weird when it's from someone like Hunter.

My eyes fall to the key on the easel, and a flash of guilt hurts my soul. How do I explain this to Noah and even better, how can I explain it when I'm not sure which road I desire?

NOAH

Beth sunbathes on the concrete walk next to the entrance of the pool. She's soaking up the last remaining light of the evening in the two-piece Echo lent her. I sit on the curb and alternate between watching Isaiah tune up Echo's car and keeping an eye on Beth. She has a habit of attracting trouble.

"What's going on at home with her?" I ask Isaiah.

Isaiah pulls his head out from under the hood long enough to glance at Beth and switch tools. A sheen of sweat covers his forehead—the only hint that the day's been warm. "Trent's selling."

Trent: Beth's mom's sad excuse for a boyfriend. "He's always selling."

Isaiah shoots me a look that raises the hair on the back of my neck. "He hasn't sold this shit before."

Fuck. "Beth doesn't know?"

"If she did, she wouldn't be here." Isaiah yanks on something with the tool. "Do you ever feel like we're in a PlayStation war game, man? Like someone has set the clock, and the rest of the world's counting down the last seconds of this level yet we don't have a clue everything is about to go to hell?"

Right now and every damn day since my parents died. "Yeah."

Isaiah assesses Beth again. "I don't know how to save her. Not when she's so damned determined to redeem someone who doesn't want to be saved."

He's referring to Beth's constant need to protect her mother, but the dark irony of his statement nags at me. I should tell him that Beth doesn't want to be saved any more than her mother does, but it'd fall on deaf ears. Just as if he said the same words to her.

Possibly as if I said the same to Echo about her mom, or if Echo said the same to me about my mother's family. Each one of us is screwed in the head.

At the other end of the building, Echo rounds the corner with her gaze stuck to the ground and a canvas in her hands. She has that lost-in-her-own-world expression again, and my insides hollow out. That painting of Aires is going to kill her then me. I jump to my feet, causing Isaiah to snap to attention. "Trouble?"

Considering what Hunter said to me, possibly. "Echo's earlier than I thought she'd be. Will you give us a few minutes alone in the room?"

His lips turn up. "Sure."

I punch his shoulder as I pass. "I just need to talk with her."

"Some people are into that talking shit while they do it, man. I'm not here to judge."

I raise a single finger in the air as a response, and Isaiah chuckles. With a wide enough start, Echo's not in the hallway when I enter the hotel. I pull the key card out of my pocket and with a click, the colder air of the room rushes past me and into the hall.

Echo relaxes on the bed with her feet tucked underneath her, and she's focused on the newer canvas that now sits on the floor, propped against the chair. The edges of the canvas are a blue-black. It's foreign from anything I've seen her do before, especially the blank part in the middle.

Personally, I prefer the painting on the chair—the painting representing the night we made love. "S'up, baby."

"Hey." Echo sends me a smoldering smile, and I've got an instant hard-on. The door shuts, and I swear my dick moves with the sound.

"Are you ready to discuss what happened this morning?" she asks.

No. "It can wait."

"Are we alone?"

"Yeah." My body screams to stride over to her, wrap my arms around her waist, kiss her until she's drunk on me and slowly remove every article of clothing on her body. Because I love Echo, and she deserves respect, I hitch my thumbs in my pockets and cock a hip against the wall. "Homework?"

She squishes her lips to the side. "No. Yes. I don't know. If I get enough of it done in time, Hunter says he'll enter this and ten of my sketches in his work-in-progress wall at the Denver Art Festival."

This is where I bite back the crappy comment and prod for where she's at on this. Echo can give me shit all she wants about what I say and do, but in the end, I'm learning fast. "Denver—is it a good thing or a carnie sideshow?"

Echo giggles, and her laughter plays along my skin, easing some of the stress built from my conversation with Hunter. "Carnie sideshow?"

"Tilt-a-whirl, Guess Your Weight, cotton candy and

hot dog purging, Traumatized Goldfish Games. Carnie sideshow."

"It's not a carnie sideshow, but there'd be a ton less pressure on me if it was." She gets lost in the painting again.

I walk over, rest on the bed beside her and slide my fingers along the nape of her neck. "Jesus, Echo. You're cement blocks."

Echo waggles her eyebrows. "Are you going to rub the tension away?"

Any room I had before in my pants vanishes. She means the tension in her neck. In her neck alone. I cup both hands over her shoulders and begin to knead out the knots. I love how she dips her head forward, and her muscles melt under my touch.

A soft moan leaves her lips, and screw me, that sound vibrates to my toes. I clear my throat. "Denver's a good thing, then?"

Any ground I'd gained with her muscles I lost with the question, but I keep massaging her shoulders. It's not a sacrifice to have an excuse to touch her smooth skin.

"It's a good thing," she replies. "He wants to put up the sketches I did of your hands."

My fingers still. "My hands?"

"Uh...yeah... I...um..." Heat radiates from her neck, and red splotches develop. "Sometimes, after we made out and stuff, you'd fall asleep, and I'd sketch your hands because...well..." The blush spreads from her neck to her face. "I...uh...liked how you touched me so I wanted to draw your hands."

When Echo used to draw, I saw the picture on the paper. Being with her this summer, seeing her create, experiencing the same day together, I understand now that there's a meaning in what she chooses to draw. Echo wasn't drawing my hands, she was drawing us.

"You can draw my hands anytime you want." A surge of pride wells deep within me. Unable to contain it, I let the hands in question glide down her arms. I press my lips to the spot below her ear, and she leans back into me.

My hands sneak around her waist, and she links our fingers together. I pull her tight to me, and Echo admires the canvas again.

"When's the art show?" I ask.

"The end of next week."

Next week. Thursday or Friday. The time we need to leave so I can attend Jacob's last game. My teeth click together.

"If he puts my work in the show, I'd like to be there," she says quietly.

I'd miss my brother play ball. He asked me to come. I told him I'd try. "I don't know."

"I know." Echo slips away. "You don't have to decide now. He was sort of speaking gibberish by the end of the conversation, so I have no idea if it's going to happen."

Guilt eats at me over how casual she's behaving. This is important to her, but part of me is ready to head home. It's time for us to go back to our real life and figure us out there. It'll be easier when we go home. Much easier. That is if Echo wants to return home with me.

She releases my hand and turns to face me. "If my work is displayed in the show...what if I stay and you go home?"

My eyes flash to hers. "Leave without you?"

She shrugs and immediately casts her gaze down at her lap. "It's not like you enjoy the shows anyhow, and

I know you're ready to go home and see your brothers, and we'll be okay away from each other, right? Like we're okay if we don't see each other every day?"

"Are you asking for time away from me?"

"No! I'm saying there are things that are important to you, and there are things that are important to me, and we'll be okay together if we pursue them separately, right?"

It's happening. What Mia said, what Hunter said, all of my fears...Echo's moving forward...without me.

"Noah..." Her head falls back, and she stares at the ceiling like she's saying a silent prayer. "Hunter asked me to study with him here in Colorado...for the year... and I might want to do it, and I was wondering what you thought?"

I think someone slashed me open with a rusty blade, and I strive for numb. Why did I decide to feel again? I was good at numb. I survived well on numb.

Echo's eyes plead with me as she waits for an answer.

Stay with me.

Not here.

Not with him.

With me.

That's my answer. My fingers twitch with the need to grab her, shake her, tell her that she's killing me with this, but I don't. I made her a promise. A promise that I'd take care of what she had given to me.

"It shouldn't matter what I think. You've got to make this decision, and you've got to make it without worrying about me or your dad or your mom or even Hunter."

Her eyebrows pull together. "You still want me, right?

I mean...if I do this, we'll still be together? Because we have to work. I want us to work."

Long distance. Thousands of miles. Echo in an art studio where she belongs and me back flipping burgers. I drop my head, and my hands dig into my hair. "All I want is for you to be happy."

She sniffs, and her voice cracks, the sound pushing a knife through me. "What if I chose Colorado...do you think that...maybe you could...come with me?"

I'm bleeding out. "I just got my brothers back." And I have a shot at college. A chance at being something more...the more Echo deserves.

The door squeaks open. Laughing, Isaiah and Beth stumble in.

"Are you ready to go?" asks Beth.

I lift my head, and Echo stares at me. Tears pool in her eyes, and my heart is breaking. There's a thickness in my throat I try to ignore. I don't want to talk about this anymore. I don't want to think anymore.

"Yeah," I say to Beth. "Let's go."

Following the instructions on the GPS that Noah had programmed in before I told him Hunter's news, I take a right into a middle of nowhere driveway and sag with relief when I spot the lines of cars, the shadows of groups of people milling around and the bonfire in the back field. In the passenger seat beside me, Noah leans against the door. It's like he can't place enough space between us and if he had bricks, he would have already built a wall.

It's a lonely, pit-in-my-stomach sensation sitting next to someone I love and having him ignore that I exist. Hurting Noah—it cuts me deep. It somehow feels like he's asking me to choose between him and my dreams, and that causes near amputation.

I ease alongside a gray Jeep, and the moment I shift into Park, Noah's out of the car. It's like he sucked my heart from my chest, and he's dragging it on sharp rocks.

"Well, that was fun," announces Beth from the backseat. The overhead light casts dim shadows when she opens her door.

"Beth," says Isaiah.

A moment of silence.

"You wait for me."

An overly long sigh. "Yes, Dad."

"I mean it."

"I know you do." A slam of the door and Beth trails behind Noah, who's already been absorbed by the dark night.

"Let's at least get out of the car, Echo," Isaiah says.

I do and so does he. I slouch against the hood and wrap my arms around myself as if my insides will fall out if I don't. That's because they will. Everything twists out of position and tangles. I'm dying. I swear to God I'm dying.

Isaiah leaves a foot between us when he sinks beside me with his legs kicked out. "What crawled up Noah's ass and laid eggs?"

The burst of bitter laughter surprises me, but the burn in my eyes doesn't. "Hunter—the art guy I've been working with here?"

"The fucked-up stalker? Noah mentioned him."

Of course Noah informed his friends of his side of the story alone. "He's not a stalker. He's this awesome art guy who everyone admires, and he likes my paintings."

Isaiah tilts his head for the and-what-else part because it's not enough to redeem Hunter in his eyes. My hand slams to my chest. "My paintings. Mine. He sees my talent."

Nothing from Isaiah.

"Imagine you spend weeks on a car and the best car person in the world walks up to you and says, 'Isaiah, that's awesome. Come work at my shop, and you'll have the possibility to do this for life and make a lot of money doing it.'"

Isaiah pulls on the bottom hoop earring of his double row. "How much money?"

I toss my hands in the air. "Why do I try?"

"Chill. I get what you're saying. So this Hunter guy offered you a position?"

"He offered to let me study with him for the year... here in Colorado."

Isaiah scrubs both of his hands over his face, and the tiger tattooed on his arm ripples with the motion. "Noah sees you as his family, you know?"

"His brothers are his family. As are you and Beth. I'm just his girlfriend."

"That's bullshit, and you know it."

"Is it?" I ask, as anger, in the form of tiny daggers, floods my bloodstream. "Because if I was his family I highly doubt he'd be walking away from me like he just did. He'd want to talk to me, fight with me, tell me we'll figure it out or beg me to go home with him."

"Is that what you want?" Isaiah slowly studies me, and it's like how a panther must stalk an enemy from the bushes. I shiver with the gaze. "Him to decide for you?"

What pinches is my internal pause. "No." I want to decide...I think.

"Are you looking for Noah's approval?"

Yes. Even though I don't verbalize an answer, Isaiah shakes his head in disgust as if I had spoken. "You think Noah's going to leave you because you chase your dreams?"

At the very center of my being, the answer is a firm no, but there's this doubt, this lingering doubt... "I've been left before."

"He's not like that," Isaiah snaps.

"You thought he was when you found out he was searching for his mother's family."

A muscle ticks near Isaiah's eye. "I told you that was my shit. Not his and not yours."

I shrug. I should say I'm sorry for throwing it in his face, but I'm not because it's true.

"You've gotta admit," continues Isaiah, as though the last few sentences were never uttered, "what you threw at him is a lot to swallow."

He has a point.

"Give Noah space tonight. Let him blow off some steam, and I'm sure he'll get his shit straight. This relationship thing, it's new to him. Don't leave him behind because he's human."

In the distance people yell as if encouraging someone to do something. I nod in agreement with Isaiah's words, but it leaves an emptiness in my stomach. A car parks beside us, and we remain quiet as five people pile out of a four-door sedan.

One girl stops laughing the moment she notices Isaiah, and then she smiles again when she surveys me like I'm about to flirt with her boyfriend, and she knows I don't have a shot.

Isaiah stiffens. Crap, he senses a threat.

The group continues to the party and when they're far enough away I say, "What was that?"

"What?"

I gesture to the group. "That. She looked at us strange, and then you got all tight."

"Don't know what you're talking about."

He does, but he's not spilling. "You should go find Beth."

Isaiah hooks an arm around my neck, reminding me

a lot of how Aires used to treat me. "You're hanging with me and Beth tonight."

"You said I should give Noah space."

Isaiah leads me away from the crowd. "He knows some people from work. Besides, Noah's always found someone to hang with at parties. Me and you, we'll have a couple of beers and babysit Beth after she gets high. It'll be fun."

I snort. "Lots of fun."

"Two beers in, and you'll find a happy place. Besides, Noah will be shit-faced drunk in an hour and will be pathetic and will grovel on his knees because he was an ass."

A part of me aches because he won't. Another part of me wishes with all my soul that it happens.

NOAH

I raise the plastic cup to my mouth and glance at Echo from the corner of my eye. She cradles a matching red cup in her hands, and it's the same one she's nursed since she settled near the bonfire. If she's concerned about me, she sure as hell keeps it locked tight.

Occasionally, Isaiah makes her laugh. Beth causes her to drop her head, but she stays interested in that damn fire.

We've been here an hour, and I should be trashed. I should be numb, carried away by alcohol or the pot offered to me multiple times. Instead, nausea eats at my gut. No matter how many times I consider slinking back into my old life, my eyes drift to Echo, and I can't cross the line. She deserves better than me, but I guess she knows it.

She's going to leave me.

For a year.

Then forever.

Echo finally looks up and inches her gaze my way. Angling away from her, I return my attention to the group of people I work with at the Malt and Burger. Someone tells the punch line to their dirty joke, and I'm the only one who doesn't laugh. My insides shred into nothing.

Echo once said that it was easier to go back than to go forward. She's right. Anger is a hell of a lot better than pain.

"The redhead. That's your good girl, isn't it?" Mia slides up beside me like a snake in tall grass.

"She came."

"And she's not hanging out with you." Mia's eyes are glazed over, and she stumbles into me with a gust of wind. "I remembered your tattooed friend. I almost told her that we fucked each other's brains out last summer because I bet you didn't. Twenty dollars the truth would end this doomed relationship."

A rush of adrenaline and anger pushes into my veins. "What did you do, Mia?"

"Nothing, but I should have. My boy—" she points at Echo and I lower her hand to keep Echo from noticing, but Echo peers over the moment my hand touches hers "—did the same thing. After he became focused on school and started to get bored with me. I brought him to a party and he was all downer. At one point, the look on his face…"

Tears dot Mia's eyelashes, and her lower lip trembles. Damn. She's one of those emotional drunks. "He was *disgusted* with me."

I check on Echo again, and she pours the remains of her drink to the ground. Echo then stands and brushes the grass off her ass. She starts for the cars, and my heart stops. Beth jerks to life, and she calls Echo's name. Echo hesitates then crouches next to Beth. There's at least fifty high guys here and my girl doesn't need to be alone.

"Now you're interested in Echo?" Isaiah says beside me.

"Go away," slurs Mia. "That girl is no good for him. It's

ending between them, and neither one of them wants to admit it. But it's there. The last sign is there."

"What sign?" I stare at her like she possesses the most important answer in the world, and Isaiah glares at her like she's a threat.

"Remember me?" she says with a sly smile to Isaiah, ignoring my question.

"Private conversation going on between me and him," Isaiah replies.

Mia snort-laughs and points to the tree line. "I'll be over there having a good time being bad. Come find me, Noah, if you want the answer to that question."

Mia rams and shoulders her way through a group of people talking and disappears. I glance back at Echo, and she's still talking to Beth.

"She shouldn't be alone," I growl.

"No, she shouldn't. Your ass should be over there next to her doing that smooth wooing shit you're supposed to be so good at. And while we're on the topic of what you should and should not be doing, you sure as hell shouldn't be chatting it up with one of the girls you screwed last year."

Isaiah's shoulders circle back, and he lifts his chin. Damn if he's not willing to take a swing in Echo's honor.

"Does Echo know about Mia?" I ask.

"That's what you're concerned about? Whether or not she knows you're spending time with a past fuck?"

"Mia's hounding me, not the other way around. I'm asking because I don't want Echo hurt. She thinks every damned mistake I made is over a thousand miles away. For one short period of her life, Echo didn't have to walk down the street wondering if I hit the next girl she passed."

"Real noble, Noah, but she's bleeding without the past-mistake checklist. Get your ass over there and fix whatever the hell is going on."

"She's leaving me!"

"Leaving? She's been waiting for you to get your shit together."

I step into him. "That Hunter bastard is offering her the world! What do I got to give? Nothing. I've got nothing."

Isaiah slams his finger into my biceps. "She looks at you like you're the whole universe! I'd kill to have a sliver with Beth of what you have with Echo. Wake the fuck up!"

I pound my hand to my chest, mimicking the pain slicing it. "Echo's leaving me."

"No, man. You're the one leaving her," he seethes. "Get it together or she *will* walk."

Isaiah turns away, toward Beth, toward my girl. Echo lifts her head when Isaiah approaches. Her eyes wander past him and meet mine. The pain Isaiah referred to, it's there as a shadow on her face.

Three months ago, I held Echo in an ER and promised her that I'd never let her down. Two nights ago, I made that promise again. The question I never imagined her asking me is out on the table and the truth is, I don't know if I can choose living here for a year with Echo... giving up a scholarship to school...giving up a possible relationship with my brothers.

Fuck it...I do know the answer. I can't. If she chooses Colorado, I'll choose Kentucky, and then we'll both choose a long-distance relationship. That would be tough enough without this doubt weighing over me of whether Echo's moving past us as a couple.

I wouldn't put it past Echo to choose Kentucky to please me, and I can't allow that—especially if Mia is right. Echo and I could be on the downhill slide, fighting the inevitable. By dragging her up a slick mountain of mud, I could be costing Echo her career.

Running a hand through my hair, I break the connection with Echo and search for Mia.

Echo

Noah tears his gaze away from mine, and it's like he's torn my heart in two. I press my hand over my chest as if that could stop the pain. What's worse than the dizzying nausea shooting through me is that he's heading in the direction of the girl that he talked to, the one that he touched.

Disoriented and fighting a dry heave, I spin in the direction of the car. Isaiah moves in front of me. "Where are you going?"

"I don't want to be here anymore." My thoughts bounce as I try to think of a way to leave for the hotel without abandoning Isaiah, Beth and Noah. "I don't want to be here. I can't be here. I just...need to go."

A long walk can do me good, even though it will be dark and I'll be completely alone, but if I stand here any longer I'll lose my mind. I giggle, a bit of hysteria bubbling up. My mind broke once before, and Noah was the one who helped me put it back together. Funny how life changes.

I step, and Isaiah steps with me. "Let me get Noah, and we'll leave together."

One beer. I've had one beer, but I feel crazy and out of control. "He wants this party, and I want to go so I'll walk or call a cab or something, but Isaiah, I can't stay here."

I jerk my keys out of my pocket and dangle them. "Take this and let me go."

Because I'm a stupid moth drawn to destructive flames, I look over my shoulder, and Noah fades into the darkness.

I shiver. From the dread forming into a lead ball in my stomach, to how the way he walks reminds me way too much of Aires leaving me. The last time I watched Noah walk away like this, I ran after him, but this time...the ache inside me slashes further, creating a hole.

"He went after her," I snap. Like Mom chose her art, like Dad chose Ashley, like...

Isaiah forms a T with his hands. "It's not what you think."

"Then what is it?" I yell. He made love to me. Noah made love to me, and now he's chasing after some other girl.

Isaiah pops his neck to the side. "Promise me you'll stay right here. Keep an eye on Beth, I'll get him, and we'll go."

I cross my arms over my chest, but my nonverbal obviously isn't enough for him.

"Promise, Echo."

Fine... "I promise."

"Here. Wait right here." He points to the ground at my feet. "Don't make my life complicated."

When I say nothing else, Isaiah stalks off to search for Noah. The fine hair on my arms rises as if I'm on the verge of something horrible. *Please let Noah be the man I believe him to be, because I love him, and it would crush me if I'm wrong.*

Beth wanders over to me, and the last thing I need is

the Jiminy Cricket from hell yapping on my shoulder. "Not now."

"He loves you," she says.

My head whips to her. "What?"

"Noah. He loves you." In the firelight, I do my best to gauge her eyes, and they aren't bloodshot. She's not wavering and to be honest, I only saw her drink one and a half beers. She may be buzzing, but she's not drunk.

"I know," I say.

She shrugs. "Yeah, that was my best at acting girly."

I crouch to the ground and lower my face to my hands. If Beth's being nice to me, everything must be on the brink of explosion.

NOAH

I cross over the hill after Mia and pause when I notice a bunch of cars parked off to the side. A dirt road leads off into the distance. For the amount of people here, it makes sense there was a back way.

Mia holds out keys and lights flash on a Mercedes. A Mercedes. What the hell is Mia doing driving a Mercedes? She staggers to the right and rams her thigh into the hood of the car. She's blitzed, and the last thing she needs is to be behind the wheel.

"I thought you came here with other people." I clutch her door to prevent her from shutting it.

"Noah!" In the driver's seat, she glides her hand along the material of her chair. "Leather interior. For us, it'll be a brand-new experience."

"Not happening."

She shields her eyes as cars pull up from the back road and park. "When are you going to get it through your thick skull that you and that girl aren't going to work? And to answer your earlier question, I drove here myself then left with people to buuuuy—"

Mia pops open her glove compartment and produces a bag of pills "—this!"

"What's the last sign?" I demand.

Mia slides out of the car and closes the door with her

hip. Other car doors also shut, and an itch in my neck whispers at me to investigate my surroundings, to search for a threat, but I can't. Not when she knows something about me and Echo that can prevent this downward spiral.

She leans against the car, and she blatantly ogles my chest then lowers her eyes to my crotch. "Crawl with me into the backseat and I'll tell you."

"The sign. What was the last sign before it ended between you and your guy?"

She steps into me, and her clothes brush mine. The sweet scent of pot and the bitterness of alcohol waft off her. "Get high with me."

I snatch the bag from her hand. "Echo is my life. My life. I love her. If there's a chance I can make her happy...if I can save what's between us...I'll do it, so fucking tell me!"

A blaring light hits both me and Mia, and I throw up my arm as I try to spot who the hell is shining a flashlight in our eyes. "What do you got in your hands there, son?"

My stomach drops to my feet, and I swear under my breath. "It's not mine."

"Then whose is it?" With the light still on us, a guy walks toward us. His damn deputy badge glows against his dark uniform. Fuck me. Just fuck me. The plastic bag blazes hot in my hand, and there's not a damn thing I can say to make this situation disappear.

I stare at Mia, and she locks her gaze to the ground. Doesn't matter if I tell the truth. I'm the one caught holding. A pissed-off panic begins to pulse in my bloodstream. Echo can't see this. She can't know.

"Both of you, hands on your head," a bodiless voice says.

The world possesses a dreamlike quality as I move my

hands. I've been clean of drugs for months, and I'm getting arrested for possession.

With his eyes scorching a hole into my brain, the cop snatches the bag from me. He tosses it to the guy holding the flashlight. "Don't guess you have a prescription."

He's an inch smaller than me, and he's not built. My right foot angles for the tree line and damn if his eagle eyes don't catch it. His hand bolts for the gun strapped at his hip. "Don't do it."

This is a mistake. A goddamned mistake and I don't know how to rewind and redo.

Sweat breaks out along my forehead. I should have stayed with Echo. I should never have left her side. In fact, we should never have been at this party. Mia played me, and I fell for it. I'd give my left ball to be in that hotel room with Echo watching whatever boring movie for the rest of my life.

I've fucked it up. A burn roars in my throat. I've fucked it all up.

The cop assesses Mia. "You here to buy?"

My mind whirls like a tornado. With the amount of pills she had, I'm bordering on a felony, but add that up with an intent-to-sell charge, and I'm facing prison. "No."

Mia's frame trembles as her wide eyes take me in. "I'll take care of this, Noah. Stay silent, and I'll take care of this."

"Move to the hood." The cop jerks his chin for Mia to go. "Both of you, hands on the car."

"Fuck!" I say and slam both hands on the cold metal of the Mercedes. My heart pounds, and bile reaches up my throat. The cop pats me down, legs first, searching for weapons and whatever else he can find to put me in jail.

Echo. My brothers. The entire damned life I've attempted to create—all of it gone with one bad choice. By chasing the wrong person. I dip my head when the cop yanks out the lighter I carry to build the bonfires for Echo, and a strange ache in my eyes forces me to close them.

I'm losing her. I'm going to fucking lose her for good.

"What the hell is going on?" Isaiah's pissed-off voice causes the cop beside me to swing the spotlight into the darkness.

"Stop right there!" The other cop, a big son of a bitch, pops into view when another cruiser races up with headlights beaming.

In his full punked-out glory, Isaiah doesn't give a shit what anyone has to say as he keeps coming. The fingers on both cops' hands twitch, and the new guy darts out of the squad car. His hand drops to his gun.

"Stay back, Isaiah!" I shout. He halts and so does my breathing as I hunt the horizon for Echo. "Don't let her see me like this!"

The cop twists down on my wrist, rough enough that pain shoots up my arm. I don't fight him as he slaps on the handcuffs. Metal pinches and digs into my skin. This is nothing. I've heard about the courthouses. Once I'm there, they'll put me in shackles.

"Don't let her see me like this," I yell out again, and Isaiah nods once in silent agreement. "Take care of her."

"With my life." The promise isn't just words to Isaiah. It's sworn in blood.

Grabbing my biceps, the cop thrusts me forward, and we're heading for the backseat of the police cruiser. Across the field, there's more people with their hands bound. The shit I wandered into just got worse. This is a sting, a bust.

Fuck me.

A cop wanders over to Isaiah, and Isaiah holds out his arms. "I'm clean, man. Check all you want."

Hope Beth is, too. I mentally push at the cop to hurry. I want Isaiah out of here and back with Echo before she searches for him. Before she finds me.

"Noah?" Echo's uncertain voice calls from a distance.

Pain rocks through me like an aftershock of an earthquake, and I fling my body around. With Beth by her side, Echo stands at the top of the steep hill and stares down at me like she's living a bad dream. The disappointment, the pure agony slashing across her face—damn, it's annihilating.

"Let's go." The cop's rougher, sinking his fingers into my skin, as he shoves me.

"Noah!" Echo sprints down the hill, and Beth chases her—calling her name, telling her to stop. Beth finally snatches Echo's hand and whiplashes her to a stop.

"Noah!" The cracked rawness in Echo's voice almost sends me to my knees.

"Get her out!" I shout. Using his hand as pressure on my head, the cop forces me into the back of the cruiser.

Keeping her grip on Echo, Beth attempts to step in front of her, but Echo fights to break free. The misery of watching Echo come face-to-face with this reality kills me.

The cop closes the door, and I slam the back of my head on the seat. Fuck me. Fuck me for doing this to me. For doing this to Echo. I blink rapidly, trying to stall the wetness.

With damn tears cascading down Echo's face, Isaiah blocks her path. Both Isaiah and Echo gesture wildly, and the silence inside the car is deafening. Her lips frantically move, pleading with Isaiah as she points at me.

Finally ending the Shakespearean tragedy, Isaiah seizes Echo's waist and half presses, half carries her over the hill. I force my eyes away as Echo challenges him—kicking to bend him to her will, but he's doing what I asked. He's saving her from me.

A cop eases into the driver's seat and shakes my wallet in his hand. "Long way from home?"

Home.

Four years ago, I had two parents who loved me and two brothers who worshipped me.

Home.

For the past year, I've lived in a cement block basement with my two best friends.

Home.

I came to Vail searching for a connection, a place to belong.

Home.

Two nights ago, the girl I love gave me everything she had to offer. Not just her body, but her heart.

Home.

From the back of a police car, watching Isaiah drag Echo away—I've never been farther from home in my life.

Echo

Possession. Noah's been arrested for possession, and there was a mention of dealing, but the receptionist has remained vague.

The waiting area of the police station has a layer of dust and dirt and filth and is the size of a walk-in closet. Beth sits in a chair with her knees pulled up, and Isaiah watches me pace as he leans against a wall with his arms crossed over his chest.

"He wouldn't sell," I say. I barely meet Isaiah's intense gaze as I pivot on my toes to walk in the opposite direction of him again.

"You're right," he answers.

But the doubt devouring my internal organs causes me to complete my loop in front of the row of chairs faster. "I mean, he wouldn't, right?"

"If Noah was selling," says Beth, "then he sure as hell wouldn't be worried about money all the time, and he *sure* as hell wouldn't be flipping burgers."

Of course. *Of course.* I yank on a curl, causing pain at the root, ticked off that I lost faith.

"Narcotics aren't his thing, Echo." The finality in Isaiah's voice halts me midloop, and I turn to face him.

"He smoked pot." I don't know why I said it, but it's true, and the words taste bitter.

"Not tonight," Isaiah answers.

It's three in the morning. My mind wavers in this exhausted state. My vision blurs on the edges, and my muscles move like I'm wading through mud. But one clear thought causes my entire body to spasm: I'm dating a guy that could be arrested for owning drugs.

But Noah doesn't do drugs. He stopped last winter, and he hasn't used since, but I've never asked him if he quit because I assumed he quit. It all becomes confusing and overwhelming and...

"Those weren't his drugs." Isaiah breaks into my internal meltdown. "He's had a few beers, but I haven't seen Noah touch drugs in months. He's clean. You know it. I know it."

"I know," I whisper, but this dread weighs me down, and I visit that playground of insecurity I've been attempting to avoid. "Why was he with her?"

"Don't go there," Isaiah warns.

I open my mouth to respond, and Isaiah doesn't allow me the opportunity. "I mean it. He loves you. Period. So don't go there."

"I wasn't." I blink three times.

"You really would suck at poker." Isaiah chuckles and I halfway smile, but it's short-lived.

"What do we do?" I ask, because this is new to me, and there's this sinking sensation that informs me that some of this isn't new to Beth or Isaiah.

The two of them share a long look, and Beth inhales deeply. "We're going to need bail money."

I rub my eyes for so long that the sockets ache. Oh, my freaking God, bail money. "How much?"

"The charges they're talking about..." Isaiah kneads

the back of his neck, and I sort of wish I could shoot myself. "Best guess—couple thousand."

Feeling light-headed, like a balloon that has been untied and whose air is being let out, I drop into the seat beside Beth. "How much do you guys have, because I don't have that much."

Beth places a hand over my wrist, and the friendly gesture shocks me with a jolt of electricity. I stare at her, absolutely bewildered. Her blue eyes flood with sadness as she answers, "Isaiah and I would be lucky to pull fifty dollars between us."

It's like my soul split open. Noah's innocent of this. I close my eyes. He has to be. The man I love…the man I made love to…he wouldn't do this to me. He wouldn't purposely hurt me.

A slow, painful pulse begins in the center of my forehead, and I massage my temples, hoping it will force the hurt and this entire night to go away, but life is never that easy.

Noah's behind bars. A couple thousand dollars. Nausea rolls in my stomach.

I've got to get him out, and there's only one way I can do that. I stand and both Isaiah and Beth jump to be near me.

I wave them off. "This is something I have to do alone."

"What?" Isaiah asks.

I suck in a large gulp of air, but I still tremble with the idea. "I need to make a call. Just give me a few seconds alone, okay?"

Isaiah pops his head to the right as if saying he's not okay with it, but is granting permission anyway. "Stay by the door where I can see you."

I nod then step out into the night. Mist hangs and dances in the air, and I shiver. From the cold, from the situation, I don't know, but I try not to overanalyze. This isn't about me or how this call will murder the fragile relationship I've spent months developing. This is about Noah.

My cell has never felt so heavy or the buttons so hard to press. Even with the time difference, this will be a wake-up call. An unwanted one. One, to be honest, I had been told they'd be expecting.

For years I craved my father's approval. For years I sacrificed my happiness to receive it. Leaving Kentucky with Noah was one of my first real strides toward independence. Through the weeks I had been traveling, I felt my father relax his stance and side with me instead of against me, but this will cause him to be full of disapproval and anger.

I swallow when the phone rings once. Clear my throat when it rings a second time.

"Echo?" My father's voice is groggy with sleep and full of worry. "What's wrong?"

"I'm okay, but..." Deep breath before I fall off the ledge. "It's Noah. I need your help."

NOAH

With my head in my hands, I sit on a cold metal bench and count the two million ways I've fucked up not only in the past twenty-four hours, but over the past week, too.

I've been fingerprinted, photographed and processed. I had everything. Everything. Isaiah told me the path I needed to take and because I'm messed up in my damned brain, I ran in the opposite direction.

We made love. I had Echo in my arms and because I'm terrified of losing her, I've trashed everything between us.

"My dad is going to freak!" With blotched cheeks and tears streaming down his face, the guy standing beside me in the cell is seconds away from getting his ass kicked by the ticked-off mob sharing our breathing space. "What am I going to tell him?"

"Someone get him to shut the fuck up!" a guy with a Mohawk yells from the other side. Twenty of us share a large holding cell created for caging animals like me.

"Leave him alone." I win the stare-down contest with Mohawk guy in less than five seconds. I fucked it up with Echo and not a damn person here wants to mess with me—the stewing volcano.

"Thanks—" Blotched cheek guy starts, but I cut him off.

"Sit your ass down," I mumble.

"My dad—"

"Is going to be pissed if he comes here to claim you in a body bag. So shut it."

The guy's my age, honestly a few years older, but he's still got a plug-in for an umbilical cord. Most of the guys here were busted from the party. Who the hell knows if this kid was arrested for selling, holding or for stupidity, and I'll be damned if I ask.

He collapses to the bench next to me. "Dad will stop paying for college."

My head hits the back of the cinderblock wall with enough force that pain weaves through my brain like a spider's web. Fuck me—college. The only reason I'm able to go to school is because of the system. They had me sign papers that stated I understood that by receiving the money I'd stay out of trouble.

This is trouble.

What happens a thousand miles away will affect school...my future—my throat tightens—my brothers. Carrie and Joe kept me from them for two years because they thought I was bad news. This isn't think—this is know.

Pure anger races through my veins, and I bolt to my feet, searching for something to ram my fist into— someone to blame because the truth, that I've destroyed my life...I can't face it.

I pace the floor and rake my hands through my hair. This burning in my lungs, in my throat, it's a damned pressure cooker ready to explode.

In front of me is an open patch of wall. My fist rolls back and right as I'm about to lose my shit with the cinderblock... "Hutchins, Noah," a cop calls out. "Let's go."

The low murmur of conversation dies as the door to the cell slides open. It's like they're half expecting me to drop dead the moment I leave. Part of me is expecting it, too.

I wait for the bastard to cuff me again, but he doesn't. He crooks his finger for me to follow. Two steps behind and attempting to watch my back, I do. With a key, then a card, two dead bolts unlatch on a thick door, and he opens it. He walks through and so do I.

I stop breathing. Not five feet away, Echo slides her fingers along the length of her scars. The door shuts behind me, and my gaze nails the cop. "What's going on?"

Echo's head jerks up, and our eyes meet. Beth and Isaiah scrutinize me like I'm a damn ghost being resurrected.

"Charges were dropped. Both you and your girlfriend are free."

Girlfriend. Echo's forehead wrinkles, and my eyes snap shut. Girlfriend. "Echo..."

Another click and a cold draft hits my back as the door behind me opens again. Echo's sight falls beyond my shoulder, and she lifts her chin in that familiar pissed way.

Appearing pale and for the first time smaller than life, Mia walks up beside me. "I believe a thank-you is in order."

"Why does he think she's your girlfriend?" Echo demands.

There's a handful of people in the waiting room, including the receptionist behind the bulletproof window, and each one of them watches, awaiting my explanation.

"It's what I told them," Mia answers for me, and my

stomach bottoms out. "And my father when I asked him to intervene with the charges."

Echo's eyes flicker between me and Mia.

"It's not like that," I explain.

"Then why would she say that? Why would she help you?" Echo's hand trembles as she wraps her fingers around a strand of hair. "You just met."

Mia switches her footing, and I can't meet Echo's eyes. Damn me for this.

Echo recoils. "Tell me you just met. Tonight. Or at the Malt and Burger this week."

"Let's leave." With each step I take toward Echo, she mirrors a retreating step back. Her head shakes back and forth as if she already knows the truth. "I'll explain it to you in private."

Echo throws out both of her hands in a stop. "Explain it now!"

I've never felt more like dirt than in this moment. Moisture pools near the rims of her eyes, and this pulsating ache in my chest screams to comfort her. What's killing my soul is that I'm the one that's slashing her open. I'm the one causing the pain.

"Is she the reason you wanted to go to that party so badly?" Echo asks.

I nod, because I won't lie.

"Did you sleep with her?" Echo shouts.

I blink rapidly, hating myself. "A year ago. She worked in Louisville for two weeks a year ago."

Echo covers her face with her hands. "You slept with her?"

Jesus, she's gutting me. "A year ago."

Her shoulders shake, and the soft sounds of her devastation cause me to wipe at my own eyes. A sickness rolls in my stomach. The need is to touch her, to gather her into my arms, to make her better, to make us better, but I've hurt us. I've hurt her, and I can't push Rewind.

"I'm sorry." I don't recognize my voice as it cracks. "Nothing's happened since. I know I should have told you...I know I should have done a million things differently..." It's pathetic, but it's the damned truth. "Believe me, Echo."

Her head drops forward as her shoulders curl. A tear escapes from the crevices between her fingers. "I loved you." The pure agony in her muffled voice burns through me. "I loved you."

Loved. I run my hands over my head. She doesn't believe me. "I didn't sleep with her. Not this summer. I love you. You're my life."

Echo's hand darts out, and my head slams to the right. Pain across my cheek, and the waiting room vibrates with the smack.

Her chest moves too fast as silence fills the room. We stare at each other, and a glass wall builds between us—separating us.

Echo's foot angles for the door, and I jump toward her. "Don't go."

"Don't go? Don't go! So I can stay and watch you with your *girlfriend*."

"She's not my girlfriend!" I roar. "She means nothing!"

"You expect me to buy that? She bailed you out of jail!"

"Got the charges dropped," Mia butts in.

Echo whips her head to her. "Shut it."

"Go, Echo," mumbles Beth, and Isaiah slices a hand across his neck, motioning for Beth to also shut it.

Echo leans into me like she's willing to swing at me again. "I called my father and asked for bail money. I begged."

I wince as the knife she just rammed into me twists. "Echo..."

She flinches like I'm radioactive with the sound of her name on my lips. "Go to hell."

Echo turns for the exit. I'm on the move, and Isaiah blocks my path. My hand is out to shove past him, and he locks down on my arm. "Let her go."

His gray eyes morph into steel, and the guy staring me down isn't my best friend. Naw, he's peering at me like I'm the enemy.

"She's got this wrong," I say.

"You fucked up, and she needs time."

A shadow from the corner of my eye and Beth's small hand extends out, palm up. Isaiah surveys me. "Move and your ass is mine."

With a tic of my jaw, I cram my hands into my jean pockets, and Isaiah releases me. He never disengages his glare as he digs the keys out of his pocket and hands them to Beth.

Beth's fingers curl around Echo's keys. "I never thought you were an asshole, Noah. Damaged. But not an asshole."

"I didn't sleep with Mia." I overpronounce the words.

I'd welcome a million of Beth's death stares over the disappointment in her eyes. "No, but you slept with Echo."

My eyes briefly slam shut. I never told them. I never told anyone. But what I said to Echo was true. Isaiah and Beth noticed the difference. I promised Echo we wouldn't change after we made love, but we did.

Everything changed.

"When you did what you did with Echo..." Beth hesitates because speaking emotions is unfamiliar for her. "You don't get to play by the same rules as before. She deserves more than that. She deserves better."

I nod, telling her I get it. "I fucked up."

"You did." Beth won't look at me. "I'll take care of her."

With that, the last person I would have thought would be in Echo's corner walks out into the dark night.

Echo

I lie on top of the covers of the made bed and watch as the room falls into darkness then illuminates with light every other second. How long I've been lying like this or how long Beth's been messing with the light next to the bed, I don't know, but I'm just now finding it annoying.

"Can you stop that?" I snap.

Beth clicks the light off then back on. I glance over at her, and she tosses the electrical wire that contains the switch onto the bedside table. "So my plan worked."

I'm too miserable to have to deal with Beth. "What plan?"

"Are you mad at me?"

"I'm not happy," I mutter.

Beth slides her legs off the other bed and dangles them off the side. "See, that's part of your problem. You don't get pissed nearly enough. You're always trying to be proper."

I'm about to shove her proper into very unproper places. "I change my mind. Play with the light and be silent."

"Now, slapping Noah—classic move. I rate it a seven. But you should have kicked him in the nuts. That was a nut-cracking moment."

A rush of anger causes me to rise off the bed and mirror her position. "Do you think this is funny?"

Her lips turn up in that evil smirk that I've come to detest with the same fervor as people who kick puppies. "You're mad at me now, right?"

"Yes!" I scream. "I'm mad at you. You hate me. I hate you. You treat me like crap, and I forever take it. You and I can't stand the sight of one another! Are you happy now?"

"Not really." Beth appears to shrink as if my words were razor blades. "But you don't hurt now, do you?"

A painful slice at my soul as my breath catches. For a brief few seconds, I didn't hurt. I wasn't replaying tonight or any other night for the past week with Noah. I wasn't reviewing every disappointed and sarcastic comment from my father when I asked for Noah's bail. I wasn't thinking that while Noah made love to me, he had been hanging out with a girl he had previously slept with.

Especially when I told him my fear—that I wouldn't measure up to any of the girls he had left behind...or I thought he had left behind.

"Anger's better," says Beth quietly. "Anger is like a fortified wall no one can penetrate. Hurt—it's a doormat—and it lets everyone walk all over you."

"I don't hate you," I whisper. "That was mean to say."

"But it's true."

"It's not."

"I'm a bitch to you. Why would you like me?"

Because she loves Isaiah and Noah, and they love her back. "Why don't you like me?"

Beth stares at the multicolored industrial carpeting. "Because it's all changed since you came into the picture. I don't have much, Echo. Never have and never will."

"So..." My insides literally wilt with the idea. "...if this is it between me...and..." Noah. "You'd be happy?"

"I love him. He loves you. I don't want to see him hurt. Besides..." The evil smirk returns though it appears forced. "I'm the queen of displaced anger."

"So does this mean you like me?" I ask.

"It means I'm a bitch. The rest of it—" Beth shrugs and resembles seventeen for the first time ever "—it can mean whatever you want."

Closest I'll get to a yes from her, and I'll take it. We lapse into silence, and my foot taps the floor. "My father says Noah's using me."

He said that and a few more colorful things. No matter how many times I told Dad that the arrest was a mistake, my father pointed out something that struck deep: *But he's trouble. He'll always be trouble. It doesn't matter if he did it or didn't do it. He was in the scenario. You can't be arrested for something you didn't do unless you put yourself in the position of possibly doing it. Tell me, Echo, what was he even doing there?*

I don't know, and my hand presses to my heart to prevent the ache. I don't know why any of us were there. I didn't want to be there. Beth and Isaiah could have cared less. The only person who pushed for it was Noah, and I can't visit any possible reason as to why he went after that girl or how we ended up in such pain.

"I don't know what the fuck Noah was thinking tonight or even what the hell is going on between the two of you, but he loves you. I know it looked like shit when that girl walked out beside him, but I've been lying here rehashing what happened. He wouldn't cheat on you. Noah's been a dick plenty of times, but he's never been a liar."

No, he's never been a liar.

Noah has always been dark and mysterious and belonging to this world that seemed so appealing, but with the reality setting in of seeing Noah in handcuffs and the light of day beginning to creep in through the windows, I'm not sure it's the world I desire.

I'm eighteen. About to start college. I could study under one of the most brilliant artistic minds of this decade. I have a future.

A future.

I haven't slept in close to twenty-four hours, but somehow, I'm wide-awake.

NOAH

With his hands white-knuckling the armrest and his glare burning a hole through the floor, Isaiah waits for me as the guy at the counter returns my shit. Living together for over a year, Isaiah and I have annoyed the hell out of each other but until now, I've never seen my brother pissed with me.

I sign the last release form then shove my wallet into my pocket. After Echo and Beth bolted, Mia did, too. Not sure how I feel about that.

The moment I turn, Isaiah's out the door, and I follow. Cigarette smoke greets me when I step out. Mia stands under a streetlight and takes a long draw off the cigarette. The red ashes glow bright in the night. "Can we talk?"

Isaiah arches his back like a ticked-off jungle cat. "Five minutes, then I'm heading back with or without you."

He stalks toward the main road. I incline my head for Mia to talk.

"I'm sorry," she says. "That you got arrested."

"Mind telling me how you got me out?"

"Didn't I tell you? My daddy's filthy rich. Emphasis on filthy. I do the Malt and Burger travel thing just to piss him off and guess what? It does." Her entire body twitches—either the come-down from the drugs or nerves.

"News to me."

"Well...then that." She sucks the cigarette to the filter and drops it to the ground. The exhale billows out into a cloud. "There must never have been a break in the conversation for it to come up how I've made it my life's goal to be the disappointment he constantly tells me I am."

"Why'd you spring me?"

"I got you in it. It was on me to get you out."

"If we see each other again, I'm walking in the opposite direction."

She snorts. "You don't need to worry about seeing me for a while. I agreed to another stint in rehab for this bail."

"Good luck with that."

"Fourth time's a charm, right? So I'm assuming you want to know the last sign."

"Not anymore." I didn't need tips on the downward spiral of my relationship with Echo. I annihilated it fine on my own.

"Tough. You're hearing it."

No, I'm not. I pivot, choosing Isaiah's path.

"It's you," she calls out. "We destroy it all because we're so fucked up thinking that they're going to leave us that we make it happen. Self-fulfilling prophecy and all that shit. If they don't walk away then we give them a reason to leave."

The words ram like a two-by-four into my gut. I wish Mia had led with that statement in the alley, but that would have destroyed the web she was weaving. It's my own damn fault for flying straight into her trap.

Isaiah lingers near the edge of the parking lot. When I get within three feet, he angles away from me and starts alongside a narrow, forest-infested road. He's never been conversational, but pure silence isn't his style.

We're miles from the hotel. Two, maybe three, but I don't give a fuck. I'd prefer to be on foot knowing that Echo's safe. Hopefully, she's in the hotel and not halfway back to Kentucky. I don't carry much of a prayer that she'll listen to me, but I'll keep begging her forgiveness until she either grants it or yells at me to fuck off.

And if she does that, I'll take a deep breath then begin again. There's no way I'm letting Echo leave. I love her too damned much.

"Hey, Noah."

I glance up, and Isaiah's fist pulls back. The punch cracks against my jaw, and I stumble. Pain shoots through my head. Hard hits I can handle, but Isaiah's schooled on how to go fat man/little boy on a guy's ass. I wipe the blood from the corner of my mouth. I deserved that and more.

Isaiah steps into me like he's going for the tackle. "Fuck over Echo like that again, and I won't stop next time. Got it?"

"If I fuck over Echo like that again then I'll beg you to kick my ass."

"Jesus Christ, Noah, it's like you want it to be complicated. Win the girl. Then keep her. Don't let her go. Get it straight. One of us needs to get it right and, out of the two of us, you're the one who has a shot."

"I got it." I spit the metallic taste of blood to the ground.

"Do you?"

Sure as hell hope I do. "Yeah." I work my jaw. "I'm going to need time with Echo when we get back. Alone."

Isaiah nods. "I've got enough to cover a room for me and Beth."

"The room's on me. Think you could have decided not to go Old Testament?"

Isaiah cracks a crazy grin. "Naw, Echo needs to see you hurting. Maybe then she'll be soft on your sorry ass."

"Or you could have told her to give me a break."

"Could've, but you deserved a crack to the head. Let's go."

This time as we start down the road, we're walking side by side.

Standing in the hallway outside the hotel room, I rub my neck. I'd rather face a firing squad. If this goes south, it would be less painful to be shot in the head.

Isaiah slaps my back. "You ready for this?"

"No." A couple of months ago, I berated myself for being nervous over dating Echo. Now I'm terrified that I'm going to lose her. Never knew one person could twist me inside and out to the point of breaking. "But let's do it anyway."

Sliding the card through, I ease the door open. It's quiet. Too quiet. No TV. No air conditioner running. My heart picks up speed. She's gone. Damn it all to hell, Echo's gone.

I race into the room, and Beth jumps off the bed and captures my arm. "Shhh. She finally fell asleep."

Sure enough, with her hair sprawled out on the pillow, knees drawn to her chest, and in the same jeans and T-shirt as when we went to the party, Echo's asleep. A lone red curl lies across her tearstained cheek. Each intake of air is an ache in my chest.

She's so damned beautiful, and she's still here. My legs wobble. I've still got an uphill battle, but at least there's a hill to climb.

"Did she take anything to help her sleep?" I ask.

Beth surveys me like a boxer entering the ring. "Why would she take anything when crying herself to sleep works just fine?"

Point Beth. "I'm going to make this right."

Isaiah grabs his pack and stuffs some of Beth's clothes in it. "Let's go, Beth. I got us another room."

"Sounds good." Beth continues to glare at me for another second before hitting my arm with her shoulder as she walks out. "Asshole."

Looks like I'll be groveling to two females, but the one on the bed is my main concern. The door to the room closes, and I inhale deeply, trying to figure out where it went wrong.

I hurt her. I hurt Echo, and I don't know how to take away the pain.

In two steps, I fall to my knees by the bed, and her sweet scent hits my nose. Sleep is a gift to Echo. Not a promise. Every part of me begs to gather her into my arms, but I've lost all privileges.

Her lids slightly crack open, and the hollowness in her eyes rips at me. "Go back to sleep, Echo."

Little lines form between her eyes. "I thought maybe I was dreaming you came in."

"Do you want me to leave?" I hold my breath waiting for her answer.

Echo slightly rocks her head against the pillow in a no. "I want last night to have never happened."

Me, too. If I could travel back in time and beat the hell

out of the punk who permitted the hurt to control every decision, I would. "I didn't sleep with her. Not since last year. And I swear to you I've been clean since January."

The words are pouring out faster than they appear in my brain. "You want me to take a drug test to prove it, I will. I'll take a hundred of them. I'll take one every damned day. What happened last night was a mistake, and I'm sorry. I should never have been talking to her. I should have been with you. Here. Not at that party. I—"

"Stop it." The words are harsh, but there's no malice in her tone. "Just stop it."

I bow my head, searching for the right way to convince her that she's my entire world. That without her, I have nothing.

"I believe you didn't sleep with her…this week."

I wince, a blow straight to my stomach.

"As for the drugs, if you say you aren't using, I believe that as well, but I've come to realize that I never asked if you were still using, and you never told me. In fact, I told you once that I wouldn't pressure you to stop. Even if I want to be angry, I have no right to hold it against you if drugs were the reason you were with her tonight."

It's there. In her eyes. The disappointment I was so damned terrified of seeing after we made love. My throat swells, and I clear it to push forward. "I'm done. I swear to you, I'm done with all that."

Echo curls tighter into her ball. "But that's the thing. I fell in love with you for who you were. I can't ask you to change because I want…" And she snaps her mouth shut.

My pulse pounds in my ears. "What do you want?"

Her lower lip trembles, and I swear to God she's tearing out my heart.

"Just tell me." Though I already know the answer.

"I want...I want more."

More.

She wants more.

More than the punk. More than the kid with the messed-up past. More as in the guy that doesn't spend nights behind bars.

I fall back to my ass and knead my eyes in an attempt to recover from the sensation of being pulled under by a wave. Six months. I had six glorious months with her, and it wasn't enough time. For us. For me. I didn't find a way to change fast enough to be the man she craves to walk down the street with. "I'll give you more. I'll give you everything. I'm changing. Just give me more time."

Echo wipes at her eyes. "You should change because you want more for yourself, not because I asked for it. And more doesn't mean material things. I don't want what happened last night to happen again. I can't take that. I can't live that way, but you need to live your life for you, not me."

The pressure that had been building while rotting in that holding cell erupts. "You're what I want!"

With exhaustion working against her, Echo struggles to sit up against the back of the bed. "Don't you see—that's it. You're changing to make me happy, and that's going to make you miserable. It's the same thing you accuse me of. You say I make decisions based on my need for approval. You want my approval so you change. That's not healthy."

She's not getting it. "You've got it wrong. I'm changing because being with you makes me happy. You're what I think about every second of the day! You're the reason I have goals. You're why I find a reason to take a breath when I open my eyes in the morning. I wanted nothing for my life and then I found you. You showed me I could be more, and I want more."

Echo covers her face with her hands, and her shoulders roll forward. She blows air in and out. Long and deliberate. Each shaky inhale audible. Feeling the burn in my eyes, I suck in a breath like her. "I love you, Echo."

Dead silence. The hollow abyss kind. The type that convinces me I've either gone deaf or died.

"What you said—you're that for me, too." She lowers her hands. "When all the cuts on the inside have bled for too long and I'm close to death, you're the one that pulls me back. I don't like hurting over you, but I won't shove you or myself into a box we can't fit in, either."

"Tonight...that wasn't me."

Echo flattens her lips. "It was."

Fuck this. "It isn't who I want to be. Give me another chance. Let me prove to you that I'm the man you're going to be proud of. The man you want to walk down the street with."

Echo slowly smooths her curls behind her ears, staring at me like I've grown horns. "I've always been proud of you."

Now she lies. "Bullshit. If that was the case then why the fuck are we having this conversation?"

"Noah..." She slips to the side of the bed, and her leg almost touches mine. "We're having this conversation because I want you to be happy."

"Naw, we're having it because you said you wanted more." More than me.

Her knee bounces to that silent, screaming rhythm locked inside her. "I don't mind parties. I don't mind hanging out. But I don't want to wonder if I'm going to have to bail my boyfriend out of jail. That wasn't fun for me."

"I told you, that was a mistake. This entire night was a mistake. If I could take it back, I would. I'm going to become what you want."

Echo throws out her arms. "I want you to become who you want! Just like you keep saying that you want me to be happy, even if it's here in Colorado."

"I am happy!"

"You went after her," she shouts. "When push came to shove, you walked away from me and you went after her! That tells me she had something more to give than me. I don't like feeling this way. I don't want to force you to be something you're not!"

My intestines cramp, and I clamp my trap shut. I went after Mia to figure out how to keep Echo, but there's no way to say that without it sounding crazy. After several hours to think on it, it all seems like madness. "You're what I want."

"Noah...why are you becoming an architect?"

"What the hell does that have to do with anything?"

"You keep accusing me of making decisions based on my need to please, but look at yourself. Why are we even here in Vail? You're supposed to be searching for some long-lost bloodline of your mother's and instead we go to a party? You are all over the place and I don't know how to keep up. No offense, but you're searching for someone's approval, and I don't want to be on the wrong end when you figure out that my approval isn't what you're looking for."

A rush of anger tackles me hard. "Like you aren't

searching for your parents' approval? You aren't trying to prove yourself in the art world without your mom's help so you can score some sort of badge to show off to both your mom and dad?"

"At least I know why I'm pursuing art and who I'm trying to prove myself to. Can you say the same?"

The air from my body releases in a slow hiss, and I can't draw it back in.

"I'm tired," she says in a strained voice, and when I look up she's massaging her temples. "I'm tired, and we're talking in circles."

It's like watching the last remnants of sand run through the hourglass, and I'm chained to the wall unable to flip it back over. A flash of panic strikes. Echo could send me away. "Will you let me hold you?"

"No," she bites out.

I flinch and it's like she's impaled me with a sword. "Can I stay?"

A pause. A long one. *Please, Echo.*

"On the other bed." She turns off the light and plunges us into darkness. Her mattress creaks and a few seconds later, there's only the sound of her breathing.

Echo's laughter, her sighs, the tingle of her silky hair against my bare skin, each sweet and hot kiss...each one of them I've taken for granted. Not anymore. I can't live life thinking there will be a tomorrow for the two of us. "I love you, Echo."

It's like I've said it into a black hole. The silence stretches then finally she whispers, "I've never doubted the love. It's the going forward part that's blurry."

"Maybe it won't seem complicated after we rest."

"I'm taking the internship with Hunter," she says into

the darkness. "Regardless of what happens between us, I'm taking it. Just so you know when we try to figure out what's ahead—that is if we have a future."

Her words knock the wind out of me and leave me grappling to speak.

"We have one." Damn it, we do. "But good. I'm glad."

Good. It's what she wants. It's what she deserves, and there's the possibility she might not have taken it in order to please me. "You deserve it, Echo. You deserve happy."

"So do you," she whispers.

Echo asked for simple. She asked for us not to change. I thought we could slip by with both, but the truth is, we can't. I don't have the answers. I don't know how to make us right. She could have forced me to leave, but Echo decided to fight for us...at least for tonight.

That doesn't give me as much hope as it should. Sometimes you hold tighter right before you let go, and I'll be damned if I allow that to happen.

Echo

I stretch, and the pull on my muscles feels good—like a soak in a hot tub. The large intake of new air filling my lungs brings a smile to my face and I shift, snuggling closer to Noah.

His arms lock around me, and I nuzzle my face into his chest. I love his spicy scent. I love these stolen moments in the morning. I love...

A flash of pain and my eyes snap open. My entire body jolts, and Noah runs a hand along my spine in comfort, in apology. I don't love the memories of last night crashing back into my brain. I lift my head, and I'm met by Noah's dark eyes. Dear Lord, he resembles something Lila's cat would hack up.

My head whips. I'm not in my bed, but in Noah's. My eyes scrunch together. How did I...

"You crawled in bed with me." Noah answers the question before I verbalized it. "After you went to the bathroom."

The vague memory catches up. "Oh."

In my half-asleep state I had forgotten what happened between us. I had a nightmare, not a full-blown terror, but a nightmare, and I woke up, went to the bathroom and forgot why Noah wasn't in my bed.

"Go back to sleep, baby. It's still early," Noah says. "You've barely slept an hour."

I groan and scratch my fingernails into my skull. I haven't felt this heavy since the morning I had a hangover after Michael Blair's party in January.

Noah's fingers creep up and tunnel in my hair, shooing away my own fingers, and assumes the task of eradicating the discomfort.

Part of me knows I should push Noah away. That I should yell and scream and cry, but there's this sense that I'm already losing him and that these are our final moments. Moments that I don't want to miss.

I settle back onto his chest and stare at the light shining through the cracks in the curtain. There's this strange thin barrier between Noah and me that has never existed before.

"Are you mad?" Noah asks.

Mad? Should be, but... "No."

"Hurt?"

Hurt? Painfully so. "Yes." And terrified. As if I'm in a real-life horror movie. "I don't know where we go from here."

"Let's take it one step at a time."

"At some point we have to start thinking beyond the moment."

"But not now." Noah's fingers slide through my hair, down my cheek, then put the slightest pressure on my chin until I lift my head to look straight into his eyes. "I love you. I'll be strong enough for us, Echo. I wasn't before, but I am now."

I love him. So much that it aches. "The question is if

staying with me can keep you happy. I'm not convinced that's possible."

"It's possible." Noah swipes a thumb across my bottom lip. Electricity zaps down to my toes. "Very possible."

I sigh, and Noah narrows his eyes. "Don't do that."

"Do what?"

"Doubt me."

I quirk up a halfhearted grin while everything twists on the inside. "I'm not."

Blink. Blink. Blink.

"You are. I'm going to prove I mean what I say."

Noah doesn't understand. "It's not me you need to prove anything to—it's yourself."

"You're too many steps ahead. Take a deep breath and stop trying to jump into the deep end." Noah inches his head near mine and while I know that I should ease away, I can't. When it involves Noah, I've always been the moth willing to be burned.

"One of us has to jump," I whisper against his mouth.

There's a desperation inside me that screams to hold Noah as close as I can. That this boy who causes me to melt under his touch, who makes me laugh like a child, lights up my world in so many ways, will leave me soon. The need is to cling. To hold. To become one.

But the thought of kissing Noah, the thought of loving him then losing him causes tears to form. I shut my eyes, and the images of Noah walking away into the night, merging into the shadows, plague my mind.

Aires walked away. Aires couldn't fit into the mold at home. The more he tried, the more miserable he became, and he left. Not just left. He died.

My hands find Noah's chest and with all the strength I possess, I shove. "I can't."

Noah sits up. "Echo?"

I'm trembling, and the air can't enter my lungs fast enough. The room's too small, and I've got to leave. I've got to leave before Noah does. I blink to understand the thought, but everything is distorted. "Aires left."

"What?"

I run my hands over my face, and my shaking fingers stop at my lips. Aires left me. He walked off into the shadows, and I never saw him again, and Noah chose to walk in the same direction—away from me.

"You walked away, and Aires walked away, and he didn't come back."

"I didn't walk away, baby. I'm right here."

"But you will!" I yell, and bolt off the bed. "It's what happens and then...and then..." Aires died.

"Echo..." Noah says slowly, sort of like he's talking to a hurt animal. "Take a deep breath. You're breathing too fast, and you're shaking. Just sit down."

"No, you walked away last night." But he said he was sorry. Noah's saying he's chosen to stay.

"I know it sounds fucked up, but I went after Mia to talk to her. She said she knew why you and I were fighting. She said she had a relationship like ours once. I thought she could tell me how to keep you when I've got nothing to offer."

Noah's saying words. Words I should listen to, but the emotions running through me are too strong. "Did you know that Aires felt trapped at home?"

Just like Noah must feel like I'm trapping him. Noah was a different person when we met. He changed, and I liked how he changed, and I liked how he dreams of college and how he wants to build me a house and to buy me a small fluffy dog, but what if all of that is to please me and he'll feel trapped and then he'll disappear just like...

"Aires said that joining the Marines was his dream, but was it his dream? I mean, did he join because he felt like there was no other way out? And what happens when you feel trapped? What happens to you? To us? I can't lose someone like that again. I can't..."

"You aren't." Noah cuts me off. "I'm not trapped. Going to college. Being with you. Those are my choices. Not choices to prove something to you. If it was, I'd be on my knees begging you to take me back, and I'd be telling you that I'll stay with you in Colorado, but I can't. I need Kentucky, just like you need here, but, baby, I still want us together. Hear me, Echo. Hear what I'm saying. I'm not trapped. I'm exactly who I want to be...who I want to become. I wasn't chasing her last night, I was chasing you."

"Aires also said he'd never leave!" The air leaves my body faster than I'm taking it in. "He lied to me! The one person who never lied to me, lied to me! And I know you never lie so what does that mean? I'll tell you. It means that this is all going to hell."

Noah's face contorts as if I'm gutting him open. "I get it."

"You don't."

He slams his palm over his chest, over his heart. "They left me, too!"

Tears prick my eyes. "What if we'll always be broken? What if we can never be fixed? What if this is it, for the rest of our lives? Regardless of whether we're together or not? What if our past will always haunt us and makes us miserable? What if we'll never shed our baggage and weights, and we'll never be set free?"

The truth of my words is too heavy to wait for a response because I'll drown from the answer. Noah and I are trapped in a black hole. A terrible, consuming black hole.

A black hole.

I suck in a breath like I'm waking up. I slip my shoes on my feet and snatch my key card off the dresser.

"Echo..." Noah rapidly moves for me, his hand outstretched.

"It's a black hole," I tell him. "The constellation, the one I'm painting...it contains a black hole. The answers I've been searching for...the painting...I know what I need to do."

"Okay. That's good, but you need to sit—"

"No!" I desperately attempt to rein in my emotions. "No. I need to do this now. I'm going to the gallery and you stay here, and then I'll be back."

"I'll take you there."

"I'll be fine—"

"If it's not me, then I'll wake Isaiah, but I've only seen you like this once before, and I'll be damned if I let you walk out that door without someone keeping an eye on you. Kick me in the damned nuts. Break up with me a hundred times, but I'm walking you to that fucking gallery. Got it?"

Because there's no arguing with him when his eyes turn solid with determination, I grab the canvas and walk out the door with Noah.

I try the back door, and I have to fight the urge to punch it when, like the front door, it's locked. Hunter gave me a key, and I forgot it. Stupid me. Stupid, stupid me. I know what I need to do for this painting, and I'll go mad if I don't finish it. I step back from the door and assess the second story. Is there a freaking way to scale the wall?

"You've got paint in the room," says Noah. "Can you finish it there?"

"I don't have what I need there," I answer. There's a tree near the corner, but it would be a heck of a jump, and who knows if the windows are unlocked.

A sharp pain on my scalp. "Hey!" Did Noah yank out my hair?

Noah flattens out a bobby pin and leans into the door. His head swivels like an owl's up and down the back alley. "Are you sure you're allowed in here?"

"What are you doing?"

"Getting you in. I see the look on your face. You need this. So, I'm asking again. Do you have permission to be here?"

Calmer than I was in the hotel, I glance at Noah. "Do you think I'm the breaking-and-entering sort?"

With his shoulder against the door, Noah sticks the pin into the lock and begins this weird jiggling movement. "Yes."

"I can't believe you'd think that."

"If *you* think about it..." Noah halfheartedly offers his wicked grin. It doesn't quite touch his eyes, but the small attempt at playfulness does cause me to smile...a little. "You're the one who broke into a therapist's office."

I laugh, and the sound surprises me. "*You* broke in. I was saving your butt. Are you always going to rewrite history?"

"Maybe." There's a click, and both Noah and I freeze

as he opens the door. Holy crap, it worked. Noah freaking Hutchins broke into a place that he absolutely hates, after he got out of jail and did something illegal...for me... again. Just like he did last spring.

Knots form in my throat, and I'm at a loss for words.

He pushes open the door and scans the empty hallway. "If anyone asks, you had your key."

"Noah..." My mouth gapes. I close it and through the thunder of my heart, I ask, "How were you arrested for possession? Because I believe you, that you were innocent, so...how?"

He slams his hands into his pockets and half shrugs. "Mia was in her car and had a bag of pills in her hands. Part of me was pissed because she wouldn't answer me, and another part didn't want to see her behind the wheel stoned. Either way, I took the bag from her, and that's when the cops showed."

And Noah, being who he is, never would have ratted anyone out. Not even to save himself. Honorable. Loyal. Even to people who often don't give him the same respect back. "I'm sorry I slapped you."

"I'm not. Let me walk you in." Noah stalks in before I can respond. He's slow going up the circular staircase, sort of like he expects...

"I am allowed to be here," I say, holding the canvas like a shield. "No one's going to shoot."

"All the same," he answers.

Even though Hunter gave me the key, I creep up the circular staircase like I'm a burglar on the prowl. Reminiscent of how I had skulked against the lockers the night I went after Noah.

"Have you told your dad you don't need the bail money?" mutters Noah. "Because we might need it."

I shush him. Now that would be irony, me needing the money because I'm breaking in. I also like that Noah's willing to go to jail with and for me.

We reach the top of the stairs, and the hundreds of Christmas lights illuminate the room. On the far side of the room, Hunter directs his attention to us. Noah splays his arms in front of me like he's willing to take the bullet.

"Good morning, Echo," Hunter says.

I touch Noah's back to let him know that it's okay, and he eases to the side. My footsteps against the subflooring sound loud as I walk to my spot and place the canvas on the easel. With it in front of me, with everything I need within hands reach, my fingers actually twitch.

This is it. Today I'm painting Aires.

The world around me begins to tunnel, and there's a familiar voice dancing in the periphery.

"Take care of her," says Noah. "Because I'll know if you don't."

"Understood," says a voice that sounds like Hunter.

But it could have belonged to a dream as everything else fades out except for the colors.

NOAH

My mom raised us Catholic.

I never considered attending church after my parents died. God and I—we stopped talking. Not that we had many conversations before that, but anything I would have had to say to Him after my parents' deaths wouldn't have been fit for divine ears. To be honest, I don't think God exists. He's one more make-believe story in the realm of fairy tales.

Parked in the same lot as a few days before, I ignore the house that belongs to my mother's biological parents. Instead, I lean against the hood of Echo's car and stare at the church. Echo's off painting black holes, and I'm trying not to get sucked into one. It'll be a damned miracle if the two of us survive the next week.

I love her, and she loves me, but I finally understand some of those old-school movies that make Echo cry. Sometimes love isn't enough. I don't know if she can wait four years for me to prove I want to be the man she dreams of. Plus, she could be right about me. Maybe I am doing all of this for the wrong reasons.

The architect shit...

Dad loved what he did. Had a smile on his face when he went to work and when he came home. He found beauty in things that other people took for granted. Like this church. He'd appreciate how it was more than it appeared. Except for the bell tower reaching for the sky, the outside is plain brick. Most basilica-style exteriors are simple. The insides are supposed to kick ass because in truth, we all should be shinier on the inside.

At least that's how Dad explained it.

It's like Dad understood the mysteries of life because he understood a building. Maybe I'm searching for the same knowledge.

"You're back." The priest—fuck it, my uncle—carries reusable shopping bags in each hand. "In case you're wondering, I'm hearing confession in a few minutes."

"I wasn't wondering."

"Aw." Looking more human in a white T-shirt and dark pants, he chuckles as he walks past. "But you are. If you come inside, I'll tell you why your mother named you Noah."

My eyes flash to his, and he winks. "Figured she wouldn't tell you. She was the stubborn sort. Give me at least two minutes and I have a feeling you'll know where the confessional is."

Not happening. I'm not the one that needs to apologize to God. It's the other way around.

"It's a great story!" he calls before he disappears behind the door. "By the way, your mother and I used to talk. Two phone calls a year!"

My body twitches with the need to follow. It's like I'm a fish caught on a hook. A story involving my mom. One I'll never have the opportunity to hear from her. Because, as Echo pointed out this morning when she talked about her brother, Mom left, and she's never returning.

As I climb the concrete stairs for the two towering

front wooden doors, I glance up, waiting for the fire and brimstone or good old-fashioned lightning to strike me dead.

The skies remain calm, and I enter the house of the God.

It's pin-drop quiet and off to the side are rows of unattended votive candles flickering to stay alive. My dad sure as hell had one thing right: the inside of this place is immaculate. The light flowing from the stained-glass windows is like a multibeamed rainbow. Large white columns run on both sides of the center seating, and painted in the domed area over the sanctuary are pictures of the apostles.

My uncle fixes his collar and appears spiritual again in black.

"That's a fire hazard." I gesture to the prayer candle area.

That brings him up short. "I can see where you'd feel that way. We're considering moving to electric candles, but it wouldn't have the same effect, would it? Now, if you don't mind, I'm late for work."

Without another soul but the two of us, my uncle scurries into the confessional and shuts the wooden closet door.

On the ceiling, a painting of Michael the Archangel peers down at me. He's the warrior of God. The one who's called when there's a battle—a lot like the war that's about to take place the moment I step inside that confessional. Not sure if Michael is on my side or the priest's, but then I shake my head. Definitely the priest's. For the past three years, the odds have never been in my favor.

Echo

My hand rushes over the canvas, and I hear a cough behind me. I've probably got an audience again, but I don't care. Aires is missing. He's gone, and he's never coming back.

He made a promise, and he broke it.

The last thing my brother ever did was break a promise to me.

As the blues fade into a blackish-blue and as that merges into dark as midnight, there's this undercurrent of rage pushing me forward. My brother lied to me, and I'm mad.

"Echo." It's a somewhat familiar voice, but I try to block it out. "Echo."

A hand touches my arm, and all the anger bubbling inside me shoots out. "What?"

I glare at Hunter then take a step back. Oh, heck, I had shoved myself way too close into his personal territory, as in my face was a centimeter from his.

"You don't like getting pulled out of your trance," he says. "I got it, and it's filed away for future use."

There are giggles around the room, and one quick scan confirms that I've got fans. With a heavy sigh, I put my brush on the easel and stretch my back. "Sorry."

"Don't apologize, but since I disturbed you, do you mind if we talk?"

"Sure."

With a wave and a few words from Hunter, everyone moves on. "I'm going to have to shut this audience thing down soon, otherwise no one but you will get any work done."

"I am sorry about snapping at you. I won't lie—I can be hard to be pulled out, but I'm usually not so emotional, but..." I stare at the painting. "This one's different."

"What makes this one different?"

Because it's my brother. "Just is."

"You chose to leave out the star. Why?"

This thin veil that used to be a brick-and-mortar wall between me and any emotion connected with losing my brother wavers with the slightest breeze. If I wanted, the answers lie there behind the mist. All I have to do is reach for them and according to Mrs. Collins, those answers will help me keep Noah.

But there's pain behind that curtain. Pain I'm not sure I want to tackle. Pain that, hours ago in the hotel room, came close to surfacing.

Like the canvas turned into poison, I slide back from it. The veil in my head fluctuates as I focus on the colors. "Just decided to go that way."

"You're not a pushover for anyone, are you? Not even the man who can open doors for your future."

I've been wiping my hands on a towel and pause. "What did you say?"

"You. Not a pushover. How I like getting answers when I ask questions, and you don't give them. Me offering you a future and you not caring."

A smile spreads across my face. "I'm not a pushover."

"Is it because your name is Echo that you're repeating things?"

I laugh, not so much because he's funny, but because the unthinkable happened. For years my parents, my therapists, my teachers, my friends...anyone...used my need to please to get whatever they desired. I lay down and died for anyone at any time and somewhere along the way, I found a backbone.

I did change this summer. I am different.

"I'm serious, Echo. When I ask questions, I want answers. It's how this whole teacher/student relationship works."

I get it, but... "Not with this one. This one is personal, and you know it."

"They're all personal," he says.

"Some more than others. If you push me, I'll answer, but I can't promise the answers I give you on this one will be true."

"Touché. We're clear, then. Anything after this is on my terms."

"I understand."

"So the purpose of having this conversation..."

I'm nodding for him to continue though it's hard to concentrate because I'm still reeling from the I've-changed moment.

"I like the idea of you taking business courses so I'm trying to work it out with your college to see if you can take them online while you study your art here. In fact, I like the idea so much I might implement the new plan for others next fall."

That's an awesome surprise. "Great!"

Hunter eyes me warily. "So that means you're accepting?"

I bite the inside of my mouth. Noah and I are walking a tightrope, and I have no idea what's going to happen to us. Maybe we'd work if I stayed in Kentucky. Maybe we'd fall apart if I stay here. But Noah's right. The advice I gave Noah about himself is right. I need to decide for me. Noah and I will last if we truly love each other, but we'll collapse if I do everything to please him. "Yes. I'm accepting."

Hunter raises a brow. "Your boyfriend isn't talking you out of it?"

My spine goes rigid. "My boyfriend supports me." Then my stomach drops. I slapped him and pushed him away last night, then Noah broke into the gallery for me. He does support me...more than I can comprehend.

"Good," he says. "By the way, for paperwork purposes, what's your last name?"

Oh, crap. Just when things were starting to go well... There's no stopping the train wreck now. "Emerson. My name is Echo Emerson."

NOAH

After five minutes of glaring at a statue of St. Therese the Little Flower, I rub my eyes and push past the red curtain and squeeze onto the cramped wooden bench. The divider that covered the small window between us slides open. Because of how we both sit and the dim lighting from above, I can only catch a glimpse of my uncle's profile.

"In the name of the father, and the son and the holy spirit," he says, and I cross myself out of a long ago ingrained habit and hear my mother tell me that I should kneel in the confessional.

One second.

Another.

"Well," he urges.

"Forgive me, Father, for I have sinned. It's been..." This is insane. "It's been..." *Four years since my last confession.* Four years. My mother was pissed at me because I hadn't been to confession. In middle school, I had already started to question my faith.

Another way I failed my mother, and I continue the tradition by failing Echo. I scratch the spot over my eyebrow. "I don't believe in God, so it doesn't matter."

"Sorry to hear that, but for the record, He still believes in you."

Bullshit answer. "Give me the story about my name."

"Noah, I didn't bring you in here to listen to your confession, though I would be more than happy to take it. I brought you in here because there's another question you're here to ask, and I made the assumption you'd like to have this discussion with an air of anonymity."

"What's that supposed to mean?"

"It means the question you have is one that you might not want an audience for."

Uncomfortable, I bend forward and rest my hands on my knees. That tense rhythm that Echo continually harbors spreads into my veins. "Why did my mom leave?"

"And why are we aware of your existence when you didn't know about us?"

Is there anyone who isn't privy to the inner workings of my life besides me? "And that."

It's a heavy pause. Weighted enough that I consider retracting the question. My mom smiled all the time. My mom laughed almost every night. My mom had a secret that she may or may not have ever told me.

"Our father abused her."

I press both hands to my face as if I could erase his answer. "Abused her?"

"The devil is in the details with this one. There are some things that are better off left with the dead."

But the imagination could be worse. My mom.

My *mom.*

Tears fill my eyes, and I think of all the times she'd stare at me from across the room and out of nowhere say, "I love you." All the times I took for granted that I'd hear those words again. All the times that she might have craved a hug and I was too damn selfish with my life to comprehend she possessed her own demons.

"How bad?"

"Bad," he says as a whisper.

To think that someone hurt her. That someone that was supposed to love her hurt her—I slam my fist into the side wall, and when the ache slicing through my fingers doesn't disperse the anger, I punch the wall again.

"Was she in pain?" I ask, my voice breaking. "Did it haunt her?"

"There are some things that happen in life that you never forget. A branding on your soul, if you will. Like losing your parents. It's there. It happened. And it will never be taken back."

That's the insanity of the situation. The hurt that I face every morning. My foot bounces like Echo's, and I try to wipe away the moisture causing the world to blur.

"Do you want to know why she named you Noah?"

What the hell is wrong with this guy? "I don't give a..." House of God. My mother would be devastated if I cursed in a confessional in the house of God. "I don't care. Not anymore."

I try to breathe through the thoughts...that my mother was a child. That my mother was in pain.

"But this is the important part," he says in a soothing tone. "The part your mother would want you to know. She found hope. Your mother found hope and love, which is important because without love—we are nothing."

"She found Dad." And they married young. Out of college. Twenty-two. Starting out before most. Struggling for years. They had me before they could afford the rent on their first apartment, hence the gigantic gap between me and my brothers.

"Yes, she found your father, but you are the one that saved that small part of her soul that even he couldn't reach."

I freeze, no air entering my chest. "She died because of me."

He's silent, and the bench on his end creaks as he shifts. His face occupies the small window, but I focus on the wooden floorboards beneath my feet.

"I read the reports," he says. "You had nothing to do with that fire. And before you say anything, I've read the updated reports. I'm aware of the candle in the bathroom and that Jacob meant no harm."

I shake my head as if to shake away the reality. To deny what really happened. "Mom wasn't the type to stay up. My job was to be home on time for curfew."

I still remember the way my heart picked up speed when the car I was riding in turned the corner and I spotted the lick of flames shooting out of my younger brother's window on the second floor. How the car hadn't fully stopped when I bolted out of the backseat and ran up the front walk and kicked open the front door.

The girl I had been with was screaming my name and so were her parents, but they didn't follow. No one followed.

The smoke was thick, and I hunched over in a fit of coughs. The urge was to go up, into the heart of the fire, to drag out the people who meant the most to me in life, but then I heard the small voices of my brothers, and I realized in that moment that I loved them more.

My head drops, and a single tear falls down my face. I loved them more.

"You did exactly what your mother would have wanted. She loved you boys more than her own life."

"Got all that from two phone calls a year?" I attempt to shut the emotion down, but the rough sound of my voice confirms we're past that point.

"There are some things in life that you can know about a person in thirty seconds. She loved you, Noah. With all her heart, all her soul and all her mind."

"I didn't go after her or my dad," I admit, and I slam my eyes shut. *Forgive me, Father, for I have sinned. It's been four years since my last confession.* "I didn't fight hard enough."

"There was nothing you could have done. Saving your brothers was an extraordinary feat."

The sight of my mother bowing her head during service sweeps into my mind as she reverently mumbled the prayer—*that I have sinned through my own fault, in my thoughts and in my words, in what I have done, and in what I have failed to do...*

I failed in saving them. "I handed Jacob and Tyler off to neighbors. The police were there, and the firefighters just pulled up and I turned back for the door, but this guy—" it's difficult to breathe "—this guy stepped in my way."

Bigger than me, but not badder than me. I had never been in a fight. Had never thrown a punch, and the thought never crossed my mind. I never dreamed of laying out the man preventing me from rescuing my parents. A mistake, I swore after the fact, that would never happen again.

Echo's expression the day I shoved that asshole into the building and the words I said to her later replay in my mind... *No one fucks with you, Echo.* I'm protecting her the only way I know how. In ways that I was too weak to do for my parents.

"And when I tried to run past, another guy stepped in, and I let them stop me. I let them keep me from going back in."

"Your parents were already dead. They died of smoke inhalation. Not of burns. They probably drifted away in their sleep. The fire detectors weren't working. There was no warning for any of them. You saved the only people who could be saved. It's time for you to let this guilt go. It's time for you to start moving forward. Just like your mother would have wanted."

With my head in my hands, I rock in the seat, unable to keep the explosion of emotions from killing me. "I should have fought harder for her. I should have tried!"

"She would have wanted you to fight for yourself. To fight for your own life. You saved the parts of her soul that meant the world to her. You honored your mother and your father that night. You honored them with the devotion to your brothers. You honor them by sitting here, searching for people who you honestly shouldn't be searching for.

"Your mother named you Noah because you had already done what you are so desperately worried you failed at...you saved her...you gave her a second chance."

I blink, trying to understand.

"The story, son. I know your mother would have told you the Bible story."

God told Noah a flood was coming to destroy the earth and He promised to save Noah, his family and all the other creatures of the earth if Noah obeyed and built an ark.

"God gave Noah and his family a second chance," he continues. "Your father's love rescued your mother, but you, you were her first glimpse at her new world."

I lean back in the seat and let the wall handle my burden, handle my weight, because I'm too weak to shoulder it alone anymore. Echo and Beth and Isaiah. Each of us cursed with weight too heavy for anyone to carry. Troubles no one should have to face.

"If you allow me to be a priest instead of your uncle for a minute..."

When I say nothing, he goes on, "God sifts us like wheat. He refines us like flour. He works through the good in our lives and through the bad. He's preparing us to become who He wants us to be. You can look at what's happened in your young life as a burden, or you can see it for what it is—God refined you early. Made you a man before most. You have two options—you can deny it or you can embrace it. Your mother chose to embrace it. My prayer for you is that you do the same."

Run, or stand my ground and be a man.

Last night, even though I thought my intentions were correct, I ran, and I hurt Echo. I'm done running. It's time to be a man. "This doesn't mean I believe in God."

He chuckles. "Your mother was also stubborn. Stubborn as a damn mule."

I laugh, and he laughs along with me. "Dad used to say the same thing, and Mom would wear this look that said that she knew he was right, but she was too stubborn to admit it."

"I know that look," he says. "I can see it now."

The laughter fades, and I inhale deeply, strangely noticing that I sit straighter and that my insides are lighter. I guess confession is good for the soul.

"And Noah—don't think I didn't notice the cross tattooed on your arm. Deep inside, where it counts, you believe."

"Did they know?" I ask, ignoring his statement. "Mom's parents—your parents—did they know that I wasn't adopted out?"

"They knew. I discovered a few days ago that they were attempting to contact you. Right before you showed. I was in the process of trying to warn everyone I could to help keep you from getting dragged into this, but you worked faster than me. My parents got it in their heads that you'd come into money when you turned eighteen."

"There's no money," I say.

"I know, but my parents never were the type to think straight. If you want to meet them, they'll be back next week, but as your uncle I'm advising against it. I can definitely say this isn't something your mother would have wanted."

"So Mom ran, and you became a priest?"

"We both chose the paths we were meant to be on."

"Did you stay because they're worth forgiving?"

There's a long pause. "God shows all of us unmeasurable grace. As a priest, I should be able to somehow love like my God does. I tell people that I returned to my hometown and serve and live in the church across from my parents because I forgave them, but in truth, I came home to contain them. Evil like that needs to be boxed in and never let out. It's my job to make sure they never hurt anyone like they hurt me and your mother again."

In a short amount of time, my uncle gains a lot of respect.

"I couldn't protect your mother when I was younger," he says. "But I can protect others now."

I swallow. This question has to be asked or I'll regret it. "Why didn't you take me in?"

A creak of the floorboards and a long sigh. "Because that would have meant bringing you back here, and I couldn't make peace with the idea. Maybe it was a bad choice, and I don't blame you if you hate me for it. No one, including priests, is perfect."

Fair enough. I came to Vail for answers and now that I've received them, it's time I take care of the parts of my life worth saving. "Thanks. For telling me the truth."

"I wouldn't mind a phone call or two. Christmas and Easter. The house has been lonely for the past three years without that ring."

I nod, though he can't see it. "I can do that."

Without another word, I walk out of the darkness of the confessional, out of the shadows of the church, and into the sunlight.

Echo

Hunter's eyes bulge out of his head. "What did you say your last name is?"

I'm the daughter of the great Cassie Emerson. The daughter of one of the women he admires most when it pertains to painting. His eyes wander to the scars on my arms, and it's as if his mind audibly clicks. The rumors are true: I'm the daughter that the great Cassie Emerson tried to kill.

"Emerson," I repeat.

"As in Cassie Emerson."

I nod.

"You're her daughter."

I nod again.

His face flushes red. "You didn't think it was important to tell me that?"

"No." In fact, it was more important that he not know.

"No?" Hunter's fingers spread as he begins to raise his palms, then lowers them. "Get out. Take your painting and get out."

I jolt as if I had been hit by a semi. "What?"

"You heard me. Get out." Hunter turns his back to me, and it takes a moment for the shock to wear off before my feet start after him.

"What difference does it make that I'm her daughter?"

"A lot." Hunter stops at his desk in the corner and flips through a stack of invoices as if he didn't ram a spike into my dreams.

"Why? I'm totally separate from her."

"I wanted raw. I wanted an opportunity to take someone who had never been trained and say I helped create them. You're not new. You've had an advantage since birth. You learned how to write your ABCs from one of the best artistic minds. I didn't create you. Your mother did."

But my mother didn't teach me how to write. My father did. And my mother wasn't the first to teach me how to draw. My brother did. Yeah, Mom painted and when she was around she encouraged me, but she didn't teach me. Nothing beyond basics. Nothing that wouldn't make me as new as anyone else here. That would have required her to have been consistent and a stable force.

I never knew I could be so near something and watch it all slip through my fingers the moment I tried to close my fist. It's like an out-of-body experience. All the people who had sat at my feet before are now drawn back into their own worlds, pretending I don't exist.

Six months ago, I would have cowered. I would have looked at the scars and felt like I was below the scum of the earth. Instead, I return to my easel, pick up the canvas, stalk back over and slam it onto Hunter's desk. His coffee tips over and spills.

A smirk stretches across my face when the majority of it splashes onto the crotch of his pants.

Stealing a thin paint brush out of the hand of the guy working next to me, I dip it in white paint and sign my name at the right bottom corner of the painting. I flick the paintbrush at Hunter, causing little white dots to stain his crisp blue button-down shirt. "You can keep the painting because in five years, it's going to be worth more than your tired, pathetic career."

Hunter wipes at the coffee pooled on his pants. "Echo—"

"I'm not done." I cut him off and bang both of my hands on his desk, leaning forward so he knows this conversation belongs to me. "For your info, my mom never taught me to paint or to draw or much of anything. Not in the way you're thinking. So tip number one, stop making assumptions regarding me or anyone else. Tip number two, my boyfriend can and will kick your butt so don't you dare come near me again. And tip number three, most of your paintings really do suck."

The jerk actually grins as he rolls back in his seat. "I guess you've put me in my place."

Is he laughing at me? "Yeah, I guess I did."

"Do you mean what you said about my paintings?"

I wish I could scream yes, but the answer is, "No, but you're still a jerk."

"Calm down, Echo. I knew you were Cassie Emerson's daughter the day I looked at your sketchbook. Your last name was all over it. I was playing you just now. I wanted to see how you'd react when people gave you hell about your mom and, believe me, I took the nice route. Entering the art world with the rumors and stories surrounding the two of you, it's not going to be easy. So take a deep breath, rein it in and put the painting back on the easel. I'm not kicking you out."

I straighten, and people begin to laugh and talk among themselves. They're not laughing at me. I can feel that. It's supposed to be with me. It's supposed to be that relieved breath once everyone understands that this intense moment was never serious.

Hunter chuckles at something someone said as he unbuttons his shirt and grabs a new one out of the closet behind him.

"Did she fail?" someone shouts from across the room.

"No," Hunter answers with a wide, white smile. "I like girls who have fire." But then he lands his gaze on me. "I do suggest a more subtle reaction if we are in public. Some people don't find outbursts as amusing as me."

I rake a hand through my curls and stare at the man in front of me. "You know what happened with my mother?" And me?

He shrugs off the question. "I know what most people do—the rumors, but those scars are going to confirm what people think they know. But don't worry, none of it bothers me."

"Well, that's nice," I say absently. This was my dream. These were my goals. Hunter knows the rumors, and he made it into a show.

"Before you get angry, know that I did it to prepare you."

It's like I'm walking in a fog. "Prepare me?"

"What happened between you and your mom in my opinion is between you and your mom, but those scars will open you up to more speculation. Consider this my first lesson to you about life in general. People don't care what really happened—the truth—they care about what makes them feel better, what puts them higher on the scorecard than someone else—even if it's a lie. So I'm preparing you, because your mother is scheduled to show at and attend the Denver festival. The same festival you'll be attending and showing at."

I stumble back as if I've been struck by a wave. Hunter has angled away from me and doesn't notice how I'm drowning in the currents. Flashes of different emotions jerk me around like a riptide. Each time I try to kick up, another thought, another volley of feelings, yanks me back down into the depths.

My mother is coming.

Hunter has put me in the show, so that means that I'm good enough. For art. For someone...I matter. The people in Denver—they'll be watching, they'll be judging—they'll be waiting for the confrontation between me and my mother.

"Long story short," Hunter continues. "While your scars don't bother me or anyone here and you don't owe me any explanations about how you got them, you're going to run into plenty of people who will be bothered. There will be people who feel like you owe them every secret in your mind. If you don't want to deal with that at the showing, I suggest you wear long sleeves. Attending the festival with your mom around and your skin exposed will be a brave move. While you've got fire inside you, I'll be honest, I don't see you as that type of a risk-taker."

Not brave.

Not a risk-taker.

Long sleeves.

My eyes jump to his as my entire body stings like a slap to the face.

Hunter has opened his mouth again, and words of some sort are coming out, but I've settled into this numb.

I like numb. I like losing the ability to hear or understand or comprehend what others are saying.

Numb is safe.

Numb doesn't contain pain.

Numb helps me walk out the door.

NOAH

For the second time in my life, I purchase a dozen roses in the hotel lobby, but this time they're pink instead of red. The roses made Echo melt last time, and I'm hoping for the same reaction now, or at least a half smile.

Echo can zone when she paints, and part of becoming the man she needs is to learn to give her the space she requires, even if she's asked for a year. But that doesn't mean I can't woo the shit out of her when she returns.

I've got a hell of a hole to dig myself out of. Echo told me last night—this morning—she wanted more. I thought she wanted more as in the guy with the money, the guy with the job. What I didn't get was that she was no longer interested in a boy; she desired a man.

Taking care of myself, throwing a punch—it's what I thought being a man was, but what Echo craves is the guy who has the balls to walk toward her, talk out our crap and stick when it gets tough.

Not the guy who accepted dating advice from a messed-up girl with motives of her own. Not the guy who freaks each time another guy peeks in Echo's direction. She deserves the man who will not just stand by her on the easy calls—the sitting in hospital rooms, the attending of gallery showings—she deserves the man who will stand by her when it hurts like hell to do it.

The moments when I have to suck up my pride. The moments when I have to push past my feelings and think about hers. The moment when I let her tear out my heart for one year because that's what's going to make her happy.

Isaiah emerges from the hallway leading to the rooms, and his eyes narrow when he sees me. "What's going on?"

The gift shop clerk hands me back my change, and I shake the roses at Isaiah. "Groveling."

"Then you must be doing a pathetic job. Echo just busted ass out of your hotel room."

My hand freezes in my pocket as I had been shoving the money back in. "Echo's back?"

"Fuck, man. She left after you came back this morning? I was hoping she'd at least hear you out."

Not allowing Echo enough of a head start to stop to explain to Isaiah, I race for the exit. "Busted ass as in leaving the hotel?"

"Yeah. I called her name, but she kept going like she was on a mission. Said something about how she can take a risk and that she'd see me soon."

Take a risk? I tear past the front doors and into the parking lot. My muscles turn to stone when I notice the empty spot where I left Echo's car five minutes ago. We barely missed each other.

"Noah," says Isaiah in a low voice that causes my instincts to flare. "We've got trouble. Nine o'clock."

In slow motion, my head turns to the left. That damned Hunter's coming in fast. My grip on Echo's roses tightens, and a thorn slices through my skin.

"Where's Echo?" Hunter demands.

Isaiah rolls his shoulders back and tips his chin up. My brother is willing to take on this fight.

"Don't know," I answer. "Heard she tore out of here like the devil was chasing her so how about you and I cut the shit and you tell me what the fuck you did."

Hunter's eyes swing between me and Isaiah. Possibly wondering if he should notify next of kin about which of us he thinks is going to pull the trigger. "I brought up her mom, and she left."

Isaiah pops his neck to the side, and I contain the urge to rip Hunter's arms out of his sockets. "Left how?"

"I was testing Echo. To see how'd she react if someone taunted her about her mother."

I step into him, and Hunter takes a step back. Isaiah places his hand on my arm. "Let him finish. Then we'll kill him."

Right. Find out the damage then tear out his windpipe. "Continue."

"Her mother is going to be at the art show in Denver. I entered Echo two days ago, and the rumors are already building. I'll admit, my tact isn't the best, and the news freaked her out. It's why I'm here. No one who looks that dazed should be alone."

Damn him. He fucked her up then came here to be her savior. My cell's out of my pocket before he finishes talking. In fact, the bastard's still talking, now only to Isaiah, who's looking as friendly as a mangy, starved wolf.

The numbers finish dialing, and I go straight into voice mail. "It's Echo. Leave a message and I'll call you back."

"You didn't power your phone again, did you, Echo," I growl. "I know we got stuff to work out, but I don't like how you left. If you can't call me to let me know you're fine, then you call Isaiah. Fuck it, you can call Beth. Call your dad. Just someone."

I pause. In order to chase her dreams, Echo has to confront the one person that has given her nightmares. The one relationship she doesn't know how to handle. I glare at Hunter. He starts to say something, but stops when Isaiah pins him with one sharp glance.

I've stayed on Echo's cell for too long—long enough that if she did power up her phone, she would have ended the call by now, but regardless I say the words, "I love you."

And hang up.

"That's it," I say to Isaiah. "That's all she said? Take a risk?"

"Yeah, that's it."

Take a risk. What the hell is Echo going to do to prove she's a risk-taker? The last time Echo got bold, she broke into school to stop me from stealing her file. Echo keeps thinking she's not a risk-taker, but when my girl goes, she goes big and falls hard.

My eyes slam shut. Goes big. Falls hard. "Fuck me."

"What?" Isaiah asks.

"I need a car. I think I know where she went, and we need to get there before she does."

"I bet you the asshole has a car." Isaiah jacks his thumb toward Hunter.

We both assess him, and he presses his hands into his pockets. "Tell me where she went, and I'll take you."

"Naw," says Isaiah. "You give us the keys, I'll drive, he'll save the girl and I'll let you live." Isaiah looks over at me. "One of us is getting the happy ending."

Because there's never a discussion when Isaiah appears this pissed, Hunter pulls out his keys, and I smirk at Isaiah. "You're driving?"

"Out of the two of us, I'm the one who knows how to drive fast."

We had to walk back to Vail village to get Hunter's car so Echo got a hell of a head start—even with Isaiah cruising beyond the speed limit. He passed cars like half of them were sitting still. It'll be a miracle if Isaiah doesn't burn out the engine.

I called Echo's cell again and again. From the backseat of the energy-efficient car, Beth tried from her cell and used Isaiah's twice. Didn't make a damn bit of difference. Echo was either ignoring us or her phone was dead.

Longest two-hour drive in my life, and these last ten miles were going to murder me. With a forest ranger on our ass, Isaiah's had to follow the fifteen-mile-per-hour speed limit.

"Want to tell us what's going on?" Isaiah asks.

With her head against the window, Beth opens her eyes, ending what I thought had been a cat nap. One hundred and fifty miles. It's what we've traveled, and every mile between here and Vail I've thought how I could be wrong. Maybe this isn't where she went. Maybe she's someplace else, hurting, alone...I punch the door...doing something stupid without me.

"We were here a few nights ago. Some guys were jumping off a cliff into a pool of water. I wanted to. Echo wouldn't. She's trying to prove something."

Isaiah raises an eyebrow. "Why didn't she wait for you?"

"She's not proving something to me." I knead my eyes

as the images of the hundred things that could have gone wrong torture me in slow motion. "She's proving something to herself."

Echo finally understands it's not about pleasing Hunter or her dad or me, and when she figures it out, she takes a risk that could kill her.

"There." I point to the entrance to the campsite. "Park there."

My heart pounds hard when I see Echo's car. Barely placing it in park, all three of us fall out, and I'm already on the path. "This is on me. Stay here."

"Her engine's still hot, Noah," yells out Isaiah. "She's not far ahead."

With that, I run. Down the path, through the trees, praying she's over a bend, past a clearing. Hoping she'll be there right before my eyes, but she never is. She's out of reach. Just like my parents were.

"What do you see when you look down?" I asked.

"You sound way too much like Mrs. Collins." That sexy irritation leaked into Echo's voice. "And that's not a compliment."

"Answer the question."

"Rocks. Lots of sharp, kill-me-by-impaling rocks."

I'm through the woods, and sweat breaks out along my hairline as I spot Echo teetering on the rock wall.

"You can call it uptight all you want, but I call it not being suicidal. I have a four-inch—thick file in my therapist's office, and I can guarantee not once does the word suicidal *appear. Depressed? Withdrawn? Freak of nature? Sure. But not suicidal."*

I made love to her. I made love to her, and I made a promise. One that I broke the moment I walked away from her at the party. Echo's been dealt a tough hand,

and she's always been strong. She has a fighter's heart, but this week could have been the final push over the edge.

"S'up, baby." My body practically quakes with the urge to grab her, but with her toes dangling off the cliff, I'm frightened I'll spook her, and she'll accidentally go over.

As if she's in a dream, Echo slowly assesses me from over her shoulder. "You found my note?"

Jesus Christ, the thought of a note sends chills along my spine. "What type of note?"

"The one in our room? The one telling you I was coming here?"

"Nope." Though I wish I would have thought of checking the room before we left. Maybe it would have saved a few years off my life. Or it could have fucked with me harder. "What are you doing here?"

"I want to jump." Echo returns her gaze to the pool below. I ease up to the edge but still three feet from her. One slow inch at a time, and I'll hold on to her and never let go.

"Why didn't you wait for me? You know I like a good rush." Not anymore. I've never been so sick at the thought of a high in my life.

"I was scared I'd lose my nerve." Echo inhales deeply, and her fingers close tight then release several times, as if she's considering jumping then not jumping then considering it again.

"You don't need to do this, Echo."

"I do," she says plainly but then sucks in a quivering breath. "My mom is going to be in Denver."

"I know."

This forces her focus in my direction, and I'll do anything to keep those gorgeous emerald eyes on me.

"How?" she asks.

"Hunter came looking for you. He said you left upset."

Her forehead wrinkles, and I lose her to the water again. "He probably thinks I'm nuts."

"Doesn't matter what he thinks."

Echo's shoulders roll forward, and she appears to shrink. "That's it, Noah. That's why I'm here. I spent an entire summer searching for someone who'd tell me that I was good. To tell me that I had talent, and do you know where it got me?"

Me eating out of the palm of her hand? "Where?"

"Nowhere. I'm in the same exact place as I was before. Aires is still dead. The scars are still on my arms, and this big fat gaping wound in my chest is still there. I've tried everything to fill the void. I've tried art, and I've tried regaining the memories. I've tried pretending that I'm okay and that going forward is better.

"But nothing can replace Aires. Not you. Not the memories I fought so hard to recover. Not a relationship with my mother or father. Nothing. And to realize that he's gone and that there's nothing I can do about it..."

Echo's voice breaks, and my soul cracks along with it. "It hurts, Noah. It hurts, and it's here, and it's becoming overwhelming, and Mrs. Collins is wrong because this whole talking-about-it crap hurts like hell!"

The word *hell* vibrates off the rock walls and repeats in the wind. We both jerk our heads to the sound.

"It's an echo," I tell her. Echo manically giggles, and I grab hold of that one thread. "Remember when you told me what your name meant?"

"I beat you at pool, and you stared at my chest."

And her ass. "I let you win."

"I handed your manhood to you on a platter."

Yes, she did. "Echo was the girl who lost her voice, right?"

She nods.

"Then tell me who Aires was."

Her forehead crumples. "Did you not hear me? This hurts. This whole Aires thing hurts. It doesn't feel better to remember him. It doesn't feel better to talk about him. It feels like someone is torturing me."

"I know." I press a hand over my chest, over my heart, understanding the exact location of the ache she's referring to. "I get it. It's like a pain you can't stop suffering through. You think it has to stop at some point, but it doesn't. I get it, Echo, and I'm telling you to tell me about Aires. Tell me the story."

Echo's lower lip trembles, and I don't dare advance in her direction again because she keeps edging away the closer I try to get. I swear she wavers with the breeze. "Aires..."

"Come on, Echo. You can do it."

"Aires...Aires was a ram." She sadly smiles. "Which is fitting because he was so stubborn."

"Just like you?" I ask, with a slight tease, and Echo blushes. I'm getting to her. I'm slowly sliding past the hurt to her heart. One step at a time. "Keep going."

"A king took on a second wife." The statement strangled with sarcasm. "And she hated the daughter and son that he had conceived from a previous marriage."

I kick at a stone, and it bounces off the wall before it lands next to a protruding rock at the bottom. That's a long way down. "Is that how you feel about Ashley?"

I expect a fast yes, but Echo winces. "No. It used to be,

but no...I used to believe she hated me, but...anyhow...the stepmother devised this plan where the son was going to be sacrificed, and the son's mother prayed to Zeus for him to stop it and Zeus sent Aires, the golden ram, to save them."

"So this is one of the good stories." Not like Echo's name where the girl loses her voice then fades away into nothing.

"No..." Echo pauses. "It's not. Aires saves the brother and the sister, but the girl still falls to her death, while the boy lived." She trails off, and the wind whips through the trees, through Echo's hair, and I hate that it pushes in the direction of over.

"Do you know what I used to think?" she asks.

I think I want her away from the edge. "What?"

"That the brother had to be mad at Aires."

"Why?"

Echo's eyes harden into stone. "Aires's one job was to save both of them, and he only saved one."

"I'm mad at my mom." Damn me to hell, I said the words. I admitted it, and the guilt of feeling this way about someone I loved and who is dead destroys me. "I'm mad my mom didn't tell me about her family. I'm mad at both of my parents for not having a will. For not figuring out their shit enough to secure a future for me and my brothers in case they died. I'm fucking pissed that they didn't change the batteries in the fire detectors, and I'm even more fucking pissed that they died."

My chest pumps rapidly, and I can't control the intake of air. Echo seems to mimic the same ability to not breathe, and her hand goes to the nape of her neck as if she can wrench free the invisible noose. "I can't be mad."

"Why not?" I shout. "Because I am. And here's the thing. It doesn't change that I loved them."

I dig deep, thinking of what my uncle said. It's not my fault my parents died. My mother would be proud of me... even if I'm pissed. Especially that I'm pissed. "Being mad doesn't change that they died. Not being mad, acting like they were perfect...it doesn't bring them back."

A sob racks Echo's body, and she slams her hand over her mouth to prevent it, but it doesn't stop. Her entire body shudders, and she wipes at the tears as if that one act will wipe away the pain she's been harboring since her brother died.

"Then what will bring them back?" Echo begs. "Because I'm terrified to go forward thinking that this is what it feels like to lose, and going forward means that I'll always lose something. I can't lose like this again. I can't."

"You can!" I force myself to soften my voice. "You can."

I reach out, the need to touch her overwhelming me, and this time when I move forward, she doesn't step back. My fingers caress her sweet face. As Echo always does, she fits perfectly.

"You can," I repeat. "Remember what I told you. We've been through too much for something like this to get us down. For anything to get us down."

She rocks her head in a no, as if she doesn't believe me.

"We're going to lose again," I tell her. "It doesn't matter if we walk away from each other now or in seventy years after we've had ten kids and fifty grandkids. Someday, one of us is going to go. Either by choice or death. Everyone we love meets the same fate. You and I, we know this. We can either run from it and let it decide our future for us, or we can say fuck it and live for this moment now. I'm done permitting anything other than me to control my life.

"You told me that I wouldn't be happy if I was changing for you. You're right. But the changes you've seen, the changes that will be coming, they're happening because I want them. I want to be an architect because I want to build you that house. I want to build a lot of houses. I want a lot of things out of life, Echo, and I want you with me when I do them. The question is...can you put up with me when I fuck up and go asshole?"

With tears cascading down her face, Echo laughs. "You are the only person who is capable of apologizing while using profanity and it still sounds sweet."

Using my thumbs, I dry the tears from her face. "Damn straight, baby."

The fleeting smile falls. "I miss Aires, and I'm mad at him. I feel so awful that I'm mad at him."

"Me, too. Maybe Mrs. Collins will be into that group therapy crap with the two of us."

She giggles and leans into my chest. My arms wrap around Echo, and I've never felt so relieved in my life. Her soft body holding on to mine, her scent filling each intake of air. I kiss the top of her head. I've never belonged with anyone like I belong with Echo.

"I love you," she whispers. "I love you, and I'd prefer to do the whole kid and grandkid thing, but I love you enough that I'll stay with you even if we last for six more months."

"We're the long haul," I tell her.

"Even if we aren't. I'm going to stop questioning when it ends because you're right. It does all end. The question I should ask is what I'm going to do with the time in between."

Which brings me to what's going to kill my pride... possibly kill me. "You're wrong. You did get something from this summer."

"What's that?" she mumbles into my chest.

I comb my fingers through her silky hair. It's an automatic gesture. One I've done a million times. With this statement, the act will no longer be one I get to take for granted. "You get to study for a full year under one of the best artists in the country. It got you into one of the biggest art shows of the year."

Echo pulls back to look at me, and a hint of happiness lights her face. "You do listen."

"Baby," I say, exasperated. "I listen to every damn thing that falls out of your mouth. Your every sigh. Every small, sexy sound when we kiss and every hitch of your breath when you sleep. Echo..."

Say it, asshole. "I want you to stay here for the year. When you told me..." It ripped my damn heart out and it shredded my soul. "This means something to you, and you mean everything to me. We'll make it work. Skype. Phone calls. I'll visit you. You'll visit home. I'm behind you. Every step of the way."

She does it. She fucking does it. Echo steps back from the edge, and her eyes are wider than I've seen. "You're serious?"

"Never been more serious in my life."

Echo

My mind spins. Noah's promising me everything I've ever fantasized about. He's encouraging me to chase my dreams and will stand by me...at least emotionally. This, for Noah, is epic.

Like the last time we visited here, the evening is closing in around us. The night sky is fading into orange and reds. Soon, the shadows will overtake us, but this time, the darkness doesn't frighten me. Just because I may not be able to see Noah, it doesn't mean that he's not beside me.

My fingers slide along his cheek, and I relish the way his stubble sweetly scratches my palm. I craved more, and Noah's given me more.

Noah tilts his head into my touch. He also feels this connection...this magnetic force calling us home.

Home.

Noah's become a man and has built us a home. Not a structure. Not a physical place to lay our heads, but a home in the sense that it completely matters...we belong to each other.

I inch higher on my toes. Noah begins to lean down to me, but I don't want him reaching for me. I need to be the one who kisses him first. To be the one that starts the first night that begins without the baggage I've been carrying.

Before Noah has a chance to lead, I brush my mouth against his and slip my tongue between the part of his lips. Noah immediately fists my hair, and the gentle pull sends shivers through my bloodstream.

I inhale, and Noah's spicy scent fills my lungs, and it's intoxicating. Hands roam, cooler air pricks at my skin, and the pads of my fingertips skim above the goose bumps rising on his back.

The wind whips through my hair, stinging me and evidently stinging Noah as his strong hand smoothes back the curls and he begins this slow, seductive descent of kisses along my jawline and down my neck.

My body cries for more and arches into him, but I drove here for a reason. With a hand on Noah's chest and a lot of willpower, I ease back. "I want to jump."

It's like watching a train speeding at two hundred miles per hour slam on the brakes, and I stifle a giggle as Noah attempts to switch gears. He's totally disheveled thanks to my exploring. His hair completely mussed. His shirt hitched up on one side, exposing the muscles of his abs. "What?"

"Hunter said I wasn't a risk-taker, and I am. He said that I should wear long sleeves to hide my scars because it would be easier. I don't want easy because I know I'm strong. I went on this trip with you, and I've begged gallery owner after gallery owner to give me a chance, and I told Hunter his paintings sucked twice."

Noah laughs, and the smile on my face grows. He hitches a finger in the loop of my jean cut offs and draws me near. "That's my girl."

His girl. My cheeks warm with a bit of shyness and joyous embarrassment. His girl. "Your girl wants to jump off this ledge into a pool of water."

Noah peers over. "Know what I see when I look down?"

"Water?" I grin way too wide and innocently.

"Rocks," he answers as his other hand claims my waist. "Sharp rocks."

"What happened to Noah Hutchins—thrill-seeker, rush-finder, willing to do whatever?"

I meant to make him smile, but the opposite happens. His face falls, and his hold on me tightens. "I thought I messed us up, Echo. Beyond repair and the thought of not being with you anymore..." He briefly closes his eyes and swallows. "I'm not anxious to watch you jump toward rocks."

I reach around and link his hands with mine then swing them at our sides. "What if we jump together? You can scare the bad rocks away."

Half of his mouth tips up. "What's the deal, baby? Why this? Why now? You don't need to do this to prove anything to anybody."

Ugh...and that would be the reason why. "I want to jump. To prove it to me. Not to Hunter. Not to you. Not to anyone else. I'm sort of mad at myself. I spent an entire summer trying to prove that I had talent by waiting for someone else to tell me that I did. That I was someone separate from my mother and you know where it got me? Right back where I started. With her in my face."

Noah scratches the stubble and seems to be weighing his words. "What's that have to do with jumping?"

"Because she wouldn't have jumped."

When Noah raises a questioning eyebrow, I push forward. "Mom wasn't the type that would have left an art gallery. She made every decision about her life based on her art—a showing came first over dance recitals or kindergarten orientation. Her number one most stated reason for coming off her meds was because they supposedly killed her creativity.

"She came off in order to create, and she almost killed me, and she has yet to say she's sorry. If I go to this showing, she'll be there, and I'll have to face her again so I need to jump. I need to know, when I'm standing face-to-face with Mom, that I'm not her. That I realize there's more to life than a job."

"You're not her," says Noah.

"I know that," I answer honestly. "I know that now, but sometimes a girl has to jump." I stare at the ground and nudge a pebble. "And I'd like you to jump with me—and before you say no, you already promised you would."

"I did."

Because I have this problem with not stopping while I'm ahead... "And as I explained in the note that you obviously didn't read, I'd like you to be with me, by my side, when I go to the showing in Denver and when I see Mom. I realized that...you've always supported me. You left Louisville, your brothers, Isaiah and Beth, your home and family to follow me. You've always supported me, and I'm being selfish and asking you to support me some more. Please be with me in Denver."

A shadow crosses Noah's face, and my heart plummets. "I know that you'll have to miss Jacob and Tyler's game, and that makes me feel awful, but this means a lot to me, Noah, and—"

"You're asking me to come with you to Denver for when you see your mom?"

Aw, crap. Here I thought we were doing well. I shift my footing. "I also told you to come here. I was going to set up camp and be waiting for you and everything...you know, to surprise you. I found out that a bus was leaving Vail for here an hour after I left and—"

Noah's hands fly up and cup my face, and I snap my mouth shut because if I tried to continue it'd be this weird muted mumble.

His dark eyes flare with unwavering intensity. "You left a note asking me to come here then to be with you when you meet with your mom?"

I nod, but it's more of a centimeter since he still has control over my head.

"Echo Emerson..." Noah moves into me. His feet brush mine and so do many other amazing parts of him. "I love you."

Not the reaction I was expecting, but one I'll definitely take. "So you'll come?" It comes out garbled, but he seems to understand.

"I wouldn't miss it for the world."

"But your brothers—"

Noah glides his thumb over my lips. "I made a promise to you, Echo. Months ago in that hospital room and the night we made love. I've been waiting for you to let me keep it."

He's so near that I lick my lips, waiting for him to kiss me. Begging for him to kiss me. Thinking I'm going to combust if he doesn't kiss me. But with one inhale, Noah steps back and grips my hand. "Ready to get wet?"

"Definitely."

With my fingers safely locked in his, Noah and I jump.

NOAH

It's midnight, and Echo's hair is still damp from our swim. Back in Vail, Echo sits beside me on the curb under a streetlight and stares at the broken-down house my mother grew up in. The grass is taller. The windows no less cracked. The house no less decayed.

Echo's been silent, listening to me download the conversation with my uncle. All the truths that I thought I knew and all the truths I know now.

As I finish recounting every word that was said, Echo reaches over and presses her hand over mine. "I'm sorry, Noah."

"It's okay." It's not, and the sad softness in her eyes tells me that what happened to my mom isn't okay, but she believes that I will be. Hell, for the first time in my life I believe I'm going to be okay, too.

The moment Echo and I finished playing in the water, I pulled Echo out and brought her here. Tonight was evidently about spilling our guts. Taking what was the most raw and broken inside us and offering it to the other as a show of what we can't heal on our own. It's the most simple and heartbreaking of vulnerabilities...to admit that you need someone else.

I need Echo.

She needs me.

Together we're in love.

"Are you going to reach out to them, then?" Echo asks quietly. "Your mother's parents?"

"No. I'm pissed at Mom for not telling me about them, but I understand why she didn't. In this case no family is definitely better than a bad one."

"And your uncle?"

I glance over at the church, and a light shines in the rectory. The curtain in the window moves as if someone was there and now doesn't want to be seen. "Yeah. Him I'll reach out to. I don't agree with his choice, but that's a case of keeping bad family with a shot at redemption."

"You're not alone." Echo scoots closer to me and rests her head on my shoulder. "You have your brothers and you have me, Beth and Isaiah."

My lips turn up at the thought of Isaiah returning the car to that prick Hunter. I drove Echo's car back while Isaiah did his best to wear the engine out on Hunter's. "That's a damn good family to have."

"It is," she agrees. "Makes you realize that home isn't a place, doesn't it? That it's all about the people."

It's like Echo flipped on a light in my mind. This building in front of me—it's not a home. Never was and never will be. I stand and offer my hand to Echo. "Let's go home."

Echo's mouth curves into that sexy siren smile that has owned me since the first day she flashed it in my direction. "I'm assuming you're referring to the hotel, not Kentucky."

"As you said, it's the people, baby, not the place. And where I belong is with you and a lot less clothes."

Echo accepts my hand with a wicked glint in her eyes. "Then let's go."

Every time Noah and I have entered a hotel room this summer, a cocoon of nerves has formed in my stomach, and the moment his lips touched mine, millions of butterflies have spread their wings and flown in this fast race of nervous adrenaline and lust.

But tonight...it's different.

Noah's different.

I'm different.

Together...we're different.

Noah shuts the door behind him, and the click becomes this familiar sound that causes me to smile. Noah struts past, and the quick sweep of my body tells me he's already devoured me in eight different ways in his mind. Just guessing his fantasies, my body temperature peaks. Heat gathers in every single delicious right area.

We left Louisville with two high school diplomas, a couple hundred dollars in cash and a lot of faith that we'd survive the summer. I left a girl, and he left a boy in a man's body. This person in front of me, he's no longer a boy, he's fully a man.

It's what I wanted for the summer...to change. I did change, but not in any of the ways I imagined. I changed in ways far better.

Noah's phone pings, and he slips it out of his back pocket. He reads a message, and with a smirk he types something in return. "Isaiah and Beth are in for the night."

"Tell him thanks for me. Beth, too."

He drops the phone onto the bedside table, pulls his shirt over his head and tosses it to the ground, divulging each and every gorgeous ripped-out ab muscle. "Already have."

Noah sinks onto the bed, and the expectant look in his eye tells me that he's ready for me to join him. I'm ready, too. Standing a foot from him, I slide off my shirt, and his eyes darken with the movement. It's not the first time I've done this in front of him, but the rest of it is new.

There's an undercurrent of excitement in my belly. With a flick of a button, I shimmy off my cutoffs, with a lot less grace than desired, and leave on my bra and underwear. I hope that he enjoys whatever little show I put on, but more important, I love what Noah sees as I strip—the girl he fell in love with...the girl who loves him.

Before walking over to him, I study my scars, and what unnerves me is that the flash of disgust is missing. When it comes to the scars, there's nothing lurking. No hidden hate. No surge of embarrassment. No sadness. There's nothing more, either. No giddiness. No awe, but I'm okay with that. It's just an acknowledgement. A presence.

I glance up at Noah. "They don't bother me. Not now, at least." Hopefully, not ever again.

Noah stands and takes my hands, stretching my arms out in front of me. "Can I show you something?"

I nod, curious about why Noah's pushed pause when we're so close to naked and in bed. Keeping his eyes locked on mine, he brings us over to the mirror. Then from behind me, he gently flips over my arms to reveal the scars and he brings my arms together as if I was shielding myself. "Do you see it?"

"See what?"

"How you fell."

My eyes shoot straight to my scars, and my heart pounds so quickly that it skips beats.

Noah swipes his thumb over the pulse point on my wrist. "Easy, baby. Just take it slow."

I breathe in, and Noah exhales along with me. Releasing one of my hands, Noah traces one finger along a scar on my right arm then connects that scar directly to the one on the left.

"This one must have been the deepest," he says gently. "It's the longest, too. There are some that don't connect, but these..." Another slow caress against my skin, then another highlighting of areas. "They're the same cut. You must have brought your arms up to shield yourself."

My mouth dries out and like the constellations in the sky, I notice how the lines connect, how a gut reaction probably saved my life. I prevented those sharp pieces of glass from piercing my lungs, my heart.

"Do they ever bother you?" I ask.

Noah draws my arm toward his lips. "Never."

Letting him handle my weight, I lean back against Noah. I stare at our image in the mirror and see two people who love each other very much and will do anything to help heal old wounds.

There's an intimacy in this moment, and it's not the kind I originally thought we would share when we first walked in. It's a better type. The kind that lasts. "What if I said I just need you to hold me tonight?"

"I'd say that I could do that every night for the rest of my life and die a happy man."

Noah takes my hand and leads me to the bed. "There's something else I'd like to tell you."

"I'm listening."

"My mom named me Noah for a reason."

With my head on his chest and our arms and legs tangled, I close my eyes and listen to Noah recall the rest of what his uncle had to say. I smile with the newfound hope in his voice. Noah was his mother's second chance, and I wonder if he knows that he's also my second chance at happiness.

I cuddle closer to him and rest, knowing that Noah is mine.

NOAH

"I'm going to take a shower." Echo blows me a kiss then grabs her robe.

I sit at the desk and wait for Echo's laptop to boot. We checked in an hour ago at the hotel in Denver, Colorado. Beth and Isaiah left five minutes ago to scout out what trouble they could find since we're in the heart of the city.

"Want me to join you?" I swivel in the chair and enjoy the sight of her tight ass swaying from side to side.

"I have an hour to get ready, Noah. Walk in this door, and I'll redefine frigid."

I chuckle and turn back to the computer. With a swishing sound, Skype automatically loads, and as I click on the browser to check my email, my eyes drift to the list of people signed in to Skype. Mrs. Collins is one of them.

Figures. She and Echo have a session scheduled so Echo can drop her worries on Mrs. Collins before we head to the gallery.

Rehashing the crap that's happened this past week, I select her name and wait to see if she accepts the call. Two seconds later, I'm greeted by my overenthusiastic therapist.

"I thought it would be you," says Mrs. Collins. "How are you, Noah?"

"Good." And it's an honest answer. "Got a few minutes?"

She's wearing a Poison T-shirt and no makeup. "For you, I've got plenty of time. What's going on?"

I inhale deeply and jump, telling her about the party, getting arrested, getting free and meeting my uncle. Watching her reaction was like seeing snapshots of a person on a rollercoaster determined not to let the rider next to them know that they are terrified of the hills. Mrs. Collins is good at hiding her expressions, but meeting with her so much has taught me that her eyes can betray her. In them I've read disappointment and elation.

I shut the hell up, and there's a moment of silence. Mrs. Collins nods like I'm still talking then says, "So where does that leave you now?"

"Here. In a hotel room with Echo, Isaiah and Beth. Getting ready to stand with Echo at the showing and preparing to be her shoulder for when she sees her mom."

"How do you feel about everything that's happened?"

I lean forward. "Like shit for hurting Echo. With my mom's family, I feel like I've been run over by an oil tanker. Knowing that Echo and I can walk through hell together and come out stronger on the other side..." I halfway smile. "It's the closest I've been to being a king."

The smile falls, and I rub my hands together as I relax back in the seat. Mrs. Collins tilts her head. "What?"

"Do you believe in happy-ever-afters?" I ask.

"I believe I've seen a few movies in my time, but I'd like to know your thoughts."

"Do you ever answer a question?" I push.

"Yes. I answered that one. What are your thoughts on happy-ever-afters?"

I pause. "I believe in happy for now. I want Echo and me to work. She loves me. I love her. I've seen enough already to know that life isn't always shits and giggles. Life is hard, but it's going to be easier with Echo by my side."

"Even with Echo a thousand miles away?"

"Even with that," I answer. "There's no reason that we still can't be happy."

"That's all any of us can ask for, isn't it?" She grins.

I glance over at the closed door of the bathroom. "When this started, Echo covered her arms again. Hunter thinks she should cover them tonight. She doesn't want to, and I'm in agreement with her, but am I wrong on this?"

"It's healthy for Echo to accept her scars. There will be people who can never understand Echo because of it, and then there will be people like you that love her regardless. It's something she'll have to learn to deal with."

I nod to let her know I get it.

"And Noah?"

"Yeah?"

"There will be times that she backtracks. There will be days that it's easier to cover them. A few days of doing so out of months isn't a backslide. Sometimes we all need a moment to lick our wounds. And sometimes she might just be cold."

I chuckle. "True." After a few beats: "I'm mad at my mom." Though not as much as I was.

Mrs. Collins places a hand over her heart. "It's okay to be mad at her."

"I know." I clear my throat when it threatens to choke me up. "When I get back, could I stop by? Maybe talk about it?"

I swear the head shrink wags her tail and pants. "You paid me in advance, remember? Let's schedule an appointment now."

The bell rings, and the elevator doors open to the lobby. With marble floors and shiny shit everywhere, it's by far the best hotel Echo and I've stayed since we've started this trip. The reason we're here is because Hunter's paying for the rooms for his artists in the show.

I didn't like the idea of accepting Hunter's charity, but Echo described it as a business perk. That explanation I can respect, plus it's something I'm going to have to get used to. That is until I make enough money to pay for anything Echo craves.

I walk out of the lobby and into the late-evening sunlight. Isaiah texted me fifteen minutes ago, asking me to meet him in the parking lot. He and Beth bailed out of our joint room two hours ago so I could help calm Echo's nerves and to allow us time to get ready.

"Going to prom again?" Isaiah asks as I walk up to Echo's car. He extends a cold beer to me. Condensation drips down the bottle.

"Fuck you," I mumble, but I take the beer. Isaiah and Beth continue to rip my outfit: white button-down shirt, black slacks, dress shoes. The works.

"Is that a tie?" Beth cracks a rare genuine smile.

"Yeah." I stare her down.

"Noah Hutchins has gone like the beer," she says, "domestic."

"Got a problem with that?"

She shrugs. "I'll have a problem with it later. Today, I have beer."

I can deal with that.

"Where you'd score this?" I motion to the beer in my hand then at the bottles they hold in theirs.

"I have my ways," says Isaiah. "Figured you'd need it. Got an extra one for Echo if she wants it."

"She might." My gaze wanders to the eighth floor. Echo's talking with Mrs. Collins for some last-minute pointers on how to handle tonight. I'm also nervous as fuck, but I'm going to follow the advice Mrs. Collins gave me—stick tight to Echo, yet give her space. Love and accept her needs and wants. While the woman can't predict what will happen, she makes me better at facing it.

Isaiah runs a hand along the tattoo of the tiger on his arm and peers out onto the traffic moving at a snail's pace on the road in front of the hotel. "I don't feel right about Echo paying for these tickets."

My stomach twists, and I pop off the top of the beer. The small cap clanks when I toss it into the bag. Isaiah and Beth thought they'd be hitching a ride back to Louisville with me and Echo. I thought that was the plan, too, but Echo prefers to keep the car in Colorado then fly back so she doesn't have to drive back by herself after she returns home to pack for the year. I offered to drive from Louisville to Colorado with her and then ride the bus home, but Echo didn't want me to miss the first week of college.

"Echo feels bad she's not driving back so let her do this," I tell Isaiah. Because I'm eating my damn pride by letting her pay for my bus ticket, too. It's a partnership, she told me, and Echo's right. Some days she'll be on an upswing, some days she'll be on the down. This is her upswing.

"I'll pay her back," says Isaiah.

"I know." So will I. With a big-ass house on the tallest mountain and all the damn little dogs she desires. But they're still not sleeping on my bed. "And Echo knows. It's all good, bro."

When Isaiah cracks his neck to the right, I try again. "We're family, Isaiah. You, me, Beth and Echo. I know we've all had shit handed to us, but we have something now. I've got your backs and you've got mine, which means every now and then you've got to let us help you out, too. You got it?"

Beth dips her head so that her hair hides her face, a sign the words I said breached that damn wall she keeps guarded, and Isaiah won't meet my eyes. Emotion... someone giving a shit...we're not used to it and when anyone offers any semblance of affection, none of us, including Echo, have a clue what to do with it.

But those days are over. Long gone. It's time the four of us start writing our own stories...our own destinies. I raise my beer in the air. "To family."

Beth's head jerks up. "Are you fucking kidding me? Are we seriously doing this?"

"Are you going to leave me hanging?"

She laughs, and her beer joins mine. "You're a crazy son of a bitch."

We both look to Isaiah. He scrubs his knuckles against his jaw then raises his bottle to ours and repeats, "To family."

With a clink, each one of us swallows from the long neck then scrambles for another topic, but I don't care. I've finally found what I've been searching for...a family.

Echo wears blue. Royal blue, and I love how it makes her green eyes shine. The dress is simple, made of smooth fabric, and is cut in ways that highlights her curves. She's drop-dead gorgeous, but she's nervous as hell.

We're inside the largest gallery known to man with towering walls, a black ceiling and the best lighting available. In a few minutes, the doors will open, and Echo has been reduced to wringing her hands.

"Mrs. Collins told me to breathe," Echo says.

"Then I suggest trying it. Air in. Then air out. I hear it helps." I'm not kidding.

Evil glare from my girl.

"Echo?" A woman in a black dress approaches us. "Do you have a few minutes? I'd like to ask your opinion on the lighting on your painting."

Echo agrees, and when she looks at me I gesture to the woman who has already left. "I'll stay here. You can find me when you're ready."

She flashes that glorious smile. "Thanks."

Damn, Echo's sexy as hell when she walks—especially in heels. When she rounds the corner, I push off the wall and pretend to understand the painting with red-and-black marks slashed across the canvas. Some things I just don't get.

"But you said there was room!" A girl's voice grabs my attention and farther down the hallway Hunter and a dark-haired girl I've seen from his studio are deep in conversation. "You said last month that I could extend past the summer session for the year."

I should move so I won't be accused of eavesdropping, but I told Echo I'd stay put. Plus, they're the ones talking loud enough for people in China to hear.

"Meredith," Hunter starts. "There was room. An artist I had seen potential in earlier in the year decided along with me that it was best that we didn't work together."

"So they came back?" Her voice breaks.

"No, they didn't." Hunter crosses his arms over his chest, and the poor girl crumples against the wall.

"You're giving my spot to Echo." The girl sways on her feet like the statement was a blow to the head.

"Next year, Meredith. I promise you'll have a spot for the one-year program next year."

Hunter turns away from Meredith, and my stomach drops. Fuck. This is the girl that Echo had told me asked her to lunch. The girl that Echo felt could have been her friend. There's no way Echo will be okay with this, and there's no way gossip like this won't eventually be burning her ears.

"Noah?" Echo rounds the corner on her way back to me, and her eyes are wide with concern. "Did I hear that correctly?"

The urge is to tell her no. To keep her protected. To keep her happy. But I tried keeping something once from Echo in the name of not hurting her, and it almost destroyed us.

"Echo," Hunter calls. "Are you ready?"

She glances at him then at me. "I didn't hear it all, but I think you did. I need you to tell me what happened."

"I will. I promise."

Echo

The three people studying my painting, gesturing at my painting, talking in front of my painting are three of the biggest gallery owners in the world. I'm going to puke everywhere then die.

Near the wall opposite them, Noah and I watch. My foot taps continually against the floor, and the clicking sound from my high-heeled shoe is probably driving Noah to the brink of insanity.

Instead of telling me to chill out, he places a hand on the small of my back, leans down and whispers, "Let's go see something else."

I nod and with a gentle nudge, Noah guides us through the throngs of people. I smooth down my blue dress and berate myself for the hundredth time for wearing something that rides up when I walk.

"Stop it," Noah breathes into my ear, and the fine hairs along the nape of my neck deliciously stand on end. "You look great."

"You're fine if my butt hangs out."

Noah chuckles. "Not if other people can see it. And since you brought it up, there's a broom closet to the left..."

He trails off, and I imagine all of the sweet, sweet naughty things Noah and I could do in a small, private space. For three point one seconds, I consider it. My nerves were shot fifteen minutes into this showing. That was when the first person approached me and told me they loved my work.

Hearing something like that—it's comparable to being drunk on a high wire. It's an overwhelming high, and I'm learning I don't handle overwhelmed well. It sort of makes everything on the inside feel stretched while the smile on the outside becomes bigger.

But one look at Noah, and the sounds and chaos fade away. He's my secret weapon tonight. The reason I haven't run screaming from the building. I wish I wasn't going to be away from him so much this coming year.

"Outside?" Noah jacks his thumb to a door leading to a patio, and I immediately turn right, cutting off a waiter with a tray full of drinks.

I inhale deeply the moment the cool evening air nips at the exposed skin on my arms. The scars have received a few pointed stares, but for the first time in my life I've felt nothing about it. I can't change my scars any more than I can change the color of my eyes. They're a part of me. It's who I am, and I like the person I've become.

"You cold?" Noah rubs his hands up and down my arms.

I shiver, not from the cold, but from the heat of his palms on my skin. It's like a flick of a switch and the attraction awakens. "Not when you're around."

He cocks his head to the brick wall behind me. "You know, I've got a thing about backing you up against walls. It'd be a shame to let that wall go to waste."

I laugh, and as I start to wind my arms around his neck, I remember Meredith. The high crashes. Meredith and Hunter were arguing. They mentioned me and Meredith and the spot for the program, but... "What happened between Meredith and Hunter?"

Noah rolls his shoulders, attempting to ease the tension. Oh, crap. This is going to be bad.

"Before I tell you this, I want you to know that it's okay to stay. You earned everything that's happening to you, but I want you to be prepared for the fallout."

"Now you're scaring me."

"Hunter's pushing off Meredith's spot in the program for a year. That's how he created a space for you."

My intestines cramp. I had no idea I was stealing anyone's place, much less Meredith's. "This is awful. She left her home over this. Her family practically kicked her out." Panic causes adrenaline to rush in my veins. "Noah, I don't think she has anywhere else to go."

Noah cups my face and inches it up so that I'm staring straight into his eyes. "This does not diminish what you've worked for. No one can fault you for choices Hunter makes. You didn't know that you were bumping Meredith out when you accepted, and you still wouldn't if I hadn't told you."

"Until I started the program." Then plenty of people would have been more than happy to gossip about it, hence why Noah mentioned a fallout. He's preparing me for the impending rumors.

"You've done nothing wrong, Echo. Find Meredith. Make peace with her then take the spot and hold your head high."

I open my mouth to argue, but the patio door opens. With one glance, my heart jumps to my throat, inhibiting my ability to breathe. Going rigid, Noah wraps an arm around my waist and brings me closer to him.

"Your call on this," he says so only I can hear.

I nod, because I can't talk.

"Hello, Echo," Mom says as she releases the door from her grasp and steps into the night. She's wearing a form-fitting red dress that spills out near her ankles. Sort of like she was a sparkly mermaid. Her hair is a blazing red and just as curly as mine, but she wears it up, and I wore mine down.

I'm not my mom. My choices are different.

"Hi." It comes out garbled, and I clear my throat to try again. "Hi."

"You look beautiful tonight," Mom offers softly. "And may I ask who your friend is?"

"This..." Can't seem to think or talk. "This...ah...is Noah. He's my boyfriend."

Mom surveys him like he's one of the paintings in the gallery, and I can't tell if she likes what she sees. "I'm Cassie, Echo's mother. It's nice to meet you."

I blow out a long stream of air. I can imagine the two million replies Noah would prefer to give her, and I'd bet my brother's car that most of them begin with a word that starts with the letter *f*.

"Echo said you would be here," Noah says.

Oh, Noah, I could kiss you. No bad words. No telling her she's the antichrist. I don't kiss him, but I do peek up at him in appreciation. It's lost on him as his focus remains on my mother.

Mom points behind her, to the gallery. "I saw your work. It's beautiful. Especially the constellation Aires."

Her forehead wrinkles, and she readjusts the silver bag

attached to her wrist. "I like that you painted Aires, and I like your technique, with the deep black around where the star Hamal is...like you created a hole."

"Thanks," I say, and the word tastes weird. All summer I've been searching for other people's approval. To be honest, part of me was hoping for her approval, but now that I'm here, listening to her, listening to other people, I realize the approval I desired was my own.

"But what I really appreciated," she continues, "was how you portrayed Hamal as a new star, like it had just been born out of the dark hole. It spoke to me, Echo."

I altered the constellation. It's something I did after Noah and I laid out our pain. The spot where Hamal should have been is dark, but off to the side...close by but far enough away to alter Aires, I painted a new star. One that had just been born. One to show that new things can come to life after there's a death.

"Your painting spoke to me," Mom repeats. "It spoke to me and, from listening to others, it's reaching them, as well."

I know. It's what I want to say, but I don't. This is where I experience the high, the giddiness. Not that people like my work, but that my work spoke to them. That there was a part of their soul that was touched.

"It made me feel like anything is possible," she says so quietly that I strain into the night, wondering if I heard her correctly.

I added the star to the painting because I lost a piece of me I'll never reclaim. The blackness of the loss will always be there, but I've gained new things in my life. A new path. A new love. A new outlook. Like the star, I've been reborn.

Mom's gaze flickers between me and Noah. "Can I talk to you alone?"

"No." But I do ease away from Noah. "But we can talk over here while Noah stands over there."

The patio is the size of my father's living room, and there's no doubt Noah will hear everything we say, but it will give Mom the illusion of privacy, and it will confirm I'm not alone.

With a kiss to my temple, Noah heads to the wall that had shown lots of promise moments before and leans his back against it. His eyes narrow on us, a hawk set on the mice.

"I'm proud of you." Mom motions to a rock wall, and the two of us sit. Me two feet away from her. "I heard of everything you've done this summer and how you're now studying under Hunter Gray. I can't express the pride I have inside."

I nod as she talks, but then I shake my head. "You shouldn't have done it. Made the phone calls asking people to buy my work."

Mom's eyes widen. "Who told you?"

The Wicked Witch of the West. "It doesn't matter. I wish you would have let me do this on my own."

"Echo..." Mom clutches her handbag. "I don't know how to make things better between us."

A heaviness overtakes my lungs. "You can say you're sorry."

"But it's not my fault—"

I throw up my hand, and she stops.

"Having bipolar disorder—no, that isn't your fault, and you should never apologize for that. What happened that night between us—the night that left me scarred—I know you were hurting. I came over to visit you because I was hurting, too. We both lost Aires."

Mom pales at the sound of his name, but I continue, "You made a mistake. You came off your meds. You were hurting, and I was hurting, and we both ended up in more pain. And here's the truth...I used to think that all the hurt I had inside me was about that night, but it's not... Forget that night. Let's look at you, Mom. Just you. There were periods in my life that you were given a choice between me and something else, and the something else always won."

"You don't understand," she interjects, not denying my words. "Those opportunities were life-altering with my art—"

"I'm not allowing you to sweep our past under the rug or dismiss me. It happened. I'm glad that you're doing well, and I'm glad that your career has taken off, but I can't be your daughter until you look me in the eye as my mother and tell me that you're sorry. Mom—I deserved to be number one at some point in your life, at least once. Not second or third behind your art and your career."

I suck in a breath and say what has to be said, even if it could be a stake to her heart. "And even if you do say you're sorry, you have to be okay with whatever type of relationship we can figure out because this—" I gesture to us "—will probably always be complicated because you hurt me. Not just that night—not just physically—"

It's so hard to say the words when they're like leftover shards of glass in my bloodstream that were so small the hospital had to leave them in. "All those years...all the times you chose something else... You broke my heart."

Mom presses a hand over her face, and a strangled

sound escapes from her. I close my eyes, willing away my own tears.

"I'm sorry, Echo," she says in a cracked voice. "You have no idea how sorry I am."

Her words unravel whatever facade I'd been trying to maintain. Mom mumbles it again and because of her pain, my pain, I reach over and take the hand on her lap. She squeezes my fingers. I squeeze her hand back.

We sit like that—Mom holding my hand, me holding her hand back—for longer than I would have liked while still not long enough. There are so many good memories I have of my mother...so many more than the bad. But the bad are beyond bad. They were—what were Mom's words?—life-altering.

Mom glances down at my scars, and I wonder what she sees. Our past? My future? Her mistakes?

"Do they still hurt?" she whispers. "Your arms? I've always wondered if the glass did something to the nerves that has kept you in pain."

There's still pain, just not the kind she's referring to, but it somehow helps to know that she's thought of me while we've been apart. "No, there's no pain."

What's going on between us is a quiet acceptance of how life will always be—a give and a take. A phone call here and there. Visits over coffee as I grow stronger. It'll be slow, it'll be hard, and who knows if it will ever work. But as I look down at my scars I see the pattern I never saw before, and as I glance over at Noah, I see a love I never thought I could experience.

I'm the girl who jumps off cliffs into water. I'm the girl who is going to live not for her talent, but for the people in her life.

I turn to my mother and utter the only words that I can truthfully say. "I know that you never meant to hurt me."

"I didn't," she whispers. "If I could undo it all, I would."

"I know," I whisper back.

The door to the patio opens again, and my mother moves so no one can spot the tear tracks on her cheeks.

"Echo?" asks Hunter as he stumbles into the middle of a family minefield.

I walk over to Hunter to give my mother the moment she needs. "Is everything okay?"

"Yes," he says in a way that indicates he's aware that everything out here is not okay. Then Hunter notices my mother. "Oh."

Oh.

"You must be Hunter Gray." Mom extends her hand to him as she joins us. All smiles and good cheer. Only a smidge of mascara near the corner of her eye indicates we were melting down over our past family drama.

"I am." Hunter graciously accepts her hand. "You have no idea how honored I am to meet you, Ms. Emerson. I'm a huge fan of your work."

"Cassie," she says. "Call me Cassie."

A wave of disorientation hits me. Mom's been divorced from Dad since I was in elementary school. That's been years and years and... "Hunter, can you give me a few more minutes with my mother?"

He surveys us both then makes direct eye contact with Noah. When Noah nods, it's like the two of them have reached some sort of weird male agreement.

"Find me when you're done, Echo," says Hunter. "There are people who would like to meet you."

Hunter leaves us, and before Mom can say anything,

I drop the question. "Why didn't you change your last name?"

"Because," Mom starts then stops.

"Because why?"

"Because..." Mom studies Noah, then the ground. "Because..."

The silence becomes strained until finally Mom stares straight into my eyes. "Don't ever do what I did. Don't take for granted what you have because it can slip away. I thought this—" she flutters her hand at the gallery "—was important. This is what I defined myself by. I loved your father, but if you want me to be honest with you, I didn't love him enough, and he knew it. That's why he fell for Ashley."

Her face falls, and it's painfully clear that she's forcing the smile. "Now, if you don't mind, I think I should visit the powder room, and I believe you have people to meet. Maybe we'll meet up again before the showing ends?"

I nod slightly, and Mom pivots on her feet and heads for the door.

"Mom," I call out the moment her hand is on the door handle.

She peers at me from over her shoulder.

"Thank you for answering my question...for being honest. Can I ask a random question now?"

"I'd prefer random."

"If you had a friend who was going to lose a great opportunity because of you, what would you do? Would you take it yourself, or step back to let them have it?"

Mom steps toward me. "Echo, no. Whatever it is that you're thinking, don't. This spot with Hunter will change your life and your career. Friendships come and go. It's the way of the business. Shots like this come along once in a lifetime."

And I have my answer. "Okay. I hear you."

Mom blows out a long stream of air then releases a forced smile. "Just so you know, in case you contact me again, I prefer conversations other than most of the ones we've had this evening. I don't like talking about what hurts."

Like she did when I was younger, she tucks a stray curl behind my ear and lightly pats my face. For a second, I feel like I'm five as she gives me a genuine smile. "Enjoy tonight, Echo. You deserve it."

As quickly as she swept into my life, she sweeps out. Mrs. Collins is right...locking up the pain has to be the worst way to live.

I blink, and it's like the evening drops twenty degrees. Goose bumps form on my arms, and I run my hands over them. Mom said she did it wrong. Mom told me not to repeat her mistakes, but then she told me not to abandon the spot. A flood of nausea rolls through me. What am I doing?

With his eyes narrowed on me, Noah pushes off the wall. "Are you okay?"

"I need to talk to Hunter."

A thousand handshakes later, one continual plastered-on smile, and a couple of not so forced laughs thanks to Noah, and I survived the evening...with a sold painting. A painting that's still a work in progress.

Even though I'm dead on my feet, feeling as wound as a spring, and as strong as a jellyfish, I'm giddy. Very, very giddy.

I bounce on my toes, and Noah laughs one more time at me as I say goodbye to the painting of Aires. Its new home, once I'm done, will be in a gallery in New York City.

"Tell me we'll go visit it," I say again.

"We'll go visit it," Noah appeases me.

Hunter shakes the hands of a lingering couple, tells them goodbye then walks in our direction.

"Do you mind giving us a second?" I ask Noah. His response is a quick peck on my lips, and I watch as he exits to the patio.

I won't make my mother's decisions. I'm someone else. I'm who I want to be. And as I admire the painting again, I realize I'm eighteen, and Meredith is twenty-one, and I have a family, and she doesn't.

"What did you think of the showing?" asks Hunter.

"It was great." It was. "Is it always like this?"

"Yes. No. You've been to smaller shows, but the game is the same when your work is on the line. It'll get easier with time, but you have to remember that it's a business, and the smart people know how to play the game. That's why I like the idea of you taking business courses."

It's the reason I like the idea of enrolling in business courses, too.

"I didn't have time to contact the University of Louisville, but I'm still hoping to see if they'll allow you to take your business courses online while you study under me for the year."

My eyebrows lift as I brighten. Here's something I hadn't thought of. "You're not against the idea of long-distance education?"

"No." His eyebrows pull closer together as he assesses me. "Why would I be? With technology as it is, I don't see the need for person to person. You can get the same effect online, through Skype, through the phone. There are a million different ways to connect now."

"So..." *Come on, Echo, you can do this. You are a risk-taker.* "If, for instance, I wanted to go to college in Louisville, and I wanted to study underneath you for the year, I could do it?"

His eyes narrow in suspicion. "It's not the same."

"But it is," I push. "I can send you photos of my works in progress, and we can use all that technology you listed. I mean, I won't be working at your coffee shop, but I don't see how I'm missing out there."

"Did you knock my coffee shop?"

Maybe. "You like girls with fire, remember?"

Hunter goes silent, and I don't like it. "I heard I'm taking Meredith's spot."

"Did she tell you that?"

"No," I rush out. "I overheard it. Hunter, why are you pushing Meredith off a year? Why not just ask me for next year?"

He leans into me. "Because if I don't snatch you up now, someone else will."

Um... "What?"

"I want to be the one that discovered you."

Okay... "You did."

"But if I pushed you off a year, then someone else will figure out your talent, and then you'll study under them. At that point, I've lost the prize."

I'm a prize? Doesn't matter. "I don't feel right taking her spot."

"Why not?" Hunter has that same annoyed set of his

jaw that my father does when he's ticked at me, but I'm not shrinking.

"Because she's my friend. Because if you're willing to work it out for me to take online business courses for a year, there's no reason we can't set up the same in reverse. Because while Meredith needs this now, I'm okay delaying this for a year. I'm not saying no to working with you. I'm saying that I'm not okay hurting people in the process."

He pinches the bridge of his nose. "And if I tell you that this is your lone opportunity?"

My throat tightens, and I have to swallow to breathe. He's offering everything I've ever desired. All of my dreams, all of my hopes are in his hands, but how can I live with myself if I hurt people—if I break hearts just like my mother shattered mine? "Then I'll tell you I'm still not okay with hurting people in the process."

Hunter tugs on his ear like he can't trust what he's hearing, then pivots away from me and starts down the hall. My stomach sinks, and I look to my feet, expecting to find it on the floor. The urge is to charge him and tell him I made a mistake. To tell him that I didn't mean it. That my morals and values and everything that makes me, me, aren't worth it. That my dreams are more important, but I don't.

I stay solid in my spot, completely crushed, because I could never live with myself if I sold my soul.

"One year," Hunter calls out.

My heart stutters. "What?"

He slowly strides back to me. "I'm only going to do this long-distance thing for one year, and that's because I want you to focus on the business courses. I don't care what your schedule looks like now. You wipe it clean, and you fill it with business courses. In fact, send the catalog to me, and I'm picking the courses for you. After that, you're mine for the year. Do you understand?"

Do I understand? I smack my hand over my lips to stop the squeal and when I remove it, my mouth pops open with no sound.

"Breathe, Echo," says Hunter. "I'm not going to have your boyfriend angry at me because you faint."

The first sound that falls out of my mouth might be a "thank you" and by the expression on Hunter's face, he's not sure, either.

"So Meredith's back in?"

"Yes," he answers.

"Starting this year?"

"Yes," he repeats.

I hug him. Not long. Very quick. And when he touches me, I jump back. "Thank you! Will you tell her? Tonight?"

Hunter pulls out his phone and begins scrolling. "Yes, but you and I are working out the details of this arrangement tomorrow."

"No problem!" I say goodbye then race down the hall, running faster than I have in my entire life. Even faster than when I broke into school to save Noah from being arrested. I burst through the door of the patio, and Noah turns away from studying the night sky to focus on me.

"Meredith's in the program, and I'm in the program and oh, my freaking gosh..." It hits me like a tidal wave, and my heart stalls. "I'm going home with you."

Noah waits outside the car in the gallery's parking lot as he gives me space to talk to my father, and I'm holding my breath in the passenger seat. I've told my father everything, from Noah and the charges being dropped, to my conversation with my mother, to my success tonight at the gallery, to the agreement Hunter and I reached.

Now there's silence. It's been silent for so long I look at the phone to see if the call was dropped. It wasn't. Seconds are still ticking away on the screen.

"Dad?" I nudge. "Are you there?"

"Yes," he says. "I am. I don't know where to start or what to say. That was a lot to take in."

Yes, it was, and now if he could only imagine me living through it, maybe he'll find some compassion.

"Are you okay?" he asks. "After talking with your mother, are you okay?"

A relieved breath escapes my mouth. I guess I'm not the only one who's been learning things this summer. A year ago, my father would have lost his mind if I merely mentioned her, and now Dad appears to be letting the tyrant side of himself go.

"I survived," I say. "It was weird and emotional and I'm a little scared of where we go from here, but it was good."

"I'm here." Concern ravages his tone. "If things get

rough with her or if you need someone to intervene on your behalf—I'm here."

And that's all I've ever wanted from him. "Thank you."

"No need to thank me—protecting you is my job."

I glance over to Noah, who's watching the stars above. Maybe it was Dad's job and, because he's human, there are a few times he messed up, but somehow that job seems to belong to Noah now more than it does to my father. It's also my job to protect myself as I'm hardly a damsel in distress. I've proven I'm capable of fighting some of my battles on my own, but it's nice to know I don't always have to.

"When you get home," Dad starts, and now the disapproval is back in his voice, "I think we should sit down and discuss this opportunity in Colorado. I'd also like some further clarification on this situation with Noah."

I wince. The urge is to lash out and let him know that I don't need his advice, but for the millionth time I remind myself I'm no longer a child, which means I should act like an adult. Children yell. Adults talk. At least that's the theory.

"We can talk, but just to let you know, my decision is made. I respect you, Dad, but this is my life, and these are my choices...not yours."

A weighted sigh and a creak from the chair he's sitting in. "You were easier when you were five."

My lips immediately lift up. "Really?"

"No, but with the passing of time, it sometimes feels that way. At least then I could pick you up when you stomped your foot. I'd probably throw my back out if I tried that now."

I laugh, and Noah must catch the sound as he turns to

look at me. He grins at my expression then turns back around.

"I love you," I tell my father.

He clears his throat. Words like that from me are still hard for him to process. "Be safe on the way home."

"I will."

"Don't speed."

"I won't."

"Tell Noah I'm still having a conversation with him when he returns. That's nonnegotiable."

I sigh. "Still doesn't change how I feel about him."

"I'm aware. And Echo?"

"Yeah?"

"I love you, too. I should go. Alexander's waking up. Call me when you get to your next stop."

"I will." And then my father is gone. I stare at the phone, thinking about how much things can change in a year.

I lean forward and knock on the windshield. It's time for Noah and me to move forward.

NOAH

I open the trunk of Echo's car, and she appears beside me, reaching in for a blanket. "We don't need the tent."

It's late, past midnight. Echo changed out of her blue dress and into a cotton skirt and tank top. The type of top that teases me with peeks of her black bra strap. The moment we got in her car, Echo told me to return to the campsite where we jumped off a cliff. Happy as I could fucking be that Echo's going to be chasing her dream plus be beside me for the next year, I didn't ask one question. I turned onto the freeway and drove.

"It's late, baby. I have a feeling neither one of us is going to want to put it up later."

Echo grabs another blanket and two pillows. "We're sleeping in the open tonight."

She has that damned sexy, under-the-eyelash hooded look as she says it, and any room I had in my pants disappears. I twine my fingers with hers and pull Echo close. "You don't have to do this. Jumping from a cliff—that's hardcore risk-taking."

Confronting her mother. Standing up to Hunter. That's even harder core.

In the moonlight, her eyes shine bright. "I want to look at stars tonight."

Then stars it is. I release Echo long enough to take the

blankets and a pillow from her, tuck them under my arm then reclaim her hand. We leave the parking lot and enter the campsite, heading straight for the path.

The campground is packed with campers. Fires crackle. Children laugh and shout. The scent of hot dogs fills the air. As we walk hand in hand, Echo squeezes my fingers. "This is my boyfriend."

I turn my head, wondering who the hell she's talking to then see her making eye contact with a middle-aged couple that has three kids around a campfire.

"He's got two younger brothers," she continues, "and he adores them."

The couple laughs, but doesn't say anything. As I open my mouth to ask what the hell that was about, she starts again with two guys fixing fishing rods. "My boyfriend just spent hours at an art gallery because he supports me."

They also laugh because what the fuck else is there to say to that? "What are you doing?"

"Letting you know that you're the man I want to walk down the street with."

Her words stop me short, and a tug on my hand urges me to continue walking. "Of all the things I say, that's what you grab on to?"

"I grabbed on to it all, but that's the one I knew I could easily fix."

The moon lights our path. Each time we've stayed in a park like this, we've played the game where she hides and I hunt, but there's a silent agreement that the game is over. Neither of us will hide anymore.

When the trees give way to the field we played in days before, Echo changes our direction, heading toward its center. The grass hits our legs, and when we're far enough in for no prying eyes to see, Echo draws the blanket from me and spreads it out onto the ground.

From the other side, I drink Echo in. She's a slender goddess in the shadows created by the moonlight, and the way she gazes at me reminds me how much she owns me. It's a sexy look. One that dances along my skin before the actual touch.

Maybe she is a wood nymph. Maybe she belongs to some long-lost bloodline and being here in this field, in these woods, brings that special spark to the surface.

Or maybe it's because for the first time since I've met her, Echo's taken control of her destiny. She's learned how to put herself first while still being the girl I love.

"What you did tonight, for Meredith..." There's no words. "I'm not sure I could love you more."

Echo smiles and glances away, too proud of her deeds to accept the compliment. "She's my friend."

"If the world lived by your personal code, there'd be a lot less fighting."

Echo kneels on the blanket and situates the pillows near the top and unfolds the other cover. "As I said, she's my friend."

I sit beside her and help arrange our bed. "Do you regret it? That you have to wait to study here for a year?"

"To be honest, I'm more excited than I was before. Hunter is giving me a great opportunity, but he reminds me a lot of my dad. It feels powerful to know that I negotiated my own future. Does that make sense?"

"Yes." It's how I feel about my brothers and my newfound uncle. I've got a future now—on my terms.

"Hey, Noah," she says.

"Yeah?"

Her mouth moves up into this sensual smile. "I sold a painting today to a gallery in New York City."

Damn, I like her happy. "You did."

"So for about thirty seconds today, that made me a rock star."

I chuckle and sweep her hair over her shoulder, letting the soft strands drift from my fingers. "You're always a rock star."

"Hey, Noah," she says in this soft voice that licks fire into my veins.

I raise my eyebrows at her in response.

"I'm sort of done talking."

And so am I.

Echo

We haven't made love since the first time and part of me expects nerves, but what I'm shocked at is the lack of them. Maybe it's because I'm too happy. Maybe it's because it's late, and I'm a bit drunk on the high of saving not only Meredith's dreams, but my own. Or maybe it's because I love Noah, and he loves me, and I'm not afraid to trust our future.

In the middle of this field, far off the trail that's forever away from the campground, it's like we've created our own world. No one else exists—only the two of us, and that's completely fine with me.

Noah lays a hand on the curve of my waist, next to my hip, and I wiggle closer to him. The heat of his palm rushes past my clothes and straight into my bloodstream.

I raise my head, and Noah's right there. His breath hot on my face, his lips mere centimeters from mine. There's an electricity that develops between us. A hypnotic force field pulling us into each other. My heart picks up speed. I swallow then lick my lips.

Noah watches the movement. His brown eyes darken, and a thrill runs through me when I spot the spark of lust...the hunger ...the desire...for me.

"Will we ever stop being drawn to each other?" I ask.

Noah barely shifts his head in a no, and the movement

causes his lips to slightly brush against mine. My heart stutters then starts again. Once he kisses me, we'll never be able to stop, and I don't ever want this to end.

"Never," he whispers, his voice the right amount of husky.

I tilt my head up, Noah bends down, and the first taste of his lips causes a small sound of pleasure to escape from my throat. His fingers burrow into my hair in response, and our mouths move in time.

There's this build inside me as hands roam. A surge of warmth in my veins, and all of it leads to places that I consider begging Noah to caress. Hands wander over then underneath. My fingers explore with as much greed as Noah's.

My hips sway. A reaction to Noah's touch. A reaction to me touching him. I rub my hand down the plane of Noah's stomach, and I have no problem lifting his shirt over his head so I can play without barriers. Noah doesn't take long to follow the change in the dance as he fists the bottom of my tank and slips it off.

Noah pauses and stares at me...my face then my chest then back up again. "You're so damn beautiful."

I blush, and Noah smiles. He reaches over and skims the bare skin of my shoulder. Goose bumps form along my arms. One bra strap falls to my arm then the other, and the world tunnels in a pleasing haze. The material of my bra drops a little, but not enough to show all that I possess, and as Noah stretches around to my back, I'm reminded that he's definitely about all.

With a flick, the pressure around my body gives, and the sweet release of no longer being confined eases across my midsection. His fingertips trace the area where my bra had been, and I shiver as he reaches the front.

Noah leans forward and kisses my neck. The hot sensation of his mouth makes me light-headed. I wrap my arms around him and pull at his hair to stay upright. I revel in the feeling of pure skin against skin.

Using his body, Noah guides me to lie on the blanket, and the moment my head connects with the pillow, his mouth begins this delicious dance down.

Cool air nips at my skin, but Noah's caresses set me on fire. He does things that he's done before, and then he does things that he hasn't. Things with my breasts... places below. Touches and kisses and things that urge me to clutch the blanket as my back arches, things that cause the breath to rush out of my body, things that encourage me and Noah to find a rhythm.

What started off as slow becomes faster.

When he lifts his head back to mine, I swear to God the world explodes. We're rolling and shedding more clothes until there is absolutely nothing left between us but the night.

And then Noah's there. Near that special part of me that's warm and ready, and I have to force my mouth away from Noah's as I gasp, "Protection."

I smile when he mumbles a curse word into my shoulder, then giggle when he gently nips my neck. Faster than even I thought Noah could move, he's yanked his wallet out of his discarded jeans, found a condom and has it on.

He rolls back on top of me, smoothing the hair away from my face. "I love you, Echo Emerson."

"I love you." I do. So much that saying the words doesn't seem like I'm doing the high inside me justice.

"You sure about this?" he asks.

I wiggle, becoming impatient with how my body is pulsating and how Noah's not acting. He grins and I smoosh my lips to the right. "I want you, and you're not playing right."

Noah chuckles, but wastes no time reclaiming my lips. He begins this silent rhythm with his body that's in time with my pulse. My arms tangle around his neck, my legs hook with his, and I move along with him, increasing the speed at exactly the same time.

There's no warning. One moment Noah was out and then he's in. I suck in a breath and Noah stills. The burning from the first time...it's there, then it fades.

Noah skims his nose along my cheek, feathering kisses along my skin. My hands roam along his back, and after another second of readjustment, I inch my hips down, and it doesn't take long for Noah to nudge his body up.

Unable to keep silent anymore, I breathe out his name. One time. Another. And each time I say it, Noah holds on to me tighter. His hands slip lower and right as the entire world grows dizzyingly out of control, Noah rocks forward hard.

My eyes shut tight, warmth explodes through me, colors appear behind my closed lids, and as my entire body tenses with pleasure, Noah takes his turn saying my name.

We hug each other as we catch our breath, then we lazily kiss as our muscles slowly lose the ability to function. He shifts off me, rolling away to take care of things, and when he turns back, Noah pulls me into his chest.

We lie there. My fingertips trace the muscles of his chest. His fingers play with my hair. The blanket keeps us from being fully exposed. The sound of his heart against my ear joins the sound of the frogs and crickets in the still night.

"Promise me we'll come back here," I say to him. "Promise me that someday we'll make love here again."

"I swear it." Noah bunches my hair into his hand, and when I look up at him he kisses my lips. "I'll bring you back here every damn year."

My mouth tilts up. "I like the sound of that."

NOAH

This has been the craziest damn summer of my life, and it sucks it's coming to an end. Isaiah pats my back and tosses Beth's bag over his shoulder. "First call, man."

I nod and watch as Echo waves an awkward goodbye to Beth and hugs my best friend.

Echo drove the three of us to the bus station this morning. As part of their agreement for Echo to study long-distance with Hunter for a year, Echo's going to stay for an additional week as Hunter crams as much art shit as he can down her throat before she returns home. Then she'll have to visit Colorado four more times throughout the year. One week each time.

I still don't trust Hunter when it comes to his attraction to Echo, but I trust my girl. I believe him when he says he can open doors for her and teach her about the world she loves, and I want her happy. He can daydream about her all he wants, but at the end of the day, she loves me.

I hate being away from her, but I'll take it. Five weeks away beats the hell out of being separated for a year. Which is what we'll face next September, but the two of us will be ready.

Beth and Isaiah board the bus, and Echo turns to me. Her lower lip trembles, and she glances away. She promised me no tears, but how can she promise something like that?

"Come here," I say, and Echo falls into my arms.

I enfold her into me and nuzzle her hair, enjoying the feeling of peace that floods my body whenever she's this close. Echo squeezes her arms around me, and I wish she'd never let go.

"I love you," she whispers.

"It's only a week," I tell her, but I loathe this separation as much as she does.

Echo looks at me with those pleading green eyes. I twine my fingers into her curls. The first taste of her lips is sweet. The second makes me forget there's a bus terminal full of people. The third causes me to lift her feet off the ground and deepen our kiss.

"Noah," she whispers in reprimand as she breaks away. "We're causing a scene."

"Not my problem." But I lower her to the ground anyhow. "Besides, it wasn't my fault. You're the one looking at me with take-me-to-bed eyes, and I felt you kissing me back. Once again, you're the one getting us into trouble."

Echo grins. "You are so impossible."

"Damn straight, baby." I could stay with her in Colorado, but if I go home today, I can watch my brothers play their last baseball game of the year. I've never been so happy to hear the word rainout. Plus, if I head back now, Isaiah and I can settle into our new apartment. I'll also be able to get together what Echo and I need to start school as she'll miss orientation.

I'm not thrilled with the idea of her driving from Colorado to Louisville on her own, but she's determined she can do this, and I need to trust her judgment. We weighed the pros and cons over and over again and this...this is what we need to do. I have no doubt it's the best decision because Echo and me, we're for keeps.

"Last call," says the driver.

I cup Echo's face in my hand. "You keep your cell charged."

"I will, and you tell Jacob and Tyler I said hi."

"I love you, Echo."

A soft smile spreads across her lips, and my damn heart nearly explodes when we kiss one last time.

"I love you," she whispers.

"One week," I say.

"One week," she says back.

As I sling my bag over my shoulder and board the bus, I walk on with a confidence I've never had before when it comes to me and Echo.

In my seat, I press my hand to the window, and Echo stretches out her arm to me. Someday me and her, we'll come back here. Maybe she'll be an artist. Maybe she won't. Maybe I'll be an architect. Maybe I won't. What I know for sure is that Echo will be by my side, and that our love is forever.

* * * * *

ACKNOWLEDGEMENTS

To God: NIV Isaiah 43:18—Forget the former things; do not dwell on the past.

For Dave: Because real love means walking hand in hand even during the rough times and during the questions that feel impossible to answer. There is no other person on earth I'd rather have by my side in those difficult moments, as you forever bring me hope.

Thank you to…

Kevan Lyon—This journey would be close to impossible without you. Thank you just doesn't feel like enough.

Margo Lipschultz—I have loved Echo and Noah from the moment they appeared on the page, and I wasn't sure anyone else could love them as much as I do until I met you. Thank you for all your faith in me and in them.

For everyone at Harlequin and MIRA Ink who has helped me with this book and the others in this series. I am honored to have such an amazing team surrounding my books.

Angela Annalaro-Murphy—I am truly blessed to have you as a friend, a best friend…a sister.

To Kristen Simmons and Colette Ballard—One of the best parts of this journey has been meeting the two of you. Thank you for your fantastic friendship. I love you both!

Kelly Creagh, Bethany Griffin, Kurt Hampe, Bill Wolfe and the Louisville Romance Writers: Thank you for your continued love and support!

To my readers: Echo and Noah's continuing story is possible because of your support. You have no idea how much I appreciate you all!

As always, to my parents, my sister, my Mount Washington family and my entire in-law family—I love you.

Q&A

How did you decide on Aires's name, out of all the myths to choose from?

Honestly, Aires was originally named Ares, after the Greek god of war, but I changed it for two reasons. First, I wasn't convinced that Echo's mother would have named her son after war, and then my early readers had a hard time pronouncing the name.

I read through the myths again and was captured by the one behind the constellation Aires. It told the story of two siblings who were to be saved by Aires the Ram, but only one of those siblings lived through the rescue attempt. I thought this was a fitting name for Echo's brother since only one of them is alive at the beginning of *Pushing the Limits*.

If the takeaway from *Pushing the Limits* is that there's always hope, what do you want readers to take away from *Breaking the Rules*? How are the themes of the two books similar, and how are they different?

The theme of *Pushing the Limits* is that there is definitely hope. While this theme continues in *Breaking the Rules*, this time I also tackled the idea of letting the past go.

A lot of us have had something happen in our lives that becomes baggage—chains that weigh us down. If we hold on to those emotions, they can hinder our future. These emotions can impact how we deal with new experiences and relationships, and potentially can color them in a negative light.

In order to find true happiness, Noah must find a way to let go of his guilt, and Echo must face her grief. They also grapple with the question of what forgiveness means.

Through dealing with their emotions and their past baggage, Echo and Noah are free to forge ahead with their future without anything weighing them down.

We know that Noah's mother's name was Sarah, but we never learn his uncle's name. Was that a deliberate choice on your part and if so, why?

It was a deliberate choice. There are certain titles in our lives that carry great weight. For instance—mom and dad. For most of us, just saying or hearing those words can bring up a ton of emotion.

Noah is an orphan. He lost his parents to a house fire at the end of his freshman year of high school, and he believed that he had no other blood relatives. In *Pushing the Limits*, he learns that this isn't the case.

I didn't give Noah's uncle a name because I wanted the reader to focus on the relationship itself. Noah has an uncle—a living blood relative. A link to the world, and this is important to him because he believed that beyond the life he had created for himself, he had nothing that rooted him—no place he was wanted. The discovery of his uncle is a huge revelation to Noah, and I wanted the reader to feel that impact.

How do you think Echo's relationship with her mother changes between the end of *Pushing the Limits* and the end of *Breaking the Rules*, if it changes at all?

Because of the incident between Echo and her mother that left Echo scarred, their relationship will always be complicated. In *Breaking the Rules*, Echo struggles with the meaning of forgiveness and with her need for her mother to accept responsibility for their damaged relationship.

Echo slowly realizes that her issues with her mother extend far beyond the night she was scarred, to her mother's general attitude of hardly ever putting her daughter first. Echo initially realizes this is her issue with her mother at the end of *Pushing the Limits*, and she deals with this epiphany in *Breaking the Rules*.

At the end of *Breaking the Rules*, we see Echo's mother take baby steps toward accepting responsibility for her role in the broken relationship with her daughter, and we see Echo extending forgiveness. Forgiveness for Echo means putting the past behind her, yet setting boundaries with her mother that will keep any possible future relationship healthy.

After all they've been through in *Pushing the Limits* and *Breaking the Rules*, is there still more to Echo and Noah's story?

One of the most popular questions from readers after they finished *Pushing the Limits* was: Are you going to continue Echo and Noah's story? So I wouldn't be surprised if readers ask the same question at the end of *Breaking the Rules*.

To be honest, I know every twist and turn in Echo's and Noah's lives. They became living, breathing people to me, and I love them so much that I often couldn't help but peek into their future to see how they fared.

I wrote *Pushing the Limits* as a young adult novel. *Breaking the Rules*, because of its more mature themes, pushes the boundaries of young adult; Echo and Noah start off as teens at the beginning of the novel, then grow emotionally into adults by the end. This means that any future book about the two of them would no longer be in YA territory, and that's a factor I'd have to consider before continuing their story.

Will I write another novel about them? I don't know. If the opportunity arises, the timing is right, and I feel that the next chapter of their lives is a story that needs to be told, I wouldn't rule it out. But for now, I'm going to focus on the other characters in my head who are begging for their story to be told.

PLAYLIST FOR
BREAKING THE RULES

Theme:

"Can't Hold Us" (feat. Ray Dalton) by Macklemore & Ryan Lewis
"Try" by P!nk
"November Rain" by Guns N' Roses
"One of Those Nights" by Tim McGraw
"Wake Me Up" by Avicii

Noah:

"Why Don't You & I" (feat. Alex Band of the Calling) by Santana
"It Will Rain" by Bruno Mars
"Some Nights" by Fun.
"My Own Worst Enemy" by Lit
"Hard to Love" by Lee Brice

Echo:

"The Game of Love" (feat. Michelle Branch) by Santana
"Glass" by Thompson Square
"Wide Awake" by Katy Perry
"We Belong" by Pat Benatar

Songs for Specific Scenes:

Echo and Noah play in Colorado Springs: "We Owned the Night" by Lady Antebellum
When Noah meets the priest: "Something to Believe In" by Poison
Noah at the police station: "Against All Odds" by Phil Collins
The night after the party: "Just Give Me a Reason" (feat. Nate Ruess) by P!nk
When Noah goes to the church: "From the Inside Out (Live)" by Hillsong UNITED
Noah goes after Echo: "Highway Don't Care" (feat. Taylor Swift) by Tim McGraw

Songs to describe Echo and Noah's future:

"Bless the Broken Road" by Rascal Flatts
"Home" by Phillip Phillips

*Katie McGarry and MIRA Ink
are thrilled to introduce a brand-new series.*

Read on for an exclusive sneak peek of

NOWHERE BUT HERE,

coming soon!

Oz

It's three in the morning, and Mom and I continue to wait. The two of us deal with the heaviness of each passing second differently. She paces our tiny living room at the front of our double-wide while I polish my combat boots in my room. Regardless of what happens tonight, we have a wake to attend in the morning.

The scratching of the old scrub brush against my black boot is the lone sound that fills the blackened house. We both pretend that the other isn't awake. Neither of us has turned on a lamp. Instead, we rely on the rays of the full moon to see. It's easier this way. Neither of us wants to discuss the meaning of Dad's absence or his cell phone silence.

I sit on the edge of my twin mattress. If I stretched my leg, my toe would hit the faux-wooden-paneled wall. I'm tall like my dad, and the room is compact and narrow. Large enough to hold my bed and an old stack of milk crates that I use as shelves.

Mom's phone pings, and my hands freeze. Through the crack in my door, I spot her black form as she grabs her cell. The screen glows to life, and a bluish light illuminates Mom's face. I quit breathing and strain to listen to her reaction or at least hear the roar of motorcycle engines.

Nothing. More silence. Adrenaline begins to pump into my veins. Dad should have been home by now. They all should have been home. Especially with Olivia's wake in the morning.

Unable to stomach the quiet any longer, I set the boot on the floor and open my door. The squeak of the hinges screeches through the trailer. In two steps, I'm in the living room.

Mom continues to scroll through her phone. She's a small thing, under five four, and has long, straight hair. It's black. Just like mine and just like Dad's. Mom and Dad are only thirty-seven. I'm seventeen. Needless to say, my mom was young when she had me. But the way she slumps her shoulders, she appears ten years older.

"Any word?" I ask.

"It's Nina." My best friend Chevy's mom. "Wondering if we had heard anything." Which implies neither Eli nor Cyrus have returned home.

From behind her, I place a hand on Mom's shoulder, and she covers my fingers with hers.

"I'll be out there watching their backs soon." Now that I've graduated from high school, I'll finally be allowed to enter the family business.

A job with the security company and a patch-in to the club is all I've thought about since I was twelve. All I've craved since I turned sixteen and earned my motorcycle license. "They're fine. Like I'll be when I join them."

Mom pats my hand, walks into the space that serves as our kitchen and busies herself with a stack of mail.

I rest my shoulder against the wall near the window.

The backs of my legs bump the only piece of furniture in the room besides the flat screen—a sectional bought last year before Olivia became ill.

Without trying to be obvious, I glance beyond the lace curtains and assess the road leading to our trailer. I'm also worried, but it's my job to alleviate her concern.

I force a tease into my voice. "I bet you can't wait until Chevy graduates next year. Then there will be two more of us protecting the old men."

Mom coughs out a laugh and takes a drink to control the choking. "I can't begin to imagine the two of you riding in the pack when the image in my mind is of both of you as toddlers, covered in mud from head to toe."

"Not hard to remember. That was last week's front yard football game," I joke.

She smiles. Long enough to chase away the gravity of tonight's situation, but then reality catches up. If humor won't work, I'll go for serious. "Chevy would like to GED out."

"Nina would skin him alive. Each of you promised Olivia you'd finish high school."

Because it broke Olivia's heart when Eli, her son, opted out of finishing high school and instead tested to gain his GED years ago. Eli's parents, Olivia and Cyrus, aren't blood to me, but they gave my mom and dad a safe place to lay low years ago when their own parents went self-destructive. Olivia and I aren't related, but she's the closest I have to a grandmother.

"Chevy wanting to take his GED." Mom tsks. "It's bad enough you won't consider college."

The muscles in my neck tighten, and I ignore her jab. She and Olivia are ticked I won't engage them in conversation about college. I know my future, and it's not four more years of books and rules. I want the club. As it is, a patch-in—membership into the club—isn't a guarantee. I still have to prove myself before they'll let me join.

My dad belongs to the Reign of Terror. They're a motorcycle club that formed a security business when I was eleven. Their main business comes from escorting semi loads of high-priced goods through highly pirated areas.

Imagine a couple thousand dollars of fine Kentucky bourbon in the back of a Mac truck and, at some point, the driver has to take a piss. My dad and the rest of the club—they make sure the driver can eat his Big Mac in peace and return to the parking lot to find his rig intact and his merchandise still safely inside.

What they do can be dangerous, but I'll be proud to stand alongside my father and the only other people I consider family.

Mom rubs her hands up and down her arms. She's edgy when the club is out on a protection run, but this time, Mom's dangling from a cliff, and she's not the only one. The entire club has been acting like they're preparing to jump without parachutes.

"You're acting as if they're the ones that could be caught doing something illegal."

Mom's eyes shoot straight to mine like my comment was serious. "You know better than that."

I do. It's what the club prides themselves on. All that TV bull about anyone who rides a bike is a felon—they don't understand what the club stands for. The club is a brotherhood, a family. It means belonging to something bigger than myself.

Still, Olivia has mounting medical bills and between

me, Chevy, my parents, Eli, Cyrus and other guys from the club giving all we have, we still don't have enough to make a dent in what we owe. "I hear that 1 club a couple of hours north of here makes bank."

"Oz."

As if keeping watch will help Dad return faster, I move the curtain to get a better view of the road that leads away from our house and into the woods. "Yeah?"

"This club is legit."

And 1 clubs are not legit. They don't mind doing the illegal to make cash or get their way. "Okay."

"I'm serious. This club is legit."

I drop the curtain. "What? You don't want gangsta in the family?"

Mom slaps her hand on the counter. "I don't want to hear you talk like this!"

My head snaps in her direction. Mom's not a yeller. Even when she's stressed, she maintains her cool. "I was messing with you."

"This club is legit, and it will stay legit. You are legit. Do you understand?"

"I got it. I'm clean. The club's clean. We're so jacked up on suds that we squeak when we walk. I know this, so would you care to explain why you're freaking out?"

A motorcycle growls in the distance, cutting off our conversation. Mom releases a long breath, as if she's been given the news that a loved one survived surgery. "He's home."

She charges the front door and throws it open. The elation slips from her face, and my stomach cramps. "What is it?"

"Someone's riding double."

More rumbles of engines join the lead one, multiple headlights flash onto the trailer, and not one of those bikes belong to Dad. Fuck. I rush past Mom and jump off the steps as Mom brightens the yard with a flip of the porch light. Eli swings off his bike. "Oz! Get over here!"

I'm there before he can finish his statement, and I shoulder my father's weight to help him off the bike. He's able to stand, but leans into me, and that scares me more than any monster that hid under my bed as a child.

"What happened?" Mom's voice shakes, and Eli says nothing. He supports Dad's other side as Dad's knees buckle.

"What happened!" she demands, and the fear in her voice vibrates against my insides. I'm wondering the same damn thing, but I'm more concerned with the blood dripping from my father's head.

"Medical kit!" Eli bursts through the door and the two of us deposit Dad on the couch. Mom's less than a step behind us and runs into the kitchen. Glass shatters when Mom tosses stuff aside in search of her kit. Mom's a nurse, and I can't remember a time she hasn't been prepared.

More guys appear in the living room. Each man wearing a black leather biker cut. Not one of them would be the type to leave a brother behind.

"I'm fine, Izzy." Dad touches the skin above the three-inch-long cut on his forehead. "Just a scratch."

"Scratch, my ass." With kit in hand, Mom kneels in front of him, and I crouch beside her, popping open her supply box as she pours antiseptic onto a rag. She glares at Eli. "Why didn't you take him to the ER?"

Dad wraps his fingers around Mom's wrist. Her gaze shifts to his, and when he has Mom's attention for longer than a second, he slowly swipes his thumb against her skin. "I told him to bring me home. We didn't want it reported to the police."

Mom blinks away the tears pooling in her eyes. I fall back on my ass, realizing that Dad's not dying, but somehow cracked his head hard enough that Eli wouldn't allow him to ride home solo.

"You promised you'd wear your helmet," Mom whispers.

"I wasn't on my bike," he replies simply.

Mom pales out, and I focus solely on Eli. He holds my stare as I state the obvious. "The run went bad."

Jacking trucks for the cargo inside is a moneymaker for hustlers, and the security company is good at keeping hustlers on their toes. But sometimes the company comes up against the occasional asshole who thinks they can be badass by pulling a gun.

"Someone tried to hit us during a break at a truck stop, but we were smarter." Eli jerks his thumb in Dad's direction. "But some of us aren't as fast as others."

"Go to hell," Dad murmurs as Mom cleans the wound.

"You should have reported it," Mom says.

A weighted silence settles in the room, and Mom's lips thin out. The security business is as thick as the club. Business in both areas stays private. Everyone is on a need-to-know basis, me and Mom included...that is until I patch in. I'll likely learn more when I'm initiated as a prospect, and I'm counting down the days until I'm officially part of the larger whole.

"He okay?" Eli asks.

"You of all people should know how hardheaded he is," Mom responds. Eli's a few years younger than my parents, but the three of them have been a trio of trouble since elementary school. "I believe everyone has a wake to attend in the morning, so I suggest sleep."

That's as subtle as Mom will get before she'll stick a pointed steel-toed boot up their asses. Everyone says some sort of goodbye to Mom and Dad, but my parents are too lost in their own world to notice.

"Walk me out, Oz?" Eli inclines his head to the door, and we head onto the front porch. The muggy night air is thick with moisture, and a few bugs swarm around the porch light.

Eli digs into his leather jacket and pulls out a pack of cigarettes and a lighter. He cups his hand to his mouth as he lights one. "We need you out on the road."

"They told me they'll send my official diploma next week." I was supposed to walk at graduation tomorrow, but Olivia's wake is the priority. Not caps and gowns. "You tell me when to start, and I'm ready to go."

"Good." He cracks a rare grin. "Heard that we might be adding a new prospect this weekend."

The answering smile spreads on my face. Becoming a prospect is the initiation period before the club votes on my membership. I've been waiting for this moment my entire life.

Eli sucks in a long drag and the sleeve of his jacket hitches up, showing the trail of stars tattooed on his arm. "Keep an eye on your dad. He cracked the hell out of his head when he hit the pavement. Blacked out for a bit but then shot to his feet. When his bike began swerving, I made him pull over and double with me."

"He must have loved that," I say.

"Practically had to put a gun to his head." Eli breaths out smoke.

"Was it the RMC?" The Riot Motorcycle Club. They're an illegal club north of here. I've heard some of the guys talk when they think no one else is listening, saying that our peace treaty with them is fracturing.

Eli flicks ashes then focuses on the burning end of the cigarette. "As I said, we need you on the road."

Our club and the Riot have had an unsteady alliance from the start. We stay on our side of the state, they stay on theirs. The problem? A new client that the business has contracted with resides in the Riot's territory.

"This stays between us," says Eli. "This new client we signed is skittish and doesn't want the PR related to possible truck-jackings. We need this business, and I need people I can trust with those loads. I need you in."

"Got it." I throw out the question, not sure if Eli will answer. "You had his back, didn't you? You knew there was going to be trouble so you pushed Dad to the ground."

A hint of a smirk plays on his lips, and he hides it with another draw. He blows out the smoke and flicks the cigarette onto the ground. "Be out here at six in the morning. I'll pick you up in the truck and we'll go get your dad's bike before the wake. I want him to sleep in."

Hell, yeah. "You going to let me drive his bike home?"

"Fuck, no. I'm bringing you along to drive the truck back. No one touches a man's bike, and in desperate situations only another brother can. You know better than that." Eli pats my shoulder. "See you tomorrow, and be dressed for the wake when I pick you up."

Eli starts his bike and rocks kick up as he drives off. I watch until the red taillight fades into the darkness.

Through the screen door, I spot my mother still tending to my father. She uses special care as she tapes gauze to his head.

Mom smoothes the last strip of medical tape to his skin and when she goes to close the kit, Dad tucks a lock of her hair behind her ear. They stare at each other, longer than most people can stand, then she lays her head on his lap. Dad bends over and kisses her temple.

They need a moment together and, having nothing but time, I sit on the top step and wonder if I'll find someone who will understand and accept this life like my mother. Mom loves Dad so much that she'll take on anything. His job, this life and even the club. Maybe I'll be that lucky someday.

One girl could change four lives forever...

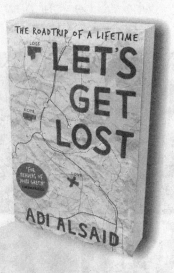

Mysterious Leila, who is on the road trip of a lifetime, has a habit of crashing into people's worlds at the moment they need someone the most.

Hudson, Bree, Elliot and Sonia find a friend in Leila. But Leila's trip could help her discover something bigger—that, sometimes, the only way to find what you're looking for is to get lost along the way...

'For readers of John Green'
—*Fresh Fiction*

www.miraink.co.uk